The Chronicles of Royal High
# The Lost Noble

R. Litfin

# DEDICATION

For Mom and Dad. You know what you did.

No, really. You gave me everything. I could not have
done this without your guidance and love.

# CONTENTS

# ACKNOWLEDGMENTS

First and foremost, I want to acknowledge and thank my mother. Had it not been for her encouragement to write early on in my life, along with the countless late night discussions and brainstormings regarding the creation of this series, then The Chronicles of Royal High may never have been.

Second, I want to thank my father as the other driving force behind this book becoming a tangibly real thing. He created all of the art and imagry, handled all the technical things, kept me sane, and helped me establish the business end of this life long venture.

I want to acknowledge my younger brother, for without him, Royal High would not have as many loveably rougish characters running around it.

I also want it known that I appreciate all of the life I have lived thus far. All of the heartaches, and all of the triumphs, have all attributed to the creation of Royal High.

I acknowledge all of the friends and loved ones who have made their impressions on my heart, and eternally encouraged my soul to see this project to completion.

To Ashley Evje, the first editor and friend to truly read the early stuff. You made me feel like I wasn't drowning anymore.

To Amanda, Charity, and Merrin, for their feed back, inspirations, and constant support.

To Aunt Cyndi and Grandma; LOOK. It's here. It's actually real. You're holding it right now. I love you both.

To M. Todd Gallowglas, for urging my dad to bring my 19 year old self to WorldCon 2011. It was there that I learned two things; just how in over my head I was, and how very badly I knew I wanted to do this. His advice and direction truly helped me find my way as an author.

To Katie, for being the most exuberant of cheerleaders and sources of sanity in my corner.

To David, for giving me the tools I needed when I felt so hopeless. Also, your constant memes, presence, sage advice, and friendship is second to none.

To the last editors and readers, Nicole and Christina. You both are such talented, giving women, and without your help I would still be lost inside my own head.

To Igor, for surprising me with the biggest shock of my life. You knew that I was ready, even when I didn't see it in myself. Thank you for loving me, and never giving up on me

R. LITFIN

# Prologue

The cloaked figure passed across the far-reaching spans of the decrepit stone courtyard. Pillars that might have previously stood proud and strong now laid ruinous and desolate all around. Perhaps a court was once held here, but it was evident a place such as this had not seen civilized customs for more than a millenia. The charred castle above him, high on the conical mountain, was the only remaining evidence of life before the darkness. Before him, a pair of foreboding iron doors were built into a facet of the cold obsidian mountain.

"Open," his ominously twisted voice commanded to the creatures who guarded the passage.

The hulking Desdem guards, golem creatures made of ashen rock and scales, stepped aside and unbolted the massive iron locks, opening the doorway.

The dark figure stepped into the forgotten stairwell. Distant lightning crackled from the dark smoking clouds in the heavens outside, and the doors rumbled shut behind him. Darkness enveloped him, and he began to descend the spiraling stone steps. Far off screams, waves of terror and anguish, echoed throughout the shadows. Mounted torches, scarce in placement, held precious flames that appeared to dance upon the walls of the passageway.

After an endless time, he came upon level ground, and swept impatiently through the corridors. His steps were frantic, and he mumbled a series of inaudible words to himself, curses from a forgotten language.

Rage and spite radiated from his very existence, creating a horrible atmosphere of its own. The intensity of his mission seemed to amplify the farther he traveled into the decaying maze, and the cries of anguish grew louder.

His heavy cloak seemed to melt and sway with the blackness that surrounded him, swathing and forming around his every move, hiding his face, as though he were one with it. The shadows whispered and babbled in the dark, voices unseen. The menacing presence of their master's anger unsettled their tortured souls.

With every corner turned, every deeper, darker hall past him, the haunting wails of agony beckoned to him. His intended passage was near as he saw a lone torch light at the end of a long, dark tunnel. He had arrived upon the final corridor, and all that was standing between him and his prisoner was a stoic iron door guarded by four more towering guards.

"Open," The Dark One's aphotic voice ordered them over the bedlam of suffering.

The thickly armored golems of Desdem stepped aside, unbolted the heavy iron locks, and swung the intimidating door free.

The agonizing screams flooded The Dark One's senses as he passed into the dungeon. Chains rattled and creaked in the darkness while the disturbed shadows around him whispered in a restless tongue that was foreign to the living.

"Silence!" The Dark One commanded fiercely.

"Gaaahh! Ahh!" Came the screams from the deepest part of the room.

"I said silence, whelp!" He bellowed as he swiftly strode the length of the grotto and backhanded the prisoner in the face.

"I-I-c-can't-Ahhh!!" The tortured captive cried out once more.

"Enough!" The Dark One's aphotic voice shrieked as he raised his hand, letting the torturers know to relent.

His minions, craven and gnarled looking beings with clammy skin and scales the color of soot, abated ever so slightly. The prisoner inhaled desperately.

The Dark One stalked around the vast cavern, his cloak of shadows trailing behind him. A couple torches barely illuminated the endless climbing walls. In the high ceiling, a crack allowed the moon to trickle through a few slim beams.

The sparse light revealed horrific things throughout the prison. In one area, an iron maiden was waiting to devour. Across from this was a wooden board, littered with nails, and adorned with leather straps. Nearby was a crank and cogs sort of contraption embedded with razor metal gears. Cages were strewn about the room with one suspended freely on chains from the ceiling. Weathered scythes, barbaric clubs, and rusted utensils of all sorts of grisly natures hung down alongside them. Shackles were fixed to the edge of the ground, dried blood coated on them all.

The Dark One paused thoughtfully, and slowly moved toward his captive. "Do you know where you are?" His aphotic tone had receded slightly, settling into a smoother, more human cadence.

"I-I-I don't know," the prisoner stuttered, gasping for air and words.

"Do you know who I am?"

"N-No."

"Oh, now that hurts!" The Dark One feigned. "You have no idea who I am?"

"No." The captive gasped.

"But we were so close in spirit and in brotherhood! You can't have forgotten me already!" He belittled.

"Wh-Who are you?"

The Dark One smirked to himself. After all these years, he had finally won. He would finally know his revenge. "I don't think you understand, so let me clarify! *I* ask the questions, and whatever I want to know, you *are* going to divulge!" His voice roared through the cavern. The phantom whispers flared, emanating his rage. "So now, tell me, who is Sealghair?"

"W-who?" The prisoner choked, confused.

"WRONG!" The Dark One exploded. The torturers tightened their hold to emphasize his threat.

"I re-really d-don't know who that i-is," the poor soul stammered out.

The Dark One was silent for a moment. He took several calculated steps back, searching for words. "Okay, we'll try this." He cleared his throat, almost like he was trying to reset himself. He began again. "Where is the Astralore staff?"

"Is that what you're after?" The prisoner asked, bewildered.

"Don't play games with me! Where is the staff?!" His aphotic voice cackled in the darkness.

"But you c-can't!" The prisoner choked, terrified, understanding the magnitude that Astralore held.

The Dark One shot across the room with inhuman speed, coming to a halt inches from the captive's face. He grabbed a fistful of his dark, sweat, and blood matted hair, and yanked the captive's head up into the slim light.

Streams of blood ran down young man's cheeks, evidence of a severe head gash he bore, but it did not hide his incredibly handsome features. His beautiful, piercing blue gaze looked up to meet the glowing crimson of his captor's eyes; they were a burning scarlet portal into his dark lost soul. It troubled the boy to stare into them, and he wanted to look away, but The Dark One held his stare.

A faint sense dawned upon the captive as he realized that this was someone he really did know, but the pain and terror of the torture clouded his head, and he struggled for the memories he needed.

The glowing eyes in The Dark One's shadowed face haunted him.

"Do *not* tell me what I can and cannot do," the captor seethed the threat between his teeth, still gripping the young man's head by his locks. "I will have the staff," he chided, "and no one will stop me. You will tell me where it is."

"I will not." The captive's voice was stronger as he gazed upon him defiantly, every bone in his body feeling like it could shatter.

Rage broiled over. "If you do not fear death," The Dark One threatened as he dropped the boy's head back with a heavy knock, "then perhaps I should just destroy everyone you love."

"Don't you dare!" The prisoner tried to hold onto any strength he had left.

"Oh, I *dare*! I *will*!" His maniacal cackle echoed in the dark.

"I don't understand w-why," the poor soul gasped hopelessly, his pain nearing its threshold.

The Dark One stepped back. Something seemed to pique his interest as he thrummed his fingers against one another and he began to pace.

"Of course you don't. Of course you wouldn't understand what is happening," he spoke at length, his condescending voice a little less sinister. "I suppose that's what happens when you grow up so sheltered. Being born with your lineage had its perks, didn't it?" He reminisced begrudgingly. "Daddy never let you get hurt. Daddy came to the rescue. Daddy was your hero. He was always there. He made sure of it.

"I remember all too well," The Dark One's voice grew distant. "The throngs of people, shouting and chanting your name, while I existed in your shadow. I easily surpassed you in so many ways, yet you had the glory," he scathed, tone nearing the point of insanity. "But *you... You* just couldn't be satisfied with the pacified and perfect life set before you. You always wanted more. And I watched your greedy hunger from your shadow as you 'unknowingly' made me your stepping stone. And I forced a smile, knowing that you were never deserving of your *power*, of your *title*," he sneered. "What *I* could have done with your life if it were *mine*."

The Dark One seemed as if he was only talking with himself, his memories consuming him. "I'm sure you now remember the day I speak of. The day everything failed. I tried to bargain with you, but anyone would have done as you had. It was, after all, treason. Honestly, what could I have offered you? You already held everything you could have ever wanted…. and I should have been more careful on my part," he mumbled absently.

His scarlet gaze flickered back to the prisoner whose mouth was agape, eyes wide with terrible realization.

The Dark One smirked. His captive had finally connected the dots. "Enough of memory lane," he nonchalantly finished. "Now, I'm going to ask you again," he moved a step closer, speaking slow and clear, "where is the staff?"

"I did always want more," the boy said as he mustered all the might he had to raise himself up against his restraints. His voice no longer wavered, and he could feel his own hot blood pool against his marred back. "I am the standard set against your kind."

"You still have the strength to challenge me?" The Dark One warned.

The young man proclaimed with all the power he had left in his lungs. "My power was never yours to begin with! It cannot be taken! I know who you are, and I do not fear you!" He cried out in a voice belonging to that of a righteous god, agony searing in his bones.

The earth rumbled and quaked as if in response to his bold statement. Stalactites careened to the ground and the phantom whispers flared fearfully in the tongue of the dead. The Dark One surged into rage and bolted across the room. He punched the captive in the stomach, making the boy let out horrific shriek. He then motioned for the torturers to continue.

"AhhHHHHH!!!" The captive screamed in anguish, as he surely felt that his limbs would be torn from his body.

The world shook fiercely once more causing part of the cavern roof and outer wall to cave in on the far side of the room. The moon's full light and a gust of cold air flooded into the grotto from the new aperture.

The Dark One's cloak of shadows faded slightly in the silver celestial stream, the hood falling back about his broad shoulders, revealing his true form. He was a young man himself, albeit older than his prisoner. His jet hair was sleek and swept back from his forehead, grazing his shoulders. His eyes were still clouded by the crimson glow, but he stood tall, and wore lavish robes of ebony and silver that ran to the ground. On his left side was sheathed a curved dagger, emanating a faint green light. His face, though distorted by evil, was deceptively handsome, and a grin, most malevolent in nature, held fast to his lips.

He watched with immense satisfaction as the boy's spirit broke.

He raised his hand toward the torturers, signaling them to relent. He needed to make sure that the boy stayed alive. "Release him," he ordered.

The slaves obeyed their master and unshackled the young man. He fell to the floor violently, still moaning, shaking, and crying.

The Dark One drew closer, the moon shining off his raven hair, and knelt down on one knee. His fingers laced into the the young man's soaked locks and brought his head up by his hair so he could whisper into his ear. "No one can hear you. No one will come to save you – you can't even save yourself," his lilting cadence was calm yet sinister. "You are mine, and never will you see any light outside of this realm again. You belong to me."

The Dark One dropped the head, letting it hit the stone cold ground.

The captive moaned in response.

"I think our little prince needs a break," he said to his torturers. "Clean him up to heal. Despite popular belief, they have their limits."

The Desdem torturers hissed lowly in obedience.

The Dark One turned to glide out the door, his cape of shadows regaining opacity as he delved deeper into the darkness.

"They'll come looking for me..." the prisoner barely voiced.

The Dark One halted, now completely in the shadow of the grotto. His voice was ice. "No. They won't."

The Desdem guards on the other side of the dungeon's door tumbled the heavy locks. The solid iron gate slowly swung open, and the Dark One walked through.

The torturers picked up the gravely wounded prince. They moved him to a pile of dark straw on the edge of the cavern and shackled his hands onto a chain connected to the wall. The faint whispers of the shadows, the soft crackling of straw, and the footsteps of the withdrawing minions were all that the prince could hear; an enormous contrast from his own screams which had been roaring in his ears a few moments ago. The torturers walked out the door and it shut behind them with a brazen clang sending chills of hopeless despair up the captive's back. With a sense of finality, the iron locks rolled back into place, and everything was still.

The moon light poured through the thick clouds, through the apertures of the ceiling and wall, and onto his broken body. The pain he felt was beyond words. He could feel his blood pooling up beneath him. His bones were going to set wrong. They'd have to be broken again.

He forced himself to open his eyes and gazed into the moon, the silvery light blinding him. All he knew was that if he could stare into the moon, then he could make it. The girl he loved was still out there. *I will hold on for her. I will leave this place. I will stop him. I must protect them all...*

The celestial body started to blur.

Everything began to swirl and float.

All went black.

# <u>One</u>

The brilliance of dawn peaked into the cottage room and through the billowing gossamer curtains, superseding the reign of night. The first rays highlighted the dust motes, and they danced around the brimming cedar bookshelves that lined the teal and grey stone walls. The light grew to touch the volumes and the trinkets that the shelves held, all of them belonging to various origins and creeds and realms, revealing their well worn spines and well handled exteriors. The golden light strengthened, casting its warmth across the wooden floor which was strewn with more books, papers, a chemise, a bodice, a sheathed dagger, a pair of boots, odds and ends. The sun reclaimed this land in totality, finally touching the artfully weather oak dresser on the far wall, and rebounded back into the room from the large oval mirror of which it held.

Within the borders of this rustic bedroom, upon a hand carved four post bed, Adella Everheart slumbered.

Her several blankets, duvet, and sheets bunched around her, halfway covering her body, halfway off her bed frame. She was rested upon her stomach, and with an arm over the side of the mattress, the sleeve of her nightgown grazed the floor. Her lengthy, golden-auburn hair splayed about her head in a tumbling cascade of tousled tangles. Her flawless skin seemed to glow, yet her mouth hung comically slack. She was indeed beautiful when awake, but the girl felt that the sentiment of "beauty sleep" could hardly be used to describe her own slumber.

Adella stirred in the growing light as her dreams began to swirl into a jumble of inexplicable colors and thoughts.

*TinklelingaTINKALinglyTINKALINGLYJINGLYTI NKLEINGY*!!! The iridescent crystal sphere on her willow bark nightstand trilled loudly in magical, harmonious chimes, demanding attention.

"Ahh!" Adella inhaled with a start as she tumbled out of bed, sheets following behind her. She mumbled sleepily to herself, rubbing her head, clamoring to silence the chimes of her crystal ball.

She grabbed the crystal and rolled it about in her hands, silencing the alarm. She yawned and studied the time for a moment, and then reality set in.

The alarm went off an hour too late.

*Crud!* Her thoughts panicked. *I forgot to set the early alarm on this thing!* She tossed the glowing ball into her sheets and blurred about her room, careful of the miscellaneous articles strewn about her floor. She grabbed the nearest bodice, skirt, and chemise hanging from her mahogany wardrobe.

Adella hastily laced herself into her clothes, and then reached for the hairbrush on the edge of her of her oak dresser. She looked into the mirror and watched herself flick the bristles through her impossibly long locks. Around the carved borders of the looking glass were wedged a few parchment renderings of her family and friends. Memories that meant the world to Adella. Her gaze settled upon one particularly painful image that she had not the heart to pull down.

She looked away before the thought could steal the air from her lungs and finished sorting her hair. She retrieved her crystal from her bedsheets and paused for a moment wanting to make the bed, but knowing there was no time, she rushed into the bathroom to quickly brush her teeth.

Her crystal started to chime wildly again.

"Hewwo?" Adella gurbled, looking into the magical sphere, her toothbrush hanging out of the corner of her mouth.

A radiant olive face with long ebony hair appeared in the glowing orb.

"Adella! Where are you? We're at Juice Palace waiting right now... Wait, are you brushing your teeth? You're still at home?"

Adella spit and wiped her mouth. "I'm so sorry, Raen! I know I was supposed to meet you guys to study but I forgot to set the alarms on my crystal." She finished washing up and ran down the stairs.

"Oh no," Raena said under her breath.

"Yeah, tell me about it," Adella agreed as she rushed around the house to gather the rest of her things.

"Della, you have got to remember stuff like this," Raena chided. "Did you just fall asleep studying again?" Her bright amethyst eyes queried.

"Umm…" Adella trailed off.

"You *were* studying for midterms, right?" Raena persisted.

"Of course. I told you yesterday I was pulling a late nighter," Adella explained, awkwardly glossing over the conversation. Truth be told, she had not opened a single textbook the previous evening.

"Always the late nighters with you," Raena sighed. "Maybe if I actually saw you crack open a book in person you might not need to stay up half the night." She smiled sadly. "You know, just throwing this out there, but I'm always here for you if you need to talk, no matter the time of night."

"I know, Raen," Adella smirked wryly. Try as she might, Adella couldn't hide everything from her best friend. But what went on inside her own head was something she felt no other person should ever be burdened with. She had made the choice to carry her grief alone until it no longer existed – even if that day would never come.

"Let's talk when you get here, kay?" Raena added.

"Alright, I'll just meet you guys at school then."

"Perfect. If you get there in time, you might be able to do some last minute cramming with us in the quad," she winked as she put a juice straw in her mouth and took a sip. "Though I'm pretty sure we're beyond hopeless at this point," she laughed and looked back at Shmitty behind her.

"Hey!" A weak protest was heard from him as he frowned in the background.

"Don't sell yourself short, Raen," Adella encouraged, "you guys are going to do great."

"Uh huh," Raena replied with a cynical playfulness.

"Hi, Adella!" Shmitty cut in from behind Raena's shoulder.

"Hey, Shmit!" Adella responded. "Okay, so I'll see you guys at school. I'm walking out the door as we speak."

"Okay, see you in a spell, Del. Ride safe."

"You too, Raen."

Adella touched the iridescent ball with her finger and it made a delicate tinkling sound. The faces faded and disappeared into the crystal ball's glittery and clouded depths. She gave a tight to squeeze to the orb in her palm and it rescinded down to its compact form. She slipped it into a pocket on her soft leather book bag.

"Bye mom! I'll see you later!" Adella called through the house to her mom upstairs. "I love you!"

"Love you too, honey," her mom echoed a replied.

Adella slung her bag around her body, hooked the clasp of a deep blue riding cape around her neck, and raced out the back door. She streaked passed their water well, through the garden path and stone arch entry, across the open field of wheat, and down the main road to the blacksmith hall at the end of their property. She flung herself through the barn's giant open doors.

"Morning, daddy! Bye daddy!" She said the words so fast that they were almost a slur. She rushed into the stable and greeted her beautiful caramel Frisian, Anisia.

"Morning princess," her father's voice called from his work on the other side of the smithy. The brash clang of a hammer hitting hot steel held a steady rhythm. "Hurry, Della," he reminded through the hammer falls.

"I know," she breathed as she hopped into the saddle in one lithe movement. "Let's go," Adella nudged forward. The horse bolted out of the stable like lightning, leaving a trail of swirling dust.

The morning air was crisp and cool as it wisped past Adella's cheeks.

"C'mon Ani, little more," she coaxed and the horse picked up pace. She could feel the pounding hooves in her heart, could hear the snaps of her cape fluttering behind.

Adella felt free, flying in the sunrise, the wind whipping through her long auburn hair. The sky was a bright cerulean, and the forest, grain fields, orchards, and vineyards blurred past in their autumn hues. The air smelled faintly of leaves and smoke, of wine and earth, of apples, dew, and pine. Her cheeks numbed with the chill. Riding her horse like this was one of the only times that Adella still felt somewhat alive. Somewhat.

Far too quickly did her beloved back roads give way to the first signs of the township. As Adella passed the entry post, *North Brook Valley*, the last of the quiet and beautiful scenic dissolved. Adella entered reality with a stoic resignation as the hustle and bustle of the town accosted her senses. The streets were a nightmare at this hour. People were shouting from tall windows and store entries, goods and foods were being sold, horses trotted loudly upon cobblestone, stands and carts with the final gatherings of harvest showcased their wares, carriage bells rang and rang and rang. The occasional 'get on with it!' was hollered.

Adella sighed to herself. *Just a few more roads to my school. I can do this. I will not be late.*

"Della!" Raena called. "You made it!"

Shmitty was with her, and they walked through the stable lots to where Adella was securing Anisia.

"Here, we brought you your favorite," Shmitty said with a big smile as he offered the smoothie to Adella in a waxed paper cup.

"Thanks, you guys," Adella replied gratefully as she finished up with her faithful companion. She then took the drink and they all started towards the quad. Raena and Shmitty chatted and quizzed each other about their last minute cramming, trying to remember all the economic and agricultural terms they could.

The blazing sun glinted off Adella's ocean eyes as she scanned all around her. The place was buzzing with people getting ready for the day to come. More students continued to fill the lot as they arrived in all kinds of modes of transportation; most of them were on horses, some were on community carts, many walked.

It was over a month into the new school year and already things had fallen into a monotonous schedule. The campus had become a familiar place once more with its sturdy buildings and columns and overhangs, all made from rust colored brick and grey stone, adorned with swaths of hanging ivy. As they walked, they passed by a row of the hundreds of tree cubbies. These lush trees, having already turned from the buoyant greens of summer to the rich reds and golds of fall, lined many of the walkways on the grounds. Each individual tree had a special carved out hole with an attached door at eye level with small locks fixed to the latches. Adella saw several first years taking out and putting away their books and supplies in these natural cubbies, chattering animatedly amongst themselves, blissful in their innocence.

Adella's nose wrinkled a little and she let out a sigh, casting her gaze down to her drink. Today was sure to be more of the same. An endless ocean of going through the motions. She brought the waxed paper straw to her lips and took a deep sip. Even her favorite smoothie seemed tasteless.

"Della?" Shmitty asked with concern. He held open on his lap a book with messy parchment notes, a last ditch effort for test cramming.

"Hmm?" Adella sounded. She did not notice when they had sat down at the benches near their first period class at the edge of the stables lot. Shmitty and Raena already had out their study materials. *How long have I been gazing into oblivion*? Adella asked herself. "Oh, sorry, Shmit. What did you need?"

"The notes for Sutton's last lecture. From Tuesday I think. Do you have them?"

"Oh, yeah," Adella shook her head, set down her smoothie, and looked into her bag. She produced them with ease and handed them off.

There was a beat, and Shmitty and Raena exchanged a wary glance. Adella had disconnected again, looking out into the distance.

"Ok, lemme see it," Raena demanded suddenly.

"See what?" Adella murmured.

"Your crystal! I'm gonna fix your settings! You *know* we decided to make Fridays our study mornings. I even tried to remind you last night," Raena said in a huff.

"I've just been beyond busy, Raen. It really did slip my mind. I'm sorry," Adella replied with a half-hearted smile.

"This coming from the girl who can multitask like no other," Shmitty said under his breath.

Adella smirked at him as she held out her orb. Raena snatched it up.

"Let me see your calendar. I'm going to set up your alarms for our study and test days this year." Raena seemed smug with her smile as she quickly touched and poked at the surface of the ball.

"Raen. I can set my alarms just fine. I'm not a techtroll," Adella scoffed, raising an eyebrow.

Raena stared at Adella and reciprocated the brow motion. "I love you, but yes. You sometimes are. Besides, your crystal is a newer one than mine and I've been dying to kidnap it from you. F.E.R.I. tech at it's best," she blissfully mused as her fingertips glided across the top. The thing let out a loud tinkling chime.

Adella's lips curved with amusement as she watched her best friend.

"Alright, you're set!" Raena handed the sphere back.

"Thank you," Adella took it and slipped it into her bag.

"So I *know* your plate is loaded pretty heavy this semester, Del. Between helping with the community shelter, the combat nights, dance and music lessons, working in the smithy with your dad – not to mention our classes and homework load–"

"What's your point, Raen?" Adella sighed, cutting her off.

"I'm just saying, if you keep up at this rate, bigger things are going to slip through the cracks," she explained. "Or worse, *you* might crack."

"Seriously," Shmitty added.

"I just like to keep busy," Adella admitted with a hollow voice.

"We've noticed, trust me," Raena laughed a little.

Adella smiled softly back but said no more. She set down her smoothie cup and looked back to the lot.

The three friends were quiet for a long moment.

"Nice weather," Shmitty finally commented.

Adella only nodded, and continued to gaze far off. Raena and Shmitty looked at each other, and then back to her.

"Okay! That's it, Della! Talk to us! You're shutting down again. I notice it comes in waves, and some days are better than others, but more than ever you've been so distant. And it's gotten worse with the start of the new school year," Raena pleaded.

"Del?" Shmitty said softly putting a hand on her shoulder. Worry filled his warm hazel eyes.

Raena squared her body to better face her best friend. "Della... it's still him, isn't it?" She asked with sad uncertainty.

Adella's eyes shot back and forth between the two of them. She barely nodded in response. Her mouth was a tight line. Even through the daily numb that she managed to cling to for sanity, the mere mention of *him* brought up so much pain.

Raena and Shmitty's faces fell with understanding and they comforted their friend.
"You haven't really mentioned it for months now and I let it be, hoping that if you needed to talk you would," Raena added softly.

Adella's voice broke. "It's just… It's been months and yet it still feels fresh. And I wish I could pretend like it never happened, but I'll never be able to pretend like he wasn't the best thing that's ever happened to me. He was a part of my heart that I didn't even know existed, and now it's a part I can never have back," her words came out in a flood, tears threatening to brim. "I don't sleep anymore. I can't help myself. I want to be strong, but I am constantly reminded of it all – especially with all the media. No matter how much I try to ignore it, he's always going to be there. He's never going to go away. I stay busy to... to..." Adella trailed as she swallowed hard. She wanted to say, *I stay busy so I don't have to think about him. I stay busy so I can try to forget.*

Her friends remained frozen, helpless. They had wanted Adella to open up, but they did not realize just how much she had been holding in.

"You're right, Raen, it does come in waves," Adella whispered finally as she looked down at her hands. "And the last few have been hard. They *keep* getting harder – not easier. It's like there is still this pull to him, like he still holds me in his grip. I don't think this is normal," she admitted, trying to keep it together. She clutched her nails into her palms, concentrating on the pain of it, willing the tears away.

"Hey, hey, hey," Raena soothed. "We're here for you. We'll always be here for you. I know it hurts, but continue to give it time. And don't feel like you have to be strong if you need to talk. We're here. Talking is *good*," she said as she gave Adella a tight hug. "You know, I don't even really hear people bring it up anymore."

"Well actually that's not completely true–"

Both girls turned to look at Shmitty. He continued, oblivious, with his story. "I was at the FERI Emporium in the mall the other day looking at the magic plasma high def mirrors and one of the mirrors had Royal Life Exposed playing on it and it showcased Brogan. Then I heard these two sophomores nearby from our fourth period saying that it must have been humiliating for you when Brogan–" Shmitty stopped himself. He realized what he was saying and that Adella was about to cry. "Err, I mean… Yeah! No one ever even mentions it ever," he mumbled.

Shmitty was never one with words, even though he always meant well; he felt awful now. He shoved his smoothie straw in his mouth, cringing as he prepared for the onslaught from hell.

Raena shot him a 'you are dead' look.

Adella sniffled, choked back tears, and turned around. She started to rummage through her book bag as she murmured something about getting to class.

"How could you say that to her?! I was trying to cheer her up and you just go on about stupid…" Raena's voice started to fade as Adella's thoughts flooded her head.

*Petty. So petty. Are random people really that bored with their own lives? Small minds just love to talk about things they know nothing of,* she thought bitterly as she tuned out Shmitty and Raena's arguing. She wasn't upset at them; it was everyone else that she couldn't stand. She looked across the grounds into the fray of students. People were laughing and hollering. She distantly heard someone say, "Dude! Where's my horse?!"

*Everything is so shallow. This school, this town. Isn't there more to life? Is it all so hollow?*

A grand commotion began at the other end of the lot, and several people went running by.

Adella, Shmitty, and Raena quickly looked up.

A flashy open top carriage was pulling up. An annoying melody was blaring from a band of pop minstrels situated towards the back of the new ivory and gold transport, and inside the front of the open air cabin sat seven royals; four pretty girls and three handsome guys. The girls wore amazing gowns of velvets and ribbons and shimmery satins, and the boys sported fine courtier attire. Their mere presence was obnoxious as they threw their heads back and boisterously laughed whilst sipping on their lattés and rocking out with their groveling entourage. They were the core of the long standing group known as *The Royal Clique*, the popular ones, at North Brook Valley High, better known by the self instituted abbreviation, *The R.C.* Conversely, this nickname evolved among the commoners into *The R.P.,* which stood for *The Royal Pains*.

"And here they come. The definitions of *perfection* – Brittney, Tiffiney, Steffney. Anthoney, Mickey, Rickey, and Gretchen," Raena cringed. She suddenly forgot about the scolding she was giving Shmitty.

"Oh, man! You know just because they have got one of those brand new open top carriages, they think that they like own the place," Shmitty commented as he sipped his smoothie, hoping Raena would forget about slugging him in the shoulder for his earlier offense.

"They do own the place, Shmitty – at least, their families do anyway. You know, if it wasn't for the fact that I really don't want to get expelled, I'd be down to go totally medieval on *The R.P.*," Raena said with disgust.

Adella scoffed in agreement and stood, turning around to face her two friends who were still seated.

Seeing The Royal Clique pull up brought forth a deeply set resentment. An anger suppressed began to burn inside her. "It's just so typical that most of the *morale-leaders* and *jocks* at this school are royalty. They ride around in the newest carriages and robes, flaunting their parent's money, while calling themselves that vacuous title. It's so pretentious, contrived... delusional!"

"Right there with you, Del," Raena nodded.

"Seriously! In no way, in any sort of universe, would I even want to be like them! I'm embarrassed to even have eaten at the same table as them, let alone to have called them friends. Even *he* wasn't any different in the end. They offer no loyalty and they act like money can buy them everything, willingly casting aside the fact that some of their families are basically bankrupt!"

"Glad to see you still have some fight in you, but Della-" Raena tried to break in.

"They're bankrupt and yet they still have the nerve to petition to tax our lands further!" Adella's wind continued and she began to pace. She hadn't felt this fiery in a long time. It felt good to let it all out. "They overspend, trying to outdo each other, all the while their selfish antics spiral their families and our economy into more debt! Seriously, if they were *real* royalty they'd be at one of the royal finishing schools - but they aren't wealthy enough to buy their way in, and their birth status doesn't carry enough merit! They are caught in a pathetic royal limbo and the only way out of their superficial title is for them to marry up in class and leech off a *real* prince or princess."

"Adella!" Raena cut in again, standing up.

"And talking of misappropriated taxes, to rule a thriving kingdom you need a strong and appreciated working class, yet they *treat* us commoners like we aren't even good enough to breathe their own air! Take away their farce of a 'title' and *The Royal Pains* are little more than obnoxious people with monumental egos."

"You really want to tell them that to their faces?" Raena said shrinking back with a worried expression.

"You *know* I would love to!" Adella said with a self satisfied smirk.

"Turn around, Adella," Shmitty said through the waxed paper smoothie straw in his mouth. He chewed on it out of fear.

Adella spun and looked. To her dismay, The R.C. had quieted their minstrels when they pulled up. They had parked right behind her and had happened to be in earshot for the butt end of her little rant.

"Hi, Adella! What's up?" Brittney haughtily announced as she was helped down from the carriage by its driver. Her loud voice drew in a crowd.

"Hey, Brittney. Uh, nothing much," Adella answered, anxiety gripping her stomach. *Oh no! Did they hear the whole thing? Should I run? No! Running is for cowards. Stand your ground. You are not intimidated,* Adella deliberated in her head.

"So, nice speech back there. The whole 'take away our titles and we are nothing more than leeches caught in a royal limbo' – you come up with that yourself?" She stepped closer while her fellow royals lingered in the carriage. "Do I sense a hint of jealousy, Adella? Or maybe it's just my brilliant imagination," Brittney sarcastically prodded, then looked back to the carriage for support.

"Just your imagination. Uh, we really should get to class. The bell is going to ring," Adella said, hoping that Brittney would drop it.

"Don't be silly, *Adella*," Brittney patronized. "The bell won't ring for several more minutes. You should stay and chat! Because it sounds to me that you actually have something to say to The R.C."

She had caught Adella and wasn't going to let her go.

"Oh, it's nothing of importance. Just, nothing. It's nothing," Adella stammered.

"Ah. Nothing then. Just like you, Adella. You're nothing," Brittney's vitriol ran deep. "Just so it's clear, if you continue to bad mouth The R.C.," Brittney paused and looked back at her audience. The whole carriage nodded at her, feeding off the malicious energy. She flashed a stuck up smirk, turned back to Adella and continued, "well, let's just say that it would be a horrible mistake on your part. You had better watch yourself, *peasant*. Know your place. You're an insignificant *commoner* in the whole large world we live in." She leaned in closer, "And that's all you'll ever be." She tossed her hair back, the blonde locks catching the sun's gleam.

"Oh hey, Raena!" Tiffiney broke in. She had just been helped out of the carriage and took her place next to Brittney. She held a thick folder with parchments almost bursting out.

"Yeah?" Raena answered cautiously. Her and Shmitty has drawn closer to where Adella stood.

Sometime back in the 4th grade, drama had occurred between Raena and Tiffiney (apparently they had once liked the same boy), and the tension mounted year after year since. The two were ultimate rivals, much in the same way as Adella and Brittney. However, the latter pair's strife went far deeper, for there was a time when Adella was once friends with Brittney and The R.C.

"Could you put up these fliers for us around the school?" Tiffiney suddenly shoved a bunch of papers from the folder she was holding into Raena's hands. "It's for auditions to get invited to Brittney's super exclusive birthday party at her family's castle next week. We're holding them at lunch today and she wants to screen every potential guest. You know, to make sure that the '*losers*' don't get invited. You can be one of our super exclusive servants for the night if you help advertise."

The whole carriage laughed. The crowd murmured – some excited voices, some angry, others entertained by the conflict unfolding. Raena just stood there, holding the papers.

Adella knew the carriage really didn't expect Raena to hand out the fliers, this was done purely for humiliation. Anger seethed in Adella's blood. She stared at a rarely stunned Raena, glanced at Shmitty who was scared stiff, and then back at The R.C.

"You people! You do this every day!" Adella asserted. The strength in her own voice surprised her.

"Adella no, it's okay, just don't. The bell's going to ring," Raena tried to cover the embarrassment. Adella wouldn't have it and continued.

"You go up to someone and debase them purely because of status when in reality, if you understood what being a royal *actually* means, you would know that you are *not* to consider yourselves better than others, but rather be servants of your realms! Are you so insecure that you must seek validation by tearing down a commoner? Well, this is what I think of your pompous farce!"

Adella took the fliers from Raena and threw them back at Tiffiney. They exploded in a dramatic flutter. Tiffiney and the whole carriage gasped, but Brittney only smirked

"Wow, Adella! If you wanted to be our servant so bad you could have just begged us. You didn't need the outburst!" Brittney smugly announced for the audience that had accumulated to hear. "And what do you mean by a *royal* being a *servant*? How does that even work? You're acting like you know what you're talking about!" Brittney challenged.

"Actually, I do know what I'm talking about Brittney!" Adella declared, forgetting that nobody actually knew the truth.

"Oh, then *enlighten* us. How would you, a *commoner*, actually know what being a *royal* is?"

"I… uh…" Adella choked on her words. *Damn it! I can't tell them how I really know! They'd never believe me and then I'd be an even worse laughing stalk than I am now!*

Everyone was waiting for an answer, but when Adella remained silent, biting her lip, Brittney leaned in and whispered, "See. I told you. You're just a lowly peasant."

Brittney then leaned out, grabbing for more attention, and announced for the world to hear, "All of this talk coming from the girl who *used* to date Prince Brogan! You all remember that, right? How he dumped her at the final rally last year?!"

Adella's cheeks burned. The crowd reacted.

"Is that it, Adella?" Brittney chided. "Is that how you know about being royal? Because you used to date Brogan? Your short run of living vicariously through him? Because we all once ate at the same table?"

The carriage roared. Much of the crowd joined in, too, but many of them just stood there, hardly believing this altercation was actually taking place. Nervous murmurs ran through like wildfire as almost everyone remembered the event that Brittney brought up.

"That news is months old, Brittney!" Adella cringed, grinding her nails into her palms, staring her down.

"But it is *oh* so satisfying to see you squirm whenever it's brought up!" Brittney laughed. "Remind me, how did it go again?" She taunted, playing to the audience. "In front of the entire North Brook Valley High student body, the words of our dear Prince Brogan; '*You are not royalty...you are so annoying...and the only reason why I went out with you is because I felt sorry for you!*'" She looked to Adella, "or something like that."

Brittney held her nose high to the sky as her icy laugh splintered. Her entourage joined in.

Adella just stood there, feeling like she was punched in the gut, near the verge of tears. The memories of Brogan, of betrayal, were flooding her, almost too fast for comprehension. It was an eternity of torture in those seconds.

The bell rang, and everyone shuffled off before the second tardy bell sounded.

"Oh, saved by the bell," Brittney cackled. The crowd was quickly thinning, teeming with chatter of what had just transpired. This showdown was sure to be fuel for many weeks of gossip. "It was nice catching up with you, Adella. Until next time," Brittney smirked and then flitted away with her friends as the now empty carriage went off to find parking. The Royal Clique's voices faded into the campus.

And Adella stood still as a statue.

"C'mon," Shmitty finally said as he put his arms through Adella's and Raena's. He escorted them, and they moved off to class, hearts heavy with defeat and sorrow.

"Yeah, they do still talk," Adella said quietly.

# Two

Adella skipped her afternoon piano lessons. She made her way to her family's property, secured Anisia in her stall in the empty smithy, glad that her father had business away in town, and grabbed the mail on her way down the road. Her mother was out in the market which meant that the house was also empty as well. She unlocked the door, passed the threshold, slammed her book bag down on the living room sofa, and ran up the stairs to her bedroom with the bundle of mail still in her hands. She tossed the contents onto her dresser, fell on her bed, and finally crumbled into her tears. And she wept so bitterly, so deeply.

"Why?" She whispered to herself through a sob as she brushed the hair away from her wet cheeks. The tears were hot and they burned like fire. "I don't understand why I'm still like this!" *It was months ago, Del, he's not someone to pine for, especially after the way he left you,* she tried to reason. *Why won't people just drop it though! I've been ridiculed before, but never has it been that bad... I guess I should have expected it... I've heard the whispers... Uhg!! I will never be able to run away...*

She laid there for a moment still contemplating, drowning in the thoughts that lead her down a heartbreaking past. After what felt like hours, and with a heavy sigh and a sniffle, she sat up and went to her dresser. She reached for the mail, desperate for a distraction, when her eye fell upon her small wooden jewelry box. She knew it was a bad idea, but she opened the lid and took out the little satin satchel, pulling out the long gold chain. The swirling filigree engraved golden heart that dangled from the end of the necklace glinted in the afternoon light.

*Her* locket. The one *he* gave to her. She dared not to open it. She hadn't held the adornment for weeks, always willing herself to get rid of it, but it called to her in that moment, and for reasons she didn't understand, she placed the locket around her neck. It made her heart feel better and worse all at once. It was one of the only tangible things she had that remained from Brogan's presence. She looked in the mirror and took a steadying breath.

*Oh spell... I've looked worse I suppose,* she thought dryly as she ran a hand through her tousled hair and wiped her tears with her fingers.

She looked down, noticing the mail once more, and grabbed it, casually thumbing through the letters and documents. She didn't normally do this, but it was the closest diversion that she could find. As she perused, she saw the month's new issue of MedievTeen. *Seriously, Del, why do you even get this crap anymore? It's not like you care...* she thought about the magazine as she pulled it out. She hadn't read one of these in months.

She stopped cold when she saw the picture on the cover.

Amidst the '*High Collars are Definitely Out*', '*How to Get that Fresh Enchanted Look*', and '*How to Tell if He's Your Prince Charming*' side bar features, Prince Brogan was the main subject of the month's issue. His beautiful face, eternally perfect, smiling a coy and flirty smirk, was right dead center. His piercing cerulean eyes stood out brightly from his artfully tousled dark mahogany hair. He was dressed in a gold and scarlet brocade doublet, advertising for some new, expensive clothing label.

"Oh man…" she moaned. "You've got to be joking. Just getting it from all sides today, aren't I?" She sighed, suddenly feeling very stupid for wearing the locket.

Up until this point she had actively avoided knowing anything about Brogan's new life. And she had done pretty well all through the last season. But, against her better judgment, she opened the twine bound parchments to his feature page, passing images of him plastered everywhere in the leafs, and began to read. The article mentioned his being an up and coming combat champion, having been named one of the best fighters of Regal High's combat league, his recent getaways and travels, his return to the world of royals from his year long hiatus, and how he's the new dreamy guy in his exclusive royal academy's campus that every princess wants to land.

Adella choked when she read the next part.

> *Prince Brogan Etherstone has already found himself in a few whirlwind romances on campus – and his sophomore year has only just begun! A stark contrast from his interim year away from the crown and spotlight, he reportedly had a secret relationship with an unnamed commoner. When we asked about it, Brogan's only statement was, 'I got my head together and realized that she was just using me… and that I was better than that…'*

Adella stopped there.

Tears rolled down her cheeks again as she flung the magazine across the room. It hit the wall with a dull thud, pages crinkling. She grabbed the locket and pulled it over her head, throwing it into her pillow. *See, this is why you have been staying away from all this crap! This is why you shut down. This is why you should have kept busy with your lessons this afternoon! You don't need the reminders!*

She fell back onto her bed and slowly drifted into an uneasy, anxious, and tear filled slumber.

"Adella? Wake up, honey," a loving voice coaxed in the twilight.

Adella's eyes slowly opened. The sun was setting, and she made out a soft face in the waning light. "Oh, hi, mom," she sleepily replied.

"Hey, Sweetpea. Sorry to wake you but can you help me make dinner?"

"Yeah, sure mom," Adella said with a yawn. The dried tears on her cheeks felt funny.

"Love you, sweetheart," her mom said as she kissed Adella's head, her billowing caramel curls lightly sweeping her daughter's nose.

Adella walked down the stairs and into the warm cottage living room. A fire was going, the magic mirror was on in the background, and the tantalizing smell of delicious chicken floated on the air. She made her way into the kitchen and grabbed a small cauldron from a cupboard.

"What do I need to make mom?" She asked.

"Peel and cut up a few large potatoes and boil them," her mother replied as she tended to the chicken on the grill in the giant, brick fireplace.

"Mashed potatoes?" Adella assumed as she filled the pot with water from the iron well pump.

Her mother nodded and Adella got to work placing the pot on the adjacent wood burning stove in the room. The quality of life in their home was abundantly blessed, but for the family of a successful blacksmith, it should come as no surprise.

When compared with the ways most other people in her town lived, Adella's home was by no means a modest abode. The two story stone cottage was detailed with fine iron accents, landscaped with a rustic garden and walkways, and adorned with diamond cut and glass stained windows with shutters. It had three chimneys, three bedrooms, a robust cozy kitchen, a living room, dining room, den, nook, stocked library, and several other amenities – all of which dignified her family as anything but lowly. Her father was a great man and worked hard to give them the best that he could for their commoner status.

Adella and her mother worked in silence for several moments and, although Adella disliked hearing any sort of media, they listened to the nightly news that was playing distantly on the magic mirror in the living room.

A woman's soothing voice stated, "Today in the Adamaris seaport of Virgo, located on the southern outskirts of the capital, Ardenthel, pirates ransacked the docks and robbed several town officials in the early hours of the morning. Among the thousands of coin stolen, they also took several priceless artifacts from the house of Devoreaux du Croix, the governing lord of the city. Ancient artwork, jewels, and sculptures that have remained with the noble family for centuries were claimed by the rogues. The specific group suspected of this crime, The Acrimony Accord, is the high seas division of the mainland band of thieves known as the Venom Blade Syndicate. It is suspected that their leader, a man known as Bane, headed up the attack himself. Officials are worried that this crime wave may head North into southern Kelemer waters. More news on these unfolding events at eleven, when–"

"How are my lovely ladies?" Adella's father announced happily as he opened the front door.

"Hi, daddy!" Adella called as her mother walked from the kitchen and into the front room to give him a hug. He took his wife by the waist and kissed her. The back of his hand stroked her cheek as he looked into her eyes.

"I love you, Rose," he whispered to her.

Rose smiled sweetly and kissed her husband once more. She took off his hat and playfully ran her fingers through his thick, dark hair with a smile. He kissed her cheek again. She then went to hang the hat on the coat rack while he walked through and hugged Adella's shoulders as she peeled the vegetables.

Despite having a teenager, Adella's parents still looked exceptionally young and beautiful.

"Hey, princess," her father heartily replied. Adella smiled as he kissed the top of her head. "So, are we still on for tonight?"

"Yeah. I still need a lot of work on that flip move you taught me," Adella replied.

"Okay, then. Let's eat this wonderful dinner you and your mother are preparing, and then we'll head out. I'm going to wash up," he said as he headed for the water basin in the backyard. He grabbed a lantern and went out the backdoor.

Adella walked over and put the potatoes in the now boiling cauldron.

"So how was school today," Rose nonchalantly asked as she looked for some spices on a shelf in the pantry.

"It was…okay…I guess," Adella trailed.

Her mom turned around and eyed her skeptically. Rose had found the spice she needed and walked over to the grilling chicken. "So, I see you skipped your lessons this afternoon," she probed as she seasoned the crackling meat.

"Yeah, I was just really tired."

"Della, did something happen?" She asked, genuinely worried.

Adella gave a long sigh. "The *Royal Pains*," she said with a grimace. "They brought *him* up. Brittney in particular. She basically told everyone that I tried to live vicariously through him. She called me a pathetic, lowly commoner. They made fun of me. I just can't believe that I'm still gossip for some people. Even the media won't drop it! It was several months ago, mom!" Adella's throat started to become thick as she said those last few words. She looked down. "Even my dreams won't let him go. I wish I'd never met him," she whispered. She dug her nails into her fists, trying to concentrate on the pain they made. It was her defense mechanism to will back the tears. She was tired of crying.

"Oh honey," Rose put the herbs down and came over to Adella. She put her arms around her child and said, "These things sometimes take time. At least one of the bright sides is that Brogan didn't compromise our having to stay hidden, especially with him being so high profile. It still hurts, though, and I know that. But even if you can't control what other people say, you *can* make a strong stand and show that it doesn't affect you on the outside. No one can make you feel inferior, Adella, unless *you* give them that power.

"And don't let those Royal Pains get to you. They don't understand the responsibility that they hold – you know that better than they do. I know for a fact that they are all just jealous that you are the smartest and most beautiful girl in all the realms."

"Mom, every parent says that about their kid," Adella countered, rolling her eyes.

"They may *think* that their kid is the best, but they are wrong. *I'm* always right and *I* say that you *are* those things," Rose grinned. "I know this may sound cliché, but remember that your father and I, and your true friends like Raena and Shmitty, are always here for you and we will always love you. And things will pass, I promise you that. Hold your head up high and hold onto hope. You truly have an amazing future before you. Just you wait and see."

With that, she hugged Adella tighter and rocked her quietly. Adella inhaled heavily, failing in her personal battle to fight her overwhelmed heart. Tears fell down her cheeks and she could smell her mom's perfume. Roses.

"Please pass me a roll, love," Adella's father asked. Rose nodded politely and reached for the bread basket.

"So, princess, how was school today?" He asked casually while he took the basket from his wife.

Rose stopped mid motion as she shook her head ever so slightly at her husband. Her eyes gave the warning that she couldn't utter. They screamed "touchy subject".

Adella didn't notice the split second exchange. She aimlessly played with the food on her plate with her fork. She had no appetite whatsoever.

"Err, I mean, princess, how did you do on your exams today?" He corrected ruefully.

"Hmm?" Adella looked up. She realized she was being addressed. "Oh. I guess I did okay. I think I could have done better…"

She looked down again and prodded a leaf of salad.

"Oh?" Her father quietly responded, carefully assessing his daughter. He looked up and Rose mouthed the word *Brogan*. Orrick thought for a moment, eyebrows pulled together.

"Adella, you remember the story of how your mother and I met, right?" He began.

"Of course. You were once a nobleman in Adamaris and she was an orphan girl in a town that your family ruled over."

"Yes, that's right," he smiled. "It was in the Sun's Tide. I had left early in the morning to go riding in the country. When I came into town, I saw her in the market. We were only teenagers at the time, but she was the most beautiful girl I'd ever seen in my life. I distinctly remember my heart stopping."

He looked over at Rose and she blushed.

"Daddy, where are you going with this?" Adella asked dryly.

"As you know, I walked up to her that morning and by some stroke of fate we fell in love. She was everything I never knew I needed."

"But when you approached your family about mom they disowned you," Adella interjected.

"Yes. They refused our love and denied me any inheritance if I pursued Rose any further. But you remember what I said to all that," he prompted with a smile as he took Rose's hand.

"You told them all to shove it," Adella smirked.

"I said a few stronger words than *that* I'll have you know," his ocean eyes twinkled with amusement. "After the rejection of my family, your mom and I set off for a new life, never looking back."

Rose looked at her husband with complete adoration.

Adella took a deep breath. She knew her father loved telling this tale, but she was in no mood to think about love stories. Her heart was hurting enough as it was.

"I'm sorry but dad why are you reminding me of this?"

"Dellabella, the point I'm trying to make is that I came from the world of royals. I knew it all too well," he gazed into his daughter's eyes with adamant understanding. "And yet I have never regretted my decision to leave. I gave up everything for true love, and by doing so I truly became the richest man in the world. I knew your mom was the one and I meant my vows. If I had gone back on my word and done what my family told me to, then I would have broken her heart and my promise.

"Any person, royal or not, should be willing to sacrifice everything for someone they really love. Those are the people we must find and hold onto. I would have died if I'd hurt your mother, especially after she had put all her trust in me. Della," he reached out and stroked his daughter's cheek. He opened his mouth to continue but Adella interjected.

"Brogan never loved me, dad." The sorrow in her declaration was crushing.

"Never mind him! *You* are such an amazing girl. You're intelligent, kind, beautiful, talented, bright, and clever. You are love and light Adella and he is *not* worth destroying your spirit. You deserve so much better than that poor excuse for a princeling. Please don't let him take away who *you* are."

Adella was quiet. She didn't know what to say.

"I saw so many similarities between what occurred with you and Brogan, and with how I pursued your mother," Orrick murmured, regret heavy in his words. "I had wondered if history was repeating itself, which is why I didn't put a stop to it… but when Brogan said those things, the day he hurt you like that, he's lucky he didn't cross my path. Any *boy* that hurts *my* little girl…" he trailed off darkly, shaking his head. His jaw flexed hard. "I wish I had put a stop to it all, but he fooled me, too. I am so sorry I didn't protect you like I should have."

"Dad, no, don't feel that way—"

"No, it's true. I should have seen it, and I didn't, and I am so sorry. But I've told you before, and I'll tell you again. Adella, he is not *worthy* of *you*. And I promise you, he will regret all that he has done because one day, you are going to do great things, and he's going to see them, and he will die inside knowing what a fool he had been."

Adella smiled at his sweet words, a huge lump in her throat. "Thank you, daddy," she said as she grabbed his hand and gave it a squeeze.

"Anytime, princess," Orrick replied as he leaned in and kissed her head.

# Three

The hour had grown late. The sky was a midnight blanket that glittered with millions of breathtaking stars. The moon was almost full and it shone a silver light upon everything it touched. A cool wind blew through the bordering forest trees which were black silhouettes against the nightscape; they rustled uneasily.

"Dad?" Adella began.

"Yes, Del?" He replied.

Adella and her father walked lightly along the field towards the smithy down the road. The glass lantern Adella held, fixed from a long gold chain, swung back and forth, shifting shadows in its iridescent light.

"Do you feel that? The wind? Hear it rustling in the trees?" She asked.

Orrick nodded. Adella proceeded.

"I don't know. Maybe it's just me or something, but it almost feels like change is coming. Like the world is about to shift. Like the winds are bringing it."

"You never know, princess," Orrick agreed quietly in the silvery, dark night. "You're at an age where life really does change a lot. Paths become clear, purposes are made known."

"Really? You think I could be right about this feeling then?"

Orrick nodded again, just as pensive as his daughter.

Adella sighed and muttered, "Well I sure could use a change."

They continued to walk in silence amongst the winds as they approached the warmly lit windows of the smithy. From within they could hear a booming laugh followed by the clang of swords. Adella smiled broadly as her father let loose a chuckle and he shook his head. They entered the wide barn doors and they saw Shmitty and his father sparring with swords.

Dust was swirling around the two duelists as they jumped back and paced in circumference of one another in a makeshift battle ring. Then, once more, they both lunged and circled as their blades crossed in intricate patterns.

Ducking and slashing, back and forth, they went at it over and over again. A hard slice was dealt by Shmitty's father; Shmitty parried it back. His father lunged forward for another hefty strike, but Shmitty was faster and dodged out of the way.

Shmitty, surprisingly, was quite the fighter. He was quicker than you'd expect him to be, and he could deal a swift, deadly strike. The problem was getting him to hit his target and dodge attacks. He was rather timid, tall, gangly – to the point of endearment – and unsure of himself most of the time. He would often falter in his decision making, missing crucial opportunities to make contact, usually tripping on his own feet. But, when he did manage a strike, it almost always took the wind out of his opponent, many times knocking them to the floor.

The match grew faster, intensifying. His father advanced in a pattern of fancy footwork. Shmitty tried to fall back and match the maneuver so he could adequately retaliate, but at the last moment, he tripped over his own legs and landed on his back. His father then put in the final strike, but purposely stopped short before it actually hit his son. The dust settled.

"Ahhh!! Shmit!" His dad exclaimed as he helped his son up. Shmitty took off his helmet and shook out his hair. "You would have had me that time! 'C'mon!" He said with a smile while mussing the boy's hair. "You did good though. Very good."

The two of them looked up and finally noticed Adella perched high up on some hay bails on the other side of the barn next to Anisia's stable. Her father was close by her, putting on his chest plate. They were smiling.

"Well done, Sir William and Shmitty!" Orrick said with a broad grin while he fastened his straps.

"Well, well, well! Look at that Shmit! They finally decided to show!" William's hearty laugh resounded as he came over to greet them.

"Hi, Shmitty!" Adella sweetly waved. "Hello, Mr. Yordinson," she then said to William as she jumped off the bail. Shmitty came over to where she was standing and gave her a warm hug.

"Heya Dells," he stepped back and shook her father's hand. "Hello, Mr. Redding," he said with a nod and a smile.

"Hey, Shmit," Orrick replied warmly.

William came over, and clapped Orrick on the shoulder. "My friend," he said.

"Are you ready?" Orrick smiled as he set his hand on William's opposite shoulder.

"Let's fight," William replied with a fierce grin. The two men then laughed as they walked over to the battle area to suit up for the next round.

"I'm sorry about today, Dells. They were awful. Are you doing a little better at least?" Shmitty said over the low murmur of their fathers as the teens situated themselves on the hay bails to watch the up and coming brawl.

Adella gave a sad smile. She looked down and picked at a piece of straw.

"I'm also sorry about what I said on the benches," Shmitty added. "I don't think before I speak and I'm really trying to fix that," he paused. He could sense more than the day's earlier events troubling her. "Did something else happen?"

Adella sighed. "So I get the mail, right, and the monthly MedievTeen showed up today. Guess who was on the cover."

"Brogan?" Shmitty assumed with a disgusted scoff at his name.

She nodded and continued. "What's even worse is the story they printed about him. He didn't use names, thank The Radiance, but he basically said that the commoner girl he dated was using him." Adella pulled her knees to her chest in misery and wrapped her arms around them.

"Ouch. I'm so sorry. Okay, I wish to rephrase my earlier question. Do you need a hug?" He asked shyly.

She looked up at him. "Yes, I could use one of those, Gavin."

"Gavin! Using my real name? Oh boy, it really is serious," he teased. "Do you know what?" He asked as he quietly wrapped an arm around her. "He's a freaking idiot. I couldn't imagine life without you in it."

"Really?" she asked.

"Er, yeah," Shmitty blushed, realizing he may have said a bit too much.

"Are you ready, Orrick?" William prompted cutting through the quiet of the barn.

"Bring it," Orrick said with a smug grin.

The mood immediately changed. As if in response to the challenge, the atmosphere seemed to tense up. In comparison to the battle that had just transpired, this new brawl was something entirely different. The warm lantern lights flickered as the wind whipped through the establishment, swinging them and breaking up the shadows.

The two duelists circled in a careful pattern, each one stepping in a cat like walk, gauging the distance. Then, in a flash, their blades hit like lightning. Again and again. The blade's strikes flashed and sparks flew into the dark.

Adella and Shmitty were on the edge of their seats, watching their fathers fight. Although this was nothing new from what they would do on any given week night, it never got old.

More precise and dangerous blade action; things picked up. Different slices and glints, brash clashes and sharp clangs, quick swings and swipes. A death dance, without the intent of a life being taken; one wrong move and the "dance" would surely end in a mortal wound.

The two fought as if it was for their lives. It was hard to tell who was the better fighter, or if they were holding back at all.

The men were best friends and had known each other for decades. They decided to go into the smithing business together and were very successful. However, both of them, having known the cruel nature of the world first hand through separate experiences, decided it was best to have their children skilled in the ways of combat and defense. The spreading rumors of wars brewing between the realms, the roving bands of thieves, and the increasingly frequent sightings of dark and terrible creatures haunting the forests and deep places of the world, was all reason enough for the men to train their children. The protection and self defense of their families was their first priority.

"C'mon, is that the best you've got, Orrick?" William playfully taunted.

"I'm just warming up," Orrick breathed as he lunged forward and struck back.

A lightning quick barrage rang out speckled with several harsh clangs. The swirling dust that was getting kicked up made it hard for Adella and Shmitty to fully see what was happening.

All of a sudden, somebody's sword went flying and a body rolled on the floor.

"I think you're warmed up," William said with a cough as he laid on his back, Orrick's blade tipped to his face.

"I told you," Orrick laughed. He held out his hand and helped his comrade up. Both of them burst into laughter as they dusted themselves off. Adella and Shmitty started clapping happily in applause from the hay bails.

Orrick and William bowed as they removed their helmets.

"Great duel! I want a rematch though, and soon!" William heartily proclaimed.

Adella and Shmitty just shook their heads and under their breaths muttered something about their fathers vicariously living out the glory days.

"Well then, Dellabella, you're next," Orrick smiled as he grabbed her sword and held it out for her. She got up off the hay bail, jumped down and grabbed her weapon.

"Kick his butt, Del!" Shmitty called with a laugh.

Orrick shot him a smug look.

Shmitty shrank back with a smirk.

Adella put on her chest plate, adjusted her helmet, and stepped into the boundaries of the ring. Like before, each duelist circled in careful proximity of the other; swords drawn, ready to block or strike. *Ok Del, concentrate*, she told herself. *He tends to come in on the left so–*

Clang! The sharp steel sparked. Adella blocked. Her father attacked harder. Clang. Clang. Swipe. Clang.

*Right on, Del,* she commended herself. *Okay, let's do this.*

Her father came in closer for a better striking radius. He spun into his new assault with all the grace of a seasoned warrior and made many quick jabs, all of which Adella blocked and dodged again.

Their fight was so smooth that it seemed as if it was choreographed. However, Adella still couldn't get an offensive hold on the match, she could only continue defending.

Orrick made a huge quick swing – parallel to the ground – in a shoulder to shoulder arc.

Adella was quicker, though. She sensed it was coming and at the right moment arched her back, her left arm bowing with her hand touching the ground. The world slowed down as she could feel the blade swipe over her chest. She then popped up, blocked the next attack with her sword, and took advantage of the steel contact to put into play a maneuver of her own. She attacked quickly, finally getting some offense in, keeping the jabs and swipes short and clean. Clang. Clang. Clang.

Surprisingly, she parried aside her father's sword, bent back, kicked off of her father's chest, using the contact as leverage, and back flipped over. He was propelled backward in the process, utterly stunned by a move that he had no idea that his daughter was capable of doing just yet. As soon as she landed she went in for the "kill". Orrick tried to block but she twirled lithely around his blade – flowing long hair around her – and knocked him onto his back.

She stopped with the sword at his chest.

The dust settled.

"Way to go Del!" Shmitty crowed as he jumped up from the hay bail. William's laughter was infectious as it emanated from him and filled the whole establishment with mirth. Adella offered her hand and helped her father up. Shmitty's arms instantly wound tight around her as he hugged her fiercely.

"Shmit… can't… breathe…" Adella choked out through giggles.

"That was so amazing, Del!" He exclaimed as he let her go.

"Well! Miss Adella! Amazing indeed! Have you been practicing behind our backs?" William winked as he came to where she was standing. "I haven't seen *anyone* fight like that in years. No one except, well, your father," he clapped Adella, lightly, on the shoulder.

She was still beaming.

So were Orrick and Shmitty.

"You nailed it, princess," Orrick smiled proudly at Adella who was taking off her helmet. He started to undo his bracers. "You just needed a little break for it to sink in. Evildoers beware the wrath of my daughter! I truly fear for the next person that messes with you!" Orrick shook his head as he hugged his little girl with his free arm.

"When *did* you teach her that?" William asked, having only ever seen that move done by his best friend in their younger days.

"Oh, just a few weeks ago," he replied with a smile. "She's been practicing."

"Orrick! Orrick!" The frantic cry pierced through the night.

"Rose?!" Orrick looked around desperately, instantly recognizing the voice. He turned in time to see her running through the barn doors.

"Orrick you must come quickly! Something has happened! There's no time to explain. I'll have to tell you on the way," Rose said out of breath. She grabbed her husband's hand.

"What, has someone hurt you? Who has done–"

"It's nothing like that – though I would have a dragon bare down upon us rather than face the situation that is waiting in our house!" Rose exclaimed as she pulled her husband along. He responded automatically to the movement and immediately shot for the door.

"Wait!" Adella called before they cleared the smithy's threshold. "Wait! What's happening!?" She asked in panic.

"No, Adella. Stay here!" Rose replied. She gave Orrick a look and he instantly knew what she meant by it. The only thing that they would keep from their daughter.

"Orrick what's wrong? Do you need my help?" William asked with his sword half drawn.

"Will," he nodded to his friend. "Watch her," his head jerked to Adella.

"Sure thing," William replied cautiously, his sword still poised. He jerked with his head to the weapon.

"Not needed. It will be fine," Orrick said. He then mouthed a word that Adella did not understand. Her head swung back and forth trying to decipher their instant conversation. "I'll come back for Adella." Orrick ordered William, suddenly seeming much more powerful than Adella had ever known.

Without anymore than that, the two were out the door in seconds.

Adella stood there, dumbfounded.

Everything was utterly silent, the three of them frozen in place.

"Okay. I'll say it. What just happened?" Shmitty asked. He looked like someone just hit him upside the head.

"It'll be alright, son. And don't worry, Miss Adella. Your parents are in no danger. If that was the case I would be right there with them by their side. Everything is going to be fine. For now just stay with us though, okay? I'm sure all will be explained in due time."

Adella looked at William. She nodded once, her eyes huge, brows pulled together, mouth a tight line. She walked over to the hay bails next to Anisia and took off her armor.

William and Shmitty picked up swords and started to duel again, but with far less spirit than before. It was at least something to pass the time until Orrick's return. The once sharp clangs were now dull and uninteresting as Adella became lost in her thoughts. She sat there, stewing. *I have to go. I don't know what it is but I must get home. Something is going on and I should be there! I hate not being with them. They never have kept anything from me! They are all the family I have left and family sticks together! Especially since Cayden... I must be with them!*

Adella got up off the bail and casually sauntered to Anisia's stable. She looked over her shoulder. The fight continued, nobody paying attention to her.

*Good,* she thought. She quietly unlatched the stable door, grabbed the golden and glass lantern that hung on the post of the stall, and silently bounded onto the horse's back bare.

"Yah!" She shouted with all her might, her voice cutting through the smithy.

In a flash, Adella and Anisia bolted out of the stable and through the barn towards the doors.

"Della! Wait! Nooo!" William and Shmitty both called as they reached in vain for the girl.

It was too late. She was out the door in seconds and racing through the anxious night as their calls faded into the dark. Her hair whipped around and her flowing dark blue skirt fluttered in the wind. The soft glow of her home's windows became clearer across the field.

*Okay, there is no way now that they'll catch up to me,* she thought as she slowed the haste of the creature. She trotted along briskly until she was on the edge of the backyard. She quickly dismounted and tied the reigns to the water basin.

She took the lantern and stealthily traversed the paths in their garden to the back door. She put her ear up to the crack and tried to listen. She heard bickering, muffled voices.

Nothing was clearly audible.

She slowly turned the handle and creaked the door open, peering in. She could see through the kitchen and into the large front room. Most of the lights were out, save for a few upstairs, and one large lantern lamp glowing in the far corner of the front room.

Standing in the living area were many tense figures; among them she spotted her parents, visibly stressed, eyes wide and mouths set hard. Rose was behind Orrick, almost as if he was shielding her and taking the brunt of the terse conversation. From what was he shielding her though?

Adella's gaze shot over to the figures on the other side of the room, facing her parents. Three people; two armored men standing behind one extraordinary looking woman.

She was exquisitely beautiful, but in her older years. She stood high and proud, although she must not have been taller than five and a half feet. A plush yet sleek long coat of dark fur was wrapped around her and underneath it her dress flowed out. It was the color of the sea on a bright clear day, trimmed in gold and jewels. Her bright blue-green eyes flashed and her blond hair was piled softly on her head. She was impossibly adorned with an array of jewels, rings, bracelets, and earrings. A dainty golden crown with gems of aquamarine and teal finished the look.

She was magnificent.

*Oh my gosh! What's the queen of Adamaris doing here?!* Adella freaked out mentally. She knew the woman's face. It was on the magic mirror enough.

"Aedrian, you must understand! Adamaris is in great need! An uproar is on the horizon and you know it will spread like wildfire with the people, the press. The whispers have already begun! Surely you understand this!" She reasoned.

"You come to me at this hour? Nay! After sixteen years, and expect what!?" Orrick raised his voice. "You exiled us, remember?!"

"You knew my reasons!" The woman gave a quick glance at Rose. Rose cringed back and Orrick became fiercer.

"Oh yes! I see you're truly repentant now, Cassandra!" He shot back, sarcasm seething hotly in his voice.

"Goodness! I *am* sorry Aedrian. I honestly did what I thought was best at the time but now I am truly sorry. I should have never been so hard of heart and I should have never written that decree. I never thought it would go this far. I would never have put it into existence if I knew you would run the way you did. But the law never included heirs, only you, and this matter is of grave importance. There is no one left!" She pleaded. She brought her hand to her temple and whispered, "And with your son Cayden being gone…"

"I already told you. That is very hard for us to talk about," Orrick coldly cut her off.

"Yes. Of course. Forgive me," the woman apologized fervently. "Listen, though. Adamaris must have a new heir sitting on its throne very soon and Adella–"

"That's enough, mother–"

Adella's breath caught.

"Mother!?" She gasped loudly in disbelief. She dropped the long chain lantern she was holding, the crash of glass and gold stabbing the silence.

Everyone's heads whipped to the back door, only to see the poor girl trying to put out the small fire she just created.

"Dangit, dangit, dangit! Get it out, get it out!" She stuttered as she stomped and tried to smother out the modest flames with the bottom of her skirt. It only took a moment to secure the situation, but the small black circle of her accident smoldered up a thin line of smoke as she looked to her now attentive and surprised audience. Her aqua eyes were wide and startled; her usually full lips pressed into a line.

"Oops," she softly said.

# Four

There was a rap on the back door and Orrick answered. William and Shmitty were standing there out of breath.

"Sorry about that. I thought we had her," William said in apologies.

"It's quite alright, William," Orrick affirmed while motioning for them to enter. "Della is a hard one to manage when she sets her mind to something," he added with a wry smile while glancing back at his daughter who was sitting on an armchair in the corner of the room. She still was chagrined, the result of her "fiery" entrance moments before.

William and Shmitty entered the house. When William saw the woman in the front room, he immediately fell to his knee with his head bowed. He reached a hand backwards and grabbed his son's tunic meaning for him to bow as well. Shmitty fumbled to his knees in confused shock.

"My queen," William said with reverence. He held his right hand to his heart.

"Well goodness, Sir William Sinclair! It has been years! What happened to your visits? It was ever so hard to find you!" A smile played on Cassandra's lips.

"I am sorry, my queen, but I did what I thought was best," William said, still on his knee.

"Rise and speak no more of it, brave captain. You were one of the best knights Adamaris had ever seen. I was wrong to have let you go," she paused and turned to her son. "Both of you."

William rose to his feet. "Thank you, my queen," he said with a fervent heart.

"Although," Cassandra began in a coy tone, "I would have thought that the bright and shining captain of the guard could have held captive a teen girl for a mere few moments." She laughed lightly.

"As I have already established, Adella has a mind of her own," Orrick interjected, chuckling.

"I could have told you that," Shmitty said under his breath as he looked at Adella. She glanced a smirk at him.

William's eyes wandered to the two guards in the room. His jaw suddenly hardened.

Both men were of different ages and stature, but William recognized the larger of the two. The guard was proud of stature, square jawed, middle aged, standing many inches above six feet. He was robust and muscular with broad shoulders, set with a barreled chest, and his dark ebony hair was swept back into a glossy low ponytail. He was wearing a shining silver breastplate trimmed in golden waves with matching bracers and greaves. His deep teal cape swept the ground and was held together by a gold clasp bearing the emblem of the kingdom of Adamaris. Many medals and gold chained adornments were attached to his right breast and shoulder. His matching helmet was set atop with a long, deep teal ponytail and he cradled it comfortably in his right arm. He had a relaxed, arrogant look on his face and his body language reflected this.

"I see you've done well for yourself, Haeman," William said to him, his tone tinted with bitter sarcasm. The guard smirked and chuckled.

"Yes, I have, actually." Haeman's voice was deep, smooth. He chuckled a little more. If rich, dark toffee had a laugh, it would be this sound. "Serving Adamaris as the captain of the guard does have its benefits, William. It's truly too bad you gave it up. However, things have improved since your leave, so I would say it was for the best."

William replied carefully. "So you finally secured a handle on those Venom Blades that always seem to hit your shores? I hear The Syndicate is going on a near ten year streak."

Orrick hid a smile.

Haeman became hot. "Actually, we are in fact close on their trail and have almost shut them all down," he replied, eyes narrowing. "You should know better than to believe in everything the press reports."

"Oh, I know *that* full well. But don't be so hard on yourself. A situation that massive *would* be difficult for an unseasoned captain to fend off," William said with diplomatic innocence. It didn't fool Orrick and Haeman, though.

Haeman glared at William, their eyes locked sternly.

"Well now, gentlemen," Cassandra broke in, "it is apparent that the safety and greater welfare of Adamaris is important to you both, but the syndicate is not the issue that I have come to discuss." She motioned to Adella.

"She's come for Adella, Will, although I think you've already figured as much," Orrick spoke.

"Yes, I assumed that this was why you had rushed out of the barn with hardly an explanation," William agreed. "Well, I figure we had best be going. It looks like you all have quite a bit of catching up to do." He looked to everyone. "Until next time, farewell."

He bowed lowly once more to the queen who was perched primly on the edge of an armchair. Shmitty followed his father's lead. She smiled grandly and nodded her head, likewise, to the knight and his son. As the two headed for the front door, William met the gaze of Haeman once again. If looks could kill, their split second exchange would have been lethal.

Their rivalry back in their academy years and during their service of the queen was as bitter as ever. Time had not washed it away. It deeply troubled William when he heard the news that a corrupt man like Haeman was able to raise through the ranks and become commander of the entire realm of Adamaris' security – especially after William had left the position to a *different* individual.

"Bye Dells," Shmitty said shyly. He mouthed the words 'call me' as he lingered momentarily in the threshold. William ushered his son out and followed behind. Orrick muttered a few things quietly to William and then closed the door. He walked over and sat down next to Rose on a large cushioned chair.

"So then, this is my granddaughter," Cassandra proudly ascertained, sitting tall. She was almost smug. Her aqua and jeweled dress wrapped around her legs in cascading layers of chiffon. She held her perfect, regal posture, every word articulated, and she continued to gush. "You know, if I did not know any better, I would swear she looked just like myself from my teen years. So incredibly gorgeous, and she has the eyes of the ocean. Every true Everheart bears those."

"We've always thought that Adella favored *my* features," Rose interjected. Her eyes narrowed as she spoke up for herself.

"Well, my *love*, Adella does hold resemblance from *both* her parents," Orrick said trying to quell the tension.

Adella just sat there, trying not to burst out in some sort of emotion. She could feel a cross between sobs, laughter, and anger building in her throat. She also was quite starstruck having the queen of the neighboring realm in her house. It was all too much for her. *I must have fallen asleep back in the barn. There is no way that this is for real. Anytime now daddy will walk over to me, wake me up, and we'll be go home. Right? Just a dream? Right?*

"Well none-the-less, the features of a blood ruler of Adamaris are more than enough there in her face. I can completely see the natural poise and grace of a princess abound within her. If she was just some commoner girl you would never see that," Cassandra rambled. "As I have always said, you can take the royal out of the palace, but you can't take the palace out of the royal."

"What?" Adella blurted, confused.

"'*What*' is not proper, my dear," Cassandra cheerfully corrected.

"It's all of the dance lessons," Rose interjected, looking at Casandra. "She's graceful because she dances."

"Oh, lovely she can dance!" Cassandra beamed. "This is perfect! She will be ready when the court holds–"

"My daughter is not going to rule a kingdom for a woman that she has never known, let alone for a people that she does not know!" Orrick burst out.

"Excuse me! May I please speak for *myself*?!" Adella stood up. It was the first time she had really spoken a full sentence. Cassandra, her parents, the captain of the guard, and his charge were all taken aback. "First of all, sorry for the outburst, but I am not some mindless cave troll. I can make decisions for myself. Second, I want the full story here! No one has even taken the time to explain anything. Apparently there is some sort of throne… family… secret… thing that has been kept from me! I just want to know what's happening!" She looked at her father, pleading. "Dad, just tell me the truth."

All eyes turned to Orrick for an answer.

"Okay, Adella," Orrick sighed, finally conceding. "I wasn't just some noble, as I am sure you have already figured out tonight. I was born Aedrian Aleksander Reyn Everheart – not Orrick Aedrian Redding. I was supposed to be crowned king of Adamaris, but I met your mom. And there was more to your grandmother," he nodded to the queen, "not wanting me to marry your mom. You see, Rose, or, Olynia, as she was once known, was being hunted," Orrick looked at his wife.

"Wait… The Syndicate," Adella put the pieces together. "They were after mom, right? That's why we've always had to hide but you've never told me why. Is this part of it?"

"Adella, sweetheart, we love you with all our hearts, and we have kept a lot from you to protect you. I think it's time you now know," Rose began. "I was with my mom and dad, your grandparents, until I was nine. We had a produce farm on the outskirts of Ardenthel, in a little ocean town known as Fairfield.

"The Venom Blade Syndicate had been around for only a few years then, and they were a far cry from the powerful band of thieves that you see today. They would often pillage my town. I particularly remember one of the thieves. His name was Aries. Whenever the syndicate ransacked our town, he and his group of thugs always seemed to be the same brutes my father ran off our land.

"We tried petitioning the royal council for aid, but our efforts were met with resistance," Rose looked hard at Cassandra as she said this. "With little to no help from the capital, my father ended up creating a militia made up of all the men of Fairfield. Word spread that we had created a small army, and no one had heard from the syndicate for months. We were beginning to wonder if they'd finally gotten scared off, but we couldn't have been more mistaken.

"Without warning, they came back in the middle of the night and torched most of the town, plundering all they could get their hands on. Aries and his men came to my farm and he came into my home."

Rose's voice became thicker and her eyes began to glaze. Orrick held her hands and rubbed the top one softly. "I hid behind the furniture–" she couldn't finish the thought. "My parents tried to fight them off," she stopped and cleared her throat, regaining her composure. "The murderers then turned on me and I ran to our barn. As they searched for me, I slipped out through a secret passage in the corner and ran to bar the doors. I tossed lit lanterns through the high windows into the dry hay that was piled inside.

"Before I fled, I stopped to watch it all burn, and as I watched, someone ran out through the charred barn doors. Out of the four men that followed me in, only Aries survived. He was screaming, still on fire, and he saw me standing there. I'll never forget how he stared at me. I turned to run as far as I could and hid until the sunrise. When I finally emerged, I came back to a massacred village. No one knew what became of Aries." Rose took a steadying breath.

"Mom, I had no idea," Adella whispered. Everyone in the room had not dared to speak.

Rose smiled sadly at her daughter. "It was decided that we would go to Ardenthel, myself and the other children who lost their families. We were put into the care of the city's largest orphanage. I never went back to Fairfield.

"As the years passed, I became one of the caretakers in the orphanage. I saw many seasons unfold in the heart of Adamaris' capital. But I spent my days feeling hunted, like the syndicate would always come for me to finish it all.

"Then your father came into the picture," Rose smiled as she looked at her husband. "The story we have told you on that part was true, Adella. He did come up to me one morning when I was in the marketplace. However, he had disguised himself as just a nobleman. I had no idea that he was the prince."

"You took my breath away. I just had to talk to you," Orrick smiled. "Besides, can you imagine if I hadn't?"

"Yes," Rose joked back. "You'd have been stuck with an arranged marriage." She snuck another glance at Cassandra. The queen tried to look indifferent to the comment.

"Wait, how could you not know that he was the prince of your city, mom?" Adella questioned skeptically.

"I was helping run an orphanage, Adella. We were poor, and had no magic mirrors. I wasn't one to busy myself with the events of the royals, I had too many responsibilities. It just never occurred to me."

"I also wasn't usually allowed out of the aristocratic areas of the kingdom," Orrick added.

"I see," Adella nodded.

"That whole Sun's Tide your father escaped everyday to meet with me and to help at the orphanage," Rose explained.

"Dad, if you weren't allowed into commoner areas, then how the heck did you manage to run off everyday?" Adella cut in again.

"I got William to cover for me," Orrick chuckled. "Had him act like he had been training me."

"You would," Adella smirked.

Rose smiled at her daughter. "Then one night he finally told me that he was the Crown Prince, Aedrian. I was upset at first from being deceived, but he promised that he would work it out with his family. That he would protect me."

Cassandra shuffled uneasily in her chair. The woman had been still as stone through the whole story, so the movement seemed exaggerated, even though it was subtle.

Rose continued. "That night we talked about how he wanted to approach the queen. It was a warm evening, and we had decided to take a walk along the streets that bordered the ocean. We soon realized, though, that we had wandered down a bad alleyway. The next thing we knew, we were attacked by a gang of men."

"The Syndicate?" Adella's eyes grew huge.

"The Syndicate," Rose affirmed. "As they grabbed us, *Aries* stepped forth from the shadows. The right side of his face was scarred, but I knew exactly who he was."

"Aries," Adella echoed her mother, on edge.

Rose nodded, "but his men were calling him, *Bane*."

"Wait, mom," realization hit Adella. Bane. The current overlord of the widely feared Venom Blade Syndicate, known for his burn scars on the left side of his face. "Is Aries, *Bane*?"

"Yes. They're one and the same."

"No way," Adella was stunned. Chills spread over her skin. "Is this why they've hunted us? Why we've had to stay hidden? Why we moved so much when I was little? Is this where it all started?"

"Yes, Adella. This is what we tried to protect you from. Aries, now known as Bane, had come to kidnap your father, the prince. He must have been watching us for awhile. Aries then said my name, and I realized that not only had he come for your dad, but he could now have his revenge over what I did to him all those years ago. He knew who I was.

"And just when things seemed completely lost, Adamaris knights suddenly flooded in and surrounded us. They had received news of Venom Blade activity in the city. Instead, their mission turned out to be divinely appointed. If they hadn't shown up when they did, well, only The Radiance knows what would have become of the two of us."

"That was probably one of the most reckless things you ever did, Aedrian!" Cassandra burst out. "Sneaking off, coming home late, never telling me where you were! Did you think I wouldn't find out what you *really* were doing?"

"Oh mother, give it a rest," Orrick rolled his eyes.

"As I was saying," Rose maintained, "the knights came, arrested Bane and the crew he had with him, and brought your father and myself back to the palace." She looked at her husband. "I remember like it was yesterday, waiting for you in the hall outside of the throne room. I had never set foot on the grounds of the palace, let alone been inside of it. The conversation you two had was quite… colorful," she mused.

"Colorful indeed," Orrick mumbled shaking his head.

"For Fate's sake, Aedrian! I'm a mother, can you blame me? You had had me worried sick!" Cassandra defended.

"Yeah. *Sick* enough to disown me if I followed my heart," Orrick argued.

"Well you can't have expected me to just accept some *common* girl who was on the hit list of an organization that rules a lawless underworld! It would have ruined the kingdom!"

"Everyone knows Adamaris' guard is one of the most elite and well trained in all the realms. The Syndicate could have used the challenge!" He looked to

Haeman. "Maybe it would have stopped them from becoming the thriving force they are today." His intense voice shook as it rose. "All you had to do was say the word, mother," he turned to Cassandra. "William would have had them all executed in an instant."

"Aedrian, did you really want to bring the concentrated wrath of all the Venom Blades on us?" Cassandra replied. "It would not have stopped them from regrouping, as bandits and cultists normally do."

"If I may cut in, but could we please finish the story?" Adella spoke up. She was sick of the bickering and wanted to get down to the bottom of things. It was disturbing for her to hear how much of a hand the Venom Blades had in her parent's past. "What happened to you and mom?" She carefully asked.

Orrick took a breath as he tried to cool down; Cassandra looked like she was biting her cheek. "That night I told the queen about your mother. To my surprise, she had known all along that I wasn't really where I said I was. She had figured it out within the first week."

"Of course I did. William was your best friend, I wasn't going to take him at face value!"

Orrick rolled his eyes and continued. "Unbeknownst to me, she made sure I was followed everyday," he explained. "She thought I would become repulsed by the commoner life, come to my senses, and run back to the palace."

"I had hoped you would get it out of your system," Cassandra offered softly. "I didn't anticipate you falling in love."

"We *never* saw eye to eye though," Orrick looked at Cassandra sadly. "And you gave me the ultimatum."

His words hung in the air, and mother and son gazed upon one another, wordless, pain beyond measure in their eyes.

"So you left," Adella finally understood.

"We left," Orrick nodded. "William made sure Bane and his men were all locked away, giving us the chance we needed to vanish."

Orrick continued to look at Cassandra. "Days later I heard about my banishment. From the throne, from all of the inheritance. The decree was absolutely unbreakable."

"I'm so sorry," was all Cassandra could mouth. Her regal appearance had diminished, and left in its place was that of a sad, old woman who had much regret.

Orrick's expression softened. "William came to you after that and resigned his position."

"Yes. He did. He wanted to go with you, to protect you."

Orrick looked at Adella. "We changed our names, banded together, and went into the smithing business. William ended up finding Ellyn, we had you only a year later, and they had Shmitty around the same time."

Adella was quiet as everything sunk in. Her mind was racing. "How did you find us? We moved a few times," she sternly asked Cassandra. It was the first time she had directly addressed the woman.

"Sir William would come visit me every few years," Cassandra replied.

"William used to go into Ardenthel for business purposes," Orrick added.

"Did you know he would tell me about you?" Cassandra asked her son cautiously.

"I didn't stop him, did I?" Orrick shrugged.

"That's how you knew about me," Adella stated.

"Yes, Adella," Cassandra beamed.

Adella was trying to process everything.

"Are you okay, Adella?" Orrick could tell that she was overloading.

"If… If Bane was supposedly in prison… then how did he escape because he's obviously still out there! It all makes sense now, why we always had to hide. The Syndicate went after us… they had come for us when I was little… they… they," Adella couldn't finish her sentence as she started to sob. The missing pieces were all there and it hurt to understand it all. "Why wasn't he executed?!" She burst out.

"Shh," Orrick grabbed Adella and pulled her into his strong arms while Rose rubbed her back. "Bane was *supposed* to be executed, but he escaped from prison soon after William's resignation. The man William left in charge died shortly after and, actually, Haeman," Orrick addressed the arrogant knight who stood in the corner, "weren't *you* named the new captain of the guard around this same time? Huh, interesting." The sarcasm in his observation was biting.

Haeman rolled his eyes.

Orrick looked to his daughter again and dried her tears. "There, there, princess," he wiped her cheeks. "This is all that we have kept from you, Adella, and we are so sorry. We only meant to protect you." His expression became pained, "and even then I feel like we failed in that."

"No, daddy. You mustn't think that," Adella's voice was thick as she fought to find her composure.

"I regretted letting you go, Aedrian," Cassandra spoke softly. "I can't believe I had acted so rashly. I had never been so wrong in my life. I never resented William for his resignation. He followed you because he wanted to protect you, knowing you would always be the prince, banishment or not. I don't blame you for taking back your life the way you wanted to live it. I understand now, only, too little too late. I should have offered you all the protection Adamaris could give."

The room was absolutely silent. Orrick was stunned, his eyes wide with fire. Rose put her hand to her mouth. Cassandra was so candid in her confession; they hardly believed that this was the same woman.

"You really mean this?" He whispered.

"I do, Aedrian. I wish I could have told William whenever he visited me, but I never did. I was still prideful. But now, I have nothing to be proud of. And by the time I finally formed the resolution to reach out for reconciliation, William's visits ceased. He sent one last letter explaining the grave news of Cayden and that he would not visit again. No more explanation was given," Cassandra explained.

"Yes, that was when we moved to Kelemer," Orrick affirmed, his eyes tight with pain.

"I am so sorry," Cassandra said sadly.

Adella could not let herself think about it further. The memories of Cayden had already managed to slip past her mental barriers several times tonight, and she was still fighting to shove them back down. She couldn't afford another breach in mental security if she was to remain whole. Those memories she had to keep locked away. She dug her nails hard into her palm, willing away the emotional pain with the physical pain, walling it all back up.

"Aedrian, I have come, not only to apologize, profusely, but to also ask if Adella…" the queen trailed, unsure of how to phrase her query.

"You want her to take the throne," Orrick finished her thought. It was a sure statement, no question in his voice.

Cassandra nodded seriously.

"What?" Adella was in disbelief, head whipping back and forth between the two.

"My dear," Cassandra turned to her granddaughter. "You are the true heir to Adamaris, and I will not be here for much longer. Like I said earlier, the decree never included heirs, so you are very much the rightful successor. This is the second reason why I have come. Not only to reconcile, but to also ask if you would rise up and take the throne."

Orrick opened his mouth to disagree but Cassandra continued, cutting him off, "Aedrian, without Adella, Adamaris will be broken up by different kingdoms, most of which will go to your cousins in Adaar. I do not wish to see this happen. Having met Adella tonight, I can see that she is the perfect fit, regardless of born status. This is her destiny. It's in her blood."

"So what are you proposing, then? That she steal away this very night to take the throne? Court and parliament would eat her alive," Orrick's resentful tone startled Adella.

"Oh, heavens, of course not," she replied taken aback. "Even the best rulers go to school, Aedrian. You know this. No, I would have her enroll into one of the royal academies."

"But how is that possible?" Adella interjected. "I hardly know a thing about living in the world of royals.

Ruling a kingdom? I've lived a peasant life for fifteen years!"

"She has a point, mother," Orrick agreed, challenging the queen.

"That is exactly why she must attend a royal school. It would prepare her for everything she could ever need, or encounter. By the end of it all, she would be more than ready to rule Adamaris."

"Well, what are you going to do then? Just trot around the world, barge into an academy's doors and demand Adella's acceptance? I'm sure they would all be very welcoming of a *Peasant* turned *Princess*," he emphasized sarcastically.

"Well, actually," Cassandra defended in a quiet, almost timid voice, "I have already made the full arrangements to take her with me for the six day journey into Varinth."

"Royal High?" Orrick's eyes widened as he breathed the name in disbelief.

"Yes. Your old school. The first of the four royal high schools ever built. I still have connections with them," Cassandra added.

Orrick looked down, his brow furrowed, and he pressed his thumbs to his lips. "Six day journey?" He muttered through them. "You don't intend to collocate out of Ebenhold then?"

"I felt it might be best for Adella if she has some time to adjust beforehand," Cassandra explained.

Orrick was silent, deep in thought.

Adella looked between her parents, then lastly at Cassandra whose gaze was fixated on her son.

"But she's all I have left!" Rose cried out, stabbing the silence. Orrick put his arms around his wife. Adella grabbed her mother's hands.

Orrick rocked his Rose for a moment as she calmed down. "Cassandra, you come here after nearly two decades, and expect us to relinquish our last child to the world of royals?" His words were careful, almost grave.

Cassandra gazed at him with a sincerity he had never known.

"And Adamaris will break up and go to Adaar if she doesn't take it," Orrick mumbled in thought to himself as he released his wife. Adella remained by her mother's side.

"Yes," Cassandra breathed.

"*If* she emerges from hiding, she *will* be hunted. We believe Bane might still have a vendetta and Adella taking the throne would only stoke those fires."

"She will be protected all the days of her life if she decides to go," Cassandra promised. "Think of all I could offer her in protection – so much more so than if she stays here."

"Orrick," Rose said quietly, "she would always be taken care of. Hard as it is to let go, this will offer her more than we ever could."

"Adella," Orrick looked at his daughter, "I don't want you to choose this path out of desperation because you *think* we are in danger."

"Then I will offer this as well," Cassandra added, looking to her granddaughter. "Regardless of your choice, child, you and your family are now under the protection of Adamaris. We will make sure no harm ever comes to them. You can be free to choose your own path without fearing for your safety."

"You mean this?" Adella's heart skipped a beat.

Orrick couldn't believe his ears. This woman couldn't be the same person who had wronged him all those years ago.

"I do. Adella, I want you to choose this because *you* want it. I believe it is your destiny to take your place on our throne. However, if you choose not to, then I understand, but I still want to right my wrongs. So, if you desire, Adamaris will protect you and yours." Cassandra was strong in her promise.

Adella was silent. "My family will be protected no matter my choice?"

"Absolutely," Cassandra affirmed. "But, for what it's worth, I do hope that you choose to come with me." She gave a coy smile.

"Dad?" Adella turned to her father.

He hesitated. "It's *your* life, Adella." He looked at Rose and she nodded. He continued. "Who are we to make this decision for you? You know the truth now, and you know why we have kept it from you. And I know you can comprehend what an undertaking ruling a realm will be if you decide to own your birthright."

Adella gazed at her father. Even after all the turmoil he had seen, Adella could tell that he still loved Adamaris, his home, and did not want to see it fall into the hands of foreign kingdoms like the Adaar cousins – whoever the heck those people were. But was he really leaving this choice up to her?

"It's your decision," he spoke once more, "one that will decide your destiny and ultimately alter the very future of Adamaris. Whatever you choose, we will always be behind you." He took Rose's hand and she squeezed back.

Adella looked around the room to the faces awaiting her reply, a reply that would indeed alter the future of Adamaris, and her own, forever.

# Five

Adella looked out the window from her bedroom to the road in front of her house. The Autumn Tide's dawn was brisk and misty, and the moon was beginning to disappear over the deep amethyst mountains on the horizon. The cloudy sky was periwinkle laced with hints of scarlet and amber. Adella hugged her silvery organza and brocade coat tighter about her as she watched an extravagant carriage pull up, followed by a smaller modest carriage behind it. Haeman, a footman, and a lady's maid stepped out of the smaller transport and came to the front door.

*Six am. Right on the dot*, Adella thought. *And she brought help. Wow.*

The girl turned and gave one wistful last look to her room as she headed downstairs – careful not to trip on the beautiful teal gown that she was wearing, courtesy of Cassandra.

Adella didn't sleep that night. She had called Raena and Shmitty only hours before, waking each of them up, and filled them in on the circumstances. The goodbyes were hard and tear filled, but she promised to visit and call when she could. She wished that she could at least give them one last hug, but according to Cassandra, they were on an incredibly tight schedule.

Her parents were in the front room getting her things situated. Haeman was talking with Orrick and grabbing Adella's bags. The footman was already walking out to the carriage with a case of Adella's belongings. Rose stood quietly by the open front door, hugging a pale taupe shawl around her petite folded arms. A wispy breeze played in her beautiful caramel curls. She looked cold.

Adella went and stood by her. Rose looked up and smiled sadly at her daughter.

Adella could tell that she had been crying.

"My gown is way too big for me," Adella whispered. "I feel like it's gonna fall off my chest. Is it noticeable?" A slight joking effort to make her mother laugh.

"You look beautiful," she murmured, her throat a little thick. "No one will be able to tell. You're so beautiful, they'll only be looking at your face." Rose smiled a little more as she reached out and gently stroked through one of her daughters long locks.

"Got ya to grin," Adella smiled wryly back. Seeing her mother like this was about to make her break, but Adella was determined to keep it together, for everyone's sakes. Her time to cry was done. She needed to reclaim the name of Everheart and make everything right. She had to do this for her family – for her mom and dad.

*Everheart. Huh.* It felt so foreign to her.

"Are you sure you want to do this? We will support you, no matter your choice," Rose added.

"I want to do this, momma," Adella nodded with a determined look as she touched her mother's arm in an effort to comfort her.

"I love you, Dellabella," Rose pulled her in for a hug.

"I love you too, momma," Adella replied with a lump in her throat as she hugged back. She did not feel strong enough for this goodbye, but she reminded herself once again that she had to be.

"Okay Dells, let's get you out there," Orrick broke in. Haeman shuffled past them and out the door with one more small case.

"Okay, dad," Adella choked a little as she put her arms around him.

"Hey," Orrick hugged her tightly back then looked her in the eyes, "you're going to be amazing. This isn't going to be easy, but don't be discouraged. The world of royals is a completely different realm – literally," he laughed a little. "But you are strong, Del, and beautiful. You're going to see things in a whole new light that those other royals won't. Now that you know the truth, you can set things right. I have faith in you. You have made me so proud," Orrick kissed her head. "We'll always be a crystal call away."

Adella smiled wistfully.

Orrick offered his arm to his little girl – overtly chivalrous in his gestures – and she took it. He winked at Adella, then escorted her out to the front with Rose following close. Cassandra was waiting outside of the carriage. She was speaking with Haeman.

"We are ready when you are," Haeman murmured to the queen.

"Very well," Cassandra whispered back. She then turned and smiled. "Ah, Adella my dear, you look marvelous! I knew teal was your color."

Adella smiled back. "Thank you, grandmother."

"Well, I see everything is situated. We must make haste if we are to arrive at our first stop before nightfall," Cassandra motioned for the guards to help Adella into the carriage.

Orrick and Rose hugged and kissed Adella once more, and then Adella took Haeman's hand and she stepped up into the coach.

Orrick watched her disappear inside. He looked to Haeman, a dry and stern expression on his face. "This is all you brought?" He remarked, nodding his head at the meager two guards Haeman had assisting them for the trip.

Haeman raised an eyebrow, offended at the question. "We've got it covered," he sarcastically dismissed the notion that he was not prepared.

Orrick stared him down. "You had better." Haeman only nodded, and looked to Cassandra, effectively ending the the conversation.

When Adella had stepped inside, she gasped a little to herself. "Whoa," she breathed.

The massive carriage was fully cushioned with luxurious pillows and seats of rich teal velvet. There was a lit up bar area where food, drink, and wine glasses were kept. Over that area sat a magic mirror. Glowing crystal faerie lights were set throughout the ceiling and wall panels while opulent, silky teal and silver trimmed curtains lined the many darkened glass windows. In an area adjacent to the bar was a mirrored vanity set with an array of perfumes and cosmetics. Everything about the spacious carriage was lavish beyond description.

Adella sat in one of the corners of the cabin, curling up against the comfy velvet. She looked out of the window and saw Cassandra saying farewell. Rose had tears in her eyes and Orrick wore a solemn look of loss. Seeing them like that almost made her break down, but she managed to remain strong while

Cassandra turned and was helped into the carriage. The queen settled into a seat across from Adella.

"Well, are you ready my dear?" The woman asked breathlessly as she removed her gloves.

Adella only nodded.

Cassandra looked upon her granddaughter with sympathy. "You've made the right choice. I promise you."

"I hope so," Adella barely whispered.

She heard the whip of the driver crack and the carriage started to roll. She looked out of the windows one last time and watched her home and her parents disappear into the pale dawn.

They traveled with haste through eastern Kelemer. Wistfully, but with an awed wonder, Adella watched her time pass with the cobblestone towns, rustic villages, and countrysides that blurred by. Some nights, when Cassandra didn't fancy sleeping in the carriage, they would stay at an inn or tavern, incognito, under assumed names. They were not only protected by their guards that drove their carriage, but also by many hidden agents of the kingdom of Adamaris. These adept protectors traveled seemingly unseen along the roads ahead and behind, making sure that the paths and stops were secure for the Everheart journey.

Though things were awkward at first, with conversation being sparse and disjointed, the ice finally broke by the end of the first night as the queen and Adella settled down for the evening in a modest tavern room.

Adella wanted to speak about something that had been gnawing at her since they left.

"Grandmother?" Adella began as she emerged from the changing room wearing an aristocratic nightgown. The expensive silk felt different on her skin. She sat upon her bed to brush out her brunette locks, their natural red and gold highlights glinting in the fire light of the flickering hearth. "Grandmother, with going to Royal High, I just… I know I am not ready to pose for pictures, let alone be in an interview. I'm getting this sinking feeling because what if they–"

"Don't worry about the press," Cassandra cut in. She walked in from the washroom, dressed in a glamorous sleeping gown trimmed in light blue fur. Her soft blonde and silver hair was tied up with a silk scarf on her head. She sat upon a chair near her bed and took off her jewelry, "Not yet, at least. I will prepare you the best I can on our journey for when the time comes, but right now our main focus it to get you into the school doors. Besides, the media has to abide by the laws of the realm, and Varinth is a part of the Interkingdom Accords. They are strict on protecting underage royals. Anything you see on the mirror about Royal High is because it's been tightly controlled coverage. They don't show you anything on the teen royals that you're not supposed to see."

"Good," she breathed a sigh of relief. "I knew the underage royal media laws were strict in Kelemer, but I wasn't so sure about Varinth." When she had dated Brogan, the media adhered to the law. No one knew in the public eye knew anything except that Brogan was taking a sabbatical in the countryside. Adella silently thanked The Radiance for that. Outside of her town, no one had any clue of her past. She hoped that it would remain as such.

"Yes, indeed. As well, I have not made anything about you public. No one but the school knows that you are coming. When the media does find out about you, which they will eventually, know that while you are underage, they cannot stalk you in the realm of Varinth."

"What about in Adamaris?"

"Adamaris, is also part of The Accords."

"Okay," Adella nodded, her anxiety subsiding only slightly.

"When you are ultimately revealed, I know Adamaris will love you. You'll see." Cassandra's eyes twinkled.

Adella nodded again. It made her feel better to know that she wasn't going to be thrust into the spotlight until she was adequately prepared. Although, with this fear put to rest, there were numerous more to replace it. She put her day dress away in her case and crawled back onto her bed and got into the covers.

She swallowed hard trying to get a grip on the next question that was racing through her head. Although she knew she had to do this for her family, her confidence wavered constantly, warring between strengths and self doubts. "So, you are *really* confident that I'll be okay to go to *Royal High?* I mean, everything you've told me about royal life in the carriage so far will help so much," *not to mention all the time I spent with Brogan and his cousins,* she censored herself before the words tumbled out, "but it still doesn't make up for the last fifteen years of my life." *Besides, if Brogan didn't want me, then why do you?* Her thoughts tortured her.

"Adella," Cassandra said, sensing her granddaughter's restless heart. "Just because you were peasant borne does not negate your blood right. You are an Everheart princess by blood, and being an Everheart comes with an innate brilliance at all you set your hand to."

Adella rolled her eyes at the arrogance of her grandmother's statement.

Cassandra didn't notice. "And what is a school for, if not for *learning*? I would not venture to put you out there if I thought you would not flourish. I knew it from the moment we met."

"Really?" Adella asked earnestly.

"Yes. And I'm sure as we become more acquainted, I shall know it all the more. Your parents have said that you are the type of girl that rises to an occasion, and I believe them. They think very highly of you."

"Every parent thinks that their kid is amazing, but it doesn't mean it's true," the girl retorted, thinking back to how her family had seen her wallow in defeat over the last few months. She fell back on her pillows and closed her eyes.

"No, not every parent believes that about their child. Adella do you not realize how rare it is to have the sort of support they have given you?" Cassandra's voice broke, thinking to how she had disowned her own son. She cleared her throat. "Adella, they know you better than anyone so I believe their assessment is to be trusted." She was offended by the amount of self deprecation and ignorance coming from her granddaughter. She got up and perched on the edge of the Adella's bed.

Adella sat up, pulled her knees to her chest, and gazed at this woman that she barely knew. Cassandra was the epitome of everything royal; beautiful, strong willed, shallow, stiff upper lip, but a true sincerity rang behind all that she did. "Well," the girl replied, "if you think I can do this, then I do, too."

Cassandra smirked coyly. "This school will refine you, Adella. You're remarkably intelligent for your age, so you will undoubtedly do well in the academic portion of your attendance. This will leave you time to concentrate on the areas you do need improvement in – areas like etiquette and protocol and more."

"Besides academics and etiquette, what else could there be?" Adella's interest peaked.

"Oh there's *so* much more, Adella," Cassandra enthused. "One of the most important aspects of any royal finishing school is the social life you'll develop. It is another part of your education. You're going to Royal High not only to learn to rule a realm, but to also build relationships with the future rulers of other realms and kingdoms. Your goal is to make alliances."

"Oh, I didn't think of that," Adella realized. Indeed making alliances would be as important as her academic work. This worried Adella more than anything.

The clock on the wall suddenly chimed a soothing tone.

"And by the sound of it, we should be getting to bed," Cassandra added. "The hour is late, and we have an early morning. We'll have much to talk about tomorrow." She stood and paused for a second, as if not knowing what to do, then leaned over Adella's head and swiftly kissed it.

The affection took Adella by surprise, but she accepted the awkward gesture, knowing it was Cassandra's attempt at being motherly, and crawled under her covers as her grandmother took to the second bed. Cassandra blew out the candle on their night stand and Adella stared into the darkness.

Deep down, she knew that all these insecurities were really stemming from what had happened over the Sun's Tide. If a revelation like this had befallen her a year ago, she would have been ecstatic. She was a much different girl back then; full of life, optimistic, confident, friendly... But now? She was being brought back from an emotional numbness she had created for her own protection. It was terrifying to her, and she hoped that she had made the right decision to step into that carriage.

To Adella, it seemed as if fate was determined to bring her back into the world of royals.

With these anxious thoughts, her mind drifted off.

When they crossed into the borders of Varinth on their fourth day of travel, Adella was excited to see the lush rolling landscapes and mountain sides the empire was famed for. Wondrous forests and deep valleys, waterfalls, rivers, and lakes, and mixed greenery sprinkled with the colors of the up and coming Autumn's Tide, were all a far cry from the valleys she knew her whole life. The sky was the most exhilarating color of azure, accented with airy, snow white clouds, stretching out as far as the eye could see. The new province enthralled her; it was a land seemingly sprung from enchantment.

By the sixth and last day of travel, Adella's building anxiety and excitement from the journey, coupled with the carriage fever of the road, had wrecked havoc on her nerves. It was barely noon, and they were on track to arrive at Royal High in just a few hours. Adella was really looking forward to using her legs again.

Cassandra and her had kept up a well paced conversation since breakfast, much of which entailed more of Cassandra's history lessons of Adamaris. Adella had to keep from rolling her eyes a few times because Cassandra's version of realm changing events were things along the lines of fashion trends turning with the decades, divorce scandals, who begat who, and who married who. Adella found some interest in those things, but it's not what she wanted to hear. The girl wanted the deeper intrigues of the stories, and the woman who sat in front of her knew nothing of the battles, motivations, trade deals, and monarchy changes that define a realm. Adella at least appreciated that her grandmother was trying.

Adella loved it, though, when Cassandra would tell stories of her early days with her late husband, King Aedonis Everheart the Magnanimous. The man had died when Aedrian was very little, but Adella could tell by the way Cassandra lit up when she spoke of him that he seemed like he was an amazing person. Adella lamented never knowing him, lamented his not being alive to stand up for his son when he brought her mother home to the palace.

"I do wish you could have known him. Aedonis would have loved you, just as he loved Aedrian. Goodness, I can't believe that Aedrian never told you everything from the start," Cassandra added sadly. "If he meant to protect you from the crown, then why in the world did he give you a proper *royal* name at your birth! Adella Olynia Gwendolyn Claire Everheart," Cassandra said with pride and then sighed. "He must have had a feeling that the past could come back for you."

"That's the only reason I could think of," Adella agreed. "He probably wanted me to be prepared. I've gone my whole life thinking my name was just Adella Olynia Redding," the girl remarked pensively as she sipped on sparkling water from of a gold rimmed wine glass. "I love that my mom at least kept her birth name alive with my middle name. After all these years I had no idea just how important it was."

"Yes, interesting how life works in its little ways," Cassandra mused.

Adella beamed. "You know, when father told me my name that night, he also said I was named for one of my ancestors, Gwendolyn. Do you know who she was?" Adella had a feeling that Cassandra wouldn't but figured she would ask.

"No idea, dear. I think we may have had a Gwendolyn eons of years back but, then again, your father was always the bookworm in our family. When he was a boy he would spend hours pouring over ancient maps and the genealogies of Adamaris. He would always talk of traveling to see the places of our ancestry. He wanted to explore the realms."

"That sounds just like him," Adella murmured, assessing the way that Cassandra wistfully remembered her son. "He still does that, you know," she offered. "When he's not in the shop, he'll spend hours pouring over books and things. I've always thought he'd make a great teacher."

"Yes, I suppose," Cassandra placated. "He has the heart for it."

Adella grinned broadly at these words.

The carriage became quiet for a while and Adella found herself gazing around once more. She had spent six days cooped up in the opulent transport, yet she still was not used to the luxury of it all. The magic mirror was playing, the sound of music barely audible in the background. The soft glow of the interior light orbs were ambient. Everything she could ever need while in travel was at her fingertips. She still had not had the need to open all of the nooks in it. She glanced out the window to admire the unfamiliar scenery once more.

"Adella?" Cassandra spoke, breaking the silence.

"Yes, grandmother?" The girl turned to look at the queen.

"There is something I've been meaning to give to you and I feel that now is the time."

Adella wondered what her grandmother could possibly mean. Cassandra took out a teal velvet box from a compartment next to her. She gently placed it into Adella's hands.

Adella looked at her inquisitively then opened the mysterious lid.

Inside was set an exquisitely sparkling teal gemstone cut into the faceted shape of a heart. The gem, quite large in size, was delicately held in place by three golden prongs, two on top, and one at the bottom point. On the two lower straight edges of the heart's setting was curled an elegant gold "E" on either side. The gold band of the ring was made up of intricate swirling waves that formed a lattice like base that the gem sat upon.

"This is the heart of Adamaris. A teal diamond hewn from the very same vein that every Everheart ring has been made from. This vein has been guarded in Adamaris for hundreds of years with a select chosen few who know of its location. All of the bloodline rulers of Adamaris have had one bestowed upon them by the ruling king or, in our case, queen. And now you shall have one, too."

Adella felt like crying. She did not know what to say.

Cassandra gently took her granddaughter's right hand and slipped the priceless adornment onto Adella's right ring finger. It was a perfect fit.

As Adella gazed with awe into its beautiful, teal facets and prisms, she felt an overwhelming pride – she never wanted it to come off. Now wearing this ring, it was almost as if she officially belonged in Adamaris, to the line of Everhearts. A symbol of her right to rule.

Cassandra beamed to see Adella's face light up with the confidence and pride she had hoped to see in the next ruler of Adamaris. She began to prepare some tea as she let Adella have her moment.

Adella marveled for a while, enjoying the way the beautiful ring shined in the light of the cabin. She glanced at Cassandra's hands and amongst the many rings the woman never seemed to take off, she saw that one of them was indeed a teal diamond in the facet of a heart. She had never noticed until now.

An indescribable feeling spread through Adella's bones, telling her that she was at the right place at the right time. She always knew that her family had to keep a low profile, especially after their move when she was a child, but she never knew why. Now, knowing who she was, and finding out that her mother and father had a serious history with Bane, the bloodthirsty crime lord himself, knowing the reason why these monsters had haunted her family all these years, it made perfect sense to her to rise to the occasion, becoming the crown ruler of Adamaris. She could take care of those she loved the most.

However, now knowing this dark family secret also made Adella feel guilty for jeopardizing her family's anonymity by having dated such a high profile prince. Sure, Kelemer was strict in its mandates that Brogan's privacy was to be well protected during his attendance at her commoner school, but she should have listened to the warning her father gave her about keeping lowkey. It was the first time she had ever brushed off his wise words and now she regretted it.

"Five generations of Everhearts have been in attendance at Royal High Academy, including your father and myself," Cassandra suddenly murmured as she stirred her tea in a delicate china cup. She was obviously deep in thought and Adella wasn't sure if she meant to say those words out loud.

Cassandra took a long sip of the steaming liquid.

Adella felt the gravitas over what was just said. The blood legacy of the Everhearts was truly in her hands. Her fingers found her crystal ball, an absent minded habit to roll it back and forth beneath her palms, and she turned to look out the window as it helped to pass the hours. Faint chimes could be heard from the orb's movement as the foreign weight of the Everheart ring, now on her finger, contacted with the crystal's cool surface.

Her bright eyes grew wide as the scenery outside of the glass grabbed her attention. She could see now that the road was on a slope up pretty high off the valley ground. They were on a cliff side that was beginning to climb steeply. Adella then noticed that on this particular road, there seemed to be no traffic. In fact, she could not remember seeing traffic anywhere for a long while. They continued to climb the steep, rocky canyon road for what felt like hours when the carriage finally came over a peak, allowing Adella to see this new land in a different way.

Expanding out before her were lakes and rivers, flowing and sparkling from mountain side waterfalls, which ended in distant, shining pools which sat beneath cliffs and coves. There were long running meadows nestled within forests which were bustling with life and color amidst the treetops. She could see even more villages and towns connected by webs of roads. Being this high up on the mountain side was like seeing the realm from a birds eye view. And then she saw it; the breathtaking castle that had manifested itself in the distance.

It was built on a plateau in a nearby mountain side, and a thick layer of woods surrounded it. It fit so perfectly with the landscape, that it was almost as if when the world had formed Varinth, the castle materialized with it. Adella then noticed a far off cluster of scintillating pinnacles, spires, and high rises, on the valley floor, all set about another castle, just as grand as the one in the mountain. A sparkling utopia.

"Like it?" Cassandra broke through the quiet. Adella's head whipped around and looked at her grandmother. The girl softly bobbed her head in amazed silence, ocean eyes full of wonder. Cassandra motioned with a proud smile, and a nod to keep looking. "Welcome to Vryndolne of Varinth, Adella," she whispered. "Home of Royal High."

Adella, still beaming, yet never looking away from the window said, "So that's it, huh? The castle in the mountain is Royal High." Her statement was sure.

"Are you disappointed?" Cassandra said, musing.

"A little," Adella teased lightly, smirking. Cassandra, suddenly shocked, opened her mouth to object, but when she realized Adella's game, she settled, giving a wry expression. "I have seen it before," Adella continued, "on the mirror and whatnot, but never in person. Being here now, though, I can't say that I could even begin to describe it all. Royal High," she breathed the name in a whisper as she gazed upon the castle citadel in the mountain. Her sights then fell upon the utopia in the valley once more.

"And that city, in the valley, that's Vryndolne?"

"All of this valley you see before you is Vryndolne itself, but that cluster of spires you are noting is the heart of Vyrndolne, the capital. It is a rather convenient distance from Royal High, as you can tell, and if I had to guess, you will most likely spend quite a bit of time there," Cassandra explained with a slight laugh. "The city is also the home of the Thelreds, the emperors of Varinth. I've already mentioned that their daughter, the

Empress Vivian Thelred, is in attendance this year at Royal High. Their family line has *built* the school, so naturally every Thelred goes. It would be in your best interest, Adella, to make friends with her if possible, seeing as Adamaris and Varinth have always been friendly towards one another for the past several centuries."

Adella made mental note of her grandmother's explanation as she continued to take in the view. The details of the castle high school dawned into visibility as they drew ever closer. In the beaming sun, she could barely make out the different balconies and basic architecture of the school. The forest on the back side of the castle almost cocooned it, and spanned into the plateau on the mountain behind.

The carriage began up another long slope following the arc that the small mountain range made around the Valley of Vryndolne. Adella had a feeling that they were taking the long way around as she could clearly see that the roads in the valley looked to be quicker routes. Adella then noticed a peculiar thing on all the roads that she hadn't noticed before. With the exception of the path that they were traversing, but especially on all of the roads leading from the distant spires of Vryndolne up to Royal High, there seemed to be masses of dark movement – and it became all the more intense the closer it got to the castle high school. Adella leaned forward, trying to make out what the darkness was. One of her eyebrows arched, eyes narrowing…

*Tinklingytinktinktink…* sang Cassandra's crystal. The delicate chimes broke through the silence. Adella turned around, slightly startled, as Cassandra reached for the aqua orb that was resting on the velvet seat next to her. The woman's finger touched the top and answering chime was heard.

"Yes," she answered as she put the ball to her ear. She preferred private audio on most of her calls. She listened for a moment as Adella peered curiously at her.

"What?!" Cassandra gasped. It made Adella jump again. "What do you mean the roads are blocked?! We've hardly had a single passerby today on our way over!" She exclaimed, her voice raising incredulously. She waited for a second, listening, stressed.

Adella was now wide eyed and her anxiety gripped her.

"Who called them? This was not supposed to turn into this!" Cassandra's face fell. "There are laws about this..." she warned in an almost growl.

Adella's heart began to beat like a hammer in her chest. She grabbed the edge of her seat and then looked out of the window again. *It's people...* she realized as she gaped at the swarming dark masses once more.

"Well then, they took the route out of the capital. It's obvious," she retorted, still stressed. "Yes," she said affirming some unheard question. "Vryndolne." She nodded and listened. "Well I don't care, make sure my granddaughter can get into the school gates at least! There will be retribution for this! Let it be known that Adamaris will take to court any media that puts this into print!" She said hotly. "Oh is that so? Is that what they're saying? Well we'll see about that!" She snipped harshly, touched the ball with a finger, and ended the call. She sighed, letting the orb fall in her lap. She put her head back, fingers touching her temples, and closed her eyes for a moment.

Adella sat there, frozen. The moment stretched.

Cassandra's eyes then snapped open and she looked at her granddaughter. "Adella, darling, your entrance is going to be much more… *grandiose*, than we had anticipated," she began slowly.

Adella's heart picked up speed. "What do you mean?"

"The public now know we are arriving," Cassandra sighed heavily. "This is what I was afraid of. *Someone* has tipped them off and they have swarmed the area. Pixierazzi and all."

"Well you said there were laws, right? There are laws to protect underage royals from the media, right?" Adella desperately reasoned.

"Yes, there are. However, there is already rumor that you are not truly the heir, merely some girl that I have plucked off the street. They believe they have found a loophole, allowing them a field day. The gall!" Cassandra grimaced. "It is going to be difficult to get you through the portcullis and into the foyer in one piece. You must do exactly as I say if we are to make it through without giving them what they want," she gravely instructed.

"What do they want?" Adella whispered.

"Anything. A picture, a quote, a story – anything they can use to make headlines with," Cassandra answered. "Do not be anxious, though. Like I said, just do exactly as I say when the time comes. Once you are situated behind closed doors, I will release an *official* press statement, proving that you are who you are."

"How can you prove that if they won't even take your word for it?" Adella countered.

"Well, I have half a mind to invite your father to do a press conference. I'll use the collocation portals in

Vryndolne to Ebenhold. It'll only be a day's ride for your father to meet me there. Once the world sees the former crown prince of Adamaris claiming you as his own, that should quiet them once and for all." Cassandra sighed again, cracks showing in her perfect facade, "I just wanted a quiet entry for you, at least until we could get you absolutely ready for public reveal. But," the queen straightened herself out, sitting up, "as royals, we are to accept any circumstance and operate effortlessly through them."

Adella nodded, eyes still wide with fear and shock. The girl felt as if those final words were more for her grandmother's peace of mind rather than her own. Her heart was bursting at Cassandra's mention of her father talking to the media. Her father, after years of hiding, would come back out? Travel all the way to Ebenhold, the capital of Kelemer, to be in the public eye once more? She hoped that Cassandra's promises about her family's safety would be enough.

Cassandra pulled out her crystal again and made several more calls, trying to get a handle on the situation. Adella turned to peer out the window once more, eyes fixated on her fate. Her head was spinning as everything else started to blur out.

She watched as the ever morphing mass of distant crowds continue to grow.

She began to tremble.

*They're going to eat me alive,* she thought. All of the confidence she had begun to build up within the last few days suddenly drained from her. *What am I doing? I can't make it in royal finishing school!* She was suddenly self conscious of her appearance and pulled up on the intricate brocade bodice of her grey and gold dress – one of the many Cassandra had kindly thought to provide for her on their travels. *This is too big in the chest,* she sighed to herself.

"We have fifteen minutes," Cassandra said as she finished up another call. She put her orb in her purse and began to pull out her powder. "The word of your arrival did in fact come from Vryndolne. This is why we did not see this coming. We took backroads while the *masses* took to the main road." Cassandra explained in a tense clipped tone as she reached for the vanity in the carriage. "Freshen up, Adella. Put on your best face out there."

Adella shook her head incredulously and slowly turned back around to the window.

The royal high castle was much closer now, and outside the streets had begun swarming with people and horses and carriages. It was like they all manifested out of nowhere. Their carriage was going to have to fight its way through the teeming masses, all of which were there to get a glimpse of the princess. Officials were urging people to stay on the sides of the road so that traffic could get through.

Adella eased back to face her grandmother. She drew in shallow breaths and refused to glance out the window again until it was time to get out.

The carriage came to a bit of a crawl as it made its way through the awaiting people on the long stretch of drive leading up to the castle courtyard.

An eternity seemingly passed and Adella could only hear the pounding of her heart with her uneven breaths as they crossed under the ostentatious Royal High arch. They were now on the school's property. The carriage jostled, startling Adella, making her look out into the chaos that her grandmother had warned of. Their carriage began up the sloping drive of the school's road.

"Oh my gosh," she breathed.

"Yes, this is what I was afraid of," Cassandra sighed once more, seeming to be a veteran of this sort of thing, while pulling on her gloves. "Adella, just breathe."

Adella could hardly believe her eyes as she took in the immaculate and massive castle while throngs of onlookers, reporters, and pixierazzi inundated its pristine outer courtyards. Several knights of Varinth and the Royal High guard were attempting to keep order, all the while lining themselves outside of the carriage's path, offering their assistance.

Cassandra reached over to tuck a piece of Adella's hair behind her ear and adjusted the girl's dainty golden tiara. "When we come to a full stop, Haeman is going come over and open the door. I will precede you, and then he will help you out. When that happens, stay on my heels and stop for nothing. If all else fails, just smile," she informed. She pulled out some shimmering rouge, put a little on Adella's lips, and then showered her with a sweet and light smelling fragrance.

The carriage suddenly halted. They were several yards away from the portcullis gate that encompassed Royal High's inner courtyard and foyer. The masses were prohibited from entering that area.

"The crowd is too thick. This is as far as we are going. Are you ready?"

Adella gazed at her grandmother, trying to find her resolve, heart a hammer, ocean eyes wide. She couldn't stop trembling.

"Grandmother," Adella tried, but before the she could say anymore, the door opened and a roar that the girl had never heard before reached her ears. Grandmother was swiftly out in seconds, and then a lone hand reached in to help Adella out as well. Adella grasped the offer, and was blinded by the light that reached her eyes.

# Six

Everything happened simultaneously. Adella stepped out and looked up, her fluffy tulle and brocade dress settling around her. The pandemonium was disorienting. Her expression echoed that of a deer caught in the midst of a meadow full of predators. Masses of people and media were waiting, hungry, all shouting her name with a million questions in voices that overlapped. Not to mention the several F.E.R.I. imaging orbs that they attempted to shove in her face. In the bedlam, however, nothing was truly audible. All she knew was that she had to keep her mouth shut.

She let go of Haeman's hand after she found some sort of balance. She then gasped in wonderment as she finally looked past the masses and took in her surroundings. Everything was more beautiful than she could have ever dreamed possible. The rising castle, the court, the glittering fountains, waterfalls gleaming in the sun – all the things of magic mirrors, though the magic mirrors did not do them justice. Adella felt that the beauty of it all was sadly marred by the unruly mob.

Adella looked and saw Cassandra ahead, her eyes begging her granddaughter to stick with the plan, regained her composure, and trailed swiftly behind. The guards followed them and blocked as much media as they could, but it still didn't help the fact that this was practically an all out assault.

Adella glided along, taking up the front of her dress as daintily as she could, trying to remember the way that Cassandra said it was done. All the while

Cassandra lead the way through, smiling genially and stopping for nothing. Everything felt to be happening in slow motion, and yet in double time, all at once.

Before Adella could even register it, they somehow made it past the guards that were keeping the media out of the inner court wall, and the portcullis came down as quickly they cleared it with a sharp clang.

The stretch from the carriage to the gate seemed to last an eternity, but, in all reality, the ordeal was over in less than a minute.

Adella was now safe inside the inner courts of the high school. She looked up into the towering reaches of the spires that seemed to touch the clouds.

"Grandmother?" Adella whispered.

"Yes?" Cassandra replied.

"Does that stuff out there always happen for a royal arrival?" She asked breathlessly.

"Not…" Cassandra searched for words, "usually." She smiled apologetically at her granddaughter.

"Ah," Adella replied. *So it's just me then…* she trailed in her thoughts.

The bedlam from the outside world steadily faded as they moved along at a more composed pace. With the press contained outside, Adella observed that royals walked about freely here, and most looked to be about her age. Some held their books or supplies, few were shadowed by servants carrying their things, while others just talked, walked, and laughed to wherever their destination called. She realized that several had stopped to stare at her.

"Grandmother? Where are we going now? Who am I meeting?" Adella added softly, now very aware of the mounting attention on her.

"This way. We have an appointment in the grand foyer with the Headmistress." The queen answered in a hushed tone, signaling that this was the end of the conversation.

Without another word they continued on, followed by their murmuring entourage.

Adella looked around, noting what many of the royals were wearing. Stunning, flowing, frilled, shimmering, immaculate gowns and capes of the brightest colors – all of which, she felt, put her own dress to shame. Everyone was outrageous and over the top and utterly perfect.

Adella caught a few of the haughty glances from some of the prettiest girls she had ever seen. They snickered behind her back as she passed. Other girls glared at her with... jealousy? Though few smiled invitingly if she met their gaze. But a good number of the royals continued along with their business, pretending that she did not exist, despite the obvious fact that she was the reason for the chaos naught but a wall away.

Adella looked away, trying to seem nonchalant and cool, cheeks burning, and glanced up to take in more of her surroundings, in awe of the towering institution. From slender flag poles, floating high in the wind, waved royal purple banners bearing the golden seal of Varinth's Royal High. There were numerous velvet swag trimmed balconies overlooking the courtyard area. More royals peered out from these high terraces.

One girl especially stood out from the rest. Her red silk hair sat around her shoulders and, even far away, her eyes seemed dark. Her face was arrogant like many of the other nobles around her, but it held a different light than the rest. Her gaze on Adella was beyond unsettling. Her arms were folded over her deep crimson gown which was more satiny, and less frill, than the other girls. A deep glower was set on her face.

Adella looked away and tried to concentrate on Cassandra's murmurs to the Royal High assistant that had just joined them, though she could not help herself glancing over the two guys she passed nearby.

They nodded flirtatiously at her. One had sandy blonde hair, wavy and textured and carefree, that stopped short of falling about his very broad shoulders. The other had dark hair, shorter, and perfectly tousled. Both were insanely cute. The brown haired one winked at her and the blonde waved – both grinning wide bright smiles. She looked around herself, wondering if this flirting was meant for her, and upon realizing it was, she blushed, waved timidly back, and faced forward once more, determined to make it to the foyer in one emotional piece.

However, she could not help the contagious little smirk that played upon her lips.

The entourage finally reached a set of broad stone steps leading up to an arched entryway with two grand oak doors. One of them was already propped open, an inviting signal to come in. Cassandra led the way, Adella close on her heels, while their entourage lingered outside.

Their footsteps echoed on the vast marble floor, and Adella marveled at the infrastructure of the hall. The inside matched the same grey marble and stone that made up the outside of the castle. The chandeliers and candelabras among the walls cast a regal glow while rich, royal purple and gold trimmed velvet draperies and banners hung and adorned the walls and ceiling. Golden accents and filigree seemed to touch everything. Paintings and suits of armor, expensive vases, ornate tables and carved oak doors sprawled out through the huge hall.

A plump woman, wearing the most elaborate, poofiest, frilliest, purple dress that Adella had ever seen, emerged out from a door in the hall with what Adella assumed to be the proper poise and accented grace of a learned royal.

"Welcome, welcome," her proudly overbearing voice rang in the grand foyer.

*Why is she sticking her chest out so far?* Adella raised an eyebrow.

The bustle on the back of this woman's dress made her rear jut out, too.

Adella wondered what would happen if this lady attempted to clear a door frame sideways…

The woman drew closer, and Adella saw that her enormous dress was ornamented all over with peacock feathers, and adorned with countless gems and brooches. Necklaces and other articles of jewelry literally hung off of her. *This is supposed to be fashionable?* Adella wondered as she continued her examination of this new and frightening creature.

Too much violet and lime eye make up surrounded her bright, cabbage green eyes, and her foundation and powder were layered on heavily, actually accentuating the opposite of what the woman was clearly trying to hide – wrinkles. *She's gotta be way older than grandmother,* Adella thought.

The woman's blonde, almost white hair was swirled up in a cotton candy bouffant on top of her head, while more long peacock feathers and gem adornments were fastened on each side of the mound. Her shiny red lips were in a wide, plastered looking smile, exposing her large teeth. Her long red nails looked sharp enough to slice through bone. She was holding a brown and leather bound portfolio, thick with papers.

"Welcome, Queen Cassandra Everheart of Adamaris! It has been far too long since we last held conference! And welcome to you, Princess Adella Everheart, future ruler of Adamaris," she bowed so ridiculously low that Adella thought her hair was going to fall over. "I am Baroness Bianca Gertrude Von Derdenmyer, Headmistress of Royal High Academy."

"Well met, Baroness," Cassandra replied as she nodded her head in approval. Adella noticed how subtle Cassandra's grace was; far more elegant than this garish, overkill purple woman before them. The queen smiled and continued, "And yes, it has been years. Thank you for accepting Adella on such short notice," Cassandra smiled at her granddaughter. Adella smiled back, though still bewildered by this ridiculous new lady.

"Ah yes, the prodigal princess," the baroness announced flamboyantly.

*Does she always have to be that loud?* Adella curbed the need to plug her ears.

"Welcome, princess," the baroness continued, "to Royal High Academy. We are so glad to have your presence with us here." She smiled her obviously practiced fake smile.

"I am sure you have been briefed on the special circumstances surrounding our arrival, Baroness,"

Cassandra ascertained, glossing over the niceties. "Do you know why the entire realm of Varinth and the rest of the continental media of Narcinion is waiting on your doorstep?" Cassandra raised an eyebrow.

"Oh I *am* terribly sorry about all the fuss! We expect the media for our balls and galas, but not for arriving royals. We hold very close the law of Varinth and underage royals. The magnitude of this turn out surprised even us. And all for just one royal," she looked at Adella with her peculiar cabbage gaze.

"Anonymity was stressed in our agreement," Cassandra pressed. Her beautiful face was fierce.

"And we were blindsided this morning. My deepest apologies," the Baroness maintained. "We will get to the bottom of the breach of contract and once we do you can rest assured that whomever revealed her arrival shall have the law of Varinth to answer to."

"See that you do," Cassandra's words were more threat than response.

"Well we are delighted that you chose Royal High once more for your family's education," the Baroness attempted to transition away from her blunder. "It is a great honor to have you, Princess Adella, in our warm and open arms."

Cassandra arched her eyebrow once more and nodded genially. Adella could tell her grandmother was irritated.

A silence fell.

"Well, Princess, enough introduction," the Baroness broke it awkwardly. "Let's get you situated, shall we?" She motioned with her hand and servants came out instantly. "They will get your things and in just a moment, I shall give you the grand tour," she explained as she walked over to some more Royal High servants standing by. "Now would be the time to say your farewells." She turned to talk quietly with the help at the other side of the room, giving the staff instructions.

Adella looked at Cassandra who smiled sympathetically at her granddaughter.

"Farewell?" Adella asked with surprised sadness.

"Yes. I cannot stay, my dear. I must make haste to Ebenhold to arrange a meeting with your father. From there I must go back to Ardenthel. I haven't been on the throne, so to speak, for several weeks now. Not a good thing," she explained as she grasped one of her granddaughter's hands. "I also need to let the people know that I have officially found you, the *true* heir. I must sort the media frenzy outside. Adella, if I could have introduced you anywhere into this new world, this is exactly where I would have opted for you to start. You'll do just fine. Follow the rules, and don't be afraid to ask questions. The headmistress will get you started."

"I see," Adella said with sad understanding. She knew this was coming, but it didn't dawn on her that she'd have to be parted so soon. She had only just met her a week ago and although she still wasn't quite sure of anything, she didn't want this familiar face to disappear just yet. She had to be brave, though. This was what was best, wasn't it? She felt the Everheart ring heavy on her finger.

Cassandra laughed a little and whispered, "On a lighter note," she began, as she noticed Adella's bewildered gaze fall on the headmistress, "did you know she was actually the headmistress when your father was here? And back when I was in attendance, she was in my class!" She motioned over to the Baroness who was animatedly explaining something to the help. "She hasn't changed one bit, though I should say *her* age is showing." Cassandra seemed smug. Adella knew that it was because Cassandra had aged so beautifully – especially when compared with the Baroness.

Adella laughed a little. It all made sense, now, as to why Cassandra and the baroness seemed so acquainted. She sighed. "I'm going to miss you," Adella admitted.

Cassandra's face softened. Her words took the queen by surprise. "As will I, my sweet child," Cassandra replied as she brushed Adella's cheek, and lightly kissed the top of the girl's head. "Take care. I love you, sweet girl."

Adella's breath choked a little when she heard her say this. "I love you, too, grandmother," she whispered. It was the first time they had uttered such words. Cassandra was always flipping from stoic to soft; it was hard to keep up.

The headmistress started to walk over. "Are we ready?" She chirped.

"Yes," Adella nodded.

The Headmistress looked at the queen.

"I take my leave," Cassandra answered.

"Then farewell, Queen of Adamaris. Until we meet again," the purple woman said with another unreasonably low bow.

"Farewell," the queen answered with a benevolent wave of her hand. Haeman and a few members of the staff came up to escort her out. She reached over and grabbed Adella's hand once more, squeezed, and let go.

She was then gone very swiftly and the giant carved oak doors closed behind her.

Adella instantly felt alone.

She looked around and noticed all the different wings the halls lead to. She determined that the foyer she was standing in must be one of the central connecting points for the whole establishment.

"Let's begin, princess," the Headmistress broke the silence. "And welcome, once again, to your home away from home for the next year!" She flashed her plastered smile as she motioned for Adella to follow.

Adella gracefully swept up a part of her dress in the front with one hand, and fell into step behind the woman who led her off into one of the ornately decorated halls.

The tour seemed to go on for hours but, when Adella had the chance to slyly glance at her crystal in her little satin purse, she was quite mistaken. She groaned internally, but kept her bright eyed composure and continued to nod and *mhmm* at the right times.

One of their stops was meeting The Dean of Royal High. He was the head of the school's board, and the brother to the Queen of Varinth.

"Oh, Dean Welford, there you are," the headmistress announced grandly over the constant swish of her purple layers. They found him talking in the hall with a servant outside of his office quarters.

"Headmistress," Welford nodded to her, acknowledging her presence. He was a proud looking man, average height, and exceptionally dressed in his deep violet brocade tailcoat and tall boots. His willow brown hair, streaked with silver, was slicked back into a low ponytail, and his rather round face seemed almost tired. "I was just taking my leave for the day," he spoke with an air of extreme importance.

"Well, do forgive us for the delay. I had only wanted to acquaint you with Adella Everheart–"

"Yes, I see. The Adamaris princess," he cut her off, looking Adella up and down rather disapprovingly.

"Yes," the headmistress responded uneasily, seeming taken aback.

"Good day to you, Dean Welford," Adella greeted in her most courteous manner. She curtsied as gracefully as she could manage.

The Dean raised an eyebrow. "Good to see you made it through that media mess out there. We were not sure whether you would even pass the gates."

"Er," Adella paused. She was caught off guard by his clipped and disinterested manner. "Well, I am very glad to be able to be here right now."

"Yes, of course," The Dean nodded once. He then looked to the headmistress. "You obviously have your work cut out for you. I'll leave you to it, headmistress Von Durdenmyer. Please excuse me." He nodded to his servant who followed him down the hall.

Adella just stood there, dumbfounded.

The headmistress looked down at her portfolio for a few moments and ticked a few things off. "Done and done," she murmured to herself. She then snapped the leather bound parchments shut. "Moving on!" She announced proudly, stepping off into a new hall.

Adella gazed at her retreating form, incredulous at the insensitive manner of these people, and made haste to keep in step behind.

The afternoon passed slowly, and the headmistress rambled on about the school's manifesto. She emphasized the *natural welcoming nature* of all royals, boasted about the *benevolent* student body, and rambled about how *grand and prestigious and world renown this school has been since its creation*. Not to mention the *hundreds of years of history*. The baroness stressed how *rules and protocol are meant to be followed,* and *how things ought to be done the proper way,* and that *the Royal Handbook* will soon be issued to Adella. Von Durdenmyer especially stressed the importance of the dress code.

"All royals must look their utmost best at all times and to ensure this is executed in the proper fashion, we have the dress code of all royals," she vehemently declared. "Image is everything, and the dress code determines every detail of how a royal should look. You will find all of that in your handbook as well."

She then moved onto the histories of all the deans, headmasters, and lords that had ruled and formed the establishment since its beginning.

Adella's head was overloaded. All she wanted was to get into the swing of things with as little fuss over her presence as possible. However, the reception that had awaited her as she arrived only hours earlier wasn't exactly promising to this ideal.

They turned down another long hall and towards its end was a peculiar, giant oak door. A red and gold patterned carpet ran down the corridor, and many rows of gilded framed paintings hung upon the walls. Below the art, pedestals of busts and important figures in the school's history lined the long stretch of hall. It was then that Adella noticed that the number of royals she had seen around had dwindled substantially. These halls were practically deserted. Not that she was particularly missing the stares, and the snickers, and the haughty glances…

"I said, did you want to be taken to your room now?" The headmistress spoke again.

"Huh?" Adella said looking up.

"'*Huh*' is not proper my dear," she said with a sigh. "Yes, everything you are will most definitely have to be improved upon. Our work really is cut out for us here." She shook her head in disapproval.

"Oh, I'm sorry," Adella replied, worried.

"Never apologize to someone who is lower than your class, princess," the baroness reminded sourly, "I was only stating the obvious."

Anxiety gripped Adella's stomach. She nodded.

"Nevertheless, I was asking if you wish to be taken up to your room," she restated. "The tour is complete and most of the other royals have begun to go down to the dinner hall. You will want to freshen up before you join them."

Adella looked around at the countless stained glass windows that surrounded them. Through their intricately cut glass radiated a sunset glow. She realized she was actually a little hungry. She hadn't eaten much all day.

"Yes, thank you, umm…" Adella was suddenly disoriented.

"No '*umms*'," the headmistress reminded, uptight. "And your room is in the Demasque wing. That is where all the lady royals stay. This way," she motioned to follow.

Adella wondered when the headmistress had decided to drop the nice act. She got the impression that the woman was not particularly fond of her, either.

The two made their way back over to the central foyer, and began to ascend the one of the two beautiful grand staircases in the hall. Slowly, and growing stronger, a sweet, perfumed scent began to float on the air. Adella wondered if this was because they were drawing closer to the girl's living quarters. They reached the top of the stair, and continued through a stretching corridor that had many different halls diverging every so often.

They passed several sets of double wooden doors in the hall. Adella noticed golden plaques near them that read what royals inhabited each room. She realized that these were the dorms.

Just like the rest of the castle, the Demasque wing was opulent. Throughout ran intricate violet and gold brocade tapestries, held together by giant gold and lavender bows, spanning from crystal chandelier to chandelier. Tall porcelain vases stood outside the doors of each dorm and held bouquets of the most exotic, fragrant flowers. On the outer wall, across from the living quarters, through the elegant windows and balconies, Adella caught the breathtaking sunset over Vryndolne and the Valley. The entrances to these terraces were set with long curtains of plum velvet and lavender gossamer, held open with golden sashes. Adella thought that she could faintly hear the famed Varinth waterfalls in the distance.

# The Chronicles of Royal High

# The Lost Noble

## R. Litfin

With her peasant life stripped away,
and a crown thrust upon her,
Adella Everheart must face the
darkness haunting her at
Royal High before it consumes
everything she loves.
Who would have thought
high school could be so easy?

Having been born into a family of nerds from a slice of the Shire in Northern California, Rachel Litfin cultivated a love of all things fantasy from a very young age. Inspired by dressing up with her family at renaissance faires, to losing herself in Tolkien, to playing World of Warcraft into the wee hours of the morning, Rachel created the very beginnings of The Chronicles of Royal High in her freshman English class. You can find her today in the realm of Southern California, often adventuring her way through Disneyland, reading by firelight, swimming in the ocean like a mermaid, and, of course, writing about the many stories that exist within Edenarth.

@rachellitfin    finonfire.wordpress.com
R. Litfin    R_Litfin

"Ah, here we are," the headmistress spoke. "This is your room, suite nineteen."

Adella saw the shining plaque on the side of the dorm. It said that a princess named Diamara Tyrandaa of the realm of Desevry resided within.

Von Durdenmyer pulled a stylized bronze key from her pocket and opened the double doors.

Adella gasped as the two of them stepped through.

The headmistress looked entirely indifferent as she handed the key to the girl. She glanced down to thumb through her papers in her portfolio, checking things off.

Adella continued to walk into the enormous room, key in hand, marveling at the splendor of such living accommodations. She wondered if all the quarters were like this.

On opposite sides from one another were two huge, identical beds, each with red and black satin sheets. The frames they each sat upon were of dark wrought iron, winding up into four lattice like posts, from which matching silk and velvet draperies made a canopy. Several matching pillows were piled neatly and rested at the base of each curling metal headboard.

Lined on the wall next to each bed, stretching almost the length of the room, were carved black wood wardrobes. Adella couldn't explain why, but they looked menacing to her. The burgundy candle sticks and iron candelabras on the walls, combined with a dimly glowing chandelier in the middle of the ceiling, threw a subdued, almost haunting light upon everything. The stone walls were of the same grey throughout the castle, and sets of thick, red curtains were drawn over what Adella assumed to be the windows.

The room was magnificent, and elegant, but it felt dark, and not only because the drapes were closed.

"If you have any questions or comments concerning your accommodation, feel free to contact the help down at the service desk. Or, just ring the enchanted bell," the headmistress instructed while pointing a red clawed finger at a tarnished bronze bell with a long black rope by the door. She looked at her paperwork again. "Diamara's not in here I see. I'll send the help up to set up your things," she nodded and wrote something down. She then glanced up, looked at Adella critically, and added, "And I suggest you wear something, *suitable*, for your first dinner."

"Isn't this okay?" Adella asked, slightly hurt, while gently running her hand over the tulle and brocade of her grey and gold dress.

The headmistress only shook her head. "I'll just send your bags up – *and* a Royal Handbook," she stressed the last thing with pursed lips and a raised eyebrow. "Now, if you'll excuse me, I am off schedule and my presence is needed in the grand dining hall. I shall see you downstairs." She closed her portfolio and turned quickly on her heels, her huge tent of a dress swishing with her movement, and shut the double doors behind her. They rattled mutely.

Everything was eerily quiet and Adella found herself quite alone.

The room seemed chilled, yet stifled.

The candle lights flickered slightly, and Adella thought she heard the shadows move behind her – if that were even possible.

Her hands grew cold and her hair stood on end.

When she turned around, she saw nothing.

# Seven

*Okay, deep breath. Just hold your head high, walk down, grab some food, and find a seat. Don't make eye contact. Just grab some food,* Adella silently chanted in her head.

After changing into a gorgeous teal dress that Cassandra had packed, something she hoped fit well enough into the guidelines that she quickly managed to skim, Adella paced silently and quickly to the end of the dorm hall and proceeded down the grand staircase. She was trying to make peace with the fact that she would be living in that unsettling room; she still hadn't met her roommate yet and wasn't quite sure that she wanted to. She took the corridor that she hoped would lead over to the dining hall.

She soon came upon a sleek butler who was standing behind a podium that was in front of dual giant doors.

"Good evening, princess, I am ze Maitre D François. What may I do for you tonight?" He spoke as Adella drew near. His accent was thick and his thin imperial mustache effortlessly completed his uptight suit.

"Dinner?" Adella asked as she paused and smiled.

"Of course, right zis way. You are ze new princess, Adella Everheart, of ze realm Adamaris, yes?" He motioned with his hand to come closer.

"You know who I am?" Adella asked with surprise as she stepped forward.

"But of course!" He laughed a little through his nose like Adella was missing something very obvious. "You're *Ze Lost Princess*!" He quickly zinged a bell on his stand. "If you have a seating preference for ze meal, please notify Detré," the Maitre D requested while another stuffy butler came up to escort the girl.

Detré lead her past the stunning double doors and through the connecting ante chamber.

"Any seating preferences, Princess?"

"Anywhere is fine," Adella replied as she went with Detré. "I'll just trust… your… judgment…" her voice trailed as she entered the great dining hall.

Her eyes grew with wonder as the music and the voices of the room filled her ears. Hundreds of royals all sat about round lavish tables full of food. They were all laughing and interacting in a way that she never expected from royals; they looked like normal teenagers. Royal and rich teenagers, but teens none-the-less. They were flirting and joking and eating and seemed like they had not a care in the world. As she passed through, she caught some boys throwing food at each other when the teachers, who were seated at one long arced table at the head of the room, were not looking.

The golden chandeliers gave the hall a lively, amber glow, while the centers of each table were set with white candle sticks in ornate golden settings. Around these were an ever evolving palate of plates and platters. Waiters whisked about bringing out more dishes while taking away the empty ones.

The room itself was deeply immense. On its left side were in and out doors, leading to what Adella assumed was the kitchen, and on the right side of the room were two antechambers, one closer, the other further to the back. They led to what looked like another gathering hall of some sort. The walls in the dining hall were set with huge paintings of Varinth's scenery and founders. Around these artworks were royal purple and gold trimmed tapestries and banners, all bearing the emblem of Royal High.

At the end of the hall, behind the teacher's table, was a paneled bay window that reach all the way to the ceiling. It overlooked the back quad of the school, and through it, Adella could see the very last of the setting sun's light. The sky beyond was already beginning to give way to the darkness of twilight.

Adella realized she must look idiotic, glancing and gaping at everything around her. She was suddenly aware of the stares from her peers, though, many of the royals still went about their own business. They, themselves, were the center of *their own* worlds, and no *commoner* princess was more important than that.

"And what are your meal preferences for tonight, Princess?" Detré asked her quietly as he pulled out an empty seat at a table full of other royals.

"Um, whatever the kitchen is serving?" She asked as she sat down rather gracefully.

Detré gave her the weirdest of looks, but cleared his throat and replied respectfully. "I'll see what I can do. I'll be right back with your plate." He poured a red liquid into her golden wine glass and then made haste to disappear through the kitchen doors.

Adella sat for a moment, looking to where the waiter disappeared to.

"Hi," one of the boys at the table slyly called.

Adella looked up and across to him. He was one of the guys that had waved at her when she first arrived outside in the court. He was smiling that same huge, gleaming white grin, and his dark brown hair played around his gorgeous cheekbones. His eyes were the most enchanting shade of sapphire.

"You're Adella, right?" The boy next to him asked. He was the same blonde who had winked at her in the courtyard. His bright chestnut eyes were warm and inviting; a slight dusting of tiny freckles graced across his nose, and his skin was golden tanned. He, too, was smiling an impossibly perfect white smile.

Adella had never known what to do with flirty attention from guys. Put a sword in her hand and she'll perry your heart out of your chest. But this? She struggled to find her voice. "Yes, I am," she finally managed to reply. "Hi."

"She speaks! Alright!" The blonde one laughed.

"Sweet," the dark haired one smirked.

"Well of course she speaks! She probably wouldn't have even been admitted to this school if she was a mute. Not that it would have made a difference anyway," one of the girls at the table interrupted. She had tight black ringlets that shaped a thin sour face.

"Thanks for the unsolicited opinion, Luce," the dark haired boy rolled his eyes.

"Oh come off it, Luce! Just because she didn't find out that she was the *Lost Princess* until, like, *today* doesn't make her any less of a royal!" The blonde boy added.

He said something else to Luce, but Adella didn't catch it.

"Hi, I'm Princess Kate Fendraid of Daeleron. You're Adella Everheart?" The beautiful girl to Adella's right leaned over to whisper. Her large caramel curls were half swept up, and her soft blue eyes were kind. Her pale, porcelain skin was kissed everywhere with freckles. She smiled.

Adella nodded earnestly, still happily shocked at how the blonde boy came to her defense. "Yes, I'm Adella. It seems everyone here already knows that, though."

"Well, the media did swarm our school today," Kate laughed a little. "It's really nice to meet you, Adella." Her greeting was genuine.

"It's nice to meet you, too, Kate," Adella smiled warmly.

"Hi guys, sorry I'm late," a new voice chimed in. "I was having a meeting with my uncle. He said not to worry about the spill in the alchemy lab." Her incredibly long blonde hair seemed to float around her as she arrived at the table. A servant pulled out the empty chair next to Adella and she sat down. Her cream and deep emerald dress was absolutely stunning. It made her own emerald eyes stand out. "I told him it was completely unintentional," she flashed a smug, almost scolding look to the two boys across from her and Adella. "He bought the accident story, but seriously, guys, you got off lucky. We're only like six weeks into the new year!" She chastised as she picked up her glass and took a sip of the red liquid that was poured for her.

"Oh come on, Viv," the blonde boy teased. "You wanted to see what was going to happen just as much as the rest of us. And you have to admit, it was nice getting out of alchemy for the rest of the day. And did you see Harding's toupee?! It caught fire for a second! Classic! I wonder what his Realms and Accounting class is going to be like for a while?" He laughed at the thought of Professor Harding in an even worse toupee.

"That was so awesome man!" The dark haired boy held out his fist to his buddy, and the blonde one bumped it with his own.

"Well, the explosion *was* pretty cool… And Harding is kind of the worst ever," the blonde girl admitted with a sheepish grin. "It was worth it," she allowed.

The two boys laughed.

"But," she continued, holding up a finger, "Kate and I aren't going to be the distraction next time, alright? And I don't care if it's in the name of *enlightenment*." The two boys laughed harder. She glanced to Adella next to her. "Oh my! *The Lost Princess!*" She realized. "Princess Adella Everheart!"

"Hello," Adella replied, smiling timidly.

"Oh, where are my manners? I'm Viv Thelred," she nodded and held out her delicate hand.

"Nice to meet you, Viv," Adella took it gingerly, remembering what her grandmother had taught her about greetings, and shook a delicate handshake fit for lady royals. She hoped she did it right. Adella then looked inquisitively at the other two boys across from her. She felt like she was in a fog. Everything was so surreal.

"Apologies," the blonde one said as he glanced to his friend then back to Adella. "I'm Jason Renlorre, Prince of Rivenlaes," he smirked at her.

"And I'm Blake Telarn," the dark haired one winked, blue eyes twinkling, "Prince of Itheria."

"Most of us are sophomores, like you," Jason said, motioning to everyone at the table. By now the majority of the other teens in the general area had slowed their conversations to listen in on the introductions.

"Okay, so Kate, Viv, Jason, and Blake?" Adella slowly repeated as she looked at each one. "Got it," she smiled. "So, uh, what's a *Lost Princess*? Is that something that happens here a lot?"

Everyone within earshot halted in their tracks, some dropping their forks with a clink, others stopping mid drink or mid chew, and looked at her incredulously.

"You've never heard of *The Lost Princess*?" Viv asked in shock.

"Uh, no? There's only one?" Adella said with uncertainty as she reevaluated the stress Viv had put on the word *the*. She raised her eyebrows.

"Haven't they been talking about it in the press? The pixierazzi? Especially recently?" Kate asked.

"Uh, not that I know of," Adella replied. In that moment she tried to think back to when she did pay attention to things like royal news. She was drawing a blank. Since the Sun's Tide, she had tuned out on all of the royal world's happenings. What reason was there to keep up with it all when it only brought her painful memories? She really had been living under a rock for the last several months.

"Of course there is only *one*. Don't know of any *other* realms on the continent that had their royal heir exiled in the last 20 years," Jason interjected. He laughed a little in disbelief.

Adella shook her head, her eyes burning with curiosity.

"It has long been rumored," Kate interjected, "that the Adamaris heir was a *princess*, living as a common girl," she motioned to Adella.

"Only no one knew who or where she was!" Viv explained excitedly. "The whispers of a Lost Princess have been in circulation for awhile now, and word has been going around the royal circles that your grandmother had been abroad searching for you over this last Sun's Tide. And now you're finally found! Why else do you think this palace was completely swamped with media today like it was?"

"They did that because of the legend?" Adella's head was spinning.

"She has no idea, does she?" Blake murmured, marveling at her sheltered state.

"Okay, Adella," Viv leveled in a quiet voice, bringing the conversation to a one on one. She leaned in close. "Listen. You may not have known who you are, but you are more than just The Lost Princess. You're a *crown* princess. Not everyone is next in line for their realm's throne. Whatever you once knew your life to be is now gone. There is no going back," Viv motioned around. "All of the realms and kingdoms are connected, and many are interdependent. Whenever a kingdom is having a crisis, or, in your case, missing an heir," she smiled, "well, it's kind of a big deal."

"I didn't think of it that way," Adella murmured, her ocean eyes huge with realization. The girl was taken aback at Viv's sudden candor.

"Yes," Viv affirmed. "You're a big deal."

While Viv had been explaining all of this, their food was brought out. Naturally, it was the most fancy meal Adella had ever seen up until this point. There was a bright tangy salad bursting with fresh garden fare, appetizers swimming in delicate juices and meaty bits, crispy roasted vegetables, and of course, the main dish, steaming hot, wrapped in bacon, topped with lemon slices and garnish.

"This fork, right?" Adella whispered. She had picked up the smaller four pronged fork, the first from the outside in a long line of silverware to her left.

Viv laughed a little. "Yes. You work your way in," she encouraged.

Adella beamed and took a small bite of the expertly seasoned vegetables.

"Oh geez, here she comes," Blake said, startled, as he dropped his fork on his plate with a loud clatter.

"Dude, dude, hide me," Jason said in a loud whisper while jostling Blake. He tried to sink down while Blake pretended to shove him under the table.

"Wait, what?" Adella asked, looking around, wondering what they were doing. They straightened up all of a sudden, trying to look nonchalant, when a high, snobby voice spoke from behind.

"Good evening, Viv."

"Good evening, Dia!" Viv greeted brightly.

Adella turned behind her to see the scarlet girl from the balcony, wearing the same silky crimson and charcoal gown. She was a peculiar type of pretty, in an ethereal way, with too large eyes in the queerest shade of green. Her glossy flame hair framed her shoulders which were thrust into perfect posture. Two other girls dressed in similar colors shadowed behind her.

"Prince Jason. Prince Blake," Dia smirked at them, flirting.

"Hey, Dia," the boys chorused in unison, uninterested.

"So Viv, I have a favor to ask of you," Dia began, her voice sickeningly sweet.

"Yes?" Viv encouraged.

"I'm wanting to throw a get together in my dorm sometime soon for our group of friends, and I was wondering if you would help me set it up? You did such a great job putting together the Autumn Ball this last weekend. You have the best ideas when it comes to these types of things, so you were the first person that came to mind," she smiled enthusiastically.

"I'll have to check when I am free, but that sounds like fun. Can I get back to you?" Viv asked.

"Of course! Get back to me whenever you can. I already have Anna and Kylie helping me get the guest list *just right*," she winked as she gestured to the two girls who flanked her.

"I understand," Viv responded.

Adella was suddenly reminded of Brittney. *What is it with royals and fine tuning their stupid guest lists?* She rolled her eyes.

"And, of course, you guys are invited," she looked at Jason and Blake who, when Dia hadn't been looking, pretended to gag themselves behind her. She smiled cutely at them, completely oblivious.

"Thanks," Jason smiled fakely.

"Can't wait," Blake said, smiling in the same way.

"Well, I'm off to get some beauty rest. The session I had in The City today *exhausted* me. Design Haus has been begging me to be their muse for *months* now.

They're making me the face of their upcoming Green's Tide fashion week," she looked down at Adella. "Sometimes it's hard being so in demand!" She sighed dramatically.

"Well, don't let *us* keep you from your *beauty* rest. A couple more weeks would do you wonders," Jason's smirk was too handsome for his own good.

Dia's eyes narrowed at him, unsure of the underhanded compliment. "Anyway, Vivian, I'll keep you posted on the party. And again, invite only the *right* people." She glanced to Adella once more. It was not a kind look.

Adella knew what Dia meant. She knew she wouldn't be invited to this "get together."

"Oh, how absent of me. Dia, did you meet Adella yet?" Viv asked eagerly. "The heir to the Adamaris throne? You know, the reason for that whole media mess today?"

"So you mean *this* is the rumored *Lost Princess*? How could I have missed that?" Dia exclaimed. "I mean, with your *dress choice* for tonight's dinner, I had thought you were some commoner here for a charity cause. I had no idea! It's so nice to finally meet you!"

"Uh, it's nice to meet you, too," Adella tried to ignore the backhanded comment.

"Actually, Dia, her dress was created by my cousin's fashion house," Vivian gushed. "We're looking to add the style to our handbook next year," she smirked. "Adella's ahead of the curve."

"And Adella's far from common," Blake broke in. "She's too good looking to not be royalty," he added with a wink.

Adella was speechless. These royal kids she had known for all of five minutes just stuck up for her.

"Yes, I see," Dia raised a petulant eyebrow. She said nothing more as her gaze caught on a silvery blonde girl that came into view. She sauntered by with several boys in tow, glanced once at Adella, turned her nose up, and kept walking, basking in the attention of her rowdy "mantourage".

"Well, I'll be off," Dia's attention diverted back to the table. "It was interesting to have met you, Adella." She gave a forced smile and then turned and called out, "Sadie!" as she quickly made her way over to the icy blonde, but not before her own foot *accidentally* gave a hard kick to Adella's chair, rattling the poor girl. Anna and Kylie followed close behind her.

"Is she gone?" Jason asked. Adella, Viv, and Kate turned to see the boys hiding behind a little piece of the table cloth they were holding up.

"Oh knock it off you two," Viv scolded.

"Yeah, she's gone," Kate shook her head.

"Seriously, Viv, why do you even deal with her?" Jason asked as he straightened up.

"Well, for starters, you would know *why* if you guys had read the diplomacy chapter in our etiquette class last week," Viv replied.

"Who even reads?" Jason scoffed, laughing, as he started a lively banter with their table.

Adella was quiet for a moment, absorbing everything around her. She knew not why, but The Radiance seemed to bless her to sit at this specific place in the middle of the room. These new people were *warm* to her. It gave her spirits a much needed lift, especially after how she was received earlier that day. She lifted her glass and took a sip.

"Hey," Viv leaned over and whispered in Adella's ear. "I need to use the restroom, do you want to come with?"

Just when Adella was about to respond, she started to choke.

She was choking because she inhaled her drink.

She inhaled her drink because the last person in the world she thought would be in this room was walking by.

The last person she would ever expect to be at Royal High, was *walking to her table.*

"Are you okay?" Viv said with worry as she patted Adella's back.

"Yeah," cough, "I'm fine," cough, cough.

"Sweetie, you're supposed to drink the cranberry juice," Viv laughed a little, "not inhale it." She smiled worriedly, "Are you okay?"

"Yes, I'm good," Adella said, sputtering a little. Luckily, her minor episode wasn't noticed. Her coughs were quiet and quick, lost in the noise of the dining hall.

Seeing *him* walk by, however, was an eternity for Adella. Like a slow motion tidal wave you cannot run away from.

The layer of emotional numbness that had silently grown over her during the Sun's Tide suddenly disintegrated. Everything was raw, vivid, sharp. Her ears were ringing. Countless feelings ran chaotically through her blood; bewilderment, despair, fear, self loathing, heartbreak.

Her face drained white.

Viv's breath suddenly caught as she looked up. "By The Fates," she murmured, her eyes glittering, as an adorable smirk spread on her face. "Can we wait for a few more seconds on that break?" She ran her fingers through her hair to shake out the locks.

Adella stared at her hands, hoping that he would just pass by. *What's he doing here?! I thought he was attending Regal High! That's what the stupid article said! What the spell?! WHAT THE SPELL?!? Should I talk to him? Confront him? Can I even say hello? I'm a royal now – same as him. What would he say?*

"Hello? Adella?" Viv whispered, eying her.

Adella's head snapped up only to see that he was indeed coming right up to them.

"Good evening, friends," Brogan greeted, his voice smooth like hot spiced wine, smile utterly intoxicating. After all this time, he was still charming perfection, and it sent chills up Adella's spine to see him in person once more. "How are you all this evening?" He asked the table, charisma radiating from within. His fingertips touched the collar of his ornate brocade doublet and passed over the incredible deep ruby pendant he wore. The table responded to him with more enthusiasm than Adella would have guessed appropriate.

Luce sparkled as she batted her dark eyes at him. "Our evening is lovely, Prince Brogan. Won't you join us?" She giggled.

"I am afraid that I cannot linger, Luce," he smiled with heartbreaking flair. "Merely passing by." He then looked to Viv.

"Good evening, Prince Brogan," Viv greeted him breathlessly.

"Vivian," he ardently replied, "that emerald dress lights up your eyes." He lightly took the girl's hand and kissed it. "The sunset we just had could not compare."

Adella sat there, her jaw agape. Her ears were still ringing, everything too clear. She closed her mouth and faced forward only to see Jason looking upset. He was staring at the interaction between Brogan and Viv. His lips were in a tight line and his brow furrowed hard over his eyes. He gripped his fork in his hand, knuckles white.

Blake seemed upset as well. Not as intense as Jason, but still displeased. He stole a glance to Adella, confusion crossing his face when their gaze met.

*Oh no. I wonder what I look like right now...* Adella thought with panic as she tried to work a nonchalant expression into place. Her breathing was quiet, but shallow and fast. She concluded that she must have looked like someone just punched her in the gut – because that's exactly what she felt.

Viv blushed at Brogan's advance.

"By the way, nice work in the Alchemy Lab, guys. I heard it was a pretty epic job," Brogan looked up and joked to the table.

"Yeah, you know when your plan is a success when you catch a teacher's toupee on fire," Blake added dryly.

"Oh, Prince Brogan," his name rolled off of Viv's lips with a burning passion. Adella wasn't sure if Viv did this on purpose, or if she honestly couldn't help speaking that way to him; and if the reason was for the latter, Adella really couldn't blame her. It was hard *not* to feel like that when around him. "Did you meet Adella Everheart? The *Lost Princess*?"

Adella looked to him, her ocean eyes bewildered and wide.

She wasn't expecting this.

"No, actually, I don't believe I have had the pleasure," he answered as his gaze finally fell upon her. "Good evening, Princess Adella. I'm Prince Brogan Etherstone. So you are the lost Everheart that Adamaris has long been searching for?"

Adella could only nod, wondering what in the realms was going on. *Is he really going to pretend that he doesn't know me!?* She mentally screamed. It was debilitating to feel the internal beating of the raw heart that she had smothered for months.

"I am glad you have been found then," he chuckled as if he was laughing at some secret joke. "My realm, Kelemer," he explained, "has very close relations with yours, Adamaris. You're our southern neighbor and we have been worried for your monarchy. This really is joyous news."

"Yes, well, I am so very glad that my discovery has eased your mind, *Prince Brogan*," Adella replied with a strong voice. She surprised herself at how sure she sounded, happy that her tone did not betray how she really felt inside. Every nerve within her was fire.

She looked into his eyes, trying to figure out what game he was playing. They were the cerulean hue she had memorized, but there was a light that was missing. They were cold and apprehensive. Walled. It was the same icy look he held on the day he ended it with her; the last time they saw each other.

Adella's piercing gaze could not hold him, though, and he swiftly looked to Viv.

"Oh, Viv, speaking of Alchemy, before I forget, there was an assignment," Brogan glossed over Adella's reply, "is that due in the morning? The one with the Blurberry Formulas? My partner has been out sick. Will you help me?"

Adella's stomach turned knots again seeing the way he interacted with Viv. Adella had known her new friends all of twenty minutes, and Viv had been nothing but kind to her, sticking up for her even; but Viv knew nothing of her past history with *this* boy, and Adella knew that she could hold no hard feelings towards her. Brogan, on the other hand, was worthy of the wrath Adella felt building inside. Was he really going to pretend that he did not know the *commoner* girl from his past?

"Of course! I completed the assignment already," Viv grinned. "Come see me in the morning really quick before first period. It doesn't take long."

"Thank you," he replied.

"Prince Brogan," a waiter holding a platter of desserts approached. "The headmistress has requested your presence at the professor's table." He nodded to the long table at the front of the room where all the teachers were being served.

"Ah yes, thank you," Brogan replied to the servant. He turned back to the table of his peers. "It appears that I have been summoned. Until next time," he bowed and then looked to Adella, coming closer for a moment, and spoke only so she could hear. "I am glad that your *true* identity has come to light. I hope to get to know you better as the year progresses, *Princess Adella*."

Adella's heart stopped.

He *did* know.

He looked around once more and spoke to his audience, "I bid you all a goodnight." He turned on his heel and set off, his cape fluttering behind.

Adella turned back around and touched her stomach. Her heart was hammering out of her rib cage, stomach churning, threatening to give up her dinner. She hadn't felt this raw since the day he left her. Not even when her grandmother came to drop the bombshell of a lifetime. She stole a glance back to Jason whose fork was now bent and somewhat folded in his napkin, tucked off to the side. Blake shook his head to himself.

"What did he tell you?" Kate leaned over to ask, a sincere question in her eyes.

"Just something about our realms working together," Adella tried to brush it off. Kate seemed satisfied by the answer, and the table resumed to its trivial banter. The girls were lively over Prince Brogan while the guys – except for the now brooding Jason and Blake – slyly conferred about the new *prospect* that was the *Lost Princess*.

Adella needed to leave. All of the overlapping voices; anecdoche. The ringing in her ears, the foods suddenly too pungent, the feel of her heavy dress pressing into her tingling flesh, her hair brushing against her cheeks which felt like they had been slapped flush, the lights around her that were like concentrated sun rays…

She turned to Viv who was beaming to herself as she absently twirled her fork through the decadent strawberry cake set before her. "So, bathroom break?" Adella suggested, trying to ignore her internal meltdown. She smiled, and she hoped she looked happy.

"Yes, let's go," Viv perked up.

They stood, and Jason and Blake took to their feet as well, out of courtesy, as the girls took their leave.

"Hey, Adella, are you holding up okay?" Viv asked as she washed her hands in one of the golden basins set in a long marble countertop.

Like the rest of the castle, the restrooms were no exception to the far reaching opulence of royals. As soon as Adella saw that the lavatory *thrones* were trimmed in the purest gold and made of the most priceless porcelain, she accepted the fact that there was nothing in the entire establishment that was not touched with a lavish extravagance.

"Yeah, it's just a lot to take in," Adella admitted as she joined her at the counter vanity. What she wanted to say was that she was about to have a mental snap from having just spoken to her crown prince ex-boyfriend whom she had not seen since their traumatic public break up back in her peasant hometown of North Brook Valley. To add insult to injury, he apparently had the nerve to pretend that he didn't even know her. "I'm glad, though," Adella added, trying to be positive, "that I was lucky enough to sit with you and Kate and Jason and Blake. You have been the nicest people I have met since my arrival."

"Really?" Viv smiled. "Well, usually our dinner table is always full. Guess it's a good thing that you got down there when you did, huh?" She laughed a little,

"Honestly, I was really hoping to get a chance to meet with you today. I'm really happy with how it all worked out. I'm thinking that we'll definitely have to save a seat for you from now on."

"I'd love that," Adella smiled, once again taken by surprise with Viv's kindness. She wondered if she should be suspicious.

"Don't mention it," Viv returned the grin.

Viv turned to touch up her hair. Adella looked in the mirror and straightened her dress.

"Uh, Viv," she began.

"Hmm?"

"Is there something wrong with my dress?" Adella asked ruefully. She honestly loved the beautiful teal and gold gown that she found in her luggage. It was one of the only dresses that Cassandra had packed for her that actually fit her well. And Vivian said it was from her cousin's fashion line. Was that true?

"Ohh, are you referring to what Dia had said? Yes, she was way out of line with that. I'm going to speak with her," Viv said the last part under her breath as she shook her head in disapproval. "No, there isn't anything *wrong* with your dress. I wasn't lying. It really is from my cousin's fashion line. I've been pulling to get the admin to add it to our dress code. But as of right now, it's not technically approved," she rolled her eyes as she mentioned this.

"So it's not dress code approved?" Adella asked hesitantly.

"It's not from an '*approved designer*'," Viv admitted, resentment in her tone, turning around to lean against the counter. "Which I think is stupid because my cousin makes such great work. You've got good taste, Adella." She winked.

"My grandmother chose it," Adella blurted. She paused, then asked, "So all the approved designers we can wear are listed in the handbook?"

"Yes," Viv confirmed. "But like I said, it's dumb. There are so many beautiful styles out there that I wish we could wear, but it's not allowed because they prefer to have 'sponsored' products for us. And the handbook changes every year. So a dress that you could have worn last year, may be completely unapproved this year. One of my absolute favorite dresses that I used to wear last term is not allowed at all right now. It's getting ridiculous. Half of the stuff they have picked for us is hideous."

Adella nodded thoughtfully. This all seemed entirely silly.

"Don't pay it too much mind. We'll get you up and running. Besides, you get extra points in my book for wearing a creation of my cousin. Everyone thought that you were making a great statement," Viv smiled, trying to make Adella feel better.

"Well in that case, I totally was," Adella laughed.

"By the way, I never asked you, do you know who you are sharing your room with yet?" Viv unscrewed her lip gloss and began to put it on.

"I only have a name and a realm. Diamara Tyrandaa of the realm of Desevry."

Viv dropped her makeup and it landed in the basin on the counter with a loud clatter. "Are you serious?" She asked incredulously.

"Yes?" Adella replied, nervousness taking hold.

"You're rooming with *Dia*?"

"What the spell," Adella said realizing. "*That's* Diamara?" She groaned. Adella was connecting the dots. "I'm betting that she knew she was rooming with me, too, when she found out who I was at the dinner table. She didn't even say a word," Adella speculated, upset, as she remembered the way Dia had treated her in the dining hall.

"Well, an announcement was made at breakfast that you were coming this morning. They had to explain to us why the media was plaguing our school. She totally knew," Viv admitted.

"An announcement?!" Adella gasped.

"Yeahhh," Viv replied cautiously. "Your arrival has been the biggest thing to happen since the year started – even bigger than last week's Autumn Ball," she smiled ruefully.

"Why is this Lost Princess thing such a big deal? Everyone else has their own lives, surely they don't need to be caught up with mine!"

"Adella, I already told you," Viv explained, sounding slightly exasperated. "Kingdoms are interdependent on each other. And yours is one of the most important on this side of the hemisphere. You're an ocean realm with vast agricultural resources and sea trade. If you weren't found, Adamaris would have been broken up. No way your awkward cousins in Adaar could have kept it all together."

"You know my awkward cousins?" Adella scoffed. She'd never even met these people but apparently Viv knew about them, too.

"Let's just say they're infamous for their… conduct in court," Viv smirked oddly. "Remind me to tell you about them sometime."

Adella just shook her head and sighed. Viv was very well informed; she said almost exactly what grandmother had reported. *How does she know all this?* Skepticism grew deeper in Adella's mind. *Who is Viv?*

"Anyways, I'm guessing you don't wish to room with Dia then?" Viv brought the subject back, a bigger smile spreading on her face.

"Well, not particularly, but I don't think there is anything I could do to change this situation," Adella said sadly as she looked in the mirror. She sighed as she grasped the counter top. "I'll make due, it's okay. I don't want to put people out with changing around accommodations. I've made enough waves as it is. I'll just have to suck it up."

It was then that Viv started to laugh. Really laugh. The sound was light and beautiful in the marble powder room.

"You most certainly do have a lot to learn when it comes to being a royal, Adella," she continued to giggle.

"What's so funny?" Adella asked petulantly.

"*'Putting people out?'*" Viv echoed in disbelief. Adella nodded.

"Adella, do you want to room with me? I was never reassigned a dormie for this year. The girl I was supposed to have transferred at the last moment to Monarch High. The school never imposed a new one on me."

"Really? You mean it?"

"Totally!" Viv said, a sparkle in her eyes. "I really like you, Adella. Plus, you're going to need all the help you can get coming into this. I *want* to help you."

"Wait," Adella paused. This girl really seemed too good to be true. It all did. "How?"

"I have my ways," Viv smirked shyly.

"I'm curious because you make this sound so easy. Is it like that for all royals here?" Adella questioned. Who did this girl think she was, anyway? Knowing everything about everyone, seemingly having an *in* with everybody, special privileges...

"Well, no. People here can't do half of what I do most of the time."

There was a moment of silence. Viv sighed.

"My family owns the school, Adella."

"Wait," Adella realized. "Viv... Thelred? *Empress* Vivian Thelred? Heiress to the Varinth Empire?" How did she not see it before?! The long day and endless introductions really had done a number on her!

"The one and only," Viv looked at her hands "I kind of didn't want to just tell you, you know? I think it sounds kind of stuck up going around telling people you're an empress."

"I totally understand," Adella nodded. "Aren't our realms super close, then? I mean, Adamaris and Varinth are good friends, right?" Adella had remembered what her grandmother had said about alliances with Varinth. How could she not have known who this girl was!

"Most definitely," Vivian beamed. "Which is another good reason why we should room together. Honestly, I'm sort of surprised you didn't recognize a lot of us around here already. Despite the laws, we do tend to pop up in the media from time to time."

"Well, a few of you I did recognize," Adella paused, thinking mainly of Brogan, "but I've been so overwhelmed since this whole whirlwind started!" She added, "The media makes you all look a bit different, I think."

"You're not wrong there," Viv sighed. "We're either falling out of carriages half drunk or groomed for a ball. There's no inbetween." She smirked and motioned to the door. "Come on. Oh, and remind me when we get the chance. I'll show you a spread that MedievTeen did on me awhile back. You'll see what I'm talking about."

I think I had that one!" Adella exclaimed. Vivian laughed. "So, now," she nodded to a lady servant who opened the restroom doors. Adella hadn't even noticed her standing in the shadows. "Are you ready?"

"Ready?" Adella asked as she followed.

"Let's go change your dorm!" Viv giggled excitedly as she grabbed her hand.

With her new friend by her side, Adella stepped back into the grand halls and back into the unknown.

# <u>Eight</u>

Adella felt alive as she ran with abandon through the maze of the fantastic forest. The enchanting violet and azure foliage, fragrant blooms, flickering fireflies, and endless trees called to her. She saw her way through by the silvery cast of the full moon and by the glittering essence of the stars. The soft carpet of grass and moss beneath her bare feet was exhilarating freedom. Every breath felt like magic in her lungs.

This world resembled the forests of Varinth, however, Adella could not recall having ever run through a forest so grand, especially in the night like this. But for some reason, it felt familiar. If that were possible.

She was following the note exactly, written in *his* handwriting; it even smelled like him. His intoxicating scent, unmistakable.

*Meet me at the waterfall.*

After rereading the message, Adella looked up, and suddenly it was there. She stepped out of the dark edge of the wild forest and into the velvety grass of the verdant clearing, gazing in wonder upon the waterfall. The moonlight, streaming through the wispy clouds, gave the serene scene an ethereal shimmer. The crystal waters cascaded down the moss of the ivy covered mountain and emptied into a pool as silver and round as the celestial body that governed the night above it.

Her chest rose erratically as she tried to steady her breath. Her elegant pewter dress clung to her slight form and trailed behind her like a river of silk. She neared the edge of the water.

"Adella?" He said her name with the relief of one who had finally recovered their long lost love.

Adella knew this voice immediately.

"Brogan?" She breathlessly called. She turned around and scanned the gorgeous view, but could not see a soul.

"I'm right here, my love," he murmured ardently in her ear as his arms slid in around her waist from behind.

"Oh," Adella gasped, her surprised eyes sparkling like the starlight above them.

Brogan laughed lightly as he pulled her close and rested his chin in the curve of her shoulder and neck. He inhaled deeply at her skin.

"Why are you doing this?" Adella whispered, still surprised, and now a bit upset. Her trembling hands reached down to touch his which had remained around her waist.

"Doing what?" Brogan murmured as he softly kissed her neck.

Adella froze. She could not remember her train of thought. She could not remember her own name.

He gently turned her around to face him, still in his arms. Adella looked up into his deep cerulean eyes, warm with love and desire. His dark hair, playfully disarrayed, framed his forehead and Radiance blessed cheekbones. He gazed down at her with an insatiable grin.

"Doing what?" She repeated, dazed.

"Breathe, Adella," he reminded playfully as he stroked her cheek. He inclined his head closer, and Adella was instantly aware of his strong jawline and full lips.

She inhaled a breath and held it longer than necessary. It helped clear her mind. She remembered.

"Why did you summon me here?" She asked, trying to be petulant, as she held up the note. "And why are you pretending that you don't know me–"

Before she knew what was happening, his lips crashed down upon hers. He pulled her closer against him and trailed the fingertips of his free hand softly down her cheek; and he continued to kiss her with a rhythm that Adella knew all too well.

"Adella, I've missed you so much," he whispered, passion burning from within. Her hands, frozen on his chest at first, made their way up to his locks, running through them, fingers intertwining themselves with the hair at his neck; and she found herself kissing him back with a well matched passion, their mouths moving perfectly together. A heart song they once wrote together, dormant deep in their souls, was given life once more by this most yearned for kiss.

His lips tasted indescribably wonderful and Adella couldn't help but grin as he started to kiss her cheeks, her nose, her forehead, her jaw. His hands felt along her hips, up her back, pressing her into him, longing for more.

Finally, her hands rested back onto his chest, and his hands found each side of her face, gently cradling it. He kissed her lips once more, sweetly, lightly, lingering. "Now, what were you saying?" He asked.

Adella's breath was lost. In his arms, this place, his warmth, his kiss…

"Why are you doing this?" She managed to repeat her question. With the way he had treated her over the last few months, none of this made sense.

"Why not?" He asked, genuinely confused. "Don't we always do this? Haven't you missed me?"

Adella paused, looking into his eyes.

*Not anymore we don't! Does he not know?* Her thoughts echoed. *I couldn't have dreamed the last few months, could I? Did I? This all feels so real right now. This here is reality, isn't it? It feels like I have been away from him for an eternity!*

"Oh, Brogan," she sighed, a sob in her throat. "I have missed you so much!" She buried her face into his chest, inhaling.

He rested his head on top of hers. "I've always been right by your heart, Adella," he whispered, hugging her tightly.

"Oh, but I had the most horrible dream!" She explained through her sobs, heart exploding. "You didn't want me anymore, and you left me in front of everyone, and now I'm at Royal High with you but you are so different!" He smoothed her hair and comforted her, kissing her head.

"Royal High? Della, how could all of that happen?" He sadly asked, confused himself. "I would never willingly leave you! You are my life! How could I be different?"

"But, you *are*. I think?" Adella stared up at him with frightened, tear filled eyes. "Unless… is this here the dream?"

Brogan's eyes narrowed as he put the pieces to together. "Something is wrong," he murmured, fear burning in his voice. He suddenly jerked away as if in pain, leaving Adella's arms.

"Brogan?" Adella cried.

The world began to shimmer and shake and pass into darkness. The vivid colors melted into black as the earth raged around them and cracked open into red, fiery chasms.

"There is much wrong in the waking world, Adella. Everything is not as it seems. Don't trust me–"

"What?! No, wait!" Adella tried to grasp onto him, but he began to fade into the nothingness, mouthing words she could not understand. She tried to run after him.

"No! Please! Come back! I miss you! I love you! Please!" Her grief overwhelmed her as she fell into the dark abyss.

"No!" She gasped as she hit something hard and shot up from her pillow. "No," she gasped again.

Everything was quiet, and the only sound she heard over the pounding pulse in her ears was Vivian's quiet breaths from her bed on the other side of the room.

The moon's light poured in through their open balcony, and the gossamer curtains danced in the midnight breezes.

She gripped her silk blue blankets as she sat up in her golden canopy bed. The tears poured down her cheeks, and she choked back a sob, not wanting to wake up Viv.

*What does that mean?! Don't trust me? I've never dreamed of Brogan like this; it felt real; it felt like he called to me. But he doesn't love me. He never did... He made that very clear in North Brook, and he confirmed it by his actions in the hall tonight.*

She threw back the blankets and stepped barefoot onto the floor, her thin nightgown flowing behind, and went onto the balcony. The moon and stars bathed her in their glow as she touched the marble banister edge. A chill breeze blew her long hair over the tears on her cheeks. A hollow emptiness enveloped her.

She looked across the lands of Varinth and saw the forests and mountain ranges below. They looked just like her dream. She heard waterfalls in the distance.

She sighed and gazed up into the sky, into the same celestial bodies that she had known her whole life. Here, in the cold night, the innumerable pinpoints of brilliant reason glittered with untold secrets. The Scar, a smattering streak of stars and cosmos, was the most prominent constellation to the North, and she found herself gazing into its nebulous reaches when something caught her attention. A red star started to move. It hovered across the sky at first, then started to draw closer to the land, as if it were falling. It ghosted quietly, slowly, across the nightscape.

"What the…" she whispered raising an eyebrow. As she watched this peculiar phenomenon, the star seemed as if it was on fire, or rather like fire was shooting from it. As she watched it, and it drew closer, she realized that that this was no star. Her pupils narrowed as her face fell into disbelief.

The celestial phenomenon developed a pair of fiery red wings, and a tail that whipped around viciously in its descent. It silently careened faster to the land as it tucked in its wings to drop in a death spiral.

"By The Radiance," Adella gasped. She could not believe what she was seeing. "A dragon?" She whispered in terror. She grasped the balcony as every hair on her body stood on end.

The breeze blew more fiercely, splaying her hair everywhere, blowing her sleeping gown behind. She now understood why she thought it was a falling star at first, for the moon beamed off of its shimmering scales.

The wings flared before it hit the forests, and it began to soar towards the school. Smoke rose from its nose and it shot a silent spout of fire once more. Its talons were bared and it seemed to snarl as it hurtled closer.

Adella wanted to run, she wanted to scream, she wanted a sword in her hand, but dread gripped her to the point of paralyzation.

The bloodcurdling creature's speed reduced significantly to a light soar. The wind stopped and everything seemed utterly still.

It hovered over the school momentarily, perhaps only five hundred yards away from Adella's terror gripped stance, and threw what seemed to be hideous grimace toward the girl. The eyes were dark, knowledgeable, and rimmed with bright green irises. Its crimson red scales faded in parts to deep violet and black. It quietly snorted smoke – almost like it knew it wasn't allowed to make a noise – and then stealthily flew upward, seeming to head behind a wall over the school.

*BOOM!!!!!!*

Adella's head snapped to where the noise of the explosion emanated from, somewhere deep in the forest. It sounded like the world shattered for just a moment. She then remembered the dragon and looked back over to where it had been headed.

It had vanished.

The boom cleared Adella's senses, and she was no longer hypnotized by the fear of the drake. She sprang into action.

"Viv! Viv!" She cried as she ran back into the room. Viv was already sitting up in her bed looking annoyed.

"What Adella?" She moaned, barely opening her eyes.

"Vivian!" Adella gasped as she jumped onto Viv's bed. "Did you not hear that explosion?! I think there's a dragon that's attacking the school!"

"Calm down, Adella, it's okay," Viv seemed a little more alert. "It was just the alchemist Professor Bracke performing some of his experiments in the forest. He does his more dangerous concoctions out there that way if they go awry they don't blow the alchemy lab to kingdom come. Last year it happened like five times. It's totally normal," she reassured, yawning.

"Seriously?!" Adella managed to say.

"Wait," Viv said skeptically, now fully aware, "did you just say there was a dragon attacking the school?"

"Yes!" Adella exclaimed.

"Adella, dragons have been extinct for a thousand years. You must have been dreaming, sweetie."

"I know what I saw! Though," Adella allowed, "it wasn't attacking the school, but it sure didn't look like it wanted to make friends! And I wasn't dreaming. Trust me."

"Adella, go back to sleep," Viv smiled while shaking her head. "I promise you there is nothing wrong."

Adella gave an exasperated sighed.

"Besides," Viv added, "if there was a dragon, our handsome guys can take it down." She yawned again. "Our combat team is undefeated," she sighed dreamily and lolled over.

Adella got up and rolled her eyes, shaking her head. She walked out to the balcony once more and saw a pillar of smoke rising up miles out from the school in the forest. She looked at the stars, The Scar, and then looked at the spires behind her, hoping to see something that would prove that she didn't just hallucinate the dragon.

There was nothing to prove either way.

She listlessly wandered back to her bed, suddenly very weary, and slipped back into the sheets while her mind slipped off to more unsettling dreams.

# Nine

"Adella, do you really not have anything approved to wear?" Viv questioned as the two girls got dressed the next morning.

Adella was going through the scant wardrobe that Cassandra had provided. The few dresses she had were very pretty, but none of them were within *the dress code*.

The previous night, after dinner, the two girls rushed over to the school's service desk. Within that hour, Adella and her things were settled into her new dorm with the empress. She was now to live in suite number one, the most spacious of all the girl's dorms, which was located on the top floor of the Demasque wing. The grey, gold, and violet themed quarters were open and airy with many windows and balconies – a far cry from Diamara's creepy room.

"I'm beginning to think not," Adella replied with a sigh as she turned away from her clothes to turn down the magic mirror. To no surprise, her face had been plastered all over every channel since she had arrived. The media were having a field day over her unconfirmed royal status. Adella could not wait for her father to meet with Cassandra and make the announcement once and for all.

Her parents had called to check in on her before bed, letting her know that Orrick was leaving by the first light of morning, and that Rose was going to stay with Shmitty and William until his return. Cassandra had already messaged Adella that she had successfully taken the portals out of Vryndolne and was waiting for him in Ebenhold. Until then, Adella was going to have to deal with the media just a little while longer.

"That's it," Viv said with determination as she was slipped into a petticoat by a servant of Royal High.

"That's what?" Adella asked, still wearing her silky dressing robe. She just had a bath in a huge marble tub filled with bubbles and hot jasmine scented water. As wonderful as it was, it sadly did little to ease her anxiety about the night she had. The dream and the dragon would not leave her head.

"We're going downtown to the capital after school today. Vryndolne is right down the road," Viv beamed. "I'm taking you shopping."

"Thank you, Viv," Adella was deeply touched. "But grandmother hasn't sent me money yet," she admitted. "She said funds for spending would arrive soon, though."

"Fine then," Viv smiled, "my treat. Just pay me back when you can. Go grab something out of my closet for now," she pointed to her wardrobe on her side of the room while a maid started on her corset. Another came over to powder her nose. "Pick out anything you like. They are all up to date with our handbook. Hurry, though, classes start at nine and we should be downstairs for breakfast by eight. That is, unless you wish for them to bring breakfast up here to our room," she gasped a little as the maid wound the ribbons tighter. She clutched her waist.

"No, it's fine, I want to go to the hall."

"Good, me too," Viv grinned painfully, panting a little.

A smile worked its way to Adella's face as she walked over to Vivian's side of the room. She pulled back one of the large doors set into the many panels of the massive walk-in wardrobe and looked through the endless satin, silk, velvet, chiffon, tulle, taffeta, brocade.... Any dress she could have possibly imagined, it was there, in every color. After pursuing for a moment, she decided.

"Is this one okay?" She asked, holding a shimmering lavender and gold gown out for inspection.

"Perfect, that will look wonderful on you," Viv smiled.

By the time the maids had helped them finished with the morning regiment, Adella had exchanged several crystal messages with both Raena and Shmitty who were already in their first class back in North Brook. Their entire high school was going crazy over Adella; she disappeared for a week only to emerge in the news as a *princess*, or, rather, *possible* princess – many claimed they were not convinced that Adamaris was not lying. Raena and Shmitty now had a lot of ridiculous attention from their school for being the best friends of a *possible* crown princess.

As Vivian led Adella down to breakfast in the hall, Rose messaged to let Adella know that her father had left for Ebenhold, and that she was now safe with William. Adella responded to her with a promise to talk more later that night. She then sent a quick message to her father.

*I love you. Ride safe!*

She slipped her crystal ball back into her bag. Adella missed them all terribly, but at least being able to communicate made it easier. She knew she couldn't do this alone.

Adella opened her handbook to study as Vivian led her into the grand foyer, the smell of bacon and sweet baked things floating on the air. "So let me get this right," Adella began, reading aloud. "It says here that royals are to *uphold the attributes of absolute perfection at all times*?" Her eyes were glued the dress code section in the royal handbook as she skimmed. "Wearing only the aforementioned approved designers, royals are to abide by all of Royal High's high court etiquette during the entire duration of attendance... In hopes that they retain these teachings well throughout their lives as rulers." She looked up with an eyebrow raised.

"Yeahhh," Viv smirked while shaking her head. "You'll get used to it, though. We all were raised in it," she admitted. "Though court customs can vary from kingdom to kingdom, most of everything remains the same."

The girls arrived in the dining hall and were seated for breakfast.

"Hey there, gorgeous," Blake said to Adella as she took a seat next to him.

"Good morning, Blake," Adella smiled, trying to keep on her best face, though that was an easy feat around Blake. "Hey Jason. Hey Kate," she greeted.

"Good morning, ladies," Jason replied, winking.

"Good morning, girls," Kate chimed in brightly.

"How did you sleep on your first night here?" Blake smugly prompted Adella as he took a bite of his cinnamon toast.

Adella thought back to the night's ordeal and involuntarily shuddered a little.

"Heard the bang, huh?" He asked with a laugh, mistaking her apprehension for Professor Bracke's boom.

"Who didn't hear that!?" Jason added, laughing as well. The boys then dug into their hearty breakfast platter while Vivian and Kate gossiped.

The drone of the hall's conversations brought Adella's attention everywhere. Despite everyone here having been raised in noble society since their births, she noticed that many of their morning routines reminded her of her high school at home - a far cry from the line about *perfection* she just read in the handbook.

She saw several young royals who did not look ready to embrace the new day; people who slyly hid their yawns, wore groggy faces, and strolled with the pace of an undead. Then, there were those individuals whose eyes were bright and alert, the ones that really didn't need to reach for that fifth cup of coffee. She also noticed quite a few kids who had books open on their laps as they pretended to eat. She made the correct assumption that they hadn't studied in the previous night, and now they were cramming - just like Raena and Shmitty.

Adella laughed inwardly, quickly seeing past the farce of the supposed perfectionist show that Royal High put on. Just like she had observed at dinner the previous evening, underneath all of the high society pomp, these were all teens just like herself.

Her food was brought around to her, and she inhaled deeply. It smelled like a Saturday morning at her house when her mom would cook a big breakfast. It made her think longingly of home. Her anxiety had taken away her appetite, not to mention the corset she wore left little room for anything else, but she forced herself to eat what she could. *Mom's tastes better*, she thought as she munched on a slice of french toast.

Brogan suddenly appeared, giving Adella half a heart attack once again, and greeted the table with flair and fanfare. He barely acknowledged her, though, and mentioned the assignment from the previous night to Viv. Vivian's face lit up and she giggled as the two of them left to go off and finish it.

Adella's heart pounded, feeling the after pangs of her dream, as she watched the two of them disappear. She turned back around and saw that Jason seemed upset again, though he appeared a little more composed this time around, and the silverware seemed to be in better condition.

With the way Viv would talk about Brogan, Adella knew that her past was going to be a tough subject if it ever came up. The empress couldn't contain her excitement as she regaled Adella about the Autumn Ball as the girls had gotten ready for bed. Brogan had been her date and they had had an amazing time together. Vivian even admitted that she was a little disappointed that he didn't ask her to be his girlfriend at the end of the night. Adella just dealt with the curdling feeling in her stomach and smiled along with her new friend, genuinely trying to be supportive for her.

Adella exhaled deeply like she had been holding her breath and attempted to pick at her breakfast.

*So Brogan really is going to pretend that he doesn't know me then,* she confirmed in her thoughts. *Well, I want an answer. No way is he just going to ignore our past. I wish I could talk to him. Last night really screwed me up.* Don't trust me... echoed in her ears, his last words to her in her dream.

"Where did you say you were from again, Adella?" Kate broke into Adella's thoughts. Jason, Blake, and a few of the other kids who cared enough not to be obsessed in their own world for a moment, eyed Adella curiously as she spoke.

Adella gladly answered their questions, being vague in the parts that called for it, and informative in the areas that she could afford to divulge, indulging their curious appetites for the commoner world that was so foreign to them. Soon everyone began to leave for class, and Kate took Adella to their first session.

*Alrighty, first class. At least I have it with Kate. She'll help me out. Breathe, you can do this. It's Monarchy 101. Sounds...easy?* Adella mentally prepared through the halls.

Her new friends reassured her that they would try and be there to help her find her way throughout the day. They made a schedule to see when they could tag team and switch off to help her around. Many of their periods matched up which was of great peace of mind to Adella.

As she walked into the Monarchy classroom, Kate had informed her that it was assigned seating and to be careful with this teacher. He most definitely had his favorites and was rarely compassionate. His family line had been one of the founders of the school. She smiled sadly at Adella and took her spot in the second row. Adella walked up to the teacher.

"Excuse me, Professor Landin?" Adella approached the man who was reading paperwork at his thick oak desk. The teacher, who had a bald shiny head circled by salt and pepper hair that seemed to be hanging on for dear life, addressed her.

"So you're the *Lost Princess,* hmm?" He asked, still looking at the parchments before him. "Peasant birth and upbringing, correct?" He finally glanced up. "I'm going to be honest with you, a commoner will not understand what goes on in here. Hope you're ready for this," he stated haughtily and stood.

His height was average, and a paunch belly extended from his too tight waistcoat. A prominent gap between his large two front teeth was accompanied by dark beady eyes. They peered over small squared rimmed glasses that fell to the edge of his nose. His head shape reminded Adella of an egg. He assessed the girl critically, "You are probably wondering where to sit? How about…" he trailed, eying the room. "There," he pointed to an empty seat in the third row by the giant paneled window.

Adella walked to her spot, thankful at least that some students were still trailing in. Kate was right; he wasn't even going to give her a chance. She immediately felt his downcast judgement, and it was only compounded by the furtive whispers from her peers. She could feel all sorts of eyes on her back. She looked at Kate, and Kate gave a reassuring smile in return.

Adella sat down and the teacher's assistant walked by, dropping text books onto the tables, each with a dull thud. Adella stared at the ancient aging volume: *Monarchy for the Ages* was titled in fading gilded script.

"Well, hello there, *Princess*," a familiar voice chided as he sat in the empty seat on the other side of her.

*Oh no, please don't tell me...* She took a deep breath, settling her startled heart, and looked up.

"Good morning, Brogan," she replied with the most dazzling smile she could muster.

"Interesting, we have this first class together," he surmised as he looked into her eyes.

As she gazed back, she felt something take hold inside of her. For some reason, she suddenly felt fierce. *Play the game,* she chanted to herself. *Play the game.*

"So it would seem," she agreed, raising an eyebrow, smirking in way that she hoped would steal his breath.

He chuckled a little. He seemed careful, almost tense. "Are you ready for your first day?"

"Definitely," she grinned at him again, running her fingers through her shining chestnut curls.

The tension grew as they continued to stare at each other. She hated that he was the most physically beautiful person that she had ever seen. The way that color grey looked on him, his dark silver cape that swept the ground, his broad shoulders, perfectly messy mahogany hair... Why did it hurt so much to look at him? *This pull to him is insane… no normal person should still feel this way,* she thought about herself.

But again, instead of wanting to go curl up and cry like usual, she wanted to fight. Fight the power he seemed to have on her. Fight to prove herself. Something screamed in her head to show him that she was up for the challenge of being a royal. The sad broken girl she had become after he left was non existent in this moment.

He leaned in a little closer and whispered, "Well, I'll be here if you need help then, *princess*," his cold cerulean eyes flashed.

*You want to help me? Well then I want an explanation from you. I want closure,* she thought, fire in her soul. He wanted to help her? Well then, he was going to get his wish.

"I think I got it," she shrugged confidently as she quickly thumped open her text book, pretending to scan through it, trying ignore the fluttering feeling his eyes made her nerves do.

The bell tolled, signaling the start of the day.

The period went on with painful drudgery. Landin rambled with a self righteous manner, and his many tangents were poorly misinformed. They made Adella cringe. And any time Adella glanced around, she would often catch her classmates staring at her. Worst of all, Brogan kept flirting with her throughout the session.

He picked up her quill for her when she dropped it. As he handed it back, his gaze more intense than necessary, their hands touched for the first time since her arrival. It sent the feeling of electric fire through Adella's body, making her heart jump.

She did her best to ignore him for as long as she could after that, willing herself to focus on the front of the room. She registered the faint scratch of a quill on parchment, and the subtle rustle of paper sliding to her. She glanced down at their table.

*You look stunning today.*

Shock drained through Adella. The first thing that hit was how familiar he was acting for someone she *supposedly* just met and had barely any exchange with. She had at least shared a couple meals with Blake and Jason before they pulled those one liners. Second, his handwriting was completely wrong. She examined his script, and her dream from the night before came to mind. When they were together, the two had memorized everything there was to know about each other. Adella knew his handwriting, especially after all of the love letters and funny notes they passed to each other through that time. Even so, her dream last night had replicated it exactly.

This script she saw before her was foreign.

*Don't trust me*, from her dream rang again in her head.

She glanced up to him. He was staring forward, a smirk on his lips. She looked forward indignantly.

Why was he flirting with her when he seemed so into Vivian? And Vivian felt that he was destined to ask her out? Was Viv misreading his signals?

Professor Landin asked the class to turn to page 246. Books flapped open and students shuffled.

"What page did he say again, Adella?" Brogan innocently asked.

Adella already had her volume open.

"Page two forty six," she replied cautiously.

"Thank you, beautiful," he winked.

Adella swallowed hard. As much as she hated to admit it, she had missed him; as her best friend *and* as her love. But this was not like their old times in North Brook, and though he was technically the same boy, he was now *very* different.

The rustling and movement of the students had stopped and Professor Landin continued.

Adella heard the faint slide of another piece of parchment. She looked down.

*What's your next class?*

Brogan was looking at her out of the corner of his eye. He waited for her to respond.

Adella didn't want to get into trouble. She didn't look at him.

He slyly shifted it back and scrawled.

*Talk after class?*

Adella nodded her head once. Professor Landin seemed to be eyeing their table more than all the others and she didn't want to give him any more reason not to like her. She knew that he already had an opinion about her – one that was completely wrong.

As she tried once again to concentrate on the class, she felt strong convictions against what Landin was *preaching*. His handful of favorite students would sometimes nod and engage him in conversation as he went on.

"I cannot stress this enough. To be fit for any royal position, one must *look* like a royal," Landin vehemently declared. "From your speech to your walk, but most importantly, your attire. The way a person dresses is a powerful statement to the filthy commoner masses. If you do not outwardly fit the part, then having *royal blood* truly means little at all. But, if you study hard, you will find how to execute all of these values in our royal handbook. In addition, on page 246 in our Monarchy textbook, there are some remarkable references that uphold everything I have imparted." He turned to take a sip from the goblet on his desk.

Adella did not want to be so vain as to think that this entire lecture was aimed at her, but with his snide *royal blood* sentiment, it was hard to not attribute it to herself.

"Now, for example," Landin began anew. "There is a land dispute between the location of your guard, and a local peasant farmer. Your captain of the guard wants the land for training and facilities due to its resources, but the farmer is not giving up the property that he has owned for generations. How would one handle this situation?" He paused pointedly and looked around the room. "Princess Adella," he called out.

Adella looked up from her notes, startled.

"Yes, Professor Landin," she replied.

"Since you are falling asleep in my class," he accused, "I would very much appreciate it if you would give me your thoughts on how to handle this scenario-"

Adella cordially tried to defend herself before he finished his sentence. "But I was not falling asleep Prof-"

"EXCUSE ME," he cut her off harshly, holding up a hand. "Do not *disrespect* your instructor. I do not know if this is acceptable by commoner ways, but those barbarian customs will not be tolerated in my class. Now, if you could tell us how to handle the scenario?"

Adella was taken aback, eyes huge and frightened, but she began in the kindest tone possible. "Well, I would try to buy the land for a fair price from the farmer so the guard could use it. Otherwise, it's his property. I would relocate the guard to a different and perhaps even better spot if this happened," she answered honestly.

"Okay," Landin countered, "the farmer doesn't give up his land then. You're saying you would side with the peasant? You would let him walk all over your commanding guard? Because a kingdom is only as good as its infantry."

"Well, I don't see it as letting him walk all over my guard. It *is* the farmer's land but–"

He cut her off again. "Answer the question, yes or no. Would you side with the commoner?" His eyes narrowed.

Adella sighed in defeat. "Yes, I'd side with the commoner."

The professor chuckled. The class was silent, all eyes on the two of them. Even Brogan shuffled uneasily in his chair.

"Your peasantry upbringing precedes you, clouding your judgment," he announced. He looked to the rest of the class and rolled his eyes as if to say 'that's what you get for having a peasant come into the palace'. His favorite students smirked at the overt physical prompt. He then looked back to Adella.

"No," he began, "if you were a *true* royal, you would know that nobody is to come between what you deem as law. Your army holds higher rank and you must make an example of this man. He is to be thrown into prison for his defiance, and your armies are to take the land. In the long run, this will be beneficiary for the advancement of your realm because then your forces shall be stronger for taking what they need instead of being at the mercy of some peasant." He scoffed quietly, shaking his head, and mumbled, "siding with *peasants*."

Adella was stunned. He just humiliated her in front of the entire class when he was the one in the first place to make her speak. She didn't know what to do or say.

A quiet, cold laugh escaped his lips. "Actually, please, stand up," he motioned to her.

She slowly took to her feet. He eyed her for a moment.

"Just as I thought – your attire is out of dress code," he added.

"But, I thought… what's wrong with it?" Adella questioned, bewildered.

"I should not have to explain it to you. I would write you up but we are running out of class time. You can find your short comings if you look in the hand book – assuming that you can read. Now, I'd like it if you sat down, Princess. Your interruptions today have been entirely rude," he sniped as he turned his back to write homework instructions on the board. He began about the weekly assignment, acting as if nothing had happened.

Adella sunk back into her chair. Tears welled as she picked up her note book and started to take notes.

The bell tolled soon after, signaling the period change.

"Adella, wait," Brogan called out as Adella shot out of the classroom.

"Adella?" Kate called after her.

Both of them made way into the hall as quickly as possible after her.

"You need her too, huh?" She asked as she shuffled next to Brogan.

"Uh, yeah," he replied uncomfortably.

Adella dashed around a corner into a vacant corridor, put her back against the wall, and took a deep breath trying to keep back the tears. She clenched her fist, dug her nails into her palm, willing herself to concentrate on the painful sensation.

"Adella," both Kate and Brogan said as they came up to her.

Adella looked up at them; first, incredulously at Brogan, and then to Kate. "Is Landin always like that?" She whispered, cursing herself for how thick her throat sounded.

"Only to the students he doesn't like," Kate sadly replied. "Which is a decent chunk of the population. He tends to favor the more athletic royals so a lot of us have to deal with him like that. Anyone who doesn't think like him he deems a 'problem student'. That was the harshest I've seen him. I'm so sorry."

"It's not your fault, Katie," Adella nodded thoughtfully.

"Still though," Kate pursed her lips with worry. "He's wrong."

Adella was silent for a moment. "Thank you, Kate," she kept her voice even. "But Brogan and I need to talk for a second, is that okay?" She looked at the prince.

"Yeah, sure?" Confusion flickered across Kate's face. "Er, do you know how to get to Grammar?"

"Oh, I'll show her, it won't be a problem," Brogan replied. He looked at Kate and melted her with a smile.

"Okay," Kate smiled back, suddenly dazed. She looked at Adella. "I'll see you in class?"

"Yes," Adella affirmed.

Soon Kate was out of earshot and down the hall.

"Brogan. What the spell?" Adella looked hard at him, tears gone.

"Is something wrong?" He arched an eyebrow, seeming to charm her with his confusion.

Adella was having none of it. "Something wrong!? Let's start with why you pretended to not know me last night? Or this morning? And why aren't you at Regal High? I heard you were supposed to be going there. Is this some sort of game you're playing? We haven't talked in four months and you're acting like everything's just fine!?"

"What game would I be playing?" He asked innocently.

She looked at him in disbelief.

"So you're just going to act like... like..." she could barely get the words out. "Like we were never anything? You're really going to do this?"

He was silent, eyes searching Adella intensely; he sensed her conviction was relentless. He suddenly settled into an expression of stoic resignation, feigned confusion gone.

"Okay, yes I acknowledge last year," he allowed. "I don't know where you heard I was at Regal but it was probably misinformation. As for leaving you like I did, it's a very long story," he paused. If they lingered any longer then they would risk being late to their next class. "We don't have enough time," his eyes pleaded. "But just for now, could we have a fresh start? I think we deserve that. Why bring up the past to people who don't need to know?"

Adella was surprised. She was not expecting that 'fresh start' line. She wanted to hold onto her anger, but for some reason, it was melting away.

"And besides, I really want to get to know the *Princess* Adella," he smiled enchantingly as he presented his arm for her to hold. Adella froze. "Come on, I'll walk you to Grammar and Lit."

Adella hesitated. She didn't want to be near him, and yet she felt inexplicably drawn to him.

"It's okay. Take it. I mean no ill will," he assured, brilliant eyes gleaming.

Adella took his offer hesitantly, seeing as he *was* her only way to her next class. Her arm linked with his, fingers settling on the brocade of his forearm, and he rested his opposite hand on top of hers. His skin was hot, and Adella immediately registered it. It almost burned. Her heart wanted more, to instantly lace her fingers with his, but her head screamed to run. She ignored the sensations and fell into step with him as he led on.

He had barely scratched the surface of what was burning inside her, but at least he admitted he had left her. He *knew* her. It was a start she would have to take.

The whole school was alight with how Professor Landin had called out *The Lost Princess*.

Adella heard the whispers, felt the glances, as Brogan escorted her through a few short corridors down to Grammar and Literature.

"I heard he told her that her outfit was a blatant dress code violation," a perky girl in a stark pink outfit announced rather loudly to her friends.

"Well of course it is! I mean look at her, she's a mess," one of her friends replied.

Adella rolled her eyes as she passed them.

Further down the hall she heard another girl gasp to her friends, offended, "is that *The Lost Princess* on Prince Brogan's *arm*?"

"Lost Princess? More like *Peasant Princess*."

"She's not even a confirmed Everheart," another student murmured, "and I'd have to agree. She looks *ghastly*."

Adella glanced to the last voice as she walked by and saw that it belonged to a boy who was about the same size as she. He had silk straight blonde hair, parted limp down the middle, and wore his frilly cuffs with a haughty smirk. He seemed the type to faint at the sight of blood.

Adella felt like she could take him down in a split second, but before that thought had too much entertainment, Brogan's fingers squeezed hers. She gingerly peered up to him. He seemed glad, almost smug.

He had not explained anything and yet was acting like they were the best of friends. She was not going to let him off the hook. He was going to explain himself one way or another.

They approached the room.

"Here we are," he leaned in, making Adella's heart skip. "Listen, I know you hear all of the talk around you. Don't let them get to you. Jealousy brings out the worst in people. Adella, you are someone to be admired."

"Thank you?" Adella answered cautiously, glancing around. People were still staring at the two of them.

"Don't mention it. Hopefully we'll see each other later today." He took her hand and kissed it lightly, never breaking eye contact.

"Sure," Adella whispered, mezmorized. What could she say? No? And of course they were going to see each other again considering they seemed to be friends with the same people.

He flashed his heartbreaking grin and turned to go down the hall, cape fluttering behind.

Adella was speechless as she stared at him walk away in his flamboyant stride. She absentmindedly raised the hand that he had kissed, bringing her fingertips to her lips for a moment. She shook her head, regained her composure, and scurried into her next class.

# Ten

As Adella passed the threshold for Grammar and Literature, she saw that Viv, Blake, Jason, and Kate were all sitting at the back of the room by the window, laughing very hard at something on Vivian's crystal ball. Jason was the first to notice her as he looked up.

"Hey! There she is! Adella!" He said heartily.

"Hey, over here," Viv called. "We saved you a seat."

"You made it just in time!" Kate happily exclaimed as Adella drew closer.

Adella smiled as she sat down, instantly feeling the drastic change in this classroom's emotional climate.

Landin's room was utterly oppressive with it's drawn windows and dark grey color palette. This new class was flooded with beautiful sunlight from the wide windows. Bookcases, full to their brims of volumes, ran around the room and vases full of scrolls were scattered everywhere. Banners of purple baring Royal High's signature gold emblem hung alongside artwork depicting ancient stories from literature. A huge bouquet of bright garden flowers sat upon the teacher's messy desk.

The bell tolled.

Adella looked around, waiting for the class to settle down and start, but no one shied away from their ongoing conversations. The teacher, a stocky older woman, was at her desk writing something. Several stacks of books surrounded her, almost obscuring her. She didn't even bother to look up, continuing her pace.

"Lady Raj is great. She's so chill. You're going to love this class," Blake assured Adella. He glanced down to his blue glowing crystal ball in his hands and started to check his messages. He made no effort to hide the orb even though there was a strict no crystal policy during school hours.

"Adella, I heard about what happened with Professor Landin," Viv began. "I'm so sorry. I wish I could have been there. I would have defended you."

"It's okay, Viv. Besides, I would have felt bad if you defended me. This is your family's school."

"All the more reason why I can stand up," Viv countered.

"Thank you," Adella gratefully smiled. "So, I see word travels fast around here."

"You have no idea," Viv rolled her eyes.

"Yeah," Jason agreed. "Landin's probably going to tell his next class all about it. He likes to use students as lesson examples."

"Uhg! He can't just go around doing that! It's not right!" Adella exclaimed with disgust. She then added, "and apparently this dress doesn't comply with the 'dress code'."

"No, that can't be. I just wore it a few weeks ago. It's brand new!" Viv replied, confused.

"Well not to *Landin*," Adella informed.

"I think you look fine," Jason mumbled.

"Yes, I do too," Viv agreed. "Hmm, *I'm* going to have to check on this," she toned thoughtfully. "Well, any excuse to go shopping then, right?"

"Right," Adella nodded.

"And we'll make sure Landin doesn't have any room to disagree after. What happened today won't happen again," Viv smiled confidently, flipping her long golden hair.

"Adella have you seen these?" Blake asked as he held up his crystal. He handed the ball to her. The rest of the group leaned in to look over her shoulders.

Adella groaned as she saw the first of several images on a sleazy royal gossip site. She had seen all the news coverage of her arrival on the mirror, but nothing like this had been shown by any of the reputable organizations.

The pictures on *this* particular site were bad. One showed her blinking funny when the sun first hit her eyes as she stepped out of the carriage. The next was when she turned in an odd manner, her dress cutting her wrong, making the garment seem ill-fitting and awkward. Another one showed her when she was trying to rush to the gate. She looked clumsy and ill prepared. The headline, *"The Lost Princess or a Peasant Princess?"* There were more images, but Adella didn't want to see them. She glanced further into the article.

> *Has The Lost Princess been found? Is this truly the heir to the Adamaris throne? Turns out this Lost Princess might be more the Peasant Princess type – if ever there was a thing before this day, which has lead many to wonder if she is even a legitimate Everheart...*

Adella groaned once more, handing the orb back, not wanting to read another line.

Lady Rajilaa suddenly stood up, smiled, and proclaimed an austair and welcoming, "good morning!" She took her place at the front of the room.

Grammar and Literature was one of Adella's favorite subjects back home, and it was nice to finally be in a familiar element. The teacher, true to Blake's word, was very kind to her.

She had Adella stand up for a moment and introduce herself. Lady Rajilaa warmly welcomed her, and then zealously dove right into the lecture. She spoke of the timeless legend of a love story between two star crossed teenagers from warring families.

Lady Rajilaa's voice had droll and low lull to it, despite coming from such a short stout woman, but the class hung on her every word. Adella often found herself grinning from ear to ear at the teacher's dry comedic timing as she bantered with her students. Her snarky description of the duel between the main hero and the cousin of the girl he loved, accompanied with stick figure drawings on the board, elicited countless laughs from her students. Her hilarious side commentary as to how this fight would affect the events unfolding later made the tale come to life. Adella loved every minute, and when the bell tolled, she found herself sad to leave.

Adella's next period was Arithmetic with Lady Jenson. The class was quiet and rather uneventful, with only numbers, letters, and more numbers to worry about. Lady Jenson wrote equations and formulas upon the bored, explaining how each problem set was done. Adella wasn't one for this subject, though it was still far more pleasant than Landin's class. By the end of the period, Adella decided that Lady Jenson was really pleasant, even if the subject matter did bore her. Lady Jenson even told Adella to have a wonderful day as she left the room.

Philosophy class was Adella's fourth session for the day, and as she walked with Jason to the classroom, she asked him about what to anticipate next.

"Get this," Jason began. "They just brought this guy in last year. The school has never seen anything like him. I guess a few years back, Royal High was going to be passed over for accreditation because of a lack of philosophical diversity or something. The board had a hard time keeping the claim that they were a 'diversely taught' school, especially when they were compared with the other Royal Academies. So, they ended up bringing on Professor Freelove - and yes that's actually his name. Rumors say that board doesn't like him very much, though. His ideas are," he paused, searching for the right words, "kind of controversial for the world of royals."

Adella looked at him like he was insane. *Controversial?*

Jason took in her expression and added, "You'll see."

"Good day to you, class," the man paused and inhaled deeply. "I am Professor Freelove. And I say this today because I see that we are joined by a new student."

The Professor wore a ruffled crème peasant shirt loosely opened on his chest. It was barely tucked into his tight tan breeches, which were tucked into his tall cuffed boots. A long necklace of faded colored beads fell from his neck, matching the bracelets around his wrists. He ran his fingers through his messy mane so effortlessly that Adella wondered if he tousled his long bronze hair like that on purpose, or if he had honestly just rolled out of bed. He was the most handsome teacher Adella had yet to see at Royal High, and he looked so casual and carefree in his neutral clothes. Was he even of higher birth?

The candles and incense that burned on his desk filled Adella's senses with their heady and deep aroma, inviting her into the space. Luscious plants, bright flowers, curious trinkets, and wind chimes hung around the room. A fey enchanted rock waterfall in the corner produced a tranquil rippling sound.

"You are Princess Adella Everheart of Adamaris?" He asked as he motioned to her.

"Yes," she smiled.

"Most excellent," he smiled in return. "What I cover in my lessons will probably be familiar to you, having in mind your background. A first for my class." His accent was pure, belonging to upper society, though he held no heir of pretension.

Adella looked over to Jason and he nodded.

The Professor requested the class humor him as he recounted his upbringing, having grown up belonging to a wealthy family of Lords in Vysteria as the youngest male in the successive line. He had been taught all his life that status meant everything – the typical mindset for most royals. But, after being held for ransom by bandits, and eventually being rescued by the help of the peasants in his land, he came to realize that he was brought up by a horrible lie.

"I ended up making the decision to live among my people," Freelove concluded fervently. "To embrace their way of life. I wanted to become the best representation possible for them, and I denied myself the amenities of the noble life. For you see, I am not better than any of them because of my birth or title. I am," he paused and inhaled boldly, emphasizing with passion, "*their* servant. So, for many years I did this, and I learned a different way of monarchy, refined a new philosophy of royal existence. I was not next in line to take over my realm, so I decided the best way I could better this world was to teach, to educate others, to help open the eyes of other royals to new possibilities. And so, here we are," he smiled serenely.

After Freelove's class, Adella had Etiquette, taught by the headmistress Baroness Von Durdenmeyer.

The headmistress, in many ways, was a lot like Landin. They both emphasized the same philosophies, the same hostility towards peasantry. Adella kept her mouth shut and did all that she was told, grateful to have the class on her lineup, because in spite of the smug nitpicking comments from the Baroness, Adella knew that she needed as much practice in the etiquette of royals as she could get. Luckily, she had Vivian in her period to help her out, and after an excruciating study in the nuances of footwork when in court, the bell finally released them from the torturous purple woman's lesson. Adella, arm and arm with Vivian, practically danced out of the room and down the hall.

"You don't even know where Alchemy is," Vivian giggled as she steered her friend in the correct direction. "This way."

It was their final period, and Adella could not wait to see what a royal academy's alchemy class would entail. The subject in question was an expensive and dangerous practice; as a result, alchemy was not something that was taught in commoner schools. By and large, it was considered a study only for royals, or for those with the innate ability to manipulate the elements; faeries were widely known to be the best suited in the art. Adella knew herself lucky to have had the chance to study the old alchemy books her father possessed in his library. Usually accompanied by Raena, Adella had dabbled with them off and on through the years, nearly blowing the two of them up on more than one occasion.

"All right, masters an' mistresses," Professor Bracke boomed in his heavy brogue as the girls entered the room. Adella was instantly taken aback by the hulking man she saw.

He was as tall as the door to the room, and his broad shoulders and barrelchest were barely concealed within his navy peasant shirt; tufts of chest hair spiraled out through the untied laces. Sitting on his hips, adorned with countless odd trinkets and bottles and strange artifacts, was a thick leather belt which secured his dark plaid kilt. His obviously muscular arms seemed like they could swing a double handed broadsword with ease, and his rugged and weathered face was intense with aged wisdom. Black locks, swept back and disheveled, sprinkled generously with silver strands, contrasted against his too bright grey eyes. A menacing scar ran through his right, bushy eyebrow; there was no denying that he had obviously seen battle. This man was, without a doubt, the most terrifying person Adella had seen since her arrival.

"I don't want a repeat of yesterday's shenanigans, understood?" He continued. "Harding is already threatenin' to quit, an' I'm figurin' if he loses one more of his toupees, then that's just what's goin' to happen." The professor glared at Jason and Blake as the two went to their work station. The boys just smiled back impishly.

Bracke shook his head and finished his address to the rest of the students filing in. "An' in case anyone of you were wonderin', yes, I was responsible for last night's li'l disturbance. Now go grab an apron, go to your cauldron, an' start workin' on the potion in page five eighty nine," he instructed.

When Bracke mentioned the previous night's disturbance, Adella's thoughts flashed back to the dragon. She wondered if Bracke had anything to do with the terrible creature. The timing was so odd. She shuddered.

The students were lively, completely at ease, as they thumped open their books and ran about the room for supplies.

Viv brought Adella to her usual cauldron, but before the two girls could put on their aprons, Bracke called out.

"Princess Adella?"

"Yes, Professor?" Adella replied, turning around, a little startled at hearing her name from his deep voice.

Bracke motioned for her to approach, and Adella came to the front.

"So you're our wee li'l *Lost Princess*?" He asked, a smile brimming on his lips. There was no hint of sarcasm. He seemed genuinely interested in his new pupil.

Adella smiled a little in return as she quickly assessed the man towering before her. Bracke's unexpected warmth came through his tough exterior. It made him almost handsome, and suddenly far more approachable. Adella wondered if underneath the intimidating appearance, he could possibly be just a big old softy.

"Yes, Lord Bracke," Adella affirmed.

"Well it is very nice to be havin' you in my class, princess. If you find yourself lost, please do not hesitate to ask for help. Oh, an' I have no title. Just call me professor, or Bracke will do just fine. Welcome to Alchemy," he motioned kindly with his large hand for Adella to go back to her seat. She noticed the faint scars on his palm.

"Thank you, Professor," Adella curtsied her best and turned to go to her station. *No title? But how are you here? Were you peasant born, too?* She wondered about the instructor. As she walked to her place, she realized just how expansive the classroom was; it was the biggest classroom she had seen yet.

Aside from the many rows of tables and cooking cauldrons, endless bookcases and hundreds of shelves lined the climbing walls. All were filled with dusty ancient volumes and strange things between them; aged bones, tarnished boxes, little figurines, and weathered artifacts; herbs set to dry, twine bound in hanging bunches; haphazardly set containers, jars, and vials, whose contents were odd at best and terrifying at worst. Adella managed to identify a couple of the ingredients around her at a glance; ninroots, blisterwort, gobsmouth, bats wings, Humbolt's flower, wolfsbane, nightshade, chameleon's eyes, troll eyelashes... Adella never had access to a lot of components when she would experiment with her dad's modest alchemy library, but here at Royal High was a completely stocked alchemy lab, one that she now had access to.

She inhaled deeply, trying to calm the wild blend of nervousness and excitement that ran through her. The room had a certain kind of musk, akin to that of aged books, smoke, earth, wood and... something else she could not quite place. Fog began to float off from some of the cauldrons, making the ground wispy. Adella looked above her and found the giant spire ceiling completely obscured with smoke, all of it funneling out a giant flue of sorts in the roof.

Viv was slyly scrawling on her crystal ball, hiding it behind the huge text book at their station. "Here," she looked up and smiled, handing Adella an apron as she approached.

As Adella tied the thick canvas material around her waist, she looked up to the long blackboard behind Bracke. It was filled with compounds and writings, some of it in the ancient tongues and symbols of faerie. Adella felt a little surge of confidence as she understood most of what was written.

Bracke spoke again. "Okay, class. Today, as I am sure many of you have pieced together from the text, we will be workin' on makin' elixirs of minor camouflage. Now, since the school's board doesn't allow elixirs bein' used for personal use around the premises without prior authorization, an' seeing as how it is also illegal to use such elixirs in some realms, it was like pullin' *teeth* to let them let me teach this one to yah. In other words – don't screw it up. Got that?"

The class chuckled and murmured their agreement.

Bracke turned to his board to explain the alchemy behind this elixir, how it would be useful in royal life, and what the colors of the process mean.

"Blue is the desired final color, but if you start hittin' purple, you better backup a few steps and add some extra chameleon eye. Lastly, don't even think about dawning the palette of the red spectrum," Bracke advised.

"And what happens if it goes red?" A girl chided suddenly. Adella recognized the voice, turned, and saw Dia at the back of the room.

Adella did not remember when Dia had entered the class.

For all she knew, Dia materialized back there.

"Just turn down the heat an' add some more chameleon eye," Bracke said sternly. "Unless you want to blow us all to kingdom come." His eyes flashed with the sudden graveness of his tone as he stared Dia down. In another second, he was looking up to the rest of the students, his mood lighter. "Okay class, if there are anymore questions, please ask. Other than that, have at it!"

"So, all of this is normal?" Adella asked Viv as they walked down the castle hall towards the quad.

Blake and Jason were right behind them, talking amongst themselves. The final bell for the day had just rung minutes before.

"Well, I'm not sure what your definition of *normal* is, but yeah, that's about it for a day around here," Viv smiled.

Adella shook her head, smirking. It felt like years since the beginning of he day had started, and yet it was over in flash.

"My fair princesses," Jason ran around to the front of the two girls to face them. His cape swept the ground around him dramatically as he bowed. "Myself and my fellow nobleman, Prince Blake," he paused looking back at Blake who nodded at him approvingly, "would so fancy it if you would like to accompany us for some refreshment today in the tea garden?"

It was a little past two thirty, the time of the day that classes ended, and the students were heading off to whatever afternoon activities were planned.

Adella grinned but Viv seemed apologetic.

"Oh, so formal?" She asked, looking at Jason, her eyebrows arched. He blushed a little. "Though a delight you two are, I have promised Princess Adella that I would show her around Vryndolne this afternoon. We have some things that need taken care of," she explained.

"That's right, you two are going shopping," Blake realized.

"Yes, we are. And don't you guys have combat practice?"

"Yeah, but it'll be short meeting later this afternoon. Coach wants us to save our strength because we're collocating first thing in the morning."

"Understandable. Well, we'll just see you guys at dinner, then," Vivian said. She reached into her purse for her crystal.

"Guess we have time to kill," Jason sighed.

"Wanna go skimboard the quad fountains with our practice shields?" Blake casually suggested.

"Dude, Vondurdur got pissed at us last time," Jason countered.

"And we care...?" Blake feigned shock that his best friend would even give caution.

"I'm in," Jason laughed as the two turned to leave.

"Be good!" Viv called out.

"When are we not?" Jason turned around and winked with a grin.

The boys were off, and Viv started to make a call.

"Are they always like that?" Adella asked, marveling as they walked away.

"Jason and Blake?" Viv nodded in the direction the boys went. "They're ridiculous. But I don't know what I would do without them," she sighed. "I would have loved to join them today, most likely keep them out of trouble, but we really do need to take care of your *wardrobe*," she smiled sweetly.

"You really don't have to do this," Adella said again.

"It's already done," Viv winked as the crystal finally came to life.

"Good afternoon, Empress," a polite voice emanated from the orb.

"Hello, Virgil," Vivian spoke curtly. "Prepare a carriage to Vryndolne. We'll be needing shopping assistance. Bring the largest pairs of arms you got. This one's gonna break the bank."

# Eleven

Vryndolne was breathtaking. Adella had never personally seen so much splendor in a city. She pressed up against the window of the massive carriage, similar in style to the one she traveled in with her grandmother, and marveled at the world around her; the towering pinnacles of the central castle keep, along with all the city's spires, shining in the afternoon sun, the vendors on the pristine streets, the rows of designer shops, boutiques, and fountains of sparkling waters all seemed too beautiful to be real.

"What do you think?" Viv breathed.

Adella turned around. The girls had a giant carriage to themselves while every pair of eyes standing on the street looked to them as they passed by.

"It's brilliant, Viv," Adella beamed. "You grew up here?"

"Born and raised," the blonde giggled as she touched up her lip color. "My palace is those huge spire tops over there," she pointed out the window. "I'll take you when we get a chance. You'll love my parents!"

Adella couldn't stop smiling. "And to think, this city is a half hour from Royal High."

"Right? So lucky for us we can shop whenever we want!" Viv snapped closed her makeup compact. "It's the best rule."

"Rule? From the handbook?" Adella asked flatly.

"No, silly," Vivian giggled again. "It's like, what do you do when you're feeling bad?" She prompted.

Adella hesitated, unsure of how to respond. *Uh, cry? Sword fight? Pretend like I'm not sad until maybe the sadness pretends like it's gone?*

Vivian stared at her like she was missing something. Their carriage rolled to sudden halt.

Adella sighed. "What do you do when you're sad, Vivian?"

"I shop!" Vivian smiled proudly. "Shopping is my happy place. Sad, or happy, or bored, I get out there and I treat myself. It's my rule," she explained. "Keeping that positive headspace."

Before Adella could respond their bodyguards came around to open the door, offering their helping hands to the girls as they stepped out into the city's central most plaza, right in the heart of Vryndolne.

As Adella blinked around at the reaching arches, the gleaming pinnacles and spires, the mosaics, the sparkling marble fountains, the too bright sun glinting off everything, the surrounding commoners of the plaza were stunned at the site of their empress standing with the Lost Princess. Adella's face had been on every news and gossip network in the last twenty-four hours, and she was technically still not a confirmed Everheart.

"It's the *Lost Princess*!" Somebody shouted.

"The Princess of Adamaris!" Another one exclaimed.

Adella's head whipped around as she heard the cries. She looked at Vivian, fear touching her ocean eyes.

"Follow me," Vivian breathed, grabbing Adella's hand, snapping into action.

They took off like a shot with Viv leading the way, their bodyguards barely keeping up, while a mob of onlookers started forming behind them. A million questions were fired off from the sea of voices.

The girls ran into their destination, and the designer boutique locked its doors behind them. Onlookers crowded outside.

"I take it that's not normal?" Adella breathed, making light of the situation.

"Adella, when are you going to realize that you need to redefine your version of *normal*," Viv answered, fixing a strand of out of place hair.

Adella shook her head. *Father and grandmother can't make that announcement soon enough,* she thought. *Then this will quiet down.*

"Don't worry," Viv put a hand on Adella's shoulder. "You were meant for this. It's just part of the territory sometimes."

"Good afternoon, Empress Vivian," a deeply accented voice greeted.

"Oh, Paulo!" Vivian exclaimed as a suave man, dressed in a tasteful black and white brocade vest, took her hand and kissed it.

"Adella, this is Paulo Praeva of House Praeva," Viv introduced, "one of my best designers. I've commissioned him many a time. And, luckily, he's handbook approved." She winked. "Paulo, this is Adella Everheart."

"Ah, Princess Adella Everheart? I have heard every voice in this city speak of your name today. What a pleasure I get to meet you so soon!" He took Adella's hand with flourish and kissed it. Adella beamed with surprise. "Welcome to House Praeva. What can I do for you two stunning beauties today?"

"Paulo, I need you to pull out everything you've got. She needs the works."

Adella's eyes widened, raising a brow to the term "the works".

"Well then, let us get started!" Paulo happily declared. "Yvonne, Kali, Demi," he announced as he clapped his hands twice for his assistants, "we have work to do!"

Although Adella felt like her legs were going to give out, she hadn't had this much fun in a long time. There had been reams of gorgeous materials to choose from, fittings, endless gowns, shoes, jewels and accessories. The sun had already begun to set; they would be late getting back to the school.

Vivian and Adella had chatted all afternoon, getting on fantastically, but Adella could not shake her doubts. Though Vivian had admitted to the previous encouragements from her family to make the new Adamaris heir feel welcome, she assured Adella that all pretenses were gone, and that she genuinely liked her.

*Maybe Viv is just a really kind soul,* Adella pondered. It was scary to put herself out there like this; it was scary to let someone *new* into her heart.

As the girls waited for the rest of their purchases to be transferred to the carriage, they finished up their last fitting in an ornate room paneled in every direction with gilded mirrors. Viv watched on as the wordless seamstress and a hovering fairy helped a half dressed Adella into the bottom portion of a shimmering ivory and grey dress.

"Yes, that's going to be gorgeous," Vivian noted to the fairy as the transmorphed little thing whizzed around, measuring about the bottom. "So, have I done good?" Vivian turned to Adella with big, pleading eyes.

Adella bobbed her head up and down. "Yes, you did Vivian. It's all perfect. Thank you so much," she replied gratefully. "I can't wait to go back to school with all of this."

"You are so welcome," Vivian's lips curved into an incredible smile. "So, we've purchased enough outfits to have you set for the next several weeks while the rest of the things we have commissioned will be finished at a later date. Soon we'll have enough pieces for you to fill the rest of the year, or, at least until Green's Tide's fashions come out."

"And you're sure this is all necessary?" Adella asked skeptically.

Vivian gave a lighthearted laugh like Adella had made a great joke. The empress then excused herself to step out to make a call.

Adella stood there, marveling in the mirror at the surreal, glittering fabrics that surrounded her. She absently played with the weighty Everheart ring on her finger as she watched the women around her at work.

The seamstress left for a moment while the fairy went to get more pins and fabric. They helped Adella down from the fitting platform and the princess walked over to her little satin purse which held her sparkling teal crystal ball. She checked a few of her messages, and one from Blake caught her attention.

*Hey cutie, how's shopping?*

Adella chuckled a little and responded.

> *Exhausting. But Vryndolne is amazing.*
> *Just finishing up now. Are you in trouble with*
> *Vondurdur yet?*

She smirked to herself, pleased with her jest. Her
crystal chimed back with his reply almost instantly.

> *Always in trouble.*

Adella could not help the smile on her face. She
liked Blake.

"Greetings, *Peasant Princess.*"

Adella's stomach dropped. She looked up to see
Dia enter the fitting room as a different seamstress
trailed behind her, carrying a maroon heap of tulle. It
looked like a giant skirt, the beginnings of another
gown.

"Oh. Hi, Dia," Adella responded, taken aback at
the snide nickname.

Dia proudly stepped up onto one of several tiered
platforms in the large room. She undid her scarlet silk
robe, revealing her black chemise, and the seamstress
began to slip the tulle over her head.

Everything was quiet while Adella uneasily turned
back around and continued to go through her messages,
trying to ignore the warnings going off in her head.

"You're never going to fit in, you know that,
right?"

"Excuse me?" Adella asked, bewildered, turning
back around.

Dia was staring intently at herself in the mirror while the noiseless seamstress worked on the tulle that was now flaring out from her waist.

"I'm just kidding. Royal humor," Dia smirked, playing coy. She flipped her silky flame hair back "So you certainly seem to have gotten into the swing of things," she nodded to Adella's half dressed appearance, her queer green eyes assessing her. Dia was almost beautiful in an other worldly way, with her too sharp cheekbones and a pointed chin.

"Er, I think so. I mean, Viv has been so kind to take me here and everything," Adella replied, her body tight and uneasy, heart pounding.

Dia laughed a little, musing, "So it would seem... Tell me, this is your first time among royals?"

"This many royals, yes," Adella answered, trying to be honest, but not wanting to let on about her history with Brogan and his family.

"Interesting," Dia murmured, sensing Adella's censure. "Well I personally could not fathom just jumping into royal life from your lowly beginnings! It all must be overwhelming."

"It is a little," Adella admitted, growing miffed from the constant peasant jabs.

"I'm curious, what is the most overwhelming would you say?" Dia pursed her lips in the mirror and studied her reflection pretentiously.

"Just the sudden responsibility of it all," Adella replied. She did not know why she was humoring this girl. She had the worst gut feeling about her. "Everything happened so fast, and yet here I am, getting ready to take over a kingdom in a few years."

She glanced down to her hands, the Everheart ring glimmering brightly with promise.

"Awe, look at you," Dia crooned. "I wish there was some way that I could help you get your bearings!" Her sugary tone was too much. "And to think that Vivian is only…" she trailed her thought, stopping.

"Viv is what?" Adella asked, her interest piquing more than she would like to admit.

"Oh, never mind. I shouldn't…" Dia answered, shaking her head.

Confusion flickered across Adella's eyes, unsure of where Dia was bringing this.

Dia raised an eyebrow. "With Viv doing all of this for you, it reminds me of my first few weeks of this school year, until Vivian moved on that is. I really don't know if I should even bring it up," she sighed dramatically.

Adella just stared at Dia, captivation growing

Dia continued. "Vivian probably didn't tell you this, but we were inseparable at the start of this year.

"Oh," Adella wasn't sure what to do with this news. She stood there awkwardly, already knowing how Vivian was not entirely fond of Dia.

"I was new, having only private tutoring for all of my life, and it was a first for someone of my realm to attend a royal institution-"

"Wait, your family has never attended any of the royal schools?" Adella cut her off.

"Uh no." Dia seemed perturbed.

"Why though? Are you like me?" Adella felt hopeful.

"*No*, I am not like yo-" Dia stopped herself. Her green eyes became just a little darker. She cleared her throat, and her sugary smile returned. "My realm is self sustaining. Smaller than most. We don't deal much with outsiders."

"What realm are you of?" Adella pressed. She couldn't quite recall what the placard on the side of Dia's room had read.

"*I* am the princess of Desevry. You probably haven't heard of it."

"Oh, I see," Adella murmured in chagrin. The way Dia explained made her feel inferior. And, truth be told, even with all of her geographical knowledge, Adella had not heard of it. *The realm of Desevry?* She made a note to research it.

Adella's seamstresses entered the room and led Adella back to her platform. They quietly began to work on her gown once more, but Dia's words rang through Adella's thoughts. *Vivian and Dia hung out? Vivian hasn't mentioned that. I wonder why...*

Dia was silent, her scrutinizing gaze watching her gown be made for her.

"So you and Vivian were inseparable earlier this year?" Adella spoke the words before she even realized she formed them. She felt idiotic for taking the bait, but she wanted to know what Dia had to say.

"Right when this school year started," Dia affirmed. "I was completely swarmed with media when I arrived to the school, and Vivian wanted to be my friend like right away."

"Wait, what do you mean the media swarmed you? The headmistress said that they had never experienced a situation like mine before."

"For a *peasant borne* maybe," Dia rolled her eyes. "But for weeks *my* attendance at Royal High was all the media talked about. I'm a first attendee from Desevry, remember?"

"But aren't there laws against underage royals in the media?" Adella countered, her irritation growing at Dia's one upmanship.

"Only if one's parents or sitting ruler decrees it to be okay. Varinth may be strict, but my family was perfectly fine with my being in the spotlight," Dia explained with a matter-of-fact confidence.

Adella remembered nothing of Dia or of Desevry in the media at all. In fact no one had mentioned anything about her. And didn't the school just have the Autumn Ball? The media was only allowed there because it was an organized event. No one had mentioned anything like Dia was describing.

"Anyway," Dia proceeded, "Viv wanted to be my friend, like, right away, but the famous novelty of a reclusive realm began to fade, she pulled away. And then, days before the Autumn Ball last weekend, we kind of had a little…" she searched for the right word, "*confrontation.*"

"What happened?" Adella asked cautiously.

"I only wanted to know why she was always ditching me to hang out with Jason and Blake and Kate. She never gave me a real answer so I let it go because sometimes you just need to be the bigger person. Luckily, my popularity has maintained," she sighed as she looked upon her reflection. "But, I'll admit, her betrayal hurt, especially after she made me feel so welcome. Oddly, *and you didn't hear this from me*, but I've since talked with a bunch of people and I think I've pieced something together."

Adella remained quiet, stunned with every word coming from Dia's mouth.

"This is a *cycle*. Vivian doesn't want anyone to top her. This is *her* kingdom, and she befriended me to make sure I didn't become more popular than her. I found out that she did the same thing her freshman year with another girl who doesn't attend here anymore. And it was the same story. The new girl was a popular royal that came around the middle of the year, they became fast bestfriends, then, when the novelty wore off, Vivian dropped her. It wouldn't surprise me if she drops Kate for you now," Dia sighed like she felt the weight of the world on her shoulders.

"Wow," Adella responded sadly. It was all she could say. Was Dia's story for real? The energy in the room had drained Adella's spirit.

"Don't feel bad, sweetie," Dia added. "Once the media forgets who you are, which I'm *sure* that will happen *very* soon, Viv will leave and you can go on to make real friends, closer to your *status*."

"You mean make friends who are crown royalty? I thought that's what I was already doing," Adella replied petulantly.

"Yes, but for how much of your life have you been a *peasant*? Maybe you should stay within that range."

"Excuse me?!" Adella fumed.

"Hey, calm down. I'm only telling you all this because I'm watching out for you," Dia snapped. "I call things as I see them, and this world of Royals is too much to just jump into. They'll eat you alive and I just don't want Vivian to hurt you like she has so many others."

With all of the backhanded compliments, Adella was not sure if Dia's concern was a joke. For an such uneasy acquaintance, Dia had just placed a lot of personal information onto the table. Although, true to Dia's story, everything *was* moving fast with Vivian. The friendship, the shopping, becoming roommates – maybe Dia was right. Maybe Dia *was* just being too blunt for her own good.

Before Adella could respond any further, Viv walked back into the room.

"Hey Adella, I just remembered we need to – oh, Dia," Vivian's surprise was apparent.

"Hey, Viv," Dia greeted enthusiastically.

"When did you get here?" Viv asked, not out of spitefulness, but from a place of honest curiosity. She walked over to where Adella was standing.

"A little bit ago. I decided to do some shopping today. I felt like a I needed some pretty new things to wear. You like?" Dia motioned to her inprogress gown.

"I can't wait to see it when it's done," Viv smiled amiably. "And, Adella, that is going to look amazing on you, too," she nodded to the matching bodice that Adella was now being fitted with. "I can hardly wait to show you off to everyone back at school! All eyes will be on you!"

"Thanks," Adella said, trying to sound happy. She looked up at Dia who flashed a subtle knowing smirk.

# Twelve

As the inviting violin music melted with the happy chatter and bright conversation of the dining hall, Adella felt her crystal vibrate from her purse. Upon returning back to the school, Vivian and Adella had completely missed dinner, but made it just in time for the end of dessert.

"And so then I was like, *that's not your sword!*" Jason threw his hand up into the air and looked around. The whole table roared with laughter. He fist pounded with Blake who was next to him.

"Hey, I gotta take this call. I'll be back," Adella whispered to Viv.

"Oh sure, no problem," Viv smiled.

Adella pushed herself away from the table and made her way to the side door of a hall by the bay window.

She stroked her fingers across the orb's glossy surface as she stepped outside onto the terrace.

"Raena?" Adella spoke into the glass.

"By The Radiance, Del!" Raena appeared in the translucent sphere.

"Raena! I miss you! I have so much to tell you!"

"I know you do! How were your classes? What is it like?"

"A whole new world, Raen. I can't even begin to tell you. But first I want to know what's happened at home. I'm really sorry I couldn't talk much this morning."

"No worries, Adella. Well, school was crazy today, if you couldn't tell from my messages. And I just finished dinner tonight at Shmitty's house. And Shmitty says '*hi*', by the way. He's doing the dishes right now."

"Shouldn't you be helping him?" Adella raised a playful eyebrow.

"Hey, I helped William cook, okay? Mr. Yordinson, er, well I guess it's Synclair now? Or has always been? Anyways, William explained a little more about your family's *true history*. You come from really crazy beginnings!"

"And I only just found out a week ago," Adella shook her head.

"I can only imagine, Del. We've been best friends since we were eight, and now this all hits from nowhere. We've seen you on the mirror all day. And Shmitty and I have been going through the FERI network on our crystals looking at all the pictures. It's been surreal. Your mom was really freaking out at dinner with the media contesting your authenticity. But your dad went to Ebenhold, right?"

"Yeah, grandmother is meeting dad in Ebenhold to make a press statement. It should stop all this loophole frenzy about me."

Raena scoffed. "It better."

"Varinth law will take hold then."

"Let's hope," Raena added thoughtfully. "I do wish you could have at least seen the looks on the Royal Pains' faces today," a cunning smile grew upon her lips.

"What happened?" Adella asked.

"You exploded everywhere and everyone was bombarding Shmit and I with questions. And The Royal

Pains were actually the *most* curious. Brittney in particular. She asked if we knew who you were all along and Shmit and I were like '*of course we knew!*' Hah! It was fantastic."

"I wish I could have seen that," Adella beamed. "Speaking of Shmitty, how is he taking it all? I can tell from his script messages that he's not doing so good."

"He's... overwhelmed," Raena paused. "You'll never guess what he did today. He's accident prone already, but a whole week without you and he's been worse than normal. This morning, instead of just forgetting his socks or his backpack, he walked out without pants. *Pants*, Adella. Luckily, he was riding with me, and I got him back inside before the neighbors could create a mob," Raena shook her head. "With the frenzy at school today he just sort of shut down. We stuck by each other but for the most part."

"Shmitty," Adella breathed, sadness in her voice. "We had fight night before I left. He had done really well. The best I'd seen him in a long time."

"Yeah, well, whatever you saw, he's lost it. Like, literally, he's lost it."

Adella shook her head.

"You know, he loved those fight nights," Raena stopped, choosing her words carefully. "He... cares about you."

"I know," Adella sighed. "I do care about him, too, Raen, just not in that way."

"I know – and I think he understands that. He's the biggest dork, but in his own way he's really protective of you. He doesn't want to see you get hurt, again. It's been the three of us for so long, and I don't know how he is going to cope without you there everyday. Spell, *I* don't know how I'm gonna cope without you! You spiraled so bad this last Sun's Tide and now we don't even have you at all."

"Oh, Raen, I'm so sorry-"

"No. We love you," Raena cut her off. "That's what friends are for. It's amazing though, seeing you like this. I feel like your spark is back."

"I *am* back, I promise. I'm alive. And I won't ever become that shell of a person again. I promise," Adella felt a pang of longing; the chest tightening yearn for a hug from someone held so dear. The Everheart ring on her finger felt heavier.

"I'm so proud of you," Raena said, a lump in her throat. "I wish I could hug you."

"We *will* see each other again. I'm not sure when, but soon," Adella offered, uncertain if this was even a possibility.

"We *will* find a way," Raena concurred, determination in her tone. "So, lighter note," she quickly blinked away the tears from her clear amethyst eyes. "Your dress is *amazing*!" Her face appeared bigger in the crystal as if she was trying to get a closer look.

"Thank you! I just got it today in Vryndolne!" Adella responded with a huge smile. She quickly tried to think of everything she could possibly tell Raena. Every good and bad thing since her arrival flashed through her head in an instant. It felt like a lifetime, even when it had only been a little longer than a day. "I've made friends, I think. And when I went shopping in Vryndolne today, it was because Empress Vivian Thelred took me."

"Vivian Thelred?!" Raena gasped with disbelief. "You're hanging out with *Empress Vivian Thelred*?! Heiress to the Varinth Empire?"

"Yes," Adella laughed, eyes alight. "I can't even process it all."

"That's so crazy, Del! Who else is going there?!"

Adella instantly thought of Brogan, and she had been dying to talk to her best friend about it. Now was her chance. "That is actually one of the craziest things that's happened-"

"Adella?" A curious voice called out.

Adella turned around, startled, to see Brogan walking towards her onto the terrace. She spun back around to end her call.

"Del?" Raena asked. "What's wrong? Who is there?"

"Uh. Can I call you back?" Adella's heart pounded.

"Oh, spell no. You look like you just saw a ghost–"

"It's Brogan, okay?" Adella whispered. "But I'll explain–"

"Brogan?! What the spell?! Why didn't you tell me?! How is that even–"

"Cut it, Raen! Talk later!" She whispered hastily back into the ball. And with that she slid her finger across the smooth surface of the sphere, banishing Raena away.

Adella could feel her heart working double time as she turned around to see him.

He bowed low, cape swirling around. "Good evening, Princess. I hope I'm not interrupting."

"I just stepped out to take a call," Adella cleared her throat, trying to keep calm.

"Oh, I'm sorry. Is this a bad time then?" He asked innocently.

"No, no it's fine. I was just finishing up."

"Great," he smiled. "I was worried when you didn't return to the hall."

"You? Worried about me?" Adella asked, skepticism saturating her voice.

"Why wouldn't I? It *is* quite noticeable when your presence is missing from a room."

Adella looked away, trying to still her heart. It was a quiet evening. The stars glimmered over head, distant waterfalls rushed faintly.

"Do you wish me to leave?" He sensed her hesitation.

"Why are you talking to me Brogan? I still don't understand you," Adella looked back at him, exasperated, confused. "You've never given me an explanation for leaving North Brook like you did. And today you just glossed over everything like it was no big deal. I get it, a fresh start would be nice, but sometimes it just doesn't work that way," her voice broke and she turned to look away once more.

Brogan sighed deeply.

"Adella," he searched for words. "You have no idea the amount of pressure I was under as the crown prince of Kelemer. You are so amazing and I fell so deeply for you," he hung his head. "I was so stupid. I really was. I should never have left things in that way."

"That literally makes no sense," Adella challenged, looking back to him, anger building in her chest. "Your actions go against everything you had ever said to me. My common birth didn't matter to you, remember? You loved me! We loved each other!"

"And we did! But my council pressured me. I was in too deep, and they threatened to deny me the throne if I chose you."

"You said horrible things to me in front of everyone and never talked to me again. You became a different person!" Adella's fury took over. Instead of recoiling into despair, she wanted to punch him in the face.

"I had to be convincing, they were watching."

"They were watching," Adella scoffed. "They, meaning your council?"

"Yes."

"Wow," Adella shook her head, incredulous that this was the reason behind her personal torture. "You do realize the sacrifices my own father made to be with my mother? Why I even exist in the first place?"

"I… know how bad this looks. Especially to you of all people," Brogan conceded.

"Why have you come tonight, Brogan? You got what you wanted. You kept your crown, you're going to be king of Kelemer. Why did you seek me out?"

Brogan was silent, his gaze unreadable.

Adella raised an eyebrow. "Is it because I'm actually a princess now? That I turned out to be nobility all along?"

He hesitated, a smirk on his lips. "I mean, it is convenient, right?"

"I'm done," Adella bit her cheek, gritted her nails into her palms, and marched for the door back to the hall, rage inside bubbling.

"No, wait, Adella," he called.

She hated how every time he said her name her heart would skip. She stopped and whipped back around dramatically, gown skirts swishing, long auburn hair floating around her, and crossed her arms. Even in her anger she was graceful. She glared at him.

"Adella," he stepped forward and placed his palm on his chest meaningfully, covering his ornate ruby pendant. "Please, I want to make things right. I know they won't be perfect and I know I don't deserve another chance at even being your friend, but I really do want to make amends. I've *missed* you."

Adella stared at him, his huge cerulean eyes fixed on her, pleading; and in that moment, she could feel it – feel herself *breaking*. The walls she put into place to guard her heart and mind, the walls that held her together and contained what was left of her shattered heart, the walls that she had built *because* of Brogan, were powerless against him. Like a thief in the night, he had stolen past the soundless barricade that she had built for her soul.

"Brogan," she whispered, warring within. It all felt wrong, and yet here he was. Wanting her attention. Pleading for forgiveness. Her dream from the previous night came into her head. *Don't trust me*, echoed yet again.

"Please," Brogan begged sincerely. "I came here solely to concentrate on becoming the best ruler I can be, but seeing you again has made me realize my feelings for you never left. I can't commit to anything right now, but I do want you in my life. This is, after all, my first year here, just like you."

Adella just stood there. She couldn't breathe. *He still has feelings for me*? She didn't know what to say. *What* does *one say to that*?! *He doesn't want a commitment but he wants me in his life?*

"Listen," he coaxed, reading into her hesitation. "Let's just start over. Like I said earlier, no one has to know our history. No one even has a clue. Here, you can be Princess Adella *Everheart*."

Adella was quiet. His presence was intoxicating, and she struggled to regain her breath. She wondered if she had always felt this way around him, suffocated by his perfection. The overwhelming need to hold him and simultaneously run as far away from him as she could.

"Okay," she finally managed.

"Good," Brogan flashed a smile. "We should be getting back." He held out his arm. "*Princess* Adella?"

Adella smiled gingerly and took his offer. They walked to the door they had come through, and Brogan released his arm to open it for her.

"Allow me," he grabbed the handle.

It was locked.

"Uh oh," he laughed a little. "Guess they forgot to unlock this side."

"Uhh," Adella voiced nervously.

"Don't worry, love," he flirted. "There is another entrance this way." He held out his arm again and led her onto the winding marble ramp that ended on a pathway which ran along a side of the castle. They approached a door that belonged to one of the side halls on the outer wings, somewhere past the bay window of the ballroom, Adella guessed. She had only the information of the short tour to go off of.

"Ah, here we are. This one is open," he smirked as his eyes flashed in the light of the elegant golden lanterns that lit the entire campus. He pulled the door handle and gazed intently into her eyes. She felt her heart jump and hesitated for a moment, swallowing away the urge to kiss him. She stepped through into the new hall, and he took to her side once more and led her on.

She was sure that this was a new area in the castle. She had no memory of it on the tour. Brogan laced his fingers with hers on his arm and gave it a tight squeeze. Adella tried to distract herself from the sensation by looking at all of the other things in the hall.

"Hey, what's that?" She asked as she left his side and walked closer to the banner that had piqued her interest.

"Oh, that's just left over from the Autumn's Tide Ball. I guess they forgot to take this one down," he answered with a smile.

Adella just stood there silently in the dim candle and chandelier light of the hall, staring at the decoration. He stepped up next to her.

"I don't suppose you've ever been to a ball before," he assumed quietly.

"No, I never have," Adella turned to look at him. "*Someone* had promised to take me a long time ago but…" she trailed wryly, raising an eyebrow.

"Yes, I did promise, didn't I?" He seemed sad.

"Mhmm. But that's in the past now, isn't it?" She retorted.

"Well, maybe not…" he smiled. "If you've never been to a ball before, I'd say that now you'll get your fair share. The Frost Waltz is the next one."

"Well I knew what I was signing up for," she joked.

He looked deep into her eyes, mesmerizing her. "If I remember correctly, you love to dance."

Adella barely nodded. She had a flash of a memory that she had long since buried. She was dancing with *him* in the starlight back in North Brook, twirling on the balcony of his room in his cousin's estate.

"I do," she whispered. "Dancing was something we always loved."

He smiled so warmly that Adella feared she would melt. "It was," he agreed.

Her heart swelled painfully. "Well, seeing as it'll be my first official ball, and not a waltz in the moonlight, I might be a little lost."

"Don't worry," he brushed a stray lock away from her cheek, "I'll show you how it's done." The moment was intimate, both of them reading one another. "Come on, let's get back," he finally held out his arm. She took it without thinking.

*Did he just ask me to the Frost Waltz?* Her heart leaped for joy as her logic gave way.

They continued on through, almost reaching the dining hall, when Brogan's crystal ball started to go off. He stopped just before the two of them emerged from the side hall they were in – right before any of their peers saw the two of them together. He let go of Adella and pulled out his sphere.

"Ahh," he groaned, "I gotta take this. Let's meet up later, okay?"

"Okay," Adella smiled amiably.

"Oh, Adella," he added, just before he took his leave.

"Yes?"

"Just for now, let's not seem too familiar, alright?"

"Oh. Uh, yes, of course," Adella agreed. Confusion touched her eyes.

"Thank you, beautiful," he caressed her cheek lightly and winked. He then turned on his heels and started down a different hall, away from the direction in which they were originally heading. Adella watched him for a second, completely enamored, before the sound of distant laughter snapped her out of the trance. She looked to where the sound came from and realized she needed to find her friends.

Her head was racing as she walked through a much more populated corridor. Her gut told her to listen to the warning in her dream, to listen to her confusion and hesitations, but for some inexplicable reason she still longed to be in his arms. The feeling overwhelmed her chest.

Her crystal chimed with a message.

It was from Viv.

> *Hey, where are you? We're all in Hang Hall. Did you get lost? You need us to come find you?*

Adella breathed a sigh of relief and made her way over to meet her friends.

"Hey, Adella!" Jason called out.

Adella entered Hang Hall, and having only been in this room once on her tour, she was proud of herself for finding it all on her own. As she sauntered over to where Jason had called, she was taken in by the high ceilings and flying buttress beams. They raced along the roof, carved elegantly from dark marble. Purple tapestries bearing Royal High's golden emblem were everywhere and, on the far wall, the largest marble fireplace she had ever seen was roaring. Night had indeed fallen, and the light of the tavernesque chandeliers, paired with the elaborate gold candelabras along the walls, made for a subdued, mellow atmosphere.

Several royals were scattered through the hall in various activities of leisure. A group talked and tuned their instruments together whilst others created casual, muted melodies on a stage like pavilion set in the corner.

Her attention was drawn away from the musicians when a group of students broke into a raucous. She glanced to the outcry and saw royals playing cards with game chips. Many of the kids in the group suddenly touched their noses and tried not to laugh after putting down the cards in their hands. It reminded Adella of a game she had played back home. She wondered if it was the same one. Beyond them, more students sprawled out together on clusters of couches, sofas and huge floor cushions that filled the hall.

Adella felt an evening breeze caress her skin from the open terrace doors as she arrived to where her friends were situated. Jason, Blake, Vivian, Kate, and a few others she could not name, were lounging around watching a movable on an enormous magic mirror. It was mounted high upon the wall above the fireplace for all to see.

"Hey, sorry about that," she said as Viv scooted over a to allow some room for her to sit. "I was talking to my friend from back home. I didn't realize how long I had been gone."

"Aw, don't worry about it. We were just getting worried is all," Kate answered.

"We thought we were gonna have to send a rescue party," Jason chuckled as he lazily strummed the mandolin that laid against his chest.

Adella settled into the comforting company of her new friends as they chattered away. She did her best to keep interested, but truth be told, participating was proving difficult. All she could think about was Brogan and his allusion to them becoming something more again.

*Maybe we still have a chance,* she thought hopefully. *His council wouldn't object to him being with me now, right?* Her subconscious reared its head at this notion, trying to bring up the absurdity of why he left her, but Adella banished away the thoughts. *He said he wants a fresh start,* she reasoned, heart overtaking logic.

Her subconscious reminded her how Vivian was in love with him. It stopped Adella short, making her realize what this possible love triangle could do to her brand new friendships. Her fight to belong in this world of royals was going to be one of the hardest things she was ever going to do. She was going to need every kingdom alliance she could make. With all of the odds and prejudices stacked against her, her ability to thrive was going to greatly depend on whether or not she could survive socially. And, *if* she could survive at Royal High, it would be a shining testament to her parents, to her own heart, and to her bloodline. It would prove that no matter the circumstance or upbringing, an Everheart can always rise above. The *peasant* princess would show them all.

Adella took a deep, sobering breath. There was no question. Her feelings for Brogan were going to have to take a side seat. Her overnight fame had landed her in a great niche of people and she needed to play her cards right if she was to hold onto the quickly forged friendships. As much as wanted think think the best of them all, she still wasn't so sure of everyone's intentions. Fame *is* fleeting, and Adella needed her new friends to be a permanent development. A development to prove Dia's "advice" wrong.

# Thirteen

It was just after dawn when the crystal call came through, breaking Adella from her deep slumber. She answered it groggily and heard from one of grandmother's advisor's to turn on the news. Adella sat straight up, realizing what today was. She slipped out of bed and padded barefoot past a sleeping Vivian to turn on the mirror in their spacious suite.

The FNN network came to life. They were about to hold court in Ebenhold for the Queen of Adamaris to give her statement.

As Adella waited for her grandmother to appear, she went and shrugged into a silky robe, pulled open the drapes on the balcony to let in the morning sunlight, and rang the servant's bell for tea and coffee. The knock on her door was quicker than she anticipated, and after she accepted the platter on the service cart, she quickly poured herself a cup of black coffee in an effort to will away the nerves. She wanted the caffeine.

An unseen voice through the mirror proclaimed, "Announcing her royal majesty, Cassandra Devenira Levaine Everheart, Queen of Adamaris."

Adella had barely gotten through half her cup when she looked up to see Cassandra emerge on the screen. She was shadowed by an incredibly handsome royal– *BY THE RADIANCE, THAT'S MY DAD!* Adella freaked out internally. Sure enough, Aedrian was on the interkingdom news, wearing a princely doublet of dark teal and gold, marking him as an obvious part of the Adamaris court.

"Vivian! Vivian!" Adella practically shouted, forgetting about her coffee and flinging herself across the room to spring onto Viv's bed.

"What!" Vivian shot straight up. The blonde beauty looked seriously startled. Her hair stood out comically in crazy bed-head waves.

"My dad's on the mirrorrr!" Adella sang as she hopped down and ran back to watch.

"Della," Vivian moaned petulantly. This was the second day in a row that she had been awoken by having her sleeping form tackled. She looked over to Adella who was waiting for her grandmother and father to speak. "Not to be rude, but my daddy's on the mirror all the time. *Why* is this news?"

"Vivian, my dad hasn't been in the media since before I was born. And now they're going to set the record straight about my birthright. This is big deal, remember? Please show some support. I'm sorry I glomped you."

"Forgiven," Vivian managed to mumble as she poofed back down into her sheets. She made an effort to turn over and face the magical device, halfway watching in her groggy state.

Cassandra opened her mouth to speak. "Greetings to all kingdoms of greater Edenarth, and may The Radiance bless House Etherstone for their warmth and hospitality in hosting our court. Given the sensitive nature of this matter, time has been of the essence. I speak today from the Ebenhold citadel with an announcement regarding the heir to Adamaris' crown. The man to my right is my son, Aedrian Everheart. Nearly two decades ago I had decreed he would not be my successor. However, Aedrian's line has continued, and my decree does not affect direct descendants. His daughter, Adella Everheart, is the rightful heir to the Adamaris throne. She has been enrolled in one of the royal institutions of higher learning to prepare her for her future as the new ruler of Adamaris. I have called this court to declare, once and for all, that Adella Everheart will be crowned my successor. She is an Everheart by blood, and as such, she will be protected by the Interkingdom Accords. Anyone who is found in breach of the accords shall be declared an enemy of the accords and shall be dealt with by the swiftest methods of justice in the land of offense."

Cassandra turned to whisper something to Aedrian, and the two shared a silent conversation. Murmurs ran through the unseen crowd in the mirror. Adella's father then stepped in to speak.

He cleared his throat, seeming a little nervous. "To all kingdoms, good morning. I am Duke Aedrian Everheart, former crown prince to Adamaris. I've… been away for awhile," he paused, as if looking for the right words to say. He licked his lips, hesitant, but spoke again. "My daughter, Adella Everheart, is The Lost Princess. She is of the direct Everheart bloodline, and she will be queen." His ocean eyes were serious and hard. Adella had never seen her father this polished, this grave, in all her life. "Henceforth, she is to be protected by The Accords. Any violation of this is a direct violation against the royal court of Adamaris. Let it be known. Thank you."

Aedrian stepped away from the screen and Cassandra followed him. The network cut away to their faerie reporters floating to the center of the mirror to give their commentary on the announcement.

"There you have it," Vivian said, sounding satisfied, looking to Adella.

Adella didn't move as she wordlessly watched the reporters banter.

"How do you feel?" Vivian prompted.

"Better," Adella finally let out a sigh of relief. She turned to face the empress who was still in her bed. "Much better. It's done now."

"It is," Vivian smirked. "Welcome to the club."

Within an hour after the queen's declaration, the whole dining hall was buzzing with the news. Those who had snidely remarked about Adella's authenticity were suddenly claiming that they knew she was real all along.

Adella attempted to ignore them as she finished her breakfast, though a smug smile refused to leave her lips. She wished Jason and Blake could be there with her, but they had left at dawn for their away game. They wouldn't be back until Sunday night.

After everyone had finished their morning meal, Adella slipped away back up to her room to start on her homework. She desperately wanted to catch up with all of her new classes. With a large chunk of the guys being gone for the weekend, Jason, Blake, and Brogan being among them, she felt that she finally had a moment to concentrate without distraction. She also had half a mind to explore the castle if she got a chance. Priorities, priorities of course.

Adella had barely begun to write the homework notes for her etiquette chapters when Vivian and Kate burst into the dorm. They managed to hunt her down and effectively coerced her into Saturday tea with Lord Langsly Fendelson.

When Adella arrived with her friends to the lavishly set table in the outside terrace court, she realized that Langsly was the same boy who she had seen in the hall when Brogan had walked her to Literature – the same frilly blonde one that she wanted to punch in the face. His family apparently owned some of the best gold deposits on the continent, which, in return, bought him his entry into Royal High. He was no crown prince, though he'd have you believe otherwise.

Having cakes with this pompous boy did not lessen Adella's desire to deck him. He was arrogant, foppish, kind of creepy, and his high voice grated on her every nerve. Less than a half an hour in and she had already had her fill. She longed for escape. Many marvelous things awaited around every turn in the stunning campus, and here she was entertaining this pompous fool. Vivian and Kate seemed quite pleased, though, laughing at the appropriate times, and engaging in school gossip. Adella knew that they were only playing the politics game. *Money can indeed buy friends,* she thought wryly to herself as she sipped on the last of her tea.

"Thank you for your company, Langsly, but I do believe I am going to retire. My head has steadily grown into an ache and I feel the need to lie down away from this heat," Adella lied. She politely excused herself from the sudden surliness of Langsly. Vivian and Kate seemed worried, offering to walk her up to her quarters, but Adella insisted that she'd be alright on her own. Afterall, they were having such a *lovely* tea; she didn't want to be the reason why it ended.

Adella slipped away into the halls and up to her dorm. She hastily pinned her long hair back, and changed into the most casual garments she could find in her suite; silk chemise, bodice, skirt, boots. *Probably missing a few dresscode approved layers, but hey, it's not school hours*, she thought.

Lithe on her feet and full of giddy excitement, she left her dorm as a rush of adrenaline coursed through her body. She figured if anyone discovered her wandering, she'd just say that she got "lost". She left the Demasque wing, found a random side entry on the upper levels, and burst out onto a veranda that was bathed in the warm autumn sunlight. The balcony looked out over the stunning campus; the foliage of Varinth was giving way to Autumn Tide's golden warm hues. The mixed conifers held their evergreen shade, but many of the deciduous boughs were touched with ambers, golds, scarlets, and rich burgundies.

Her eyes caught on the Royal High gardens, and she made her way down on a staircase to the ground level of the campus. She entered their winding pathways and lost herself in a botanical palace of hanging canopies and hedge mazes. Magically illuminated fairy lights, winding, curving, lattice structures, luscious flowers of every shape and color, many of which Adella had never seen before, all left her enchanted. The smell of earth and green was invigorating. She realized that apart from the bird song, the soft breeze, and sounds of rushing waters, all was quiet, not a soul around. Every so often she would stumble upon a random statue, frozen in its story; there was an ancient bronze war horse, a white marble woman in a marble veil, a golden king in a bed of roses, and a copper swan, speckled generously with patina, set in a shimmering fountain. Adella journeyed into the deepest reaches, places where the afternoon barely pierced, and found some of the waterfalls that Varinth was famed for, shimmering into serene ponds. Finally, as far as she dared to go, she came upon a gorgeously aged and ivy swathed pavilion hidden on the edge of this world. Time seemed lost here.

Adella made the decision to try and find her way back. As she followed the paths she thought led her out, she realized she was drawing near the outer reaches of the school's backyard. There was a sprawling verdant lawn, some distant buildings, and what looked to be an arena. She realized that she was on the edges of the athletic and combat fields. Beyond them stretched more of the long green lawn, and beyond that was a wall of trees, the border of the Grenvar Wood.

A chill suddenly blew through her, despite the warmth of the Autumn Tide's sun, and she decided it best to further her adventures inside the castle.

As she began her journey back to the palace, she noted how desolate and forgotten the gardens were when compared with the central quad. She could see the courtyard from a distance, lively with passing royals. She knew it best to stay away from there if she didn't want to be found. Plus, switching out her fully boned corset for an adventuring worthy bodice would probably raise a few eyebrows.

Adella stealthily entered the castle once more, and went down a hall that she hoped lead to the classrooms. She had begun to already grasp a basic familiarity with the most used areas of the school, but several odd corridors, which everyone seemed to ignore, called to her adventuring heart. She stole past the classroom halls, navigating her way through winding turrets and down long staircases, losing herself in the wings that none of the royal population seemed to ever bother going into. She passed by countless gilded paintings, lifelike busts and statues, ornate and intricate tapestries, and stunning architecture; the sheer beauty and wealth of everything left her a constant state of awe. It was like a museum that nobody ever seemed to visit, and Adella began to wonder if this was standard for castles. Artwork made, bought, and forgotten about. At times she would stumble upon a fairy enchanted suit of armor that could talk about some of the pieces they were stationed next to, discuss histories of the school, and give insights about Varinth's past. But, apart from these enchanted steel figures, Adella was very much alone, and the further she explored, the more aged and strange the artwork around her became.

One painting near a suit of armor piqued her interest in particular.

She drew closer to the overly enormous piece, hung against the marble and granite wall. Set in a beautifully gilded frame, the artwork seemed far older than anything Adella had encountered thus far in these halls.

Amidst a dark and barren landscape, a war waged on, while lightning and scarlet rivers of flame lit up the distant background. Scattered about the foreground, six armored forms were fighting; five men and one woman. Although Adella could not make out their faces, she could see that the men were handsome in stature, and the female was beautiful, with her long dark hair flying about her. Their armor and weapons, though tarnished from the soot and ash of the surrounding environment, seemed to glow in the darkness around them. They were glorious to look upon, and Adella felt a strange warmth in her heart. Her eyes drifted and she noticed the rest of the piece. The forces the six warriors fought against seemed like smeared shadows, some flying above, and others around on the ground. Adella saw that the large dark smears were all over the canvas. The things these heroes were fighting back had been smudged out, made to look like phantoms. If the six weren't in the painting, Adella realized that this art would be terrifying to look upon. An unsettling chill grew along her spine as she stepped closer to get a better look.

Adella's proximity made the nearby suit of armor glow. "Dated to have been painted almost a thousand years before today's common age," he began in his hearty metallic voice, "this painting was discovered in the Valley of Geldor, in the Realm of Kelemer, about 200 years ago. The artist is unknown, but this painting is one of the oldest in Royal High's collection. What we see here is believed to be a depiction of the fabled Astralore Wars. Not much is known about this history, only that these battles supposedly shaped many of our realms that we now know today." The suit of armor finished his tale and then turned to Adella. "Good day, Princess. Is there anything you would like to know?" He suddenly sounded like a tour guide.

"Uh, yeah," Adella jumped a little, the goosebumps on her spine settling down. "Why are there smears all

over the painting? What are those shadowy things?"
She pointed out.

The suit responded mechanically, "The painting
was found as such. The smears are believed to be the
mythical shadow creatures, The Maldeemed, who are
said to have their origins in the dark places of the far
north. Others believe that the painting may have been
altered, and that the shadows might have been orcs,
trolls, or even dragons. None can truly say." The suit
then prompted, "Is there anything else you'd like to
know, Princess?"

"Yes, can you tell me who the six fighters are?"
Adella pondered.

"They are The Champions of Old, Princess. Is
there anything else you'd like to know?"

"Who are the Champions of Old?" She pressed

"The Champions of Old are The Champions of
Old." He responded monotone. "Princess, is there
anything else you'd like to know?"

Adella could see that this was going to go nowhere.
"No, I'm fine. Thank you Suit."

"You're very welcome, Princess. Have a wonderful
day." And with that he faded back into an inanimate
object on his stand.

Adella reluctantly turned from the mysterious
painting, pushed away the inexplicable longing in her
soul, and continued her adventure.

When the afternoon began to darken, it became
apparent to Adella that finding her way back might
prove to be difficult. In the more populated areas of the

castle, servants of Royal High occasionally scurried to and fro, completing whatever task they had before them. Whenever they saw the Everheart Princess wandering, they often stopped to ask if she was alright or if she was lost (apparently her behavior was not the norm). She assured them to carry on and that she was fine.

Now that Adella needed to find her way back, she realized that she probably should have taken one of them up on their offers for she, indeed, was lost. There hadn't been a servant, or even a Suit, in quite awhile. This worried her. The aimless exploring was fun at first, but not knowing her way back, especially when she hadn't seen anyone for what felt like a very long time, was unnerving. Of course, in this worst case scenario, she had left her crystal ball behind. She deduced that she was very deep within the mysterious castle and found herself entering an area which felt forlorn and forbidding. The halls were barely lit, and she got the feeling that she was headed into sublevels of the school. She needed to find a way back up, but the way behind her seemed a worse idea–

"Ooof!!" A flurry of fairy dust and papers went everywhere as Adella collided with the fey. The two had been quickly rounding the same corner in opposite directions – Adella hadn't noticed, but she had actually started to jog in her desperation. The fey had been absent minded in his flight, whizzing quickly along, not expecting to find anyone in this area.

"By The Radiance! I am *so* sorry!" Adella pleaded as she helped pick up the papers from the floor.

"No, no it's my fault! I should have been watching where I was flying!" The fey shook his head as he nabbed more papers fluttering in the air.

He looked upon the girl he had hit and realization set in. "Princess Everheart?"

She looked up, startled he knew her name. "Yes?"

"Oh forgive me, where are my manners," he spoke quickly, but eloquently, as he broke hover and set down upon his feet. "I am Lenroe, fey in the service of Royal High, Assistant to Professor Bracke." He bowed low, thin and long iridescent wings folding down his back. When he raised up, Adella noted his slight build. He was only a couple of inches taller than she. Sandy brown hair stuck out stylishly in several directions from underneath his slouchy silk hat, almost covering his pertly pointed ears. His bright silver eyes were the prettiest and most prominent feature of his slender, sprite like face. He wore a tunic and trousers in all the shades of silvery clouds with a sash of deep periwinkle around his waist. Adella found his silken garb relaxed yet ethereal. Fairy dust lightly shimmered upon his nose and cheeks and in areas of his clothes.

"It's nice to meet you, Lenroe. And please, call me Adella," she smiled gingerly as she handed him back his papers. "I'm sorry again about the collision." She was covered in fairy dust, yearning to rub her now sore shoulders and nose. She vaguely wished that he had been flying around in his tinier, transfigured form – it wouldn't have hurt so bad to crash together then.

"Oh, it is not your fault. Wait," he said, suddenly looking around the corridor as if he was missing something. He then looked her up and down, taking in her unorthodox apparel. "Are you lost?"

Adella raised an eyebrow. "What gives you that impression?" She answered sternly, feigning confidence.

"Because the kids... I mean, the *royals,* never travel in this area of the castle. Parts like these don't usually see traffic," Lenroe shuffled his papers better together and began to hover slightly once more. Adella figured that this was probably subconscious for him.

"Well, why are *you* here then?" She smirked.

"I'm not normal traffic," he replied in a matter of fact tone. "I travel my own paths. I get around better that way."

"Oh," Adella replied.

Neither of them said a word for a moment. He smiled.

"So, are you lost? Or am I to go along on my merry flight?" He proposed, and she couldn't tell if he was teasing.

"I *am* a little disoriented," she admitted.

His expression became soft. "Well, I was just headed on my way to the alchemy lab to put these graded papers back, would you like to follow?"

"Please," she replied.

As Lenroe glided along next to her, Adella noticed how quiet he was. He made no attempt at trivial conversation like most of the people in the school. He seemed to rather enjoy the silence, and, to Adella's surprise, she actually found it comfortable. However, Lenroe was *actually* someone that Adella wanted to have conversation with. She did not know many full blooded fey like him. He had to be ancient.

"So, you're Bracke's assistant?" Adella's bubbling curiosity won out over enjoying the silence. Aside from being a fey, the assistant of her favorite teacher had to be cool, or at least close to decent, like Bracke was, right?

"I am."

More silence.

"That's cool…" She murmured after it was apparent that this was his total response. "Well, for the record, I really like Bracke and his class, even if I have only had it once."

"Yeah?" Lenroe perked up slightly, looking to her.

"Mhmm. Back where I am from we don't have alchemy classes like what they offer here."

"So I have heard," Lenroe smiled sadly.

They went along, and Adella found things familiar again.

"So what do you do, Lenroe?" She asked suddenly, sensing their time was coming to an end.

"What do you mean?" He replied.

"I mean what exactly do you assist Professor Bracke with?"

"Well someone needs to be there to keep the crazy in line," Lenroe smirked a little. He was teasing again. "I correct papers, help with supplies and experiments, get him his morning draught of ale. It's a simple life."

Adella laughed. "He drinks ale first thing in the morning?"

"Alongside his spot of tea and toasted tarts," Lenroe chuckled coolly. His wings seemed to flitter more when he was amused, even if his face was composed. The iridescent appendages shimmered and trailed sparse glittering dust behind them.

Adella saw servants scuttling about again. Lenroe had successfully led her back into more populated areas. She could tell that they were nearing the hall that had professor Bracke's class in it.

"Are you in familiar parts once more?" Lenroe playfully asked.

Adella looked to him and flippantly responded, "Yes, I do so recall that exact vase." She pointed nonchalantly to a random vessel that looked exactly like most of the others they had passed.

"Cheeky," Lenroe cracked a grin.

Adella hoped that "cheeky" was a good thing.

They arrived at Bracke's large, rustic door (a rather out of place door for such an ornate establishment), and Lenroe passed his hand over the handle, never touching the metal. The nob clicked and the hinged lumber swung open.

"Are you okay to find your way back from here?" Lenroe queried as he hesitated entering the room.

Adella looked to the windows across the hall and noticed the rapidly darkening sky. Dinner was probably within the hour and she needed to find Vivian.

"Yes, I'm good. I think I have had enough exploring for one day."

"Oh? I don't think one could ever explore enough," the fey commented wistfully.

"Oh, I'm not done. Just done for today. I need to finish my homework now," Adella added.

"What subject?"

"Alchemy." A sheepish grin grew upon her face.

"Really? How are you getting on?" He inquired, seeming nonchalant, still barely hovering.

"I'm catching on. I just need to finish the potions tomorrow and then I'll be ready for Monday."

"Finish the potions tomorrow?" Confusion flickered across his face.

"After my etiquette and monarchy studies."

Lenroe was quiet as he pursed his lips together in a thoughtful manner. He then gestured into the room and spoke.

"Well, you are welcome to use the lab–"

"No! No… er, I mean, I'm good," Adella exclaimed nervously. To her chagrin, she realized how odd her outburst must have been and explained. "I just don't want to face the other royals in the lab just yet. I'll be okay working on my own for now. But thank you!" She did not want to be around any of her peers working on the homework in front of them. She already felt self conscious and, from what she had skimmed of her Alchemy book, the class had already been covering some pretty advanced work which made her feel incredibly behind.

She thanked Lenroe once more, and he well wished her off. As she turned to leave, daintily sauntering down the hall in her best royal stride, she thought she heard him mutter as he entered the room 'but there's no one else.'

# Fourteen

It was Monday afternoon, and Adella had had to rush to retrieve her satchel. She sped through the halls, passing many peculiar and disapproving stares, as she willed herself to make it back to Bracke's class in time. Without a second to spare, she reached the door and shuffled through with the last group into the musty stone classroom.

Bracke's voice boomed, "All right! Settle in, settle in," he urged, holding up his thick hands. The bell tolled.

She made her way to her workstation where Vivian was already waiting, and began to tie an apron around her waist, covering her beautiful gown. Adella then set out some of the contents of her satchel with the supplies she needed for that day's lab assignment. She looked around for Lenroe, hopeful to see him again, but saw no sign of the fey.

Bracke continued to speak. "I hope you all have had a good weekend! Good job on winnin' your away game combat team!" He nodded to Blake and Jason and a few of the other players in the room. Many of the boys looked pretty beat up. "Heard your travels to an' from the realm of Renlyn were smooth, but I am sorry to hear you've lost two more players to injury during the tournament. Radiance willing they have a swift recovery for the remainder of the season!" He turned to write something on the board. "Now, onto the class work. Let's finish up the lesson from last Friday. Here's to hoping that you all took a deeper look into the finer details of the minor camouflage elixir…?"

The class was quiet. Someone coughed. Adella looked around puzzled. Bracke faced back to the class.

"We are supposed to finish them up today. That is considerin'," Bracke raised a bushy eyebrow, "you *did* do your homework, right?" Silence. "*Anyone* go over the material…?" More silence. "We made the first part of the potion, but did anyone finish the equations?" His last sentence was subtly laced with exasperation.

The class started to mumble and mutter excuses about how hard the assignment was and how it was difficult to understand and how most of the boys didn't have time because of combat.

Bracke sighed heavily, "If it was so hard, then why didn't I have visitors? Why weren't you all comin' into the lab? Not a soul dropped in here all weekend." He shook his head. Adella's gut did a flip.

*No one came into the lab at all?* She repeated in her head.

Bracke continued, growing irate. "Fine, alright. Take out any notes you have an' we'll finish it up in here. I did say I'd collect the theory notes at the end of this class period so I suppose we can finish the rest together. We'll put off the lab 'til tomorrow. I *was* hoping that someone would have at least–" he halted mid-sentence, noticing the vials Adella had out on her table. "Princess Adella? What have you there?" He questioned curiously.

Adella felt her stomach drop. "Uh, I did the homework, Professor," she quietly spoke. "But I see now that we were only supposed do the equations. I got a little carried away I guess…"

"You did the homework? *An'* finished the experiment?" He asked, pleasantly surprised.

"Yes," she nodded. All eyes in the room fixated upon her, making the girl wish she hadn't brought out her supplies in the first place. "I thought we were supposed to continue the lab work on our own."

One of the girls in the classroom uttered under her breath, "lab work is *only* for the lab."

The jealous girl's friend whispered to her, "know-it-all."

Adella knew all too well the sting of catty girls. The title of know-it-all was something that she had been called before, even throughout her commoner schoolings. Tongues were sure to be sent wagging after this class – and not just because of "*The Lost Princess*" thing.

She noticed Jason and Blake smirking at her, along with handful of other boys in the room.

"Well, what did you find out?" Bracke eagerly urged.

"I discovered some interesting things," she spoke cautiously, "having to do with the chameleon eye to hollowgrass ratio. There are even differences in regards to how long it is heated," she explained, halfway wishing she could disappear. "I wrote out the equations and mixtures for them all."

Bracke's smile was genuinely insatiable, crinkling the edges of his wise grey eyes. "Would you mind to come up an' show us? An' please, bring your samples."

Adella brought her notebook and six vials, all of different shades of blue, and some even of purple. One was black. She set them on Bracke's desk. He then handed her a piece of chalk and she filled up the board with the equations.

The room watched in awed silence. A few guys whistled quietly as she continued.

When she was done she turned around and gingerly placed the chalk back on his desk.

Bracke was still smiling eagerly. "Can you explain what you just wrote?"

"I think I can," she responded earnestly. She pointed to the first set of equations and held up it's corresponding vial. "This, here, is when the chameleon eye is half less than the hollowgrass, creating a more blue elixir. In theory, it won't camouflage as well, making one only slightly invisible, but movement isn't as hindered as opposed to the original mixture which inhibits movement but conceals much more. The side effects, as I remember you had said, can make one nauseated if they are concealed too long. I really didn't want to be the guinea pig for that," she laughed a little.

Dia, who had been sitting quietly at the back of the class, arms folded across her chest, sour faced, flame hair about her shoulders, mumbled bitterly, "would be a shame to throw up on your pretty new dress."

Bracke eyed her darkly. She eyed him back, her stark emerald stare too bold; she was no match for Bracke's hardened battle glare, and it shut her up effectively. His rough brogue presence, even when minutely irked, was horribly intimidating. For a split moment, Adella thought she saw something change in Dia's eyes. It was like a clashing spark between teacher and pupil. The exchange lasted but a few seconds, and for someone who wasn't looking for it, no one would have caught it. But it was there, and Adella wondered what it was. Surely something deeper than the petty comment from a mean girl.

The professor turned back to Adella, smiled, and urged her to continue.

She proceeded to explain what each of the vials and equations meant and how she achieved their outcomes. For several minutes she held the class captivated. Bracke would nod with approval, asking minimal prompt type questions.

"The black vial is different from all the rest because although it's mixture matches that of the fifth vial, I boiled it the longest on a whim. I wanted to see what would happen, and since there were no warnings in the textbook against it, I proceeded. It became that color. I have no idea what it does or means, but it looked cool so I brought it in as well," she stopped talking and smiled. "So, yeah. There's the homework."

No one in the class spoke as the bubbling of the cauldrons filled the silence. Several people's mouths were hanging open. Adella looked over to Jason and Blake who were grinning ear to ear. Blake especially.

Bracke laughed out loud. "The black doesn't mean much, other than ya just boiled it too long. Great job, Adella. Go ahead and have a seat. You have done quite well. Quite well indeed," he marveled at the board.

Adella ghosted to her place next to Viv, still wishing that the kindly but intimidating Bracke hadn't noticed her. *There you go again, drawing attention to yourself! You should have just left it all in the satchel. You want to be a know-it-all here? Jeez, Del. Why can't you just be apathetic like everyone else your age, huh? Why can't you just slack off like the rest of the kids around here? Uhhhg!!* She internally berated herself.

She sat down as quietly as she could manage and looked at her hands, looked at the Everheart ring's prisms upon her finger.

Dull murmurs were beginning to run through the room and Adella wondered why Bracke wasn't speaking. She finally looked up to see a speechless Bracke, rubbing the back of his head, studying the board. He started to scowl, and his thoughts grew deep upon his face. He turned around and began to study the vials on his desk, picking each one up and gazing upon them.

Moments passed and the murmurs grew quiet as they waited for Bracke's final word.

Bracke's pensive scowl deepened, as he planted his fists firmly on his desk.

If a pin had dropped, it would have been heard.

Suddenly, he clapped his large hands once, rubbing them together, breaking the silence, a smile spreading across his lips. "Well," he looked to the students, "seein' as Princess Adella managed to figure out most of the lesson that I was planning on goin' over today–"

The class broke into dissatisfied murmurs again. The jealous girls whispered amongst themselves, looking furtively over to the Everheart girl.

Adella moaned.

Bracke continued, "I'm figurin'," he raised his hands with his voice, trying to talk over everyone. He stared them all down under his bushy eyebrows until they were all quiet. "Thanks to Adella, class is dismissed for today," he said brightly. "Go, have a great afternoon. No homework, an' I'll see you all tomorrow." He began to sift through some papers on his desk, being careful not to disturb Adella's vials.

Nobody moved, thinking this was some kind of joke.

Bracke looked up, realizing they weren't leaving, and said, "Bye bye!"

Still, no one moved. This was completely out of the norm for him.

"Go!" He said, pointing to the exit, his eyes big, trying to convince them all.

All at once chairs scraped the floor and the royals got to their feet, chattering happily. Instantly, many of their opinions of Adella had changed, going from disdain to gratefulness.

"Hey, great job, Adella," some said as they filed out.

"Yeah, thanks for the early afternoon!" One of the cute combat boys added.

Adella just stood there, smirking in disbelief as her classmates left the room in a considerably chipper mood.

"Well, well, well," Vivian voiced as she removed her apron. "You didn't tell me you were fluent in Alchemy!"

"I'm not," Adella shrugged.

"Uh huh, sure," Blake beamed, coming over with Jason. "Wonder what else your hiding from us," he half joked.

"I bet we'll find out you're some kind of trollslayer or battlemage or something," Jason laughed.

Adella scoffed, smirking. Bracke spoke up from his desk.

"Princess Adella, can I have just a quick word?" He motioned forward.

Vivian, Jason, and Blake exchanged a cautious look with her, but voiced that they would catch her outside. Adella walked to the front of the room.

Bracke waited until everyone was out of the lab to speak.

"I let everyone go today because I realized that I might have bought you some unwanted attention. This way, they have an early day with you to thank."

"Oh. Wow. Thank you, professor," Adella replied, grateful at his reading of the situation.

Bracke nodded. "Princess, you did quite an outstandin' job," he began. "Tell me, have you ever worked with alchemy before?" His query was earnest. The bubbling cauldrons filled the silence.

"A little. It's not taught at my old school, but my best friend Raena and I would play with my father's old Alchemy books. He had some supplies in his study, but it was nothing like what you have here."

"Ahh, Aedrian did have a rather strong interest in alchemy," Bracke remarked. "It comes as no surprise that he would teach you such things."

"Oh, my father taught us a little, but Raena really taught me a lot. She's better than I am."

"Really? Your commoner friend?" Bracke's interest piqued.

"Yes. But you said you knew my father?" Adella questioned.

"Course I knew him. A wonderful student, he was. Great heart, great fighter. I was sad to see him not return for his last year."

"Yeah. My grandmother forbid him from choosing my mother," Adella affirmed. She was taken off guard at how boldly Bracke talked about it all.

"Yes, I remember well when that whole mess occurred," Bracke's eyes seemed far away. "He was only seventeen. Made my heart sad, the way it all happened. Your father was a visionary in his time here. He thought all men should be treated equal – a concept no doubt you've noticed is lost on most royals. Made me wonder what Adamaris would have become with a crown prince like him. And with him gone, and no direct blood line heir… well, I know you've heard it all already. It was quite the growing concern in the royal circles. An' yet there you were, livin' in the commoner world, hidden in plain sight."

"I can hardly believe it all myself," Adella murmured.

"And you had no idea of who you truly were?" He asked, sincerely wanting to understand.

Adella nodded. "All dad had ever said was that his noble family didn't accept my mother. So, in a sense I knew, but I didn't *know*. I just thought that somewhere out there I had some distant royal family who I'd never meet."

Bracke chuckled. "An' what are your thoughts now? Knowing you are the *crown princess* of Adamaris."

"Honestly, I'll let you know when I wake up," Adella giggled.

Bracke's chuckle turned into a booming laugh. "Well, you are very much awake, and all things aside, I can certainly say that you did a fine job today. I must ask, though, how did you manage all of this," he motioned to the vials, "without comin' into my lab? Not a soul came in all weekend."

"Oh, er…" Adella blushed, embarrassed of the means she used for her experiment.

"I did notice that your supplies an' ingredients were missing from your desk on Friday after class. You're technically not supposed to take them out of this room without permission."

"Oh, no. I'm sorry, I didn't know that," fear leaped in Adella's stomach.

"Don't worry, Princess, you are not in trouble. Not in the slightest. I am just curious as to where ya did your experiment?"

"Well, I thought there would be other people in here using the lab, too, so I, erm… I used the kitchen."

"The kitchens?" Bracke's voice boomed and his eyes grew wide. "Why in the world did you use the kitchens?!"

"I was nervous for the other royals to see me working. I didn't feel ready yet."

"You were… shy?" Bracke guessed, surprised.

"Is that bad?" She winced.

"Adella, my class is a place for learning," Bracke spoke, his deep baritone resonating through the stone room. "And to learn we must admit what we do not know. And not knowing is nothing to be ashamed of. No one can make you feel inferior without your permission, Princess. Remember that."

Adella nodded, feeling deeply touched by Bracke's sage words.

He smiled at her kindly. "Now, about the lab work. You said you used the kitchens. How exactly did that work out?"

"Well, I grabbed one of the cooking cauldrons, and there's several fireplaces going in the kitchen, so I just asked if I could use one."

Bracke laughed hard. "Boy you must have been a sight. All in the midst of the kitchen staff with your supplies. Not that I'm knocking your unorthodox way of achieving results." He was teasing her now.

"Yeah, I almost got soup spilled on me a few times. I think I freaked out the maitre D."

"Well we wouldn't want poor François to have a heart attack now, would we?" Bracke's chuckle was hearty. "Adella, please, come into the lab next time. It's safer, for one thing, but there is an agreement with the board that all alchemy experiments are to be done in lab, with mine, or Lenroe's, supervision. Besides, at least in my lab you won't have to worry about soup ruinin' your pretty li'l dresses," he beamed. "At worst it'll just be toad guts here."

"Okay," she smiled, feeling comforted.

"Also, would you mind if I examined these vials a li'l bit?" He motioned to her work, still on his desk. "I'd just like a closer look for myself," he asked.

"Oh, of course," she responded, politely surprised.

"Well, I've kept you long enough. Go, enjoy your afternoon, Princess."

Adella thanked him, curtsied, and practically skipped out of the lab with her now considerably lighter satchel.

Bracke remained at his desk for a moment, smile fading, brow growing into a furrow. He picked up the black vial. "Smart girl," he muttered, half-disbelieving, staring at the concoction in his hand.

Lenroe suddenly emerged from a back door in the classroom. Papers in one hand, mug of ale in the other.

"So, class is dismissed for the day?" He inquired skeptically as he set the jug upon Bracke's desk. He then flitted to set the papers down on a shelf.

"She did the entire experiment, an' *then* some," Bracke chuckled quietly.

Lenroe then looked over his shoulder to the vial the professor held.

"Did she… is that?" He raised an incredulous eyebrow, inspecting the vial in Bracke's hand.

"As far as you can get without breakin' any laws," Bracke shook his head. "When her supplies were missin', I had wondered what she was up to. It was a good thing you intercepted her in the hall. I cannae believe she did all this in the kitchen, though."

"She's got the touch, that's for sure," Lenroe smirked.

"Aye, the Everheart Princess does," Bracke smiled back. He set the vial down and grabbed his mug, taking a long drought.

Adella could not help her grin. Her friends, true to their word, were waiting nearby down the hall.

"So, beauty *and* brains," Blake flashed his perfect smile as she approached.

Adella was practically skipping, trying to contain her high. She blushed a little as she saw Blake's grin. "You guys," she began, "just a thought, but do people *not* do their homework around here or something?"

"Well, some do," Blake answered. "Mostly just the kids with pressure from their parents to have honors and high marks. But usually no. Most of us don't," he gave a carefree sigh of leisure.

"Oh don't paint it that way, Blake," Vivian scolded. "That's just you and Jason! A lot of us do our homework sometimes… kind of…"

Adella laughed. "So no one really takes their education seriously?"

"Ehh," Jason and Blake shrugged, walking backward through the corridor, facing the girls.

"You know, back where I am from, you are only as good as your education," Adella chided.

"Well, where we're from, you're only as good as your vaults of gold and surname," Jason countered smugly.

"Well aren't ya glad you aren't where *she's* from then, eh, Jase?" Blake playfully leered at his buddy. Jason punched his best friend in the arm, but Blake only laughed.

"Hey, Adella?" Vivian voiced over boy's snarky banter.

"Yes?"

"The Professor said he hadn't seen anyone in the lab all weekend."

Adella raised an arched eyebrow whilst looking at her blonde friend. Vivian continued. "If you didn't whip up those vials in there, where in the world did you?"

Adella only smiled and shrugged as they all continued to walk together down the hall.

# Fifteen

Through the next couple weeks, Adella found herself settling into a pattern of life at Royal High. The headmistress Von Durdenmyer seemed particularly keen to point out any and every flaw the girl possessed during her etiquette courses. Adella would often walk out of the room crushed, but, she vowed that she would *not* let the purple woman break her, because no matter what the headmistress would do, it paled in comparison to her encounters with Landin.

Landin constantly put Adella on the spot during his lectures, with a standout incident almost everyday that she had to endure. Landin was also the type of man obsessed with appearances, and Adella soon realized that he was notorious at the school for giving out "dress code" violations. He clearly enjoyed his self ordained crusade to enforce every handbook rule to the utmost letter of the law, finding any and every excuse to get kids written up. There were, of course, his *own* exceptions he made for the students that he favored; kids from the families that always donated to the school, or from households widely deemed to be powerful – especially when it came to their military, resources, and wealth. And, to no coincidence, the sons of many of these families were often key players of the combat team. Landin *loved* the combat team; he vicariously lived through their victories.

Luckily, Adella found renewed strength and encouragement in her other professors. Lady Rajilaa and Lady Jenson were kind to her if not mostly indifferent. Adella always had her homework done, and they greatly appreciated her involvement in the class time. Freelove's class was also a place where Adella felt welcome. During their class discussions, he would often ask her if she had any stories from North Brook that she could share which would correlate with the day's lesson. Many of her peers and friends got to know Adella well from these discussions, and Adella liked that she could help teach everyone about commoner life.

It was Bracke's period, however, that always seemed to be the highlight of Adella's day. No matter how bad of a berating she had received from Landin or Von Durdenmyer, it was his class that would brighten her spirits; and she quickly learned that Lenroe wasn't kidding when he talked about "the crazy." Professor Bracke was loud, hilarious, insane, sometimes terrifying, almost always kind, and easily Adella's most favorite teacher.

Following her "know-it-all" incident, Bracke's effort to extinguish the target on Adella's back had mostly worked. Many of Adella's classmates now came to her for guidance or help on the lab time assignments. Adella didn't mind, naturally, as she would always help anyone in need – it *was* partner time after all. As a result, the lab period saw her form tentative friendships with several royals who had initially never given her the time of day.

True to Dia's word, her *Lost Princess* novelty had begun to wear off. The attention bombshell that she had been on that first weekend had waned, especially following the official announcement from her grandmother and father. The pixierazzi had left her alone for the most part as she was now to be given the same regard and protection as her palace born peers. Still, the law could not keep all unwanted attention away, especially the attention of a certain boy; Brogan was a constant thorn in her side.

Vivian was head over heels for him, and Adella knew that in order to keep her friendship with the empress, then she could never act on her feelings for Brogan. This noble resolve was constantly put to the test, thought, as Brogan would often light-heartedly flirt and joke with her, giving her pangs of nostalgia for the past they shared; when Adella would later round a corner, she would witness him talking intimately with the Empress, or worse, talking a little *too* sweetly with *other* girls. The emotional whiplash was excruciating, and on a daily basis she found that she either wanted to kiss him, or punch him in the face. It was a vicious cycle.

Luckily, she had not dreamed of Brogan since the night of the dragon, and for this she was thankful. Not only was the vision far too painful and real, the words he had uttered, *don't trust me*, haunted her. When Brogan wasn't playing on her heart strings, drawing her into his spell like charms, she felt a strange sensation around him – the same sort of way that one feels when something sinister and unseen is watching from the shadows.

Sadly, Adella realized she would never be over him for good, and for this reason she loathed herself deeply.

"Hey Della!" Jason called out.

Adella was waiting outside her Wednesday morning arithmetic class when Jason and Blake approached her.

"Hey guys," she smiled as they flanked her sides, the three of them ready to go to their fourth sessions. They walked down the corridor to their destinations.

"Looking exquisite today, Adella," Blake winked. Adella blushed and looked down, a tendril of hair falling onto her jaw, her new teal and champagne gown flowing around her. "So, you slay that quiz in Jenson's class?" He queried.

"Eh, maybe. I feel decent about it," the girl beamed coyly as she tossed her cascading auburn hair over her shoulder.

"So modest," Blake laughed, his voice playful.

"I *do* have a question for the Princess," Jason began.

"Well, the *Princess* might have answer," Adella teased.

"Well," Jason paused uneasily, seeming to choose his words.

After a long enough silence, Adella prodded, "Yes?"

Blake sighed and cut in. "My mate Jason here was talking after combat yesterday, and he wants to know if Vivian is going to the Frost Waltz with anyone." He turned to Jason and uttered, "Now was that so hard?"

Jason rolled his eyes at his best friend's sarcastic add.

"Aw, is that what this is about?" Adella brightly smiled between the two.

"Yeahhh," Jason smirked back, rubbing his neck. A blush spread upon his tanned and freckled dusted cheeks.

"You like her," Adella stated.

"Is it obvious?" Jason asked nervously, wrinkling his nose.

"Well, I can tell, but I think that's only because we hangout so much. Don't worry, though. I love her, but Vivian's kind of *oblivious* to everything, so I think you're in the clear," she gave a light laugh. "On my end, I won't say a word, but you should definitely ask her! You two would be so awesome together!"

Adella was all for a development between Jason and Vivian. Even if Vivian was in love with Brogan, Adella couldn't shake her weird feelings about him, and she honestly wanted the best for her friend. Besides, as far as Adella knew, Brogan hadn't asked anyone to the ball just yet. And Jason was just as handsome and charming as Brogan, maybe if not more. He was fun, mischievous, and had a heart of gold. The more Adella thought about it, the more she knew that Jason and Vivian would be a great fit.

"You think she'd say yes?" Jason asked, his warm chestnut eyes alight with hope.

"I honestly think she would," the ocean princess nodded excitedly.

Jason seemed energized at Adella's encouragement. "Alright, I've got to ask her soon! Don't want anyone to beat me to it!" He laughed as he ran his fingers through his sandy blonde hair.

"It's still a bit away isn't it, though?" Adella asked.

"Yea, but people always ask early," Blake replied.

"Speaking of dates," Jason added, "have *you* been asked to the Frost Waltz yet, Del?"

"I," Adella suddenly thought back to the conversation she had had on her second night with Brogan. The poster in the hall came into her recollection with him nonchalantly suggesting that they should go together. *He's never brought it up again...* her thoughts chided hurtfully.

"Yeah?" Blake waited her response, his sapphire eyes bright.

"Oh, um, it's nothing. No, I am dateless thus far. Hopefully I won't be a wallflower when it comes around!" She laughed at her sad, little jest.

"Ohh I think that would be an impossibility, Del," Blake gave a nervous chuckle.

Adella blushed once more. "We'll see. I seemed to do a right job of scaring away the guys back in my old school," she sighed.

And to that comment, Jason and Blake laughed a good long measure, for it was the funniest joke that they had heard all day.

# Sixteen

Adella had just sat down for dinner in the hall, her friends laughing and feasting all around, when she spotted Vivian talking to Brogan in the shadows by the grand doors. She watched the two hug, and, in a single moment that made her stomach drop, Brogan swiftly kissed Vivian.

Adella's heart began to hammer as she watched him tenderly stroke Vivian's cheek and walk out from the hall. Vivian, her smile beyond bright, started for their table.

Adella's head snapped away, not wanting to be caught as a witness, and looked to her dining companions. All seemed oblivious to the split second exchange; everyone was still laughing at something stupid Blake had done. Adella ventured a glance back to Viv who was practically dancing over to the empty chair next to her.

"Well hello there, sunshine," Jason greeted the buoyant blonde. "Pray tell, what is the source of your happiness on this lovely evening?"

"I'll tell you later," Viv giggled as she took her seat. She then leaned over to Adella's ear. "Guesswhatguesswhatguesswhat?!" She ran her words together in an ecstatic, breathless whisper.

Adella only looked at her friend, afraid her trembling voice would betray her, and smiled a joyful grin, hoping she looked curious.

Viv drew close to whisper once more. "Brogan just asked me to the Frost Waltz! He kissed me!"

"That's so awesome!" Adella whispered back, feigning girlish glee.

"I know, right?" Vivian crooned, her cheeks pink.

"Actually, hold that thought," Adella stood up. She wasn't sure how much longer she was going to be able to keep herself together.

"Where are you going?" Vivian asked.

"I forgot my crystal upstairs," she barely choked out through her smile.

"Hey, you two, what's with all the whispers?" Blake accused, raising an eyebrow.

"You know, it's rude to tell secrets in front of other people. Chapter eleven, etiquette. Look it up," Jason added in his funny, smart-alec voice.

"Jason, you don't even read that book!" Kate laughed.

"Hey! I read!" He protested.

But Adella barely heard them all, for their voices had faded into the pounding roar of her heart in her ears. She didn't wait for Vivian's reply, slipping away out of the hall, her fluttering dress trailing behind.

The misty clouds magnified the last streaks of scarlet and gold in the western sky. Adella raced along the terrace, as fast as her legs would carry her, holding back the sobs. She was not strong enough to keep the tears from blinding her eyes, but she *would* keep them from brimming over for as long as she could. She did not know where she was going, but in her distraught state, she needed to get away.

She soon found the escape she was looking for – a winding stone stair leading out into the back end of the quad. Losing herself was better than dealing with all of the faces she didn't want to see.

She took the steps quickly, chills and shakes running down her spine, skin crawling, labored breaths, the unbearable urge to scream at the top of her lungs. Her tears over took her, racing for her chin. Her feet hit the bottom step and she broke into a sprint along on the stone paths, under the lantern lights, through the quad's outer buildings.

Her surroundings became unfamiliar.

Not a soul could be found.

She had no desire to stop.

A peculiar door, set under the awning of a mysterious curtilage, caught Adella's eye. She had been gone for awhile, though she knew not how long. She approached its entryway, lit only by a huge, rustic chandelier, suspended from the overhang, and reached out her hand to try the giant handles in the sturdy carved oak. Before her fingers touched the cold looking iron, she glanced to a weapons rack beside the door. It was set with many swords.

Her curiosity deepened upon further inspection of the weapons. The way the steel was cast, their overall aesthetic, was far too familiar. The blades were all blunt, though, something she did not immediately understand. She looked at the hilt of one of the swords and noticed her father's emblem.

"No way," she breathed, her eyes growing huge with shock.

She inspected the other swords and noticed his forge mark on all of them. For a second she forgot her grief and wondered when in the world her father had supplied Royal High with weapons!

Alas, seeing her father's swords caused a different wave of longing to flood her. She realized, more than anything, that she wanted her parents. Her legs felt weak, and she stumbled back into the wall of the building, sliding down the cold masonry, burying her head in her hands. The tulle of her gown enveloped her as she cried fresh tears.

For ages she stayed there, knees to her chest, alone with her thoughts. The sun had long set and the sky was indigo riddled through with silver.

"*I can't commit to anything right now… But I do want you in my life…*" Brogan's past words came to her, echoing in her mind like footsteps in a ruinous temple.

"I'm not good enough," Adella whispered to herself as she slowly raised her head. She uttered this statement as one who fervently realizes a deep truth. "Of course he would want Vivian… I was never good enough to begin with. *Peasant born,*" she choked a cry back. "And Vivian is *palace born*, and more worthy and more powerful and more beautiful and more… and more." Her huge, glassy eyes, reflecting the color of starlight, looked around her as she gnawed on her lip. She realized where she was; she had stumbled into the combat hall.

The words she just spoke began a churning in her soul.

The churning started to burn.

The burn of the will crushing grief became a raging inferno.

Without thinking, Adella grabbed one of her father's swords from the rack and stormed across the path, through the gate, and into an adjacent training field filled with practice targets.

"Yahhh!" She let out a cry as she let her sword strike the first one that she came within proximity of. She spun around and struck another target, and another, and another, as visions and flashbacks of every moment with Brogan filled her mind.

Adella turned quickly, rage burning inside, long locks flying around, as she leaped into the air to strike down hard on another dummy post.

"How could he?!" She gasped as she drove her fist through a suspended punching bag, making it shudder. She whirled around and sliced through another target, this time damaging it considerably, despite the blunt blade.

"Not good enough," she breathed through a sob as she spun and dealt a hard roundhouse kick to one of the largest dummies, leaving the entire pole to which it was bound, shaking.

"I wasn't good enough," another slice, taking chunks and splinters off a thick, wooden rod.

Whatever her steel, fist, or foot came in contact with, she let loose and didn't hold back. Four months of repressed emotion had finally come to a head. She should have listened to the warning from her the dream. She should have ruined him the moment she saw him again.

The rage began to recede, but not enough for it to leave completely. She started to feel numb. Utterly and hopelessly numb.

With a final effort, she shoved her sword into one last target, letting go with a hearty battle cry. It shook the post to its core, leaving it to knock back and forth.

She dropped to her knees and wrapped her arms around herself, hair blowing around, tears ceaselessly streaming.

"WHAT WAS THAT?!" A voice excitedly exclaimed.

"Shut up, dude," another one chided in. A muted punch was heard.

Adella's head snapped up and around. Jason and Blake were standing at the entrance to the training ground. When the two boys saw her tear streaked face, they immediately rushed over.

"Adella, what's wrong?" Blake asked as they made haste to aid her. He tenderly helped her up. "Did someone hurt you?"

"Whose ass are we kicking?" Jason added with a scowl.

"I don't think she'll need help in that department," Blake laughed a little.

"Truth," Jason allowed.

"It's nothing," Adella sniffled as she rubbed her nose.

Both guys scoffed. They did not buy this, obviously.

"That sure didn't look like nothing," Jason rebutted.

"Why are you so upset, my darling, fearsome lady?" Blake persisted as he wiped away the tears from Adella's cheeks.

She looked away, deliberating.

"Del," Blake said softly.

The way he said her name made her look back to him. "Did Viv tell you the news?" She whispered, voice trembling. She suddenly realized what this would mean for Jason, too. She braced herself.

"About her and Brogan?" Blake assumed sarcastically.

"Yes," Adella mouthed.

Jason's anger was evident in the harsh sigh that escaped his chest. Blake and Adella looked back to him, but he only shook his head. His eyes were closed and his jaw was clenched.

"I'm so sorry, Jase," Adella whispered.

He didn't make a noise, eyes remaining closed.

"She told us after you left," Blake looked back to Adella. "She seemed kind of hurt when you shot out of there. We asked her what was wrong when you bolted, but she wasn't sure. Said you forgot your crystal, but you never came back, so we went looking for you. Adella why are you upset about Brogan and Vivian? Are you *this* involved with Jason's love life?" He laughed a little, trying to lighten the mood.

"Shut up," Jason murmured bitterly, shooting him down.

Adella shook her head, biting her lip again.

"What this is about, then?" Blake paused as he looked her into her starlit eyes, searching for an answer. Adella was silent, but he suddenly understood. "You liked him, too." He meant it as a question, but it came out as a statement.

Adella nodded once. She took a deep breath, trying to steady her voice. "I... I know I should be happy for her – for Vivian. She has been nothing but wonderful to me since the moment I set foot in this place, but she has *no* idea the history that Brogan and I have had."

"Elaborate," Jason pleaded, breaking in. "I don't trust him at all."

Adella's eyes narrowed. "You shouldn't," she concurred coldly.

# Seventeen

"It was last year. Brogan wanted to go to a commoner high school, so North Brook, my hometown in Kelemer, was chosen to host him."

Adella, Blake, and Jason were sitting back in the courtyard against the wall where Adella had originally found the swords.

"Wait, are you saying you knew Brogan before you came here?" Jason asked skeptically.

"Yes," Adella curtly confirmed.

"Does he even remember you?" Blake ventured.

"Yes."

"But he acts like he doesn't?" Blake pushed, trying to understand.

"We dated for eight months. He's lying."

"What?!" Both boys chorused.

"How?! When?!" Jason demanded.

"Yeah, this wasn't in the news. I mean, not that it would be, I guess? I think I might remember hearing something about a country side sabbatical for the prince of Kelemer…" Blake added, trying to make sense of this.

"He wants to act like it never happened. He wouldn't have mentioned it," Adella shook her head.

"But it did happen," Jason ascertained. "He's just acting like you two never had history?"

Adella paused to collect her thoughts. "In keeping with The Accords, Pixierazzi were not allowed anywhere within the township. Hence no one having official record of my time with him. And he was only supposed to attend for the first semester of freshman year, then he was meant to go one of the royal academies."

"So he just got it in his head that he wanted to hang out with commoners?" Jason scoffed.

Adella's soft voice reminisced in the deepening night. "His mother had died a few years before, and his father had died the previous year. The Kelemer council thought Brogan was going off the deep end in his grieving process, but they decided to let him have his way. He wanted an escape from the royal bubble."

"Ahh, okay. I can see that." Jason nodded sympathetically.

"With the crown prince of the realm going to a commoner high school, he was naturally assimilated into the wannabe royal clique that's in North Brook," Adella explained.

"Yeah, the pathetic small town royalty you've told us about," Jason laughed arrogantly.

"No way are they on our level," Blake replied, mirroring his friend.

Adella continued. "I was hopelessly drawn to Brogan, but I didn't know how to talk to him. I could barely say hello. He was always kind to me, though, so when North Brook had their first school dance of the year, I got up the courage to ask him. I mean, what did I have to lose? Guys never took interest in me so I thought–"

"Wait a minute," Blake interrupted. "What do you mean *guys never took interest in you?*"

"Can I go on?" She raised an eyebrow.

Blake and Jason sighed, but nodded.

"And I mean, don't get me wrong, it wasn't like I didn't have friends at one point," Adella added, thinking aloud. "It's just, maybe, I guess I was never really worth taking note of."

"Never worth taking note of?!" An incredulous Blake broke in once more.

"Can I *finish*?" Adella smiled, wanting him to just hear her out for a moment.

Her audience sighed and waited.

"The day I was going to ask Brogan, this one girl named Brittney–"

"Oh, she's the fakey duchess, right?" Jason chuckled.

Adella nodded, amused that Jason actually remembered her stories from home. "Brittney heard that I wanted to ask him, and beat me to it before I could." She looked to Jason and gave a sorry smile.

"Go on," he replied sourly, the irony of missed opportunity not lost on him.

"So the night of the dance came, and I found myself low key heartbroken and dateless and–"

"Whoa, whoa, whoa… whoa…" Blake cut in again. "Del, just tell me this one thing, and then we'll shut up for good, but I am honestly so confused right now as to how in the *spell* does an absolutely gorgeous girl like yourself end up without a *date* for the *dance*?"

"Blake," Jason explained, "just look at her. She probably scared them all away."

"That's gotta be it," Blake shrugged. His tone was agreeable, making it seem as if this fact should have been obvious.

Adella laughed. "Why do you think I scared them all away?"

"Uh, because you're hot," Jason scoffed.

"And apparently dangerous," Blake winked.

"So, what you're saying is the reason why no one ever seemed to take interest in me, is because I *intimidated* them?" Her voice was heavy with skepticism. She had always thought herself annoying – not intimidating.

Jason and Blake shared a loaded look with each other, then looked back at Adella.

"Uh, probably, yeah," Blake responded. "I bet you had a ton of guys crushing on you. They were probably just too scared to talk to you."

"So why are *you* two talking to me then?" She arched her eyebrow as she posed her query. "You're not scared?"

"Never said that, sweetheart," Blake smiled nervously.

"Aside from the obvious codes of chivalry, we are of the rare breed that has decided that we are too mature to *not* talk to pretty girls," Jason laid it on thick with his suave voice.

Adella and Blake were quiet for a split second, and then the three of them burst out laughing.

"Now, I am sorry. We will stop interrupting," Blake amended. "Promise."

"Thank you," Adella smiled. "I went to the dance with my best friends Raena and Shmitty. The three of us had barely entered the auditorium when I saw Brittney and Brogan together on the dance floor. Brittney glanced at us and pulled him in closer, like she was trying to show off. I couldn't stand to see her stupid show so I went outside to get some fresh air. I do this thing where I don't always look where I am going when

I'm really preoccupied, and I ended up running full force into a transfigured faerie that was on the lighting guild for the dance."

"Oh crud, you must have been *covered* in fairy dust," Jason murmured.

"It was everywhere," Adella affirmed. "I finally got away outside and found a place to sit on the steps, but the door opened again behind me. I didn't bother to look over because I thought that Shmitty or Raena had followed me, but when the person didn't speak, I began to realize it wasn't either of them…"

"Hey, there. Are you – I mean, are you okay?'" He said.

Adella's heart skipped at the voice. The girl turned her head slightly to see Brogan standing near.

"Yeah, I'm fine. Just needed some air," she replied, trying to hide the lump in her throat, too scared to look him in the eyes. She didn't want him to see her in her glitter covered state.

"Oh," was all he managed to say, seeming uneasy himself.

It was quiet.

"Do you mind if I sit down, too?" He asked meekly. She looked up a little more and nodded shyly. He got down right by her and smiled. "So, you're Adella, right?'"

Shocked that he even remembered her name, she nodded once more, still not totally looking at him.

He continued to smile, "You know, I've seen you around a lot, but I don't think we have actually ever talked before."

"I think you're right," she responded, involuntarily looking at him.

"Oh wow, glitter girl," he whispered quietly in surprise, taking in her appearance.

She quickly looked away, feeling idiotic.

"No, no, it looks *beautiful*. Like you're made of starlight or something," he tried to explain.

She looked back and found him still smiling. She couldn't help but beam back in return.

"So," he began skeptically, "you're out here by yourself, and your date is still inside?" He nodded his head towards the door.

"I don't have a date," she replied sadly.

"You don't?" He asked with surprise. His brow then furrowed over his eyes, and he seemed upset. "But, I thought you went with your boyfriend, Shmitty?" He stopped, realizing that he had said too much. He tried to gloss over his reaction with an embarrassed smile, "I mean, you two are nice together. I thought he took you."

Adella giggled. She was amused at how nervous he seemed. This was the first time they had ever conversed, and she had never seen him so tangibly human.

"Shmitty isn't my boyfriend," she explained. "He's one of my best friends, but not my boyfriend. Where did you hear that he was?"

Brogan scoffed once and shook his head. "Brittney," he said flatly.

Adella cringed as she started to realize what that horrid girl had done.

"So, wait, why are *you* out here then?" Adella wanted to know why he wasn't still dancing with *Brittney*. As far as she was concerned, if he was out here, and the stuck up mean girl was still in there, then that *had* to be a good sign.

"Err," he paused, chagrin coming through, and spoke as if he was choosing his words carefully. "I don't think that the dance floor is quite big enough to hold Brittney's ego."

Adella's starlit eyes widened. She was elated at his admission. "Would you care to elaborate on that?" She asked coyly.

"In a nutshell?" He shook his head. "Some poor girl accidentally bumped into Brittney while she was dancing, and then Brittney proceeded to yell at her. She made quite the scene."

"You left Brittney in there?"

"I kindly explained," Brogan defended, "that I felt that I should go, seeing as how it appeared that Brittney needed a bigger dance floor. I apologized to the girl that she hurt and made sure that her friends took care of her. And then I went to find some air."

Adella was quiet for a moment as this sunk in. She started to smile. "And now you're out here?"

He nodded earnestly, his cerulean eyes warm and open.

Adella could hear the music from inside the auditorium change to an ethereal, mesmerizing melody.

Brogan noticed it, too. "Would you like to dance, Adella?"

Stunned, Adella nodded. He stood up and held out his hand, pulling her up close with ease. They started to turn slowly under the stars and moon, notes swelling upon the night air.

"Did you know I was out here?" She asked quietly as they revolved.

"I noticed you went towards this exit, so I followed my gut," he shrugged a little.

"You noticed me?" She asked, her heart soaring.

He smiled, completely entranced by Adella. "I've always noticed you–"

"Then why didn't *he* ask you to go to the dance then?!" Blake broke into Adella's reverie, desperate and angry, bringing her back into the present. "What. The. Spell?!"

"Dude, don't you get it? That Brittney chick lied to him the whole time. Brogan thought Adella was *with* Shmitty. Weren't you paying attention?" Jason explained as he punched his best friend in the arm.

"Sorry. Sorry. I'm still just hung up on that jester's-ass who is schmoozing with Vivian in the dining hall," Blake flippantly replied as he took a deep breath.

Jason's cheeks started to burn. He clenched his jaw.

"Hey, guys, calm down, okay? It's okay, just let me finish," Adella attempted to smooth things over.

"I'm sorry, but this just makes me even more angry with him," Blake explained apologetically.

"Even *more* angry?" Adella commented. She didn't understand why they seemed to share the same feelings of frustration as her. Yes, he just swooped in on Vivian, but there seemed to be something more on their side of things.

"Finish your story, Adella, and we'll explain our reasons after," Blake sighed.

It was quiet as both boys waited. Adella took a breath.

"Brogan asked me to be his girlfriend after that, and he decided to finish out both semesters in North Brook. He became my best friend... I thought it was true love."

"Whoa, really? You two got that *serious*?" Jason asked earnestly.

Adella nodded. "Like I had said earlier, Vivian has no idea the history him and I have had. It was very serious."

"But he's a crown prince Adella – I mean, not to diminish the fact that you're a crown princess now yourself, but, didn't he realize that he couldn't be with a commoner? He would have had to forgo his crown," Blake carefully questioned.

"His logic was that he was going to be the king, anyway, so he would make his own rules. He got to the point where he intended to finish out his remaining education in North Brook, much to the dismay of the high council."

"If you two were *so in love*, then why are you now... er, *not in love*? Obviously something happened," Blake spoke kind of nervously. He knew this part had to be a touchy subject.

Adella was quiet as she let her mind wander back to those memories.

It was the last day of Adella's freshman term in North Brook, and the whole school was gathering for one final rally. The positive energy of the student body was tangible. Thanks to Brogan, the school had seen a year of unity like never before. He had managed to make peace among every group, and everyone looked up to him. Because of this influence, as well as his key role in winning the championship for their combat team, he was to give the farewell speech before sending everyone off for Sun's Tide.

Out of the norm, Adella had not seen Brogan all morning, and as she filed into the auditorium with Raena and Shmitty, she noticed him standing near the stage in the shadows talking to Brittney. Brittney had become their class' royal representative, and although there was peace within the school, she was still a painful thorn for Adella when no one 'important' was looking. Adella was undeterred, though, because for the first time in a long, long time, she was truly happy with her life, and nothing could change that.

As Adella watched Brogan and Brittney interact, something didn't seem right. He winked at her, and she was all giggles as she touched his chest before going to take her seat. Adella's stomach turned upon seeing the exchange. A little thing like that shouldn't have bugged her, but it was the way he looked at Brittney that made her uneasy. For as long as she had been with him, he had never looked upon another girl like that.

Adella was on edge for the rest of the gathering, waiting anxiously for the rowdy teams and clubs to give their farewells, and for the goodbyes and the memories to end. All she wanted was for Brogan to say his speech so they could get out of there.

The Dean finished commemorating the graduating class, and then invited Brogan up to say a few words. The prince took the stage and the whole auditorium burst into roaring cheers.

Brogan started to speak in an effort to quell the bedlam. He smiled as if he was enjoying the attention. Adella felt strange once more, for she knew that this was not like him. He launched into his speech.

"This has been the most incredible year, getting to exist among all of you amazing people. You took me in as your own and I want to thank you!"

The cheers went crazy again. Brogan waited for it to die down to continue.

"Our combat team this year was excellent and I was honored to be your first freshman team captain. Championships you guys!" He beamed as he held up his fist.

The auditorium erupted with deafening applause and the combat team went insane with shouting, fist pumping, and whooping out crazy things and team innuendos in deep boyish voices.

One person stood up and hollered, hands cupped to his mouth, "It was all you, Bro! AWW YEAHHH!"

It was so intense, that Adella could have swore they were about to break into a riot.

"Sadly, sadly," he tried to quiet everyone. "Sadly, I shall be leaving for one of the Royal Academies next year," he barely finished the word as the whole auditorium gasped, stunned.

"What?" Adella choked out and grasped at Raena next to her. She was shocked as well, her mouth opened in silence while everyone else murmured.

"With my going to one of the Royal Academies in the Autumn's Tide, I now have something in common with the graduating class this year; I am going miss all of you so much in my absence. All of the friends I've made and the people I've gotten to know. You are all beyond amazing, but, if I am truly to rule our realm one day, I must be prepared for it, and I feel that this chapter in my life here at North Brook has ended. I will never forget all of what you have taught me and all that I have learned. Most importantly, I will not forget all of you. This was not a decision I made lightly but I feel it is the right choice. And don't let all of these memories end on a note of sadness, my friends – it is all of *you* that should be celebrated for it is all of *you* that make this school great! Let us celebrate for the Sun's Tide is upon us!"

The auditorium, despite its apparent sadness, cheered in a chorus at his final line. The combat team rushed the stage and put him on their shoulders, carrying him off.

Dumbfounded, Adella tugged Raena along and moved through the bustling crowd.

"Brogan!" Adella called in angry dismay over the chaos. "Brogan!"

He heard her and looked over his shoulder as the combat team set him down. People started to realize what this meant for the two of them, his going away, and many stopped to hear what Adella was about to say. Brittney emerged in that moment and stood by Brogan in the background. A scene in the fray was forming.

"Adella! What's up, sweetheart?" Brogan asked innocently.

"What-what's up?! What do you mean '*what's up?*'" She was so stunned she could barely get out the words. "You just said to everyone that you were going to the Royal Academies! You never told me this! You never told me any of this!"

"Listen, Del," he came up closer to her trying to calm her down.

Adella met his gaze, and fright rushed through her veins. His eyes were of someone she knew not; his eyes were cold and unwelcoming.

"Del, the small town high school thing, it's not working out," he stated.

"I... I don't understand?" She replied catatonically. "I thought... You said... You had said you–"

"Adella, you're *not* royalty. You can't keep living in my world. Yes, we had a few fun months, but I need to move on with my life. The only way I can do that is to go back to the world of royals. *Not* stay here in North Brook. It was fun, but let's be real, I'm the *crown prince* of this realm. You're just a peasant girl. For the better of the realm, I really should end up with someone of my own *kind*."

"Then you're a liar!" She burst out, tears streaming. The crowd around them had grown quiet, listening to their breakup. "Everything you said was a lie! You were my best friend!"

"Uhg, would you *stop*, Adella?!" Brogan cut her off. "You are *so* annoying!" He sighed heavily. "The only reason why I went out with you is because I felt *sorry* for you. Now, please, before you embarrass yourself any further."

Brittney stepped forward. "C'mon, Brogan," she chided as she slipped her arm through his.

"Goodbye, Adella. Have a good life," he turned and made his way through the crowds, Brittney on his arm, his entourage following behind.

Adella heard the murmurs running through the thinning crowds, but could only stand there, tears relentless and blinding, as everyone left her behind…

"If you'll excuse me," Blake jumped up and grabbed a sword from the wall.

"Wait, what? No, Blake!" Adella tried to lunge and grab for the prince, but he was quicker. Her hands grasped the air behind him, just barely missing his fluttering cape. "Jason! Grab him!"

"I'm gonna kill him!" Blake's anger surged as he ran through the grass for the nearest castle entrance.

"On it!" Jason got up, running at full force. "Dude!" He shouted.

"Oh no," Adella sighed as she held the bridge of her nose and closed her eyes.

"Oomph!" Was all she heard from across the yard followed by a muted thud.

"Dude, no!" Jason said as he held onto Blake's legs. Sounds of struggle were heard.

When Adella opened her eyes, Blake was face down on his stomach, sword still in hand in front of him. He was tackled to the ground by Jason who wasn't about to let go. Adella ran over.

"Let me go! I won't *really* kill him! Promise! I just want to maim an arm, a leg maybe – or some sort of appendage!" Blake begged desperately.

"No! You'll look like an instigator and you know that it's not the right thing to do," Jason tried to reason with his best friend.

Blake lifted his head and breathed out. "He's in there. Right now. With Vivian," he countered quietly, raising an eyebrow, yet not being able to turn around to see Jason's face. He knew his friend, though. He didn't even need to look.

"Let's get him," Jason let go, now furious himself, forgetting reason.

"Oh no you don't," Adella pushed both of them back down before they could get up fully. "Knock it off!" She put her hands on her hips. "You know this all has to remain a secret! If anyone knew I'd be ruined! No one can know. Please. *Please*," she pleaded.

The boys looked up into her eyes.

"Alright," Blake allowed, coming back to his senses, realizing he *might* have been rash.

Jason didn't speak.

"Jason?" Adella questioned. She wanted to make sure he wasn't going to try anything stupid. She gave a small smile. "You like Vivian, yes?"

"Always have," Jason smirked at her shyly.

"Well then, we gotta play this right if you're going to win her over from Brogan," Adella nodded impishly. "Actually," she realized, "you never told me why you hated him."

"Well," Blake looked back at Jason.

"He's taking Viv to the waltz," Jason elaborated, "but he's been playing hearts in this school since he arrived. And he doesn't even follow The Chivalric code. Plus, Vivian's different. You don't play a girl like Vivian." His mouth was hard.

Adella was thoroughly impressed by his devotion. He seemed like he truly would go to the ends of the earth for Viv. However, she had to ask, "The Chivalric Code?" She raised a brow.

"Yeah. It's in our Chivalry classes. One of the the codes is honor. When one of your friends likes a girl, you don't go behind his back and sweep that same girl off her feet. That's breaking the code," Jason explained.

Blake added, "If you break the code on accident, well, then it was an accident. But Brogan doesn't care and just goes after whoever he wants – even if they're already with someone. It's created more fights and drama here than all of last year put together – and we're only two months in!"

"Why have I not noticed any of this?" Adella shook her head. "I mean, I've seen him flirting with everyone, but I know nothing of–"

"Your nose is always in a book," Blake smirked, cutting her off. "And you're better off for it, trust me." He winked.

Adella blushed.

"It's unnerving that everyone still loves him despite how problematic he is," Jason clicked his tongue as he stood up.

"Why?" Adella asked.

"We have no clue. All our teammates think that he's some kind of '*combat god*'," he scoffed his reply.

"'*Combat god*'?" Adella asked skeptically.

"Yeah. That's the other reason why we can't stand him," Blake remarked.

"So, you're jealous of him because he's good at combat?" She ascertained.

"Oh, spell no. Not jealous," Jason added. "Yeah, he's an amazing fighter, but Blake and I can kick some serious arse here on our own thank you very much."

"Brogan cheats," Blake interjected. "Refs and coaches don't even see it. *We've* seen too much. He fights dirty, skirts the rules, lies. Why he does it is beyond me. He's a good fighter without having to do all of that." Jason held out his hand and Blake clasped it and rose to his feet.

"So, he plays girls, fights dirty, cheats," Adella murmured. "Why in the world doesn't the administration step in and have some words with him? Obviously he needs an intervention. He doesn't sound like the definition of a *true* royal at all."

Jason and Blake laughed out loud to this.

"Adella, love," Blake said sweetly and offered her his arm. She took it and they all started to walk back to the castle, each boy on either side of her. "You of all people should have realized by now that the administration here doesn't care. As long as you have the money and status to go here, you're as good as gold."

"So character means nothing?" Adella had an edge to her voice.

"They don't care about character," Jason added. "As long as you look good on the outside, look good on parchment, they're usually happy. Usually," he mused for a second. "Brogan's untouchable here."

"Looks to me that they just don't want to lose a star athlete of their combat team," Adella mumbled.

After her statement, no one responded. Her words left a mark of their own.

"Hmmm…" Blake's voice trailed in the silence.

"What?" Adella look up at him. He was looking over her head to Jason.

Jason was looking back at him in the same manner.

"Combat?" Blake mouthed to his best friend. They seemed to have a mental conversation.

"What?" Adella asked once more, impatiently.

"Adella do you know how the combat circuit works?" Blake inquired innocently.

"Yeah?" *Where is he going with this random question?*

"The basic rules for a match? Like, how do you win?" Jason added.

"The original rules for the games are ancient, and there's different variations." Adella replied, still confused.

"The rules the circuit usually plays by," Jason pressed.

"You have twenty minutes to either down all of your opponents or to make the allotted points. My father and I used to watch the professional circuits all the time," Adella was growing petulant. "Why do you ask?"

The two boys looked at each other, then back at her, both smiling a smile that was charming and impish in nature. Mischief gleamed in their bold sapphire and chestnut eyes.

# Eighteen

"This is not going to work."

The subtle moving of chainmail was heard from behind a thick velvet dressing room curtain.

"Yes, it will!" Blake assured. His voice sounded like it had been trying to convince her for hours. "Hurry, Del. Our detentions went over today and we're gonna be late."

"They're going to know!"

"Not if you fight the way you do!" Jason chided back.

"Just come out already," Blake pleaded.

There was a moment of silence. Finally, a sigh of surrender was heard and Adella emerged from behind the cloth wall. She was wearing leather brigandine vest on top of a long chainmail tunic. Leather pants hung off her waist while simple steel greaves adorned her legs and feet. Plate bracers and sturdy pauldrons completed the outfit.

"Wow," Blake and Jason murmured quietly.

Adella looked down at herself. "What?" She asked naively. Even through the disguise of men's armor, she still looked as radiant as if she was wearing the most beautiful ball gown. She looked up and quickly pieced together why they were speechless. "See!" She groaned. "They're *so* going to know!"

"No. No, they won't. You're going to be fine," Jason came over and put a hand on her shoulder.

She smiled a little. "I still think this is a ridiculously stupid idea."

"If by stupid, you mean brilliant, then yes, we agree," Jason laughed and Blake joined him.

Adella sighed, shaking her head in disbelief as to what she was about to attempt. "I don't know what to do about my hair, though," she pointed out. Her beautiful chestnut locks cascaded about her and down her back. She put her hand on her hips. "Come to think of it, the helmets you guys all wear don't cover much of the face."

The boys looked at each other and then back at her.

"Way ahead of you," Jason smirked.

Blake produced an artfully crafted plate helm – with a fully attached face covering.

"It's not quite like the ones we use, kinda ancient, and it's a little heavier, but I think it will do," he gave a rueful grin. "There's no way your pretty face could ever pass for a dude's, Del. So we swiped this thing off a suit of armor in a random hallway." Adella was about to protest, but he cut her off and continued. "Don't worry – we replaced it with a papier mâché helm that we found in the art room. No one will notice the difference."

"You mean Sadie's art project?" Adella dryly countered, raising an eyebrow.

"Ohhhh," the boys voiced in realization, noticing that they might have made a mistake.

"It's for a good cause," Jason shrugged it off.

Blake raised the metal helmet, poised to place it upon her head.

"Do you guys even realize that it wasn't even that good of a sculpture?!"

"No one's seemed to notice... yet," Blake laughed, thinking back to the way they couldn't really get it to set straight on the inanimate armored guard.

Trying as hard as she could to fight it, a huge smile spread across her face. She finally gave in.

"See, we got your back," Blake whispered. "Now, don't worry about paperwork. Being assistant manager, I handle a lot of the coach's affairs, so I'll make sure you're sorted, and no one will see it but me. That way, we'll put down your real name, so you don't get disqualified. You just get out there and kick some ass," he explained, drawing closer to her. He poised the helmet, and Adella twisted her hair up and hastily pinned it. He then placed the armor upon her head, concealing her true identity from the world; soft locks, sparkling eyes, and the rest of Adella's beauty, now hidden behind cold steel.

He stepped back and Adella could feel the new weight upon her shoulders. She was not used to wearing a helmet when she fought – and she wasn't particularly a fan of how impaired her vision now was – but it was definitely manageable.

"Well, how do I look?" She asked, slightly muted by the orb of steel encompassing her head.

"Short," Jason remarked curtly.

"Short," Blake agreed, "but you look like a guy." He smiled, satisfied.

"I'd better. My boobs are killing me," Adella mumbled to herself.

"What?!" Both boys leaned forward. Their eyes were huge, not quite understanding if what they thought they heard, was *really* what they just heard.

"Nothing, nothing. Come on, let's do this," she laughed to herself, thinking about how she had to bind her chest down.

"She's right, let's go," Jason nodded. "It's time for practice, *Arnie.*"

The boy's laughter echoed through the halls as they led their warrior princess out to see if they could pull off the scandal of the ages – one of which the royal academies had never seen before.

"Coach! Hey, Coach!" Blake called as he and Jason jogged over to the side lines. They were back in the combat training fields on the outer edges of the school, just across the way from the grand arena. The Grenvar Wood bordered nearby. The two boys stopped once they were standing in front of a tall middle aged man who was overlooking many of the athletes spar. He was sanguine in pallor, barrel chested, and sported a thick but short and neatly groomed salt and pepper mustache on his upper lip.

"Boys," the coach nodded in a gruff voice as they approached. He seemed to be chewing something.

"You, uh, wanted to see us, coach?" Jason asked shuffling to one side of the man. Blake took the other side.

"Yes, I did. So just who *is* that new kid over there? I saw you two come out onto the field with him." He nodded. The three of them glanced over to where a four on one spar was occurring. The coach watched as the new kid dominated the battle. His reflexes were lightning as he downed each guy one after another. The coach hadn't seen anyone fight like that in near twenty years.

"Oh, that's Arnie," Blake explained coolly. "You know, since our team is down, what is it now? Three? Four players? And with Henry's broken arm being the most recent in the injury count, we figured you could use another body, just for numbers sake."

Adella suddenly took a hit from a very large player. It was the first time she was seriously struck during the spar. The huge student had almost another foot on her own meager five foot, four inch height. Regardless of the blunt swords types the teams used, the blow hurt, but Adella recovered well, quickly rolling on the ground to avoid another strike, and then rebounded up to land a counter attack.

The coach grunted in thought as they watched, skeptical of the tiny new player. "He's a lil' small ain't he?"

"Hey," Jason placated, "Don't judge a book by it's cover."

The coach gave an daunting look towards the blonde boy and rumbled out, "What're you talkin' 'bout books for, you don't read!" He guffawed, his face turning red at the jest.

"Why does everyone say that?!" Jason asked in exasperation. The coach continued chuckling like he had just heard the best joke ever.

"Because it's true," Blake answered dryly, leaning behind the portly man to see his friend's face.

Jason rolled his eyes away from him and grimaced.

"Anyway, Coach, don't judge him by looks," Blake urged. "Just *see* how well he's doing." While Blake said this, Adella dodged a set up of attacks from two opponents. Her defense was impressive. "Not bad, huh?" Blake smirked. "We really could use him for the tournament this weekend."

The coach sighed and seemed to agree. He responded dutifully. "Well, get him over here. If he wants to join, I'm gonna have some words with him." He turned and barked out to the field, "ALRIGHT, GENTS! WATER BREAK!"

Jason and Blake nodded and ran into the dusty battlefield. The fighting stopped at the coach's call and everyone began to remove their helmets.

Adella's remained on her head.

"Man, where did you learn to fight like that?" One teammate asked, out of breath, as he took a gulp from a water skin.

"I don't remember there being an *Arnie* at this school," another voiced called out. There was an edge to its tone. Adella looked up to see Brogan stepping forward, removing his helmet. "What realm are you of again?"

Adella just shrugged, trying to avoid his inquisitive gaze, even though her helmet was all encompassing. She acted like she didn't hear the question.

"Yeah man, why didn't you try out at the beginning of the year? We could have used you the other weekend," a shaggy red headed boy added as he wiped his mouth on his sleeve and gave her back a sturdy clap. Adella had to hold back a cough. Even though she could fight, her frame was dainty underneath the armor. These boys were sturdy and tough. The clap easily took her breath away.

"Well we need him *now.* The tournament with Monarch is this weekend," a handsome student with deep skin and bright cunning eyes chimed in.

"Hey guys," Blake called out as he and Jason approached.

"Blake, man, where did you find this kid?" The redhead asked.

"Yeah, dude, take your helmet off. I need a face to a name," the first team mate spoke up again.

"Uhh, he can't do that at the moment–" Jason swooped in and grabbed Adella's shoulders, steering her towards the coach. "Kay, bye!"

"We'll be right back," Blake amended as the two hijacked the new wonder of the combat team, leaving their dumbfounded peers behind for the time being.

Adella wasn't entirely sure of what was going on, but trusted Jason and Blake to take care of things. Truth be told, the adrenaline that was coursing through her veins was exhilarating. She had never fought on a scale of that magnitude. The most opponents she ever took on was three to one and Shmitty wasn't nearly as strong as her father and Mr. Synclair. Her side throbbed from the hit she had taken earlier.

"You did *so* good," Blake murmured through her helmet as they made their way to the sidelines.

"And what exactly is all this going to prove anyway, Blake?" Adella whispered back.

He could not respond, though, because the coach was now within earshot.

"Here he is, Sir," Jason beamed as he halted her to a stop in front of the man.

"Arnie, huh?" The coach grunted. "Put 'er there." He held out his hand for a shake. Adella clasped it and heard her knuckles pop a little in the coach's vice of a grip. "Son take off that ridiculous helmet – looks like you're going to fall over."

"Uhh, uh," Jason stuttered.

"He can't exactly do that, Coach Peterson," Blake explained. "Arnie has… a… head problem…?"

"He's allergic to the sun – with lice," Jason squeezed in.

"And has a highly contagious case of headfungalitus–"

"In other words, it's best for the entire well being of the school if he keeps the helmet on," Jason whispered. "He's sensitive about it, so '*shhh*.'"

"It's why he was too shy to try out originally. He stays indoors mostly, wears hats, reads, sings… lovely singing voice. Lovely," Blake added in a whisper.

"Oh, uh, well," the coach voiced, now seeming to be nervous about his proximity to "Arnie." He looked at his hand that he used to shake with and nonchalantly wiped it on his pant leg as he cleared his throat. "Well, uh, what realm are you from, son?"

"He's from my realm, Rivenlaes. He's actually my third cousin, once removed on my… mother's side. Duke Arnold Kingsley," Jason covered quickly, eyes searching around for something to spur inspiration for a title, "Lord of–"

Blake looked at his best friend with an incredulous glance.

Jason spotted the water barrels used for the combat team – and their contents being distributed by the well endowed water maiden.

"Water… Chests," Jason smiled proudly.

Adella placed a hand on the back of her neck. A deep sigh from within the metal was only heard by Blake.

"*Duke Arnold Kingsley, Lord of Water Chests*?" The coach asked skeptically, furrowing his brow.

"It's why we don't share the same last name," Jason nodded his head, still smiling.

The coach was silent for a moment, looking at *Arnie*, sizing things up. He glanced back at Jason and Blake, two of his best combat players standing before him, then looked out onto the field to the rest of the athletes. It was true that they were down players, and he knew it. Henry, being the newest kid out for the season, was just insult to injury. A deep rumble of a sigh escaped the coach's chest.

"Arnold, huh? Well," he paused, and the corners of his mouth turned up, his eyes crinkling with the aged experience of a seasoned combat player. "Welcome to the team."

"Fantastic!" Blake chided. "I'll start his paperwork."

# Nineteen

"If you're just now joining us, welcome! Welcome all royals and country folk to the Young Royal Athletics semi-finals combat circuit!" A booming voice echoed over the sprawling Royal High stadium which was bustling with patrons. The sun was gleaming, the weather, unseasonably warm for the late Autumn's Tide, and the excitement that filled the atmosphere was catching.

"This is Steve Maguire of Vryndolne," the voice introduced over the faerie soundings set up throughout the arena.

"And I'm Bob Jones of Crown Vale. And we've been bringing you the play by plays for today's heart-stopping duels and battles between the royal academies Monarch High and Royal High." Two smartly dressed men who could pass for Lords were seen on a massive magic mirror that overlooked the stadium. They were live on site, covering the tournament from a private viewing box high above the crowds.

Transfigured uniformed faeries zipped to and fro running the media coverage for the arena. Some were mounted on hovering image recording orbs, while others concentrated on supplying the magic levels, making sure that the sound was coming through loud and clear.

"Also," Bob boomed out with a cheesy smile, "we'd like to remind everyone that this sporting event is catered by Mutton King. Remember, 'when you're running on nuttin, come grab our mutton!'"

Steve jumped in. "Also sponsored in part by Vryndolne's own William Knightly's Carriage Repair. They're the quickest fix for all your carriage related troubles – at the lowest cost!" He rushed through the last, fine print sounding sentence, "Squash based carriages cost additional fees and wait time."

"Also, Steve, don't forget to remind the folks that if they miss a moment of today's action, FSN2, the second Fairy Sports Network, will be doing a complete re-cap special tonight during Chapell's Prime Time highlights. Don't miss out! Now, back to the action!"

"That's right, Bob, and what an action filled tournament it has been. For those that are just tuning in, I wanna talk about the new comer Duke Arnold of Rivenlaes. With all of the bad luck and player injuries Royal High has endured over the last few weeks, this kid, out of nowhere, seems to be their savior!" Accompanying Steve's intro flashed playbacks of Adella, masquerading as *Arnie*. Clips from her best matches earlier that day had been stitched together as they danced across the mirror's surface. "It's the strangest thing, though, he has not removed his full plate helm since the beginning of the tournament. We have yet to get a good look at his face," Steve continued. The giant mirror then showed a close up of Arnie's head from the most recent fight, almost like it was trying to get a good look as to what was under the helmet. "What's he hiding?"

"Well, Steve, aside from his faceless gimmick, I gotta just point this out, his armor style is rather unorthodox. I mean, just chainmail and leather? As opposed to the classic breastplate armor style?" Bob gave a guffaw.

"I sure as heck wouldn't knock it, Bob, because he's currently the quickest thing out there. And with so little plate pieces on him, it is in his favor that he's hard to touch."

"Very true that."

"Mark my words, Bob, his career is for sure going to take off. It wouldn't surprise me if he is already being scouted to join the Professional Tournament Circuit when he comes of age."

"Oh, no doubt, Steve, no doubt!" Bob replied. "P.T.C. will definitely be taking an interest in him!"

"C'mon Del. Look at me. Look away from the screen. Block out their chatter," a ragged looking Jason interrupted, snapping Adella's trance and causing her to finally look away from Bob and Steve's fast talking commentary. Suddenly, the stadium went wild. Adella missed what it was. She looked back into the arena.

The majority of the patrons were all swathed in some deep shades of purple, like a moving sea of violet. Aside from the handful of royals already enrolled in the school, countless townsfolk had come straight out of Vryndolne and the surrounding provinces to show their support and spirit for their home team, Royal High.

The rivalry in the air was thick as the opposing team, Monarch High, from the across the world on the other continent of Nadromei, tried to show their presence through the raging purple masses. The players and their meager turn out of supporters sported orange, representing the hues of the regal butterfly for which their royal academy was named.

It was late afternoon, and everything had finally come down to the final match. Monarch had been giving Royal High a tough fight, always finishing each round just a couple points ahead of the home team. Things were almost tied up and the ultimate victory was anybody's game. Down on the sidelines, Adella was getting ready for the last fight.

"Look at me, Del. Listen," Jason murmured getting her to finally pay attention. "It's going to be fours, and they're sending out the that big guy, Charles, so be careful."

Adella nodded, trying to pay attention through the chaos of the announcers, the crowds, all of the distractions. Her head felt fuzzy. She wondered if she maybe had a concussion, or just some serious heat exhaustion. She did her best to suck it up and follow Jason's orders; to tune them all out and focus. She raised her plate visor a little, conscious that they were out of sight from everyone. She dabbed a towel on her forward and took a gulp of a water skin as she listened to Jason.

"We're down to the wire now," he continued. "This is the final fight and everyone that has been holding back will pull out all their final stops, their best moves. No one wants to run the clock on this. This is your first fours match and there's going to be a lot of action. You're going to be teaming up with Sean the senior, and Brogan," Jason somewhat snarled the last name. Adella rolled her eyes, lowered her towel, and put back down the visor.

Throughout the whole tournament, Brogan had been the biggest jackass on their team. Adella had only fought beside him in two other rounds, but they were the two worst rounds each of them had played. He constantly cut off his teammates for winning shots and showboated more than usual. Jason and Blake seemed to be the only guys who were not having a complete "bromance" with him; they were sick of his attitude.

"You'll have Blake with you, too, though, so don't worry," Jason added in.

"Got it. I'm good, I'm good," she replied through her all encompassing helm. She was covered in sweat, the armor was so hot. The gulps of water had helped a little, but she wished in vain for a breeze to caress her face. She had held up so far, but now, wrapping up the final round, all of the bumps, bruises, and darn near broken bones that she had incurred over the course of the tournament were really starting to wear on her.

"I know you're good," Jason winked at her confidently, echoing her words.

"Ready, *Arnie*?" Blake came up, excitement and adrenaline coursing through his chiseled body. He was decked out in Royal High's plate and chainmail, holding a shield and blunt tournament blade. He had been through several hard rounds himself that day, and his sweat matted down his dark hair. He looked handsome, if Adella was being honest with herself, but she refused to linger on the thought. He was her friend, her teammate.

"Yeah," the girl affirmed in her deepest, manliest voice. "Let's do it!"

This made Blake laugh out loud.

Brogan and Sean came up.

"Alright, ready to do this Blake? Arnie? Bro?" Sean crowed. Being that he was a senior, he was completely fired up, doing his best to absorb every last moment of his final year. He high-fived Blake, and then gave a hard slap to Adella's butt.

She jumped at the contact, but instantly gave off a deep and manly, "Yahhh!" in response. However, underneath her helm, she was bewildered. *Sean just slapped my butt.* Her eyes shot to Blake, and she saw his mouth holding a smug grin, seeming like he was dying from laughter within.

Brogan flashed an arrogant pose. "Let's do this."

"Let's go," Blake nodded. He raised up a fist, and the four of them began to walk out into the center of the arena.

The crowd's uproar was deafening to Adella. The four of them waved, greeting the spectators. She saw that the mirror was zoomed in on a shot of them. Blake looked up and winked to the audience. Several girlish cries were heard. Brogan blew a kiss and more girlish squeals followed. Adella decided to milk it, too, and pointed heroically back into the masses. A corresponding wave of cheers sounded. She smirked wildly under her helm.

"Aaand we're back from our break," Steve boomed. "Alright Bob, it looks like Royal High is ready to take on this last match of the day, and at this point, it's anybody's game! This, right here will determine who will move on in the circuit. This last battle is four versus four aaand... now it looks like Monarch High is on the field and ready as well. They are coming out, meeting in the center with the refs. Let's watch."

Even though Adella had been through this about half a dozen times this weekend, her heart still raced as she met each of these rounds. Monarch High's players were now a couple yards away from them. Adella quickly sized them up. Three out of the four guys in front of her she had already faced-off with at least once.

One of the kids, a junior named Andrew, had even met her twice in combat over the tournament. However, Charles, the one player out of the four that she had yet to fight against, also happened to be the biggest teenager that she had ever seen. Jason was right.

Charles must have been six and half feet tall, maybe inches more. His shoulder spans was easily double that of Adella's, however, the pauldrons he wore may have been adding to his  massive frame. He had a dull look, with an almost vacant, scowling stare lurking from underneath his half helm. His weapon of choice was a sword, the same size as the one Adella possessed, but in this student's massive hand the blade seemed dwarfed. The girl had heard tales of giants and trolls living out in the wild forests of distant nasty lands, and she felt as if she was seeing one up close in this moment. She reminded herself, though, that this kid wasn't a monster, and was probably a really nice person, for she had seen his good sportsmanship on the side lines across the way earlier. Regardless, meeting this player for battle made her feel as if she was facing something far more monstrous than just a student from a school of nobility.

Adella shook her head, clearing the doubt and sinister thoughts away. She found her focus and tried to recall what she could remember about this new foe. She had observed Charles fighting before in only two other rounds, and each time he wiped the floor with her teammates. His fighting style, when he wasn't swinging his sword like a lumbering brute, was to act as a brick wall and throw his weight around. Most of these boys could take a hit from him and probably walk away, but

Adella knew that this guy could accidentally kill her if she wasn't careful.

For the first time since the tournament started, she actually felt fear for her life.

All of the players lined up, chosen steel in hand, bowed in respect to their opponents, and set into their positions, ready for the referees to signal the start of the match. Shields and other arena approved weapons were set around the field, just on the off chance that someone might change their minds on their fighting style. The crowds began to settle as the head referee raised his hands.

"Alright gentleman. On your marks," the man instructed, magically projected voice echoing over the stadium. "Four versus four. First team to take down all opponents or reach forty points before the clock runs out, wins the round. On our signal." The officials began to back away, retreating to the sidelines.

Adella felt the sweat roll off the nape of her neck and temples.

*One more, Del. You can do this. Ignore the aches, ignore the pain.*

Moments seemed to slow down as she concentrated. She could hear the crowds roaring.

*It's just you...*

She looked into the arena, then back to her team.

*Your mates...*

The morale-leaders' uplifting, muffled chants sounded through the slowed stretching time. She could hear Vivian's distant voice among them.

*Your arena...*

Her heart pounding in her ears was accompanied by the far off hollers from her teammates at the side lines. The head referee lifted his hands once more as the hour stood still.

*Your sword...*

A bell tolled loudly, filling the arena with it's deep note, signalling to start.

Adella felt a fire surge inside of her as the true sense of time rushed back. The heat within propelled her forward to meet the battle head on. Everything instantly became crystal clear in her head.

"Arnie, I'll take him on the right!" Blake bellowed, pointing at the two guys heading straight for Adella. Brogan and Sean seemed to already be going in on the big guy.

The sudden crash of first steel meeting steel rang out over the dusty arena as the chaos of the four verses four match began.

"Yaaahhhh!" Adella sounded in her deepest cry as she repelled back the blade that met with her own. The opponent was Andrew, the one she had already fought against twice. Several times their steel clashed, each player setting up attacks to use.

After several sets, the Monarch student taunted, "You know, for a combat player," he huffed with exertion as he dove in to take a shot at her. Their blades met with a locked and fierce grind, face to face, "you fight like a bitch!" He spat with an evil smirk.

Adella's heart caught for a second, and she wasn't sure if he meant that he knew her secret, or if it was just an insult to get inside of *Arnie's* head.

"Thanks, I learned from watching you!" She instantly retorted, repelling him back with all her strength, never missing a beat. The girl's steel barraged him with lightning quick strikes. Her sharp comeback infuriated Andrew, but he could not keep up with her onslaught. Light on her feet, she practically danced around as she landed several solid hits. She snuck a glance at the mirror and saw the points for their side shoot up by four. "Yes!" she breathed.

Mere yards away, Blake and Sean were having a time with the mammoth Charles, whilst Brogan was perfectly happy to hold back the rest of Monarch High's team.

"Hey Blake," Brogan taunted over his shoulder as he fought. Sean was out of earshot.

"What?!" Blake seemed annoyed as he ducked away from Charles' lumbering blow.

"Looks like they love me more than you," he nodded at the mirror which was zoomed in on him and his battle. Brogan turned to an imaging orb and winked right before he heroically dodged a swinging mace, sending his fans into a frenzy. Vivian chanted his name from the sidelines where she was cheering with the Royal High morale-leaders.

"Ass! Just concentrate on the fight!" Blake spat out as he dove in to swipe at Charles. His frustration with Brogan was obvious.

"Already, Bob, Royal High is really taking the lead against Monarch here! Arnie's been quicker than we've ever seen him! And Prince Brogan's down there taking two to one! Wow!" Steve enthused. "Brogan sure has been carrying his team this season, and in this final fight here, we see exactly why!"

Adella did her best to block out the echoing commentary, but she could hear Brogan's haughty laugh nearby. "Screw this," she whispered as her internal fire fueled her. "YAHHH!" She cried out from her gut, having only one mind to finish off the Monarch player before her.

"Whoa!" Andrew yelled, not expecting the sudden rush. Try as he might, he could not hold onto his defense. "UHN!" He fell backwards as she parried his sword from his hand, remembering all that her father had taught her, and left her steel at his neck, his back flat on the dirt.

"And Monarch High's Lord Andrew Pendry of House Bydenvole had been dealt a finishing blow by Duke Arnold Fields of Rivenlaes!" The purple swathed fans gave a frenzied cheer. Adella looked to the stands and held up her fist triumphantly. "This now gives a total of ten points earned for Royal High by Arnie! The score is now Royal High twenty, Monarch High twenty-two."

"Arnie!" Blake happily crowed from across the field. "Get your ass over here!"

Adella nodded and took off at full speed to interrupt Brogan's little two on one show while the referees escorted a positively fuming Andrew off the field.

Suddenly a loud crack was heard and Adella's head shot to where Sean was. His left arm was close against his chest, pain obvious in his face, and the shield he once held was splintered into chunks about his feet. He didn't dodge out of the way in time from one of Charles' massive swings, and it landed directly on him.

"Hey! Bring your ugly face to my steel!" Blake commanded, trying to get the mountainous player's attention away from finishing off Sean, demanding to fight him one on one. It was of no use, though, as Charles took the opportunity to pin Sean to the ground, almost suffocating him, resting his sword upon Sean's head.

The refs sounded their signal.

"Oh wow, Steve, in a surprising turn of events, Royal High favorite, Lord Sean Cardiff, of House Cardiff, has been eliminated by Monarch High's Prince Charles of Morrowaith." Bob's bright grin faded as Sean and Charles' faces flashed by on the mega screen. A red "X" appeared by Sean's picture. "However, because of Sean's injury, it looks like the refs are giving Monarch a penalty for unnecessary roughness. Monarch has just had two points taken away from their score." The orange patrons protested and booed. "This now brings the score to Monarch High twenty, Royal High twenty!"

As Sean was taken off the field by the specialists from the school's infirmary, the players had a couple seconds of timeout to regroup.

"You doin' okay, Arnie?" Blake asked, out of breath.

Adella only nodded her head, too afraid to speak in such close proximity to Brogan.

"How sweet," Brogan chided flippantly. Thirty seconds were left on the clock before the round resumed.

"What?" Blake asked petulantly.

"Just wondering how you and your new spritely sized girlfriend were doing."

"What the spell? He's new, I'm just trying to make sure he's holding up okay!"

"You guys, we should regroup," Adella tried to interject in her huskiest voice.

"No, no, you know, I have been so sick of your crap, Brogan," Blake yelled, chest raising.

"Awe, you wanna pick a fight, Itherian? Go toe to toe against the unbroken king's blood line of Kelemer?" Brogan got into Blake's face.

"Dudes," Adella tried once more.

"Only if you throw the first punch," Blake challenged. "I'm no bully, but I'll finish it. Come at me, Bro."

The signal sounded for the round's resume. Adella wasted no time trying to deal with those two as she went right in for the players that Brogan had been fighting earlier. She knew that she could not go solo on Charles. Knowing how he had messed up Sean, who was wearing full plate, she knew that wearing this light armor, she would be dead. At all costs she had to stay away.

"Whoa, what is this here, Bob? Looks like Royal High is having a little bit of trouble in their own house! Prince Brogan and Prince Blake are having some heated words apparently, while Arnie has just picked up two swords and is running head long into battle!" Steve exclaimed.

"What a warrior! No fear right there!" Bob crowed.

*What are you, a coward? Take the big guy!* Her mind captiously questioned her. *No,* she answered back, *I want to* live. *I'm not taking him, at least, not without help...*

In that moment, Charles came up to Blake and Brogan and struck the dirt with the heavy mace that he had switched to. It was an invitation to fight.

"Bye," Brogan skittered off towards Adella's direction.

"What the?! You're leaving me with him?!" Blake shouted.

"Can't let our dear *Arnie* have all the glory now, can I?" Brogan called.

"Well if this isn't a sight, Steve. Duke Arnold is dual wielding blades! Every once in awhile some young champion with this amazing ability comes along and completely just blows us away. What a sight!"

"Look! The Royal High midget thinks he can dual wield! How cute!" One of the players from Monarch cackled at Adella.

"Careful with those or you'll poke your eye out!" The other one joined in as they circled round her. Adella's eyes darted back and forth, trying to see out from the cumbersome helm. She twirled her weapons with flair and poised her stance for an onslaught.

The first who spoke led the attack while his partner followed, arrogance in their movements, swords held high, ready to strike. Sparks from the metal meeting flew in flashes as Adella successfully parried them both off in mere moments, twirled around and sliced the first one in the back with her blades. If the weapons were sharp enough, they could have cut through the player's steel, surely gashing his back. As it was, she probably just inflicted a nasty bruise.

"AHHH!" The Monarch member cried out. "You little–"

Suddenly the brazen clash of steel meeting plate was heard, and it was a sound that Adella did not create.

Her head jerked to see that Brogan had caught up with her. Whether or not he wanted to work as a team remained to be seen. Adella could guess at the answer, though.

"Dual wielding, eh?" Brogan scoffed. "Isn't that trying a little hard?" He repelled back an advance effortlessly.

Adella fumed inside at his arrogance. She stepped backwards and instantly twirled her blades around her body with skilled flourish, metal gleaming in the sunlight. She heard the crowd respond to her show with applause and chants. "Arnie! Arnie!" They began to chorus. She stopped, body poised for attack in her controlled and still coil. She cocked her metal head as if to say, "I know what I am doing."

She then noticed that Blake had managed to bring Charles over into their vicinity which meant that the three remaining members on both sides were all truly fighting together.

"Whatever," she heard Brogan breathe as he began to fight on his own, trying to one up her.

"Well look at this. I cannot take my eyes away from these warriors, Steve. All together now, interchanging partners like true teamwork. This has got to be one of the best battles we've seen all season!"

"Did you see how Arnold is handling those blades, Bob? The crowds are still chanting his name! I've never seen a kid in this circuit so capable and confident as a dual wielder!"

"Oh, you've finally made it to this party, Blake," Brogan taunted.

"Fashionably late," Blake leaned away from Charles' swipe and then took his moment to hit. He had finally timed Charles' movements to the point of understanding when to hit, and when to avoid. He did not want to go out like Sean did. The well meaning senior tried to be recklessly heroic and ended up with a fractured arm.

"Arnie," Blake huffed out over his shoulder. "You could probably go," he began breathlessly, rolling out of harm's way, "at this guy... much faster than I am right now. Have a feeling," dodging a swipe, "that a quick guy would be *his* weakness."

Adella heard Blake's suggestion as she scored a point for Royal High by hitting her Monarch opponent in the shoulder. She began thinking of a way to act upon his hint.

Brogan suddenly careened wildly.

"I can't see! Dust!" He moaned as he swung his blade madly.

"There's barely anything in the air!" Adella called, confused.

"AHHHHHH!!!!!!" Blake's horrid cry pierced through arena.

"Blake," Adella breathed, her heart choking her, as she turned to look at him.

"UHHHHHHNNNN!! AHHH!!!" Blake buckled to the ground, barely missing one of Charles' lumbering strikes. He had managed to roll away from it in time, giving himself just enough space to assess what had occurred to him.

Brogan's uncontrolled swing had completely caught the side of Blake's left knee. Blake could feel the all the blood in his body rushing into his grievously injured joint. It felt like it wanted to explode.

"Oh, what's this here, Steve? The refs are calling another time out because it looks like there's been some friendly fire that just went down between Prince Brogan and Prince Blake of Royal High."

"Here," Brogan held out his hand to help Blake up with a seemingly sincere and gallant effort. Miraculously, whatever "dust" had afflicted his eyes was now gone. Blake reluctantly grasped the offered hand, and as he rose him up, Brogan's eyes locked coldly upon his supposed brethren. He whispered darkly, "first punch."

Blake inhaled sharply as rage consumed him. This was no accident. Brogan had intentionally injured him so he would opt out of the fight, or worse, be downed by another player. Then it would be just down to Brogan and "Arnie" to finish the competition.

A sudden sense of horror seized Blake, for he then thought of Brogan turning and hurting Adella in the same fashion. This panicked him more than the bone crunching pain radiating up from his wrecked patella.

Blake forced himself to fight through the pain as he resolved to protect her at all costs. He would not be forced from this match.

"Blake!" Adella called, almost forgetting to use her manly voice. She could not keep the keep the fear from it.

"Alright Bob, we now see the infirmary specialists coming out onto the field to check on Blake's injury to his left leg. The story that we're getting is that Prince Brogan had something in his eyes which panicked him to swing his weapon around wildly. Not the best strategy because as we all can see, this can injure the unintended! Luckily these kids play with blunt blades!"

Don't even want to think about if that sword had been sharp!"

"Are you okay?" One of specialists asked as he came closer to Blake.

"Yes, I'm fine." Blake gritted his teeth

"Are you sure?"

"Yes! I want to keep fighting!" Blake forcefully insisted.

The specialists looked to one another, and then back to Blake. "Don't do anything stupid. It's not worth it, kid."

"I'm staying." Blake's intense sapphire eyes bored into their wary glances.

"You come see us as soon as this is over." And with that the specialists made their way back to the sidelines and signaled the refs to continue. Thirty seconds were left on the time out clock.

"Blake," Adella spoke in her deepest manner, "Are you—"

"I'm good, Arnie. I'll keep with Charles, you just take out one of those remaining cave trolls, and then we do our thing." He gave her a knowing look. Adella could tell he was hiding his pain.

"*Your thing?*" Brogan scoffed. "Can't it wait until you reach the *bedroom*?" He laughed coldly.

Blake ignored him, and stared right at Arnie, even if he was only looking into metal plate. He knew that Adella could see his eyes.

Adella realized this was it. They were going to finish it.

The tournament bell sounded.

"Alright, Steve. It's down to the wire. Blake is opting to stay in, but no word on how traumatic his injury is. For all we know, the kid could be sporting a broken knee. Only time will tell. He just might be today's hero. And now the signal to resume has sounded. These players better wrap this up quick seeing as we only have but moments left on the clock!"

Blake's words on taking out just one more of the opposing players resounded in her head. *You got it, Blake,* she smiled to herself as all the remaining Monarch members went in on them at once. Holding nothing back, she imagined her blades as if they were extensions of her arms. She twirled in and around her foes, hitting them several times. Brogan tried to keep up, but Adella had become the player that Monarch was truly trying to defeat. In one fluid motion she had managed to score five points for Royal High, and, in another graceful turn, swept one of her opponents right off his feet, flat on his back, and held one of her blades to his throat.

The signal for a downed player sounded, but Adella gave no pause as her adrenaline pushed her to move on. Brogan's ego was completely into his own fight. He seemed to pay no heed to the newly downed player and he kept dueling with the other Monarch. Adella vaguely heard the announcers report on who she had just slayed, but she had no interest in the student's identity. The clock was coming down to a minute left, and she didn't want the round to end without downing every single one of the opposition. She wanted to finish this the old fashioned way. To her the scores didn't matter at this point.

"Blake!" She called. The horribly wounded prince ducked out from Charles, and turned to see Adella.

"Now!" He cried as he ran in her direction, steeling his body. Lucky for Blake, the fight had taken its toll on Charles as well, and he could barely chase after the hobbling prince.

With Blake's cue, Adella took off at full speed, dual blades in hand, sprinting as quick as she could for Blake's waiting arms. A crash course was imminent, and Charles was about to catch up to him. Blake then held down his hands at the last moment, catching Adella's steps, and propelled her backwards beyond himself like an airborne projectile.

Adella sailed through the air, swords held high, heart pounding and blood rushing in her ears. Time stood still as she registered the signal of a downed player, realizing that Brogan must have gotten the other Monarch kid.

"UUUuuuhhggg!!" Charles bellowed as Adella collided hard into his head and chest. Her legs wrapped around his body, throwing him off balance, bringing the giant down to the dirt on his back with an audible thud, creating a cloud of dust.

Her swords were crossed fiercely at his neck, legs straddling his chest, and she heard the signal for another downed player. A breeze blew through the arena, clearing away the dust. She could feel it through her long mahogany locks, caressing her overheated and soaked forehead and temples.

The frenzied, cheering patrons suddenly gasped in a simultaneous sound, and all across the arena, murmurs began to spread.

Up in the stands, where many of the faculty sat, a mesmerized Professor Bracke stood to his feet, clutching the balcony edge before him as he breathed in disbelief, "Gwen?"

A horrified Adella saw her helmet resting several feet away from her. Her ocean eyes flashed up to the crowds as she stood and stepped away from Charles. She clutched her weapons with white knuckles, and soot streaked across her breathtaking face. The winds blew her hair all about her as she turned to look around the arena for the first time; her vision finally unobstructed by the heavy metal helmet. Her gaze met with Vivian's across the way, whose own face held a look of shock and fear.

The silence that had grown over the crowd was poignant.

Brogan thought he won the round, but quickly realized that the stunned silence was not for him. He turned around to look behind him.

"Adella?" He mouthed.

"Lords, Ladies, gentlefolk, I'm not quite sure what we're seeing here, the officials are running onto the field, but it looks as if a young lady has been masquerading as *Arnie*, or rather, I don't even – what is *happening* here, Bob?"

"Steve, I'm getting a word, *Arnie*, is actually Princess Adella Everheart, the crown princess to the kingdom of Adamaris."

"As if we could forget The Lost Princess!" Steve realized. "She's caused quite a stir in the world of royals with her being discovered! Is this even allowed? A female on the combat field?"

"I don't know, Steve, I've never seen this before."

Blake glanced at Adella, held a positive thumbs up, and then grimaced. His knee was throbbing fiercely.

"Alright, what is this?" The head referee came out with his colleagues to talk to the players. "You aren't *Arnold*?" He surmised, taking in the beautiful petite girl before him.

"No. My name is Adella Everheart, crown princess of Adamaris," Adella stood up for herself as all the referees, Blake, and Brogan drew near. "And before you say anything, I want to let you know that nowhere in the rules of tournament combat does it say that a female cannot join in. I made the team. I can fight."

The officials were stunned. They looked to each other, and without another word, grouped up to deliberate amongst themselves for a moment. One of the referees had a huge and ancient looking book brought out to them.

"Blake," Adella finally breathed, "are you okay? What's going to happen?" She still hadn't dropped her weapons. She wasn't sure she could.

"You'll be okay. What we did is not against the rules," Blake assured her, ignoring her query about his state. "And if you do get in trouble, I'll take the fall," he gave her a painful smile.

"Blake, I–" Adella tried to speak.

"Adella," Brogan said in disbelief as he gazed upon her. It was all he could do to say her name. He looked at her like a man seeing the sun for the first time.

Adella met his eyes, her face stern and proud.

The lead referee turned to the crowds, raised up his hands, and began to speak. His voice magically projected out once more.

"We, on behalf of the official counsel of the Young Royal Athletics combat circuit, have decided, after a rigorous pouring over of the rules of these combat games, that in no place is it written that a woman should be barred from competition. With this knowledge in hand, we deem that the tournament is not void, will stand, and that the victory today belongs to Royal High!"

Before the official could even finish saying the rest of the school's name, the violet clad patrons jumped up and roared with mighty triumph.

All of Royal High's combat team rushed forward to Adella. Deafening cheers and elated hollers ensued as they raised her up on their shoulders while magical purple and gold confetti glitter flecks began to rain through the air. The masses shouted her name and the giant mirror zoomed in on her ecstatic and tear streaked face as she was carried around the field for a victory lap. The announcers rambled on about things that she could not make out in the bedlam. She knew that a lot of people were going to want to talk to her after this.

She looked over and saw Blake being carried off the field on a stretcher. Her heart yearned to go to him, to also see him on the shoulders of their companions. Today was his victory, too. She thought of what Brogan did to him.

She looked over and found Brogan on the sidelines bench, removing his armor. His marveling expression had vanished and set in its place was a brooding scowl.

She saw underneath her and realized that Jason was one of the shoulders that she was on.

"Jason!" She shouted.

"Yes, my Princess?!" He happily shouted up to her.

"Jason, take me to Blake!"

"You got it! I wanna see him, too!"

As Jason lead Adella's entourage to their injured friend, the girl couldn't help but think of the possible repercussions of her being the very first lady royal to enter the Young Royal Athletics combat circuit, especially with her being a crown princess. She shuddered to think of what the board, Vondurdenmeyer, and Landin would have to say. What would grandmother think? Or her parents?

*What a scandal I am truly becoming,* she thought with a wry smirk as her team carried her off.

# Twenty

"Are you feeling okay, Blake?" Adella had made her way through the grand Hang Hall of the castle to sit with the wounded prince. He had managed to wash up, change into some silken lounging clothes, and was comfortably situated on a soft sofa near the roaring fireplace. His injured leg was propped up with many tasseled pillows. He had a mug of hot tea on the table beside him. It was a much more intimate setting, here by the fire, away from the party that had been going for hours around them.

Even as the night began to deepen, the dancing, boisterous laughter, feasting, and merry making had not abated. The entire school was high from that day's victory.

"Yes, Adella, I'm fine, for the hundredth time," he replied with a slight laugh as she sat down near him. "How'd all your interviews go?" He gave a cheeky smirk.

Adella had endured endless pixierazzi interviews; anything having to do with the Young Royal Athletics Association was not covered by The Accords, and entry in the games meant that all involved could be subjected to media coverage.

Adella smiled shyly. "They went as well as anyone in my position could hope for. I kept as brief as possible but I'm sure grandmother is just livid. I haven't heard from her which worries me a little."

"Ah, she'll get over it. You're an anomaly to begin with, so might as well as go all out." Blake smiled. "I know you've wanted to blend in, but why should you? And, speaking of *not* blending in, you look really beautiful tonight." His sapphire eyes gleamed.

After visiting the infirmary for her battle damage, Adella had managed to clean herself up for the festivities, changing into a stunning violet, emerald, and gold dress that hugged her body and fell off her shoulders. Her hair fell down her back, a few soft braids among the long locks, and wavy curls framed her face.

"Thank you," Adella smiled, looking down at her hands, blushing. She wondered how much pain potion the infirmary had given him. He seemed a little *too* happy. She knew she had had quite a bit herself.

"So, thinking about today, something just dawned on me," Blake prompted.

"Yes?"

"Sean totally slapped your butt before we went out to the last battle. That literally almost killed me. Inside. I was dying. So hard," he cracked up and then winced from the pain in his ribs.

"You're the worst!" She playfully gave him a smack on the chest. She instantly realized what she did as he tensed a little more. She hit a bruise. "I'm sorry! Sorry!"

"No, no, I deserved it," he allowed, still snickering, rubbing his newly inflicted penance. "I almost hit it, too, out of habit, I just didn't have the same excuse that Sean did. You would have kicked my ass."

"You know I would have," she smirked arrogantly.

"You warrior princess, you," he leaned in a little, gazing intently into her eyes, challenging.

"Your knee, what did the infirmary say?" She changed the subject quickly, her heart racing. She sometimes couldn't stand it when Blake laid it on so thick.

"Luckily, there's no break. But it's really bad. It popped out of place," he leaned back again. "I'm not sure if I'll be able to play anymore games this season," he shook his head in disgust. "Brogan will pay for this."

"And you're sure he did it on purpose?"

"Del, he told me in the arena that this was his '*first punch*', whatever the spell that's supposed to mean."

"I'm so sorry, Blake," she lamented. "I don't know why but I feel like I could have prevented this but I just wish–"

"No. Don't you go blaming yourself, Del. This is between him and me. I may be down, but I'm not out. I'll be back before he knows what's hit him."

Before he could say anymore, Jason, Kate, Vivian, and Brogan came up to join the two of them.

"Blake's not gonna die, Adella!" Vivian jested.

"I know. I just needed a moment to breathe. It's been quite a day," Adella laughed. Pain flashed into her ribs; just one of the many injuries she had sustained from the weekend. She involuntarily glanced to Brogan. He looked upon her, all semblance of his earlier brooding gone. She suddenly felt very uneasy that he was among them.

"Well being *sick* in bed all weekend surely takes its toll," Vivian accused playfully. She leaned into Brogan as they all sat down together. He casually shifted so Vivian wasn't so close to him. Jason eyed them.

"Yeaahhh…" Adella's chagrin grew on her lips at the lie she had fed Vivian in order to disappear for the tournament.

"Adella I can't believe you had the guts to go out there like that!" Kate cut her off.

"Trust me, it wasn't all my idea," Adella raised an eyebrow and looked to Jason and Blake.

Both boys were grinning ear to ear. Blake especially so.

"Where did you learn to fight like that? Do all the peasants where you come from fight like you, too?" Kate's questions came out in a rush.

Adella was amused at the sweet girl's enthusiasm. "No, Katie, they all don't fight like me. I…" She looked to Brogan for a second. He knew her story. *At least, he used to. Unless he's forgotten this, too,* her thoughts bitterly gnawed.

Brogan looked puzzled, waiting to hear her next sentence.

Adella continued. "I mean, most peasant girls don't take to the sword. If they do, it's because they are either self taught, or they've had people in their lives who actually cared enough to teach them."

"Well you sure as spell weren't self taught. You fight in the royal style," Blake remarked.

"No peasant we've ever seen fights like you," Jason added.

"Well that's because my father trained me. Everything you've seen from me, I've learned from him," Adella offered a smile.

"But why?" Vivian seemed perplexed. "I've been told most commoner women don't fight. Why would your father want you to hold a sword?"

Adella paused to choose her next words carefully. The blazing fire crackled behind them all. "Bandits attacked my village when I was a young girl. I had a little brother."

"*Had*?" Vivian echoed. A sudden sadness fell over the group as that word sunk in. Everyone realized what Adella was saying.

"My village was torched," Adella's eyes grew glassy. "And in the morning we found my brother's little cape, but not him." Her voice broke, but she found the strength to keep her tears at bay. Brogan was one of the only people she had ever talked about this with; they had bonded deeply over their family losses when he was in North Brook. Yet he seemed as if he was hearing the tale for the first time. His face was surprised and seemingly full of remorse. "So," she straightened up, smoothed out her skirt, pushed away the betrayed feeling from her heart, and cleared her voice. "My father, nobility born and royally trained as he was, vowed that his daughter would never meet such a fate."

"Adella," Vivian grabbed Adella's hand while Blake placed a gentle palm upon her bare shoulder. His hand was warm against her exposed skin.

"Convenient enough," Adella tried to change the subject, smiling away the tears, "my father has lived his peasant life as a weapon's smith. So I've had no shortage of training. Lucky for you boys this weekend."

"So, in other words, don't piss you off?" Jason laughed.

The six of them drifted into other conversations, but the undertone of Adella's heavy explanation still hung in the air. Of their small group, not one of them had ever felt the loss of losing a sibling. Try as they might to be empathetic, no one could truly relate.

The ringing and tinkling chime of a crystal ball began to sound. Adella looked down and realized it was hers that was going off.

"I'll be right back, guys," she excused herself as she stood up and searched for a much quieter place; the chilled night air on the veranda that connected to the hall proved to be the perfect spot.

The girl placed her hand over the magical glass and the ball expanded to fit inside her palm. She touched the surface and a face manifested within the orb's cloudy reaches.

"Hi, daddy," Adella sheepishly greeted. She knew this was coming.

"Adella," her father's stern voice sounded.

"Uh, what brings you to call at this late hour? I was just about to go to bed."

"Adella, it's half past nine," he countered, his face serious.

"Oh, uh, you know me, I like to turn in early–"

"Adella, we saw the tournament."

The girl sighed deeply. She looked above as she leaned against the balcony. There were no stars out tonight and a looming cloud cover seemed to ghost across the sky. "I figured as much. Took you long enough to call me."

"I figured we'd give you your space today. What are things like right now?"

"What do you mean?"

"Your friends, the administration? I know your school is probably having a party right now. They always do after a win. The media is in a frenzy over you. The Accords don't protect against this. Have you been completely ostracized by your peers? The admin?"

"Dad," Adella laughed, placating him. "I'm okay. Really. The admin hasn't said anything to me yet and everyone thinks I'm pretty darn cool right now. Warrior Princess is what they've started to call me."

"No."

"What?"

"No. You cannot fight on the team, Del. No. Too dangerous."

"But dad–"

"Adella, I taught you how to fight to *protect* yourself, not to go and put yourself in danger! You are a crown princess and you need to act like it."

Adella scoffed at this. "You're sounding an awful lot like Cassandra right now, dad," she replied petulantly. "I thought you'd at least be proud of how well I fought."

Her father stopped. "I'm sorry. I don't mean to sound like her. And you fought better than I've ever seen you. It's just," he exhaled heavily. "One, you are my little girl. My child, Adella. The *only* one we have left."

Pain flashed through Adella's chest. Tonight was becoming painful with how much that part of the past was being brought up.

"Dad, I... I'm sorry."

He shook his head and continued. "Two, you are a princess, Adella. A lady. As it is you have had a lot stacked against you going into this. Fighting on the boy's team like you did, regardless of the circuit's ruling – the royal circles will not look favorably on you for this."

"Reminds me of what Vondurdur always says," Adella sighed. Then, in her best Vonderdenmyer impression, she warbled out, "Image is ev'rything."

Her father laughed. "That old bat is still there after all these years. I mean, I usually had to deal more with Landin," he shuddered. "But Vondurdur made my skin crawl. I've never been able look at peacocks the same!" He chuckled some more.

"I like how you used her nickname, dad."

"Princess, *my class* invented that name."

Adella giggled.

Aedrian continued, "Regardless, the administration *will* pull you in for this. Do you know what you're going to say for yourself? Because I think you already know that they don't want you there."

All Adella took from that was that no one wanted her at Royal High. "But lots of other people do, dad! Most of the teachers love me, and I have made so many friends! Even people that judged me at first are coming around!"

"And it's wonderful that you have that support, Adella, but when people don't understand something different, they often fear, even abhor it. The Royal High administration has been set in their ways for a long, long time. You can't blame us for being worried."

"I know, dad. I know. But the way I see it, as long as I can win over the hearts of my people, who cares if I follow protocol?"

He was quiet for a moment and then spoke softly. "Adamaris loves you already."

Adella stopped at this. "They do?"

"Your grandmother was really unpopular after my banishment. The kingdom's been crumbling. Now, having relocated back to the palace here, being among our people again, your name is on everyone's lips. Your discovery was a miracle for them. Being peasant born made you relatable. And now, with your reveal at the tournament today, they are calling you their warrior princess, too."

"So then what's the big deal? So the admin despises me? Adamaris loves me, and at least I'm finally just being me."

Aedrian shook his head a little. "And you have no idea how overjoyed I am to hear that. But your grandmother is appalled."

"She's always appalled," Adella rolled her eyes.

"Adella, you are loved, yes, but you need to take the world of royals seriously. You now live in it, and you will have to be around other royalty for the rest of your life. You must know the customs. And right now, it is extremely controversial for you to fight on the combat team."

Adella sighed. She knew he was right. "What does mom think of this whole thing? Of my fighting?"

"Exactly what I'm telling you. We're on the same page," he stated firmly.

"How is she doing by the way?"

"You almost gave her a heart attack."

"I'm sorry," Adella breathed again, truly feeling awful for putting her parents through undue stress. "But, I meant, how is she adjusting? To the palace? I haven't talked to you guys for ages. I've just been so busy."

"We could have called as well, love. Like I said, we wanted to let you have your space. And your mom is holding up," he added. "You know she is now

Duchess Olynia of the Adamaris court. She's learning all the protocol for palace life, just like you are."

"Wow. So she's going to go by her birth name?"

"Yes. We feel it's best. Olynia is who she was before we went into hiding. And the people know me as Aedrian, not Orrick. I knew the name of Aedrian for half my life. It feels right for both of us to take them in this place. We don't have to hide anymore."

Adella was quiet. "It's so weird to think of mom among all of this. In the royal world, now."

"Your mother has much grace, Adella. It suits her, like it does you," Aedrian pointed out.

"And grandmother is warming to this?" Adella pondered.

"Let's just say that she has been overly kind. She knows she's done a lot of damage. And that right there has actually been the biggest shock for your mother," Aedrian laughed a little. "She's gone from knowing that Cassandra despised her for all these years, to suddenly having to accept the instant change of heart. She is taking to it the best she can, but it's overwhelming. You really should call your mom when you get a moment. You two would have a lot to talk about."

"I will. I promise," Adella nodded fervently. A different thought suddenly came to mind. "Wait, so what's going to happen to the smithy back home?"

"Thing are quiet for now, but ultimately we are all planning to relocate together. Sir William misses Adamaris. We'll most likely close the smithy in North Brook. He thinks we can open one up in Adamaris."

"Wait, Shmitty will be leaving North Brook? To be in Adamaris?" Adella tried to comprehend what her father was telling her.

"Most likely."

"But what about Raena?" Adella suddenly felt guilty. *Raena is going to be all alone.*

"I'm not sure, Della," Aedrian replied. "But we must do what is best for our family, and Shmitty and Sir William have been family to us since the beginning. We need to stay together in Adamaris. We've packed up many of your things, by the way. I hope that's okay."

As her father said all this, it finally began to hit Adella that she really would never live in her old home again. North Brook was truly gone for her. "Yeah, dad. That's fine. It's a lot of old junk anyways." She paused awkwardly.

Aedrian sensed her hesitation.

"Adella, I just want you to know, that yours and your mother's safety are priority. With you being revealed, the Syndicate will know who we are. We can't live in North Brook anymore. We will need the protection offered here. And, as your parent, although I can never take the throne, I can still be part of the court. Trust me, you'll want me around with just how treacherous the royal world can be."

"I know, dad. Thank you. I do need you behind me on this," she gratefully whispered.

"Always, Dellabell," Aedrian smiled wistfully.

"I'm happy you're back with our people," Adella added.

"Oh, you're calling them *our* people now?" He smirked, secretly elated at Adella's word choice. "Yeah, well, I can't believe I am admitting this, but I am actually glad to be home, too. The ocean is in our blood, Adella. I can't wait for you to see it all here, where you come from, our lineage. Get out to experience Ardenthel for the first time."

"I can't wait, dad," Adella beamed. "I hope I'm good enough for it all," she whispered, uncertainty plaguing her tone.

"Adella, you are just entirely something else, and I don't think anyone quite knows what to make of you. But I also see this as a strength. You will find that line between being a royal and staying true to yourself."

Adella nodded, meditating on his words. She suddenly felt a drop on her cheek, and looked up to the sky. The wispy clouds had grown thick. The smell of rain lingered in the air. She needed to get back inside.

Adella stared back at her father in the glass orb. "Then I am going to fight on the team, dad." It was not a request.

"No, you're not," he sighed.

"Yes. I am doing this. Besides, they need me."

"This isn't up for discussion."

"You *just* said to be true to myself. This is part of who I am. You *taught* me," Adella stood her ground.

Aedrian scowled and opened his mouth to reply, only to be cut off by Vivian.

"Adella!! There you are!" She trilled loudly through the veranda as she approached, golden blonde hair bouncing all around. "By The Radiance is that your dad?!" She squealed as she saw Aedrian's face in the orb. "Hi there, Prince Everheart!!" She beamed as she waved into the crystal.

Aedrian gave a hearty laugh. "Oh you make me sound so young, Empress!"

"Well you *are* back to being a prince now, are you not? That's what I heard from my parents! Or do you just want me to call you Mister Everheart? Or Mister Adella's Dad??" Vivian ran through her words, still giggling.

Aedrian continued to laugh with her. "Word travels fast I see. I should have known your family would fill you in."

Vivian nodded, grinning.

Aedrian continued, "My title will actually be Duke, but you may address me as whatever you wish, my dear. Adella has told us so much about you already!"

"Aww! Well she talks about you guys all the time," Vivian's smile was contagious and Adella had picked it up.

"Hey Viv?" Adella murmured.

"Yeah?"

"I'll be right in okay?"

"Okay, but hurry! We wanna start a round of Sailor's Dice!"

"Count me in," Adella nodded.

Vivian turned and grinned into the glass ball. "Good night, Duke Everheart!"

"Good night, Empress Thelred," Aedrian replied politely.

And with that, Vivian bounded her way back inside.

"Boy, isn't she a ray of sunshine," Aedrian chuckled.

"Tell me about it. She's oblivious sometimes, but I love her to pieces." Adella shook her head.

"Alliances aside, the Thelreds are good people. She's a good girl to be friends with."

"I think so, too." Another raindrop hit Adella's nose. She looked up. "I had better get going, daddy."

Droplets began to patter lightly, and Adella could smell the water mixing with the dry ground. A breeze was beginning to pick up, rustling the fallen Autumn's Tide leaves. She turned to make her way back into the warm castle.

"The rain picking up?" Aedrian assumed.

"Yeah, I'm gonna turn in."

"By turn in, you mean go have some fun?" He raised a playful eyebrow.

"Something like that," Adella's nose crinkled with a mischievous grin.

"Good night, princess."

"Good night, daddy."

"I love you."

"I love you, too."

The black translucent shadows streaked across the barren landscape as they reached out their sinister claws for her running form. They barely grazed her dark hair being blown about her by the raging storm. With a foreign gleaming blade in hand, Adella tried to slice through these dark things that crossed her path. She could not see these creatures fully – only their ebony essence gave them away. Many of them seemed to have wings.

An earthquake shook her to the core and she pushed herself to move forward. Thunder rumbled and churning clouds loomed overhead. She was here for a reason. There was some purpose as to why this battle had found her.

She looked down to see that her gown had been replaced with armor. The soot marred shining plate and chainmail fit her perfectly, sleek on her body's curves. The armor easily moved with her, was made for her. Never before had she seen a more beautiful and artfully crafted set of plate. It felt like magic on her form.

Lightning crackled again as it danced around an erupting volcano in the distance. The terrifying titan spewed forth scarlet magma and ash over the scarred and grey landscape. Rivers of its rage flowed into the dead lands.

The shadowy creatures continued their onslaught as they loomed all around, swiping, diving, shrieking. Gleaming, ghost like warriors suddenly manifested from the crackled hard ground, rising up to face the darkness. Adella realized that she was not alone in this war. These warriors of light were somehow on her side, although they were just as nebulous and translucent as the dark shadows she had tried to fend off.

A need to press onward permeated her thoughts. What was she trying to find? Where was she supposed to go? Why?

Her searching gaze then fell upon *him*.

Cerulean eyes gleaming like the brightest sky, lean and muscular body adorned in the shining plate armor of Kelemer kings, and a sword in hand was held high above his tousled, dark mahogany hair.

*Brogan!* Her mouth formed his name, but her voice emitted no sound. *Brogan!* She tried again. The fire within her consumed her every sense as she realized that he was the reason this battle had found her – and she had to reach him at all costs. Slicing through a winged shade before it could ensnare her, she began to melee her way through to him.

She watched as he fought with all the skill and elegance that she had always remembered. He was fast and true in his movements, and it seemed as if nothing could touch him. He turned around and his gaze met hers.

"Adella!" His voice rang out like a faint shimmer. He seemed surprised, almost elated, to behold her. His face became frantic as he, too, fought to meet her.

Thunder roared and lightning flashed again as the volcano shook the world. Magma rained down nearby. It was as if the darkness was trying to do everything in its power to keep the two apart, but the shimmering, formless warriors, did all they could to aid the prince and princess.

Adella was drawing closer, and called out again. *Brogan!* Her voice barely audible, but he seemed to hear her call.

"Adella, I'm coming for you! Hang on!" He cried out, battling back the darkness. There was a golden aura coming forth from his very being. Brogan was physically shining, and it was the most beautiful thing she had ever seen.

The remaining distance was diminishing, they were so close now, and Adella felt the burning in her heart as she thrashed around wildly, sweat pouring down her temples, giving everything she had. She felt the dark creatures surrounding her.

There was no warning, no time to react, as a translucent claw came from behind Brogan, breaking through his armor, emerging out from his chest. The gargantuan shadow in back of him loomed over his body. Adella watched in horror as Brogan clutched his breast, slumping, sword falling from his fingers.

"Adella help me!" He breathed as the monsters began to ravage him. His pleading, piercing gaze never broke from hers as the darkness devoured his body.

"I'm coming! Brogan!" Adella tried to scream as her tears torrented down her face, almost blinding her.

"Help! Adella, help!" He cried out again, his voice becoming shimmery and distant once more. He reached for her.

"Brogan!!" Adella leaped, thrust her hands out, and dropped her sword as she lunged for him.

Lightning and thunder bellowed.

"AHHH!!" She shrieked as her hands and knees hit the stone ground. A chill wind drafted over her skin, and the darkness of the place she now found herself in was disorienting. There was little light, save for the faint golden glow of something above her.

She looked up and saw the illuminated painting of the Champions of Old.

Lightning crackled again as she felt a large hand upon her shoulder.

"Ahhh!!!" She cried out, trying to get away, startled, distraught.

"Adella, Adella," Bracke whispered, trying to calm her. "Adella!"

She looked around, frenzied, cheeks soaked with tears. He had a gentle grasp on her shoulders and was kneeling with her.

"Professor?" She croaked out softly, full lips trembling.

"Aye, princess," he quietly replied. She could barely make out his rough, weathered face in the darkness. He began to help her up. She could hardly find her stance, feet searching through the waves of her periwinkle nightgown for the ground.

The sky lit up again and the thunder rolled throughout the castle. It made her recoil for support on Bracke's arms. "'Hey, it's alright, lil' princess," the kindly teacher soothed in his thick brogue. He looked at her and then glanced past to the painting. He spoke his next words slowly. "What happened lil' one?" He looked back to her.

Adella gazed at him through the shadows. "I... I think I was dreaming," she whispered.

Bracke studied her face, choosing his reply carefully. "You were wanderin' the halls, thrashing about, when I found you. You stopped here," he nodded at the artwork.

The girl looked behind her and upon the very scene she had just found herself in. It was like she had been in the painting itself. "I dreamed this," she blurted out, still feeling adrift and out of it.

Bracke kept an even face. "You dreamed of The Guardians?"

Adella just stared at him, tears still flowing. The wind was howling fiercely outside of the castle. She looked behind once more to the painting. She left Bracke's steady arms, and walked slowly, drawn to the ancient artwork. She placed a hand upon it's gilded frame, mesmerized by the battle within. Somewhere in the palace, the hour began to chime. They were still until the notes finished. Three in the morning.

Adella finally turned back to see the professor. His brow was held in a cautious furrow. She had never seen him so concerned. He slowly offered his arm. "Let's get you back to bed, Princess. You've had a long day."

Wordless and drained, Adella nodded, and grasped his thick forearm.

As he lead her along back to her quarters, she could not erase the images that plagued her mind. Brogan, the battle, the dark creatures, the ghostly warriors. Bracke had called them *guardians*, not champions.
*Guardians...* her mind echoed.

Sooner than she could understand, they arrived at her room's double doors. She had no recollection of how they had got there so quickly. Bracke gingerly let her go, and looked her in the eyes once more.

"Will you be okay? Do you need to wake Vivian? Should I bring up some tea?"

"No. I'll be... I'll be fine." Adella tried to convince herself of those words more than she was trying to convince the Professor.

Bracke eyed her. He finally sighed. The night had worn him out as well. "Get some sleep, princess. I'll see you in the morning." He bowed.

Adella gave him a wry smile, and opened the door. "Good night, Professor Bracke," she whispered as she watched him walk back down the hall. It dawned on her that he was wearing a thick plaid robe and slippers. He had been wandering the halls at night, too.

She closed the door, padded back to her silken sheets, and slipped into their cold threads. The rain was softer, and the winds had calmed for the moment. Vivian's deep breaths were a welcome sound.

*Help me, Adella... Help...* her psyche echoed Brogan's terrifying plea once more.

"How?" She whispered desperately as she turned over.

Tears threatened.

Her mind went black.

# Twenty-One

Adella had not caught *too* much strain from the administration regarding her entry into the combat tournament. True to Blake's word, he had handled all the paperwork for her enrollment. For some reason, no one noticed Adella's name and information on the forms he had submitted. And there were no rules against fighting under a pseudonym, as some fighters in the professional circuit had done so in the past. She technically did not break a single rule by way of the Young Royal Athletics Association's standards; regarding her protocol as a princess of Royal High, however, was a different matter.

Von Durdenmyer and Landin were naturally livid as they all held a meeting with The Dean, Lord Welford, but Coach Peterson was on Adella's side, even claiming to them that he knew her secret all along. He had absolutely come around to the idea of a girl on his team, and felt that there should be an allowance for it. In his eyes, if you could fight, then you could play – and Adella was too good to let go at this point in the season. After many snide remarks and some feisty deliberation, The Dean eventually ruled that Adella would be allowed to remain on the team, but only if she did so under her real name. He feared the wrath of public opinion, and public opinion was that The Lost Princess was now a much beloved *warrior* princess. She had gained so much popularity with commoners *and* royals alike, that his hands were tied.

Adella had won her first real battle at Royal High, on *and* off the field.

It was Friday afternoon, almost a week after the tournament, and Adella, Jason, Blake, Vivian and Kate had made the decision to spend the rest of the day in the city. The weather was unseasonably balmy for the late Autumn's Tide, and combat did not have practice that afternoon as all the teachers had a meeting with the board. Being in the city seemed the perfect way to kick off the weekend.

Vivian had also invited Brogan, much to Adella's dismay; Adella knew that the more physical distance she put between herself and Brogan, the better. He had apologized to Adella for the way he had treated her during the tournament, and had been overtly trying to win her over since. Adella just wanted him to leave her alone. It was bad enough that she was dreaming about him.

Luckily, and much to her relief, Brogan had different errands to run that afternoon, and promised to meet up with them later that night. Dia was throwing her own party in honor of the combat team's victory from the previous weekend, and their group was expected to attend.

Adella looked out of their topless carriage at all the towering, sparkling spires, her heart filled with wonder. Their luxury transport clattered along the downtown Vryndolne streets. "Where are we going exactly?" She asked her friends, her ocean eyes alight. Their carriage pulled over to stop on a curb in front of a large, sparkling fountain.

"Anywhere we like," Blake smirked flirtatiously as he gallantly hopped out of the open air carriage.

"There's a door, you know," Vivian called, rolling her eyes, while one of the drivers opened it for them.

Jason followed his friend's lead and hopped out, too. The boys scrambled to assist in helping the girls out of the mobile, remembering their chivalry codes.

As Adella stepped out, she made sure to graciously thank each one of the servants that were with them. Adella's palace born friends had become so used to her typical faux paux of thanking the help that they had started to do it, too. It *did* seem polite after all.

The five teens set off together to find whatever adventures awaited them in the plaza, and after a couple of food indulgences and shopping purchases, they soon found themselves sitting along a secluded fountain wall, enjoying the final hours of the Autumn Tide's sunlight.

Vivian looked up from her crystal ball. "We'd best get back you guys. Dia's party starts soon," she reminded. She had just gotten Dia's crystal scrawl asking if she was bringing Jason and Blake.

"Uhg, her dumb party tonight," Jason moaned.

"Can we not? We celebrated last weekend, and she's only doing this for attention, " Blake grimaced.

Jason added, "Vivian, I don't even know why you cater to her. Two-faced, attention grabbing girls like that–"

"Jase," Vivian rose a hand, cutting him off before he finished the thought, "you *know* that as the Empress of this realm, I have to hold to a higher standard of geniality. Which means socializing with people like Dia."

Jason, Blake, and Kate stared blankly at her.

"She's *new* this year, and she *can* be nice sometimes," Vivian tried to reason, but to no avail.

Adella was silent. Having been a solid member of their group the last few weeks, Adella quickly pieced together that Dia's "warning" had been incredibly fake. It was easy to see that she thrived off of attention and stirring up dramatics. Quite honestly, Adella felt incredibly uneasy around the Princess of Desevry. There was something sinister hiding below her sweet and sour personality, but Adella could never pinpoint it.

Whilst her friends continued debating on whether or not they were going, something caught Adella's eye. She got up from her spot, surprisingly unnoticed, and sauntered over to a poster stuck on a pillar of the plaza.

"I'm just saying that you shouldn't have to play nice with people like her. She's all drama," Blake's remark came into earshot as she returned.

"So, I'm hearing it's an almost unanimous no on Dia's gathering?" Adella broke in. She held up the poster that she had taken down. "You all want to go to a *real* party?" She impishly smiled.

The tattered and mysterious looking parchment was an advertisement for the Nether Dusk Faire, a festival run by the roaming caravan of Nether Dusk fey.

"A carnival?" Jason seemed surprised.

"Have you ever been to a carnival?" Adella asked in a hushed, almost reverent tone. "A Nether Dusk Faire carnival?"

Jason replied, "Well, the school throws a carnival every spring but–"

"But it kind of sucks," Blake cut him off. He looked at Adella, eyes mirroring the girl's impish expression. "I've always wanted to go to one of *those*." He nodded to the poster.

"You guys, we can't," Kate chimed in. "We have to be back before nightfall. We don't have permission to be out that late."

"C'mon Katie, you don't really want to hit up Dia's party, do you?" Blake grilled.

"Well no, but–"

"Let's do it." Vivian stood up.

The group stared at her, startled by her change of mind.

"I'm sick of following rules. Dia's party will probably be nothing but drama, whether or not we show. And... I have *always* wanted to go to the Nether Dusk Faire," the empress' voice was dreamy. "Growing up in this city, I remembered seeing the posters every year. I always begged my parents to go, but I was never allowed."

Kate asked, "Have you ever been, Adella?"

"I have. They actually made it out to southern Kelemer once a year. I used to go all the time as a child, but..." she paused. "Well, it's been a long time myself."

"Well, what are we waiting for?" Jason jumped up.

The five royals looked to each other, excitement building, and they began to make plans on how to sneak back into the school after curfew. With Jason and Blake's know-how on getting around the establishment unnoticed after dark, things seemed foolproof, until Adella noticed one thing.

"Actually, you guys, we can't go," she said. They looked to her, disappointment touching their eyes.

Before they could ask why, she explained, *"Not wearing these clothes."* She motioned to their gorgeous gowns and shining capes, her lips curving into a cunning, sparkling smile.

Fire shot through several feet of space from the performer's pertly skilled mouth as giddy patron applause followed. Hovering lights, manifested by the work of the fey, glittered and illuminated the dark forest clearing. Lively ethereal music and drums floated upon the crisp, Autumn Tide's twilight air, while five cloaked figures slipped into the scene.

With peasant blouses, ruddy skirts, bodices, cotton britches, flowing maiden hair let down and boyish hair rumpled, Adella had effectively turned her royal friends into a bunch of commoner teens, out for a night of enchanting good times and adventure.

Worn yellow, purple, and green tents, flags, and stands were all around, manned by fey and human alike, all offering their services of fun and folly. Silly game stands, marvelous foreign foods, tastes and smells, future tellers, mysterious harlequin masks, costumed performers, laughter, dancing, intermittent fireworks, wooden rides powered by human muscle and fey magic – the Nether Dusk Faire was sensory overload for the sheltered royals. Even Adella couldn't remember it being so exhilarating. Their adrenaline ran high from shirking all responsibility, breaking the rules of curfew, escaping palace life, and parading around like peasants in a place that was considered forbidden.

Jason suddenly pulled Vivian into the line to ride the great wooden wheel. Kate decided she would rather stay behind on the ground – heights freaked her out. Adella offered to stay with her, but she assured them to go on, and that she would be perfectly happy to make flower wreaths with the fey children. Blake paired with Adella on the ride as the seats were only built for two.

Aside from Adella, this was the first time any of them had rode such a contraption. The two couples loaded on, and Kate waved them off with an excited smile, as the operator gave a shout, and the wheel began to turn. Suddenly, the kids were lifting off, far above the ground. Adella heard Vivian above and behind squeal with delight. Up the wheel rose, above the tops of the trees, allowing them full view of the faire and the not so distant spire tops of Vryndolne. The wheel paused to let more patrons on at the bottom, leaving them at the top for a moment.

"Amazing," Blake breathed, perfect smile flashing in the crystalline moonlight. His sapphire eyes gleamed as the two were rather taken with the view. The night sky was so perfectly clear, and they were so high up, that they could see The Scar in the northern sky. Adella shivered as an icy wind blew through her. She pulled her cloak a little tighter, letting her cascading auburn hair fall about her for extra warmth.

"Here," Blake broke into a smile as he put an arm about her, bringing her closer, rubbing her hands.

"Thank you," she breathed, her lips curving upward as well.

"It's the least I could do, *Princess*," he nudged playfully. She nudged him back.

Being so close, she could smell Blake's cologne radiating from his body heat. It was a comforting scent, cool and deep. A warmth she could not describe started to spread through her chest and into her cheeks. She was grateful for such an amazing friend like Blake.

The wheel started up and quickly lurched forward, beginning it's rotation faster this time. Adella let out a giggle and Blake gave a shout as they rapidly descended their position on the churning wheel. This happened for many more rotations, lights and colors going by in a blur, each trip giving all four kids an indescribable thrill.

All too soon, the wheel began to slow, signaling the riders' end. Vivian and Jason were let off, and then it was Adella and Blake's turn to unload. Breathless, dizzy in step, trying to regain grounded composure, they made their way back over to Kate who was laughing and twirling around with several faerie children. Some were half fey, others full blooded. Some had glittering wings, while others were transfigured, sitting upon her shoulders.

"I think they like me," Kate giggled as her friends approached. She presented Adella and Vivian with flower wreaths, much like the one she was now wearing. "They showed me how to make them!" She beamed. The girls set the wreaths upon their heads, smiling.

Fanfare began and a lively drum sounded as faire goers began to flock to the center of the grounds.

"What is happening?" Vivian murmured.

"I think I know," Adella grinned as she grabbed the empress by the hand and led them all to the source of the excitement.

Everyone in the grassy faire center began to twirl and move in rhythmic patterns with each other. The driving, drumlin beat in combination with the quick strings was almost hypnotic, as patron and faire runner alike converged in dance.

Transfigured little fey flitted above, some dancing in circles with a partner, others creating scintillating light anomalies with their near constant trails of faerie dust. As the magic cascaded around them, it felt as if the stars had come down from the heavens to dance among the revelry.

There was an energy around unlike any of them had seen or felt before.

"C'mon!" Adella laughed as she grabbed Blake and fell into step with the middle of the dance. None of the palace born kids knew the peasant dance to begin with, but after a few minutes of copying those around them, they picked right up and kept along with the driving beat of the dancers.

Weaving in and out of patrons, musical hands clapping in time, Adella knew how the dance went by heart. So many unfamiliar faces, alight with mirth, blurred past as she changed partners effortlessly over and over again.

The music picked up pace, faster, more driven. Blake found Adella again as everyone coupled up and the heat of the notes sparked a passion to dance like never before. Twirling round and around in Blake's grasp, the music's urgent beat increased tempo yet again. His knee wasn't completely healed, but he didn't let that stop him from dancing with the girl who had stolen his heart.

Blake picked her up and spun around with her in his arms. Adella let out a squeal of delight, hands clasped firmly around his neck, as their intense twirl seemed never to end. The relentless beat became frantic as Blake flipped her over, and twirled her round and about. They danced all the steps they could, as quickly as their feet would muster. He spun her about again, then back into his chest and dipped her – right as the music abruptly ended.

The crowds broke into uproarious applause and many gypsies and patrons whistled for an encore. Adella soon realized that they not only meant an encore for more music, but an encore of her dance with Blake as well! Apparently the two had quite taken center stage and many a fey started leering playfully "give her a kiss!"

Blake looked to Adella who could barely catch her breath through her laughter. He paused for a moment, looking intently into her eyes, and, realizing he still had her in a dip, brought her up slowly. He then took her hand, sweetly kissing it, never breaking away from her gaze.

Adella's smile was uncontrollable.

Everyone cheered for the innocent gesture.

A muscular fey, tall and tattooed, dressed in marvelous pantelone garb, rose up and let his booming voice cry out, "Five minutes until showtime!"

Adella had seen him striding throughout the grounds as he was distinct and hard to miss. She had guessed him to be the owner of the operation.

His call boomed again, "Five minutes until the miraculous and talented, mysterious, and unexplainable wonders in the world of the Nether Dusk fey are revealed–"

ROOOOAAAARRRRRRRRRR!!!!!!!!!!!!

The ground trembled, tents collapsed, and trees seemed to spontaneously combust, as a gale of wind accompanied the deafening roar.

Adella's spine prickled, the blood in her veins grew cold, and she looked to the heavens.

There, in all of its monstrous glory, was a scarlet and black dragon, raining hell and torment down from the sky. Time seemed to slow down. This drake looked exactly like the very same one that she thought she had hallucinated on her first night in Royal High. *This isn't real, this isn't real,* she chanted to herself.

"Adella watch out!" Blake cried as the beam of a tent began to crash down. The prince instantly dove for her, not a hair's breadth to spare, and pushed her to safety.

A second ear shattering roar sent patrons scrambling for cover. The dragon looped around again, continuing its aerial attack, leaving a path of flame.

"What the spell?!" Jason spat out as he had both Kate and Vivian under his arms, ducking for cover where Blake had Adella. The five of them found themselves hiding behind a random tent near the center of the faire. The event was in mass pandemonium as fires blazed around them.

"What is that thing?!" Vivian cried.

"A dragon!" Adella replied.

Without warning, several crackling explosions rocketed into starbursts as the flames had found their way to a stash of grounded fireworks. The kids all scattered, trying to avoid the shrapnel.

"We have to get out of here!" Blake screamed over the bedlam, eyes frantically scanning for an escape. "We need to get back through the forest to the carriage! The trees are dark enough to give us cover!"

As he said this, a score of full sized fey rose into the sky. Their bodies glowed brightly as they shot bolts of vibrant, magical energy from their hands to the beast. The drake let loose an angry bellow. The fey responded with taunts and battle cries and cheers.

"Yeah!" Jason crowed for the fighters.

Adella remembered the old tales her father used to tell her. Faeries and dragons were the fiercest of enemies. Dragons were weakened by faerie magic, and the different clans of fey used their special gifts to help the world fight them back into the darkness. There were even some humans, gifted powers by The Radiance, who could fight like the faeries did. Paladins is what her father had called them. As Adella marveled at the magical force rising up to meet this aphotic foe, in her heart she wished that she could be powerful enough to help them fight, too.

On the ground, the other faire runners were doing their best to put out the fires. The pantelone faerie directed the evacuation efforts, trying to save the lives of all who attended and worked in his caravan.

The aerial fighting continued above as the dragon moaned and fumed a fireball back at its opposition. Some of the fey seemed to naturally repel the flames with a sort of invisible force around them, though the attack did manage to scorch several warriors, causing them to career into the ground.

"No!" Adella cried.

Without thinking, she broke free of Blake's hold on her.

"Adella, no!" Blake tried to grasp her back, but it was to no avail, as the girl was already running into the clearing to help the fallen fey. Blake tripped in his attempt to follow. His knee was still injured from the combat tournament, and he couldn't run like she did. Simultaneously, Kate's cloak caught fire from floating embers. The royals worked frantically to put her out.

"Are you hurt?" Adella asked as she helped the fallen fey to his feet. His once bright faire attire was singed and tarnished with soot. On the shoulder and down the arm of his glittering skin, a burn was forming.

"I'm fine, but you should be escaping! It's not safe!" He choked out as he shook his head.

"Adella!" Blake's voice called. He was limping as fast as he could to her. Jason and the girls were in tow. "Adella what the spell?"

The hurt fey jutted back up into the battle as Blake reached her.

"I just wanted to help," Adella felt tears prick her eyes.

"Adella we *can't* fight this! This is insanity, we need to move!" Blake tried to reason with her.

The drake reared up high into the air and bellowed a deep, new sound, and it gnawed painfully at Adella's soul.

It was calling something.

Suddenly, Vivian screamed, and the kids turned to see her face to face with a looming, shadowy entity, translucent yet dark. It reached for her.

Instantly, Adella grabbed her friend and pulled her away before the dark thing could swipe at her. The teens distanced themselves from the new foe, looking for safety.

The dragon sounded out deeply, the same haunting call, once more.

The terrified screams of escaping patrons pierced the night as countless more shades began to manifest from nothingness all over the settlement. The unsheathing of blades rang through the bedlam as the clan of the Nether Dusk Faire brought forth their swords to meet these new servants of darkness.

*The drake is summoning them*, Adella realized. Suddenly, her mind flashed back to the dream she had had of Brogan. These shadows were just like the terrible, aphotic things she had fought, like the ones in the painting of The Champions of Old.

The dragon began a new circle around the faire, avoiding the faeries that tried to attack, and fumed down another inferno upon the trees surrounding them all.

"Where do we go?" Vivian cried.

"Jason, how do we get out of here?" Blake desperately questioned.

Adella's eyes frantically scanned around her. The faire was littered around with these dark shadows, making escape anywhere near impossible. The teens had nothing to defend themselves. Adella then noticed that the weapons of the Netherdusk clan seemed effective against the dark entities. They cut through them with a smoking hiss.

"Stay here!" Adella called out, making a sudden break for a sword she saw lying nearby in the grass. As the daughter of a master weaponsmith, she knew that most faerie blades possessed a special magic.

"Adella!" Blake hollered in vain.

The brave ocean princess ran as hard as her legs could carry her, and slid into the ground, grasping the hilt of the weapon. She rolled with her own momentum and missed the swiping arm of a newly appeared shadow. Her form bounded back up and she lunged toward the entity, sword poised, and pierced it deeply. It let out an otherworldly shriek, thick black smoke going up from its wispy, corporeal essence.

Adella flashed a grin, and finished off the monster with one sweeping arc of her weapon. The creature hissed a phrase in a dreadful foreign tongue, inky plumes evaporating, and collapsed upon itself, disappearing back into the oblivion from whence it came. Adella whipped around and started back for her friends, now confident that she could clear a path for them with her newly acquired blade, only to find them vanished from the spot she had left them.

"Oh no, oh no," she breathed, heart hammering, eyes searching the blazing tents and chaos. "No, no where did they–"

"Adella!" A familiar voice called to her.

Her heart stopped to see *Brogan* running to her from across the burning faire.

"Brogan what are you doing here?!" She sputtered, still gripping her blade.

"Explanations later, are you hurt, my princess?" He looked into her eyes with an intense worry that could pierce a hole straight through to her soul.

Another stomach curling roar echoed as the dragon came back around for another attack. A fey careened to the ground near them.

"You two! Find cover now!" The warrior commanded when he landed. "Follow that path," he pointed to a way out that Adella hadn't noticed. A portion of the clearing glowed blue as a few remaining patrons ran through. It was a tunnel of protective magic giving way to a part of the forest that had not been touched by the inferno or the shades.

"But my friends!" Adella tried to protest.

"Is she with you?" The fey nodded to Brogan.

"Yes!" He affirmed.

"Then get her out of here!" And with that, the muscular warrior shot back into the sky to rejoin the fight.

"Adella, we need to go," Brogan urged, curling an arm around her waist.

"No, but our friends are here!" Her head whipped around, trying to locate them.

She then saw Blake running as quickly as his knee would let him.

"Adella what were you thinking!?" Blake shouted as he got to her, only to stop his words when he realized Brogan was there. "*Brogan*?" He huffed out, utterly bewildered.

Brogan began, "I can explain, but–"

A sickening crack echoed through the clearing, halting Brogan's voice. The kid's heads snapped up to the sound's origin and found that it came from the giant wooden wheel. The flames had gotten to its infrastructure, effectively breaking it apart from its stand.

"By The Radiance," Adella whispered, realizing their immediate peril.

"Let's move!" Blake boomed as the engulfed, wooden behemoth began to roll in their direction. He grabbed Adella's free hand and pulled her along, ignoring his throbbing knee, as Brogan trailed behind.

They made only a few yards when Adella stepped wrong in the haste, her foot landing in a little divot in the grass, twisting her ankle. "Ahh!" She inhaled with pain, dropping her sword, right as the fiery wheel was nearly upon them.

"Come here," Brogan breathed as he swiftly scooped the girl up into his strong arms, leaving her breathless. He charged ahead, and Blake did all he could to keep on his heels.

Adella wrapped her arms around Brogan's neck, clinging for dear life, angry at herself for dropping the faerie blade. She hoped that the shades would not engage them.

The dark scarlet drake let loose a guttural bray as it broke through the line of airborne fey. With wings spread wide, it soared right into the faire, aiming it's wrath for the easiest targets – Blake, Brogan, and Adella were wide open. Between the cracking and clacking of the flaming contraption barreling behind them, the shades swiping at any living thing around, and the dragon incoming, they realized that there was nowhere to turn!

The drake opened it's jagged, scaly maws to rain flame upon the three teens. Adella could feel the heat of the swirling flame in the back of its throat.

Suddenly, a massive beam of magical energy, far more powerful than anything she had ever seen, hit the beast's underbelly, choking off its simmering inferno. Several of the Nether Dusk Fey had converged their magic to stave off the dragon's fire, affording the kids an escape from the flaming wheel of death.

Blake and Brogan, still holding Adella, ducked out and dashed for the enchanted safety tunnel, just as the burning wheel clattered over them.

"THIS WAY!" Jason called. Adella saw that he had Kate and Vivian under his arms and that they were way ahead of them in the clear zone.

The dragon, blinded with the barrage of faerie power, arced its powerful wings and propelled itself back, attempting an escape. Countless fey began to swarm the beast, banishing it further into the night sky. It shrieked and rose higher. The sight reminded Adella of a bee hive. Alone, a bee may not be deadly, but in numbers…

With the dragon retreating, the six teens dashed into the cover of the trees, finally leaving the flaming clearing behind.

"C'mon!" Jason urged again as he cut a path through the dark and wild woods. They ran as fast and as long they could, trying to put as much distance as possible between them and the hellish scene.

There were no flames here. In fact, it seemed as if the entire inferno was contained solely around the clearing they had left behind. Save for the huffing and puffing of terrified breaths, the crunching of leaves, and of cloaks fluttering behind, the royals were all silent. They went on for what felt like an eternity, no one daring to break the run or the silence.

Brogan still held Adella, keeping her close to his chest. It seemed like she was no burden or weight to him at all. He didn't even seem tired.

"Hold on!" Vivian finally cried out, leaning over, grabbing her side, grimacing.

"Guys wait up," Jason called. "Are you hurt, Viv?"

"No," she panted. "I just… I don't know. I'm not," she was clearly shaken. "I'm… I'm… not okay," she spiraled into a complete breakdown. "What even was *that*?" Her arms curled around her herself as she dropped to her knees, sobs wracking her body.

The teens drew together, their frantic breaths, and Vivian's cries, filling the dark night. Blake brought out his crystal to give them all some light. In the pale, glittering blue illumination, Adella could see the ragged and soot marred appearances of her friends.

"Hey, hey," Jason murmured, kneeling by Vivian, taking her into his arms, soothing her bewildered tears. She mumbled incoherently.

Adella glanced to Kate, and saw her body quivering, eyes a blank stare. She was going into shock. Blake noticed her, too, and whipped off his cloak to put around her small shoulders, for hers had burned away in the fight.

Kate seemed to barely notice the gesture. Her eyes were catatonic, teeth gnashing uncontrollably.

"We almost burned…" Vivian choked out, unable to finish the grim thought. She curled her face into Jason's arms as the flashbacks overwhelmed her.

"Brogan, I think I can walk," Adella whispered. She had grown to hate him so much, and yet a part of her did not want him to let her go. Touching him she could feel an almost painful combination of chemistry and tension.

"Are you sure, princess?" He quietly breathed, his lips so close to hers.

Adella looked into his eyes and felt herself drown in the cerulean pools...

She heard Blake clear his throat and the trance was broken. Her senses flooded back to her as she glanced to her friend. He was glaring at them.

"Yeah, I'm good. Just a sprain," she replied quietly.

Brogan softly set her down. She put some weight upon her injured foot and winced a little. It wasn't too bad. She would limp for a few days. She looked back up at Brogan. The silvery moonlight struggled to pierce through the thick canopy of trees, but with the glow from Blake's crystal, she could see the passion in his eyes for her.

She looked away and straightened, refusing to fall into his spell again. Seriously, what had come over her? They had all just endured a dragon's infernal wrath, quite literally a near death experience, and here she was daydreaming about kissing her ex-boyfriend? A boy she had spent the last few weeks growing a specific disdain for?

"Thank you for saving me," Adella managed to murmur, trying to ignore the pounding in her heart.

Brogan opened his mouth to respond but was cut off.

"Brogan, what in the spell are you doing here?" Blake demanded, stepping closer to them and away from Kate.

"I could ask you the same thing," Brogan responded coolly, looking around the group.

"No. You first. How did you find us? Your timing was *so* convenient," Blake persisted.

Jason looked up from Vivian to stare petulantly at the unwanted member of their party.

"Well, when none of you showed at Dia's party, I starting asked around the school. No one had seen any of you back from the city since you left. I had messaged Vivian a few times, but I received no reply."

"I left my crystal in the carriage," Vivian sniffled, trying to regain some composure.

"You what?" Jason looked down to her, upset.

She shrugged pitifully. "I just wanted to be free for once."

"Vivian," Jason half moaned, "not safe. You can't be doing that, okay?"

Brogan continued in his silky, even tone, "I was worried that you guys didn't make it back from the city – especially with the *empress* and *two* princesses in your midst." He shot a haughty glance towards Jason and Blake, as if chastising them for compromising the girls' safety. "I took a horse from the stables to search the city, but as I traveled into the valley, I saw the fire start in the forest. I knew that the Nether Dusk Faire was in the area, so I followed my intuition. And I see now that my intuition proved true. I seemed to have saved Adella just time." He spoke the last line with a self righteous flair.

"Oh geez," Jason rolled his eyes, exasperated, running a hand through his hair.

Blake scoffed, "I would have picked her up, too, you know."

"I came faster," Brogan smirked.

"That's not always a good thing," Blake challenged.

"Blake," Adella stopped him. "*Whatever* the reason," she looked back to Brogan, "however you found us, thank you."

Brogan smirked, the crystal light playing in his eyes. Before he could respond, Vivian broke in.

"I have to tell my father," she croaked. Her sobs had abated enough that she found some semblance of voice. "We just escaped a… dragon, right?" She looked around to her friends, pleading desperately for support or clarity. "Is this an attack on my kingdom? And those poor faeries that stayed behind? Are they all dead?"

Everyone was quiet, her words hanging heavy in the air.

"I've got to go home and warn my father!" She shouted when no one answered.

"Vivian, nothing is attacking your kingdom, love," Brogan placated her.

"Nothing is attacking my kingdom?" She blanched. "Then what was that flying fire lizard back there!?" She stood to her feet, shrugging Jason off, and stepped up to Brogan.

"It was the Nether Dusk's trick, my love. It's how they finish their shows. It must have gone wrong."

"What!?" Adella, Jason, and Blake all chorused harshly.

"What is *that* supposed to mean?" Vivian gazed at him sternly, tears still brimming down her cheeks.

Brogan grabbed her hands and locked eyes with her. "Vivian, the Nether Dusk Faire is known for their dragon show. It's all a trick – a combination of fireworks and fey magic. It must have gone awry.

Probably some misstored fire powder. Real dragons have been gone for a very long time."

"Oh," Vivian seemed to calm unnaturally at his response. "That actually makes sense." She smiled a little, staring up at the prince like he was some sort of god.

"Viv," Adella scoffed incredulously at her friend's mercurial flip. She could not believe how easily he swayed Vivian right there in front of everyone. "No, Brogan, I've been to the faire, they don't have dragons or sinister shadows at all!" She turned her anger to him, getting into his face. "Even the Nether Dusk clan themselves were freaking out!"

"And when was the last time you attended their festival, Adella?" He challenged.

Adella stopped short, knowing that the last time she had been was when she was just a little girl. She shook her head, determined to show him he was wrong. "We all know what just happened was real," a strength rang through her demand. "*That* was a *dragon*, it summoned those shadow creatures, and Varinth is in *danger*."

"Varinth is in danger?" Vivian's eyes glistened again. "It was not a show?" She looked up at Brogan. He still held her hands.

"No, it was a *show*, and *nothing* is in danger. That's the truth, I *promise*," Brogan's words intensified. "Their faire caught fire by mistake. No real threat attacked them at all. You'll see."

The teens were all silent, dumbfounded at what they were hearing from him.

"Brogan," Jason spoke at length, "you're full of troll shit!" He stepped up to him, and Brogan dropped

Vivian's hands. It seemed as if things were about to come down to blows between the boys.

"You really want to do this here?" Brogan replied, meeting Jason, practically chest to chest. "If we go back to the school in a *worse* condition than we are now, the admin will know we snuck out. You really want to bring that sort of attention upon us?"

They were silent, eying each other down, tensions flared. However, Jason knew that Brogan was right. If they came to blows, there would be evidence, for neither boy would hold back. And at this point, all everyone really wanted to do was get back to the school safe.

"Please don't tell on us," Kate meekly spoke, breaking their showdown.

"Tell on you guys?" Brogan asked innocently, looking away from Jason. He seemed bewildered. "I'd never!" He looked to them all, eyes finally settling on Vivian. "Honestly." He pleaded to her.

The kids were quiet. The heated adrenaline of the clearing wearing off, and the fears of being lost in the dark forest, and of not knowing the outcome of the drake, began to take hold. Flashbacks of the beast and the flames danced in their heads. The infernal bellows still roared in their ears.

"C'mon," Jason sighed deeply, relenting his challenge. "Let's just get back." He pulled out his green crystal ball and took the front point of their group, leading them all through the darkness.

# Twenty-Two

"Unbelievable." Dean Welford's voice was hard in the stark quiet of the room.

He was standing with his hands firmly planted upon his desk, looking far too stern and disturbed for a Saturday morning in his office quarters. He eyed down each one of the kids who stood before him.

Vivian was directly in front of his ire, as their group had decided for her to do most of the talking. Behind her was Jason, Blake, Adella, Kate – who was on the verge of tears – and Brogan, who was to the side of them all, brooding near the window balcony.

After they had made it out out of the forest and back to the school, the teens ditched their carriage down the road before the gates, and made an attempt to sneak back in. Using Jason and Blake's supposedly foolproof methods of slipping in and out of the establishment unseen, they somehow were spotted by a suspiciously awake Lord Landin. He apparently could not sleep and decided to go for a stroll along the grounds. Subsequently, the administration was alerted, the teens apprehended, and their intense and soot marred appearance earned them a one way ticket to spending the rest of the night in the infirmary, followed by a morning meeting with the Disciplinary Action Committee, or, as the teens referred to it, the D.A.C.

"Alright, let me attempt to sort this," The Dean began. "You remained out past curfew, ordered your guards to stay behind, impersonated *peasants*," he glanced to Adella as he scoffed the word, "fraternized with lowly fey gypsies, nearly burned to a crisp by some carnival trick gone awry, and got caught trying to sneak back into Royal High at two in the morning? Do I have all this right?"

The Dean had spent decades creating a finely honed sense of decorum, one of which appeared to never fluster. However, in light of the past several hours, the facade had unraveled. He had been on his crystal all morning to the angry parents of the kids who stood before him. More troublesome still, the pixierazzi somehow caught wind to a royal carriage of Vyrndolne leaving the city at dusk. And now, with the burnt out clearing in the forest down the ridge from the school, and no sign of the faire at all, things looked suspect to many outsiders, and the over all situation had worn him down. His ascot was undone and hanging round his neck, brocade vestments unbuttoned at the top, and his puffy sleeves had been rolled onto his forearms. Little beads of sweat formed upon his wrinkled forehead, and he continuously mopped them with a silken kerchief.

Behind Welford's desk were flanked on his sides the shiny headed Lord Landin, and the purple, ostentatious marshmallow that was Headmistress Von Durdenmyer. Behind those three, lingering near the bookcase in the corner of the room, was the hulking professor Bracke, arms crossed at his chest, handsome weathered face set in a deep and pensive scowl. All four administrators were a part of the school's board and served as members of the D.A.C.

"But uncle, there was a dragon!" Vivian tried to explain, ignoring all of the charges The Dean brought against them.

When Vivian was treated with Adella and Kate in the infirmary, she seemed to come to her senses. Being away from Brogan's influence allowed her to think for herself, and she was adamant that a dragon really had descended upon them at the faire. Vivian was also terrified that the monster was going to return for the rest of her kingdom, though there had yet been any reports of it resurfacing.

Adella was thankful at least that Brogan was unsuccessful in his manipulation of her friends. There was no way that he could actually believe that all that had transpired was just a trick of the fey. Adella didn't know why he was lying.

"Vivian, you of all royals should know not to spin tall tails and half truths," The Dean warned condescendingly.

With his chastising, Adella glanced to Landin and Vondurdur. Their heads nodded with arrogant approval. They seemed to relish in the conflict. *Vile people*, she thought.

The Dean continued, "I can assure you all, that the dragons have all been gone for a millennia, Vivian. There is no threat."

Adella wanted to press the matter further, to prove to this ignorant man that dragons were very much still in existence, however, she knew that if she opened her mouth, that this was not be a fight she would win. She was still a "*peasant princess*" after all, the girl who shattered so many norms that the world of royals defined themselves by. And, if they weren't believing Vivian's events of what happened, then who was she to speak up?

Adella glanced over to Bracke who seemed uneasy. Unlike Landin and Vondurdur, he was clearly not enjoying this. His slate colored eyes met Adella's, catching her bright ocean gaze.

"Now, I'm getting the impression that you all were influenced by princess Adella to go off and do this?" Welford calmly ascertained, as if this should have been obvious.

Adella's stomach dropped and the blood withdrew from her limbs making them shake. "I did not force anyone to do anything, sir," she spoke up, a knee jerk reaction to defend herself. If there was anything Adella hated, it was injustice and ignorance.

Before The Dean could reply, Vivian broke in, "Uncle, it was *my* decision to go. *I* made us go."

"Vivian?" The Dean's eyebrows raised with concerted disbelief. Landin and Von Durdenmeyer appeared shocked with the admission as well. "Vivian, this was *your* idea?" He seemed genuinely confused and dismayed at the fact that his perfect *palace born* niece would go off and break the rules of her *own* accord.

It was in that moment that Adella realized as to how the D.A.C. wanted to play this out. Clearly, in this administration's thought process, the Empress had been coerced into this sort of night by the likes of the *peasant born* princess, Adella, and those two combat ruffians, Jason and Blake. Sweet Katelyn would probably be found innocent, as she was never known to be an instigator, with her own soft spoken demeanor. And the dashing prince Brogan was only there to rescue them all.

Adella rolled her eyes.

"Yes, Uncle. *I* saw the poster in Vryndolne and wanted us all to go," Vivian stood her ground. Landin and Vondurdenmeyer were stunned, though Bracke looked like he was trying to hide a smirk.

Welford was silent, and seemed to mull everything over in his head for several seconds. He glanced to the window balcony. "Prince Brogan," his mood was considerably calmer as he called the boy's name.

"Yes, Dean Welford?" The prince was alert.

"Prince Brogan, I am understanding that your part in all of this is that you were attempting a reconnaissance?"

"Yes, sir, that is true." Brogan's voice was strong.

"Please elaborate," The Dean urged.

"I became worried when no one returned from the city before nightfall," Brogan began, glancing round the room earnestly. "I tried to reach out on my crystal but I had no response. For whatever reason, my gut told me that everyone could be in danger. I know I should have alerted the Royal High guards, but I felt that there was no time, so I went to search for them on my own. It was lucky I listened to my intuition, as I arrived in time to help save everyone from the fiery situation. I am deeply sorry I went against protocol. I guess my chivalrous instincts got the better of me." He flashed his smoldering, heartbreaking smile.

"How did you know where to find them, Prince Brogan?" The Dean indulged him.

"Lucky for me, I saw the smoke in the woods as I reached the crossroads before Vryndolne," Brogan's self assured grin never broke.

Adella was irked. Everything about Brogan's story irked her. His "showing up and saving the day" was just far *too* convenient. There were too many holes in his story, and yet the D.A.C. was buying into every word. She didn't understand it at all.

Welford responded. "And when you arrived on the scene, did *you* see a *dragon*, too?"

The whole room seemed to hold its breath as it waited for Brogan's reply, still at his place near the balcony. He was, after all, the only one of them who didn't break the rules for fun. Worse yet, Adella felt like Welford would value *his* opinion more than Vivian's. He was a *male*. Higher in birthright by technicality. Plus, he was a key player of the combat team – that alone held a lot of weight with many people.

Brogan looked around the room before looking back to The Dean. The pause was dramatic. "I'm not sure what I saw exactly."

"Of course," Jason scoffed sarcastically, glaring at Brogan across the room. Blake put his hand on Jason's shoulder to calm him.

Adella thought she heard Bracke breathe, "Oh bloody spell." She looked to the professor and saw the disbelieving scowl upon his face.

"Gentlemen," The Dean sternly glanced to Jason. It was a warning.

"What I mean is, Dean Welford," Brogan explained, "that dragons *are* extinct. There is no way that what we encountered was a drake. The only explanation I can see is that the beast that burned the clearing was indeed an illusion gone awry by the fey. The Nether Dusk clan are famed entertainers, after all."

"Are you serious, Brogan?" Jason's voice rose.

"Prince of House Rivenlaes," The Dean commanded, glaring daggers at Jason. It was a final warning.

Jason withdrew, and crossed his arms in defeat.

"If a real dragon was attacking this realm, why would it only attack the faire?" Brogan reasoned. "Not Royal High? Or the Castle Vryndolne itself?"

Adella's stomach twisted. His logic was incredibly sound. And indeed, why had this dragon mysteriously disappeared? There was no way anyone would believe them now.

They were as good as expelled.

Adella looked back to Landin and Vondurdur. They both nodded, smug, seeming entirely convinced. Von Durdenmyer's gleaming red talons folded themselves with a persnickety clicking in front of her deep plum gown.

The Dean gave a satisfied smirk. "Prince Brogan, you will make a fine king one day. It is this very reasoning that I came to myself," he agreed. "If there was any real danger, we would have known by now. Dragons do not exist anymore."

Welford leaned back, finally sitting in his ornately cushioned chair. Landin muttered something to him and The Dean looked over to Von Durdenmeyer, who nodded knowingly. He then glanced to Bracke. The professor had not changed his body language, still wearing the same enduring and weathered scowl.

Welford sat upright in his seat, folded his hands on his desk, and cleared his throat. "As I'm sure you have seen on the news this morning, the local Vryndolne media is covering the… let's just call it the 'anomaly' that happened to the now burnt out clearing. All reports of what occurred are anything but concrete. The fey who run the freakshow are nowhere to be found. Most likely they will be charged for the arson in that area of the forest. I understand that there is a warrant out for their leader. At the very least, the lowly gypsy fey won't be seen in Varinth ever again." The Dean added, "and the empire will be the better for it."

Adella wanted to scream. It wasn't the Nether Dusk Faeries' fault. It wasn't anyone's fault but the horrible aphotic beast that almost killed them! She glanced at Vivian who looked like she wanted to say something. Tears glistened in her eyes.

"Now, if your attendance of the faire had been found out by the media, the punishment for going off like you did would have to be expulsion. As of now, there's only speculation of your fraternizations, for it is widely rumored that your carriage was seen leaving the city at nightfall. Officially, the press has *no* concrete evidence on your indiscretion. As well, a sudden expulsion of this magnitude would draw more unwanted attention upon the school. For these reasons, the D.A.C. has decided that expulsion is no longer on the table."

All at once, the kids breathed a sigh of relief. Kate began to sob, the tension of her uncertain future had been too much to bear.

"Come, come dear. Sobbing is not befit of a lady," the headmistress softly chastised. She swiftly crossed the room, her bulbous layers swishing loudly, and handed the girl a silken handkerchief. "There... there." She offered awkwardly, her best attempt at soothing the stricken girl.

Kate took it and did her best to pull herself to composure.

"Continuing on," The Dean began again, "this does not mean that we, the committee, can let this act of defiance go unpunished. Taking into consideration that your peers know what you have done, we must make an example to ensure that this sort of behavior is not condoned." He paused, straightened up once more, and continued. "Having discussed many possible outcomes with the D.A.C. beforehand, we feel that the proper course of action for the students who snuck out past curfew is to have their extra curricular activities, as well as their off campus privileges, revoked for the remainder of the semester."

All at once the kids broke into protest – Brogan included. This new sentence meant that the boys would not be able to participate in the rest of their combat season, Vivian wouldn't be able to cheer on the morale squad, the winter waltz was out, and none of them could leave the campus. Adella didn't know what to do or say. She couldn't think and her head and ears were ringing as heated tears began to prick her eyes. Jason and Blake were making the biggest fuss, and instantly she felt the biggest burden of guilt as she realized that this all would never have happened if she hadn't shown her friends the poster.

"Now, now," The Dean rose his tone, hands in the air, trying to quell the voices. "This punishment would exclude the Empress Vivian and Prince Brogan, due to his attempted acts of chivalry." He explained as if these exceptions should have been understood already.

"Why?!" Vivian pressed with anger.

"Just saying *why* is not proper my dear," Von Durdenmyer clipped, obviously irked at her perceived lack of manners in Vivian.

"What do you mean, Empress?" Welford replied.

Vivian ignored the woman and continued "Why am *I* exempt, Uncle? I should be punished just the same as everyone else! I made us go!"

"Empress, you do not know what you say," Welford tried to reason. He, himself, seemed confused.

"Actually, Uncle, I do. Whatever punishment you have given, then I should have it, too. However," Vivian paused as if she was thinking out loud, "whatever will I say if my parents ask why I am not cheering, or why I cannot come home to our palace for a Sunday supper." Vivian's seemingly innocent musings rang out in the room. She had made her point in the most tactful of ways. Bracke cracked a grin; he understood what she was doing.

"*Your parents?*" Welford murmured absently, her words sinking in, fear striking in his eyes. He looked to all the kids, then back to his *sister's* daughter, Vivian. He held up a finger, got up from his desk, and motioned for the D.A.C. to have a chat in the other room of his office. The committee gathered together, The Headmistress with her endless bustle of fabrics, Landin in a deliberate self righteous saunter, and Bracke with his lumbering and reluctant stride. The four entered into the removed space, and The Dean closed the double doors behind them.

As the four administrators debated, their voices muffled through the mahogany, Adella leaned over and whispered, "Vivian, you didn't have to do that. I was the one who showed everyone the poster."

"Yes, but *I* decided we should all go," the blonde smiled apologetically.

Adella mirrored her with a cautious smile of her own. She looked back to Jason and Blake, who were whispering to one another, then to mousy Kate. The freckle dusted girl's tears had calmed, though she looked positively ill with anxiety.

"Hey," Adella whispered, catching Kate's pale blue gaze. She reached out and squeezed her hand. Kate managed a half hearted nod. Adella could tell that Kate was hitting her breaking point. The terrifying events had them all on edge.

Adella then glanced over to Brogan who remained silent at the window balcony. He seemed entirely disinterested with everything in the room and he gazed out over the grounds of Royal High. Adella was so angry with him. She wanted to say something, but she had no words. Why was he lying? Why did he seem to manipulate everyone and everything around him? Worst yet, *why* in the realms did she still have feelings for him when he so clearly turned out to be a jerk? Why did he save her?

The double doors rattled and swung open with Dean Welford striding through first. It broke everyone from their respective revelries as all eyes shot to him.

He cleared his throat and returned to the desk, Bracke to his bookcase corner, and Von Durdenmyer and Landin lingered behind. Dean Welford seemed less flushed, and his frilled ascot had been retied and tucked back into his brocade vest.

"We have decided," Welford began as he took to his seat once more, folding his manicured hands neatly in front of him, "upon a new course of action suitable for all. Much disregard was shown last night for the rules and protocol that royals should live by. Therefore, if you so desire to live like peasants, then you shall work like peasants. Maybe then will you appreciate what it means to be born of noble blood," he arched an eyebrow as he said this, looking right at Adella. "We have decided that everyone involved in breaking curfew rules will clean the Royal High establishment and grounds for the entire remainder of this weekend. Then, here on after, detention shall be served, five days a week, immediately after classes finish. It shall be an hour, carried out with Lord Landin for the men, and with the Headmistress Vondurdenmeyer for the ladies. Its duration shall last an entire month. Being the benevolent administration that we are, do not take lightly this adjustment, for, if there occurs any future infractions of this nature, publicly known or not, the next course of action will be expulsion for all involved. Have I made things clear?"

All six kids nodded their heads, stunned.

Welford looked to Vivian, "Are we clear, dear Empress?"

"Yes, Uncle, we are," Vivian replied curtly.

"Then you are dismissed to go begin your tasks." Royal High guards entered to escort the teens.

Adella looked to Lord Landin and then to the Baroness. They oozed an air of smug satisfaction. Bracke assumed an unreadable, stoic face. He seemed like he was trying to suppress what he was truly thinking.

Without another word, all six royals were escorted out of The Dean's lavish quarters and down into the Royal High kitchens for their assigned punishments.

Adella slipped away and locked herself into the servants lavatory for a moment. The kids had just received their instructions for their cleaning tasks, but she needed to make a call first.

"Adella?" Aedrian desperately answered.

"Hi, dad," Adella lowered her voice and spoke into her translucent crystal. "I don't have much time."

"Adella, what happened," Aedrian pressed firmly.

"What did the admin tell you?" Adella cautiously replied.

"That you got caught sneaking back in at two in the morning. And you were covered in soot and spent the night in the infirmary. They said you went to a faire that caught fire? What in the realms were you thinking–"

"Dad, there was a dragon," Adella stated firmly, cutting him off.

"What?" Aedrian wasn't sure he heard her right.

"A dragon, dad. We were attacked by a scarlet dragon."

"How?" Fear touched Aedrian's eyes. He instantly believed her. "Are you okay?"

"I don't know," Adella shuddered. "It was out of nowhere. I mean, we did sneak out and to go to the Nether Dusk faire, but a dragon ended up attacking the clearing. I didn't mean for any of this to happen. I'm so sorry," Adella pleaded. She looked through the crystal and into her father's wise eyes. His solemn gaze told her that he seemed to know more than he was letting on. She opened her mouth cautiously. "You know something."

Aedrian nodded grimly. "I hold an ear to the ground in many places this world over."

Adella understood what he meant. "What have you heard?" She ventured.

"My sources say there's been three attacks by a scarlet drake in Narcinion in the last year alone. Maybe more. As it's only been small settlements, nobody has gotten distinctive proof. Now, with this attack, that makes it four. I fear something is coming." Aedrian pressed his lips. "Drakes do not do this in the open. Not without a catalyst."

"The media isn't even covering this," Adella added, frustrated.

"Of course they won't. You think they want to cause mass panic in the realms? Or, more likely, become the laughing stalk of the realms? Dragons don't exist to many people, Adella."

"Yeah, the administration is completely delusional." Adella rolled her eyes. "I think Bracke might believe us, at least, but I got the impression he wasn't allowed to say that."

"Who else snuck out with you?" Aedrian questioned.

"Me, Vivian, Kate, Blake, Jason, and Brogan."

"You're hanging around with *Brogan* again?" Aedrian's voice suddenly flared with quiet anger. "I thought you had said were going to stay away from him?"

"Uhg, he came later, actually. Just showed up. Can we just not talk about him right now, dad?" Adella was petulant as she rushed through these words. "I don't have enough time. I think I hear them coming back for me."

"Time for what?" Aedrian questioned, still irate at his daughter for glossing over the fact that she was with Brogan.

"Do you remember that drake I saw my first night here? How I wasn't sure if I had dreamed or hallucinated it?"

"They are connected," he affirmed without question.

"I think so," the girl agreed.

"Way too much of a coincidence." He added, "With the school being so close to the faire, I would not be surprised if this is the very same creature."

"I knew I wasn't crazy," Adella smiled a little.

"Oh, I would not go that far. You're my child. You are definitely insane," Aedrian gave a chuckle. "But no, you are not seeing things."

"Thanks," Adella replied as she cracked a grin.

"This is troubling. The drake is becoming bolder," he shook his head. "They never went completely extinct, you know. I have begun to fear that they have only just been hiding, waiting for the right time."

A chill ran up Adella's spine, making her shake.

"I'm sorry, Adella. I shouldn't be saying such things," he realized, sensing her fear.

"No, dad. I am to be a ruler one day, I need to be informed of such things." There was a strength in her voice that caught Aedrian off guard.

"True. And in time, you will know too much, Princess. But for now, you need to focus on your classes."

Adella sighed heavily. "I'll try."

There was a sudden, heavy knock on the door. "Princess Everheart," a deep voice sounded. It was one of the guards.

"Just a minute!" Adella sounded over her shoulder. "Dad I gotta go," she whispered.

"One more thing. You said that Bracke believes you?"

"About the dragon? Yes, I think he does."

"I remember Bracke from my time there. He's a very intelligent and warm person when you get to know him. I think you would do well to make an ally of him, Adella."

"Way ahead of you, dad," she smirked, ocean eyes twinkling.

"Good girl."

"I'll talk to you later, dad. Keep your ear on that ground."

"Always," Aedrian nodded.

"Wish... we could... use... magic... or something," Adella puffed through each swipe as she scrubbed a scuffed floor tile. Her ankle was killing her, and she couldn't wait to put on the bedtime salve that Bracke gave her for it. He had run into Adella during their cleaning tasks and pulled her aside to give her a gift. In his thick brogue accent he had told her, '*No adventurer's spirit should go punished with physical ailment... But you're on your own with cleaning duty.*' She laughed to herself as she remembered his words, though she really had begun to wonder why he favored her so. It couldn't just be because she was one of the best students in his class.

"We've been scrubbing for hours," Vivian collapsed in exasperation on the icy marble floor.

Adella, Kate, and Vivian had ditched their beautiful ballgowns and poofy petticoat layers for some much simpler dressings. They tucked up their humble skirt bottoms in gathers and swags around their hips, enhancing their mobility, and tied around their waists old aprons they found in the kitchens.

Their once pristine curls and locks were pinned into hasty, messy buns, and tendrils fell into their faces every so often while they cleaned the castle. They looked much closer to the scullery maids rather than like royals. However, despite the D.A.C.'s attempt at humiliation by their punishments, some of the students saw the girls as unsung heroes for breaking the curfew in such a gallant manner.

"This is ridiculous," Kate sighed as she brushed dirt off her skirt. The three of them had been all through the bottom levels of the school, cleaning floors, beating out the tapestries, dusting trinkets, shooing away cobwebs, and shining all the surfaces of all the rooms the baroness had ushered them into. They were now in the grand ballroom, scrubbing the large marble tiles. The late Autumn Tide's sun, casting its last rays through the bay window, begged for them to take a break and come outside. "This is seriously what you grew up doing, Della? Cleaning?" Kate asked in disbelief.

"Well, not every waking hour, Katie," Adella replied dryly, looking up from her knees, raising an eyebrow, "but yeah. When you have never lived with servants before, guess who does the chores…" Adella pointed to herself.

"I've… I've never washed a floor before," Kate mumbled meekly, pursing her lips.

"Well, for never cleaning a floor, I'd say you've done a really good job today," Adella gave an encouraging smirk. "This place is shining." She stopped her scrubbing for a moment to admire their work.

"Really?" Kate perked up. "Well, I don't know if this would be a compliment or not, but we learned from the best," she admitted, obviously referring to Adella. "I had no idea that a greasy elbow was the secret." The girl held up her arm and rubbed her elbow. Her face was serious, but Adella giggled.

"I'm telling yah, the harder you scrub, the more the elbow grease flows. It really buffs out those marks!" Adella joked, laughing again. She looked to Vivian who was laying on her back, arms and legs sprawled out like a starfish. She seemed so… *common.*

"Viv?" Adella called.

"Mmmm?" The girl murmured, sounding half asleep.

"You okay?"

"I used to love this."

Kate and Adella looked at each other, confused. Vivian didn't move a muscle, nor open an eye, but continued lazily.

"When I was a little girl, on a really hot day, I used to find the most wide open places I could in my palace. Most of the time it was our ballroom. I used to spin and spin until I'd fall down, and I would lay out on the cold marble, watch the room turn above me, chandeliers blurring. I was never allowed to lay on the floor. Was

*unlady* like, mother would say. But, the cold marble
was always soothing. Like right now," she opened her
eyes and looked to her friends. "It feels so good after
the hard night like we had. I'm just glad that there
wasn't any real beast after us."

Kate plopped down and took Vivian's lead,
sprawling out herself. After a second she whispered,
"this does feel nice." She closed her eyes.

Adella stared at them for a moment, worrying
thoughts churning in her mind. The terror they had
endured the night before was beyond comprehension,
yet here they were, carrying on the best they could,
cleaning the castle like nothing was wrong. After
Brogan's logic in that meeting, Kate and Vivian swayed
to his side once more. They truly believed that there
had been no real threat. Though, to his credit, Brogan
had made the most sense. No dragon was currently
attacking the Vryndolne citadel or the high school, and
those places would be far more important than some
random faire.

But Adella could not shake the dread she felt. The
dreams, the painting of the champions, the dragons, the
strange shadows. Everything felt too connected, too
close for comfort. And the way her soul felt when she
heard the beast's awful bellow in the clearing,
summoning those dark things…

*Everyone can think I am crazy, but I know what
that was, lack of evidence be damned*, she thought as
she looked upon her friends once more.

Vivian and Kate's eyes were still closed, and they
hadn't moved an inch. They looked so utterly peaceful,
measured breaths barely raising their chests, that Adella
knew they had fallen asleep.

In that quiet moment, Adella understood it was for the best that Vivian and Kate were unaware of the reality of what they just faced. Ignorance is bliss, and better for them to exist blissfully, than to walk around in fear of a reality that they are currently powerless to change.

At least Jason and Blake were on her side.

At least they knew.

That was enough for now.

For now.

Adella exhaled a long sigh, feeling like she had been holding her breath for years. To say she was exhausted would be an understatement.

She grabbed her bucket, brush, and rag, and moved closer to the bay window. She gazed out past the glass to the setting, flaming orb of sun, magnified in the misty haze that had settled upon the vast school grounds. It lingered above all the trees, and upon the warm colored woods beyond. Frost's Tide was soon to come.

The girl sighed once more as she turned away from the scenery. She dunked her brush in the water bucket, and began to work on the tiles near the window.

Adella knew not how long she scrubbed, but she figured that this was probably their last room. Supper was within the hour and the headmistress was nowhere to be found. Adella stood, stretching her stiff limbs. She was going to wake the girls up to get ready for dinner.

"Washing floors must be nothing new for you, *peasant borne*," a quiet voice chided. "You obviously have experience with it."

Adella's head whipped around, startled. She had been so lost in her thoughts that she had heard no one approaching. A rare thing, for Adella was usually incredibly aware of her surroundings. Adella met Dia's gaze, and instantly let out a small gasp.

Underneath Dia's long flame hair, Adella could see that the skin around her left eye and cheekbone was a deep blueish, and underneath her bright green irises were the dark circles of a sleepless night. Her usual maroon and black garb was pinned up higher to allow movement for the wooden crutches that she now rested on. Her legs were visible and Adella saw her foot was in a cast. There was bruising in her wrists, stretching into her hands. She looked completely battered.

*And I thought* we *had it rough last night!* Adella thought in disbelief. "Dia, what happened to you?" Adella breathed, forgetting the bitter remark. Although Dia was one of Adella's least favorite people in Royal High, she still felt an overwhelming wave compassion for her.

"Oh, this?" Dia was nonchalant as she lifted her leg a little. "Well, after you guys were no shows at my soiree last night," she scoffed, "Brogan became worried. You know he's like my best friend and all, and he desperately wanted to stay with *me*, but he felt he should go looking for you lot just in case."

Her voice grated on Adella. *Best friends*, Adella thought skeptically. *This girl is delusional. I've barely seen Brogan interact with her. She's probably just another victim to his charms.*

Dia continued, "I begged him not to go, but he insisted. And when I decided to go after him," she lifted up her leg a little once again, "I was wearing the most expensive pair of Vysterian crystal studded heels – you obviously don't know this, but it's impossible to run in a

pair of those. I tripped and fell down the grand stair."
The anger in her voice was obvious.

"My word, Dia. I am so sorry!" Regardless of
Dia's bitter insults, Adella spoke with true empathy.

"You should be," Dia fumed, sugary front gone. "If
you guys had been there last night, instead of selfishly
going off and breaking rules, none of this would have
happened. I wouldn't have almost died, and *you*
wouldn't be scrubbing floors. However, you probably
enjoy this sort of thing, so I'm not even sure that this is
a severe enough punishment for your *kind*."

"My *kind*?" Adella dropped her brush with a dull
thunk into the water bucket. Without thinking, she
retorted, "Oh, *my* kind. You mean beautiful,
adventurous, *and* a crown royal? Yes, I am a rare *kind*.
Thanks for the *compliment*." Adella flashed her perfect
white smile. Forget the politics – she'd had enough
pandering.

Dia's intensely green eyes seemed to do the faint
quivering thing again, the same way they did in
Bracke's class on that first day. She hotly seethed,
"Well, while you enjoy your *adventurous* scullery maid
duties this weekend, you'd do well to stay away from
*Brogan*."

"What makes you think I care about what Brogan
does?" Adella scoffed incredulously.

"I've seen the way you look at him," Dia shot
back. "Oh, yes, you think no one is watching, but I can
read you like a book, *peasant borne*. Does Vivian
know?" She mocked.

"You're insane." Adella stated, completely in
disbelieve as to the turn of this conversation.

"Thank you," Dia smirked arrogantly, owning the insult. "But really, stay away from him. You're nothing but trouble, Adella Everheart. Guys like him don't need to be around the likes of you. He's mine."

"Does he know this?" Adella's eyes glanced out the the bay window as she nodded her head towards the glass. Dia looked out and saw that Brogan was with Jason and Blake. They were cutting the field grass on the back quad. Adella smirked, folding her arms. "If he was so into *you*, then he wouldn't be out there."

"*You* got him in trouble," Dia responded, undisturbed by Adella's observation.

"Wow, it's nice to see someone so undeterred about reality," Adella quipped.

"Excuse me?" Dia sputtered.

"He did that himself, Dia. He got into trouble on his *own*, by choosing to leave *you* and *save me.*" Adella raised an eyebrow and smirked.

Dia's hauntingly pretty features contorted into anger, and her queer green gaze pierced into Adella. Her bruises seemed to darken, if that was even possible.

Adella continued, "Oh, he didn't tell you? How he held me up against his chest in his *big strong arms* as he saved me from a fiery spinning wheel of death? Can't say that he did the same thing for you," Adella nodded at Dia's foot in her cast. Fire blazed in the ocean girl's heart and cheeks.

Dia's voice became low and menacing, eyes growing dark, losing their bright green light. "Listen, *peasant borne*," she spat, "you may think that you survived last night, but *I am* the one who won here–"

"Adella?" Vivian sat up and yawned. She was completely out of it, unaware of the volcanic confrontation going on just yards away.

Dia's mouth suddenly snapped closed, features morphing back into her coy and well practiced smirk.

"Oh, hey Dia – DIA!" Vivian's eyes grew huge. "Dia, what happened?!"

"I fell down the stairs last night. I'm lucky to be alive," Dia added with a sigh as if her condition was the greatest of burdens. Her flip from murderous rival to playing the victim astounded Adella. Her own blood was still racing from their heated battle.

The empress immediately got up and lamented to Dia about how sorry she was for everything. Adella was not sure how much of Vivian's apology was guilt from missing the party, or from guilt because of how badly Dia was injured. Adella went over to wake Kate while Dia relished in Vivian's attentions. Vivian offered to help her to dinner, but Dia insisted that she was fine and just passing through. Dia took her leave, and Adella watched her hobble a little too gracefully on her crutches to the doors. The girls then gathered their cleaning supplies and left to get cleaned up for supper.

However, the secret confrontation between Adella and Dia was nowhere near finished. Adella felt in her soul that this was just a taste of what was sure to come, for true colors and claws had finally come out, and they were not going back.

# Twenty-Three

"You lied, boy!" The twisted voice cackled. The Dark One whispered harshly, through clenched teeth, to his servants of Desdem. "More."

"Aaahhhh!!!!" The poor prisoner cried out as the torturers inflicted new pain.

The Dark One paced the floor, seething, mumbling to himself.

The prisoner's cries continued, nearly drowning out the cranking drone and creaks of the horrid mechanism to which he was chained. The whispers of the shadows flared frantically and the earth rumbled in the deep. Lightning from the heavens sparked and could be seen through the partially caved in roof of the morbid grotto. Another storm was brewing out in the skies. There would be no moon that night.

"Okay, enough," the Dark One held up his hand. "I can't take your noise. Usually cries of anguish invigorate my senses, but today, especially after failing to retrieve Astralore…" he trailed a craven moan as he pressed his fingers to his temples. "It just doesn't have the same *ring*."

The tormentors relented and the poor boy caught his breath. Simultaneously, the elements died down, the whispers became hushed but not muted, and the prisoner's wheezing and sputtering steadily filled the dark.

"Do you see what happens when you lie to me?" The Dark One's twisted voice was profoundly smooth after the bedlam.

"I," cough, "didn't lie," cough, wheeze. "I never *told* you *anything*," the prisoner managed, gasping.

"Oh, but you did, remember?"

"I would never."

"But you *did*. You gave me a definite *hint* as to its location," the Dark One paced closer. "I seem to remember you mumbling through your haze of tortured agony about a '*guard*'," he quoted, patronizing. He paused and added musingly, "of course, you blacked out right after."

The poor soul, covered in sweat, gashes, and dirt, looked at his captor with incredulous bewilderment, trying to put the pieces together.

"Guard?" He could barely ask.

"I went to the Ebenhold vaults," the Dark One explained nonchalantly. "Which I know is guarded by your most *elite* warriors. However, Astralore was nowhere to be found among those pathetic faerie trinkets. And Sealghair wasn't there, either." The Dark One added, "I ordered several executions for their incompetence in losing such a precious artifact."

"Th-they wouldn't have k-known," the bewildered prisoner replied. "Astralore has n-never been there."

"And do you think that stopped me? Their lives were an inconvenience. They knew the risks when they took the job."

"H-How many," the prisoner could barely get out his thought as a new wave of delayed pain was taking hold.

"Did I kill?" The Dark One presumed the captive's query.

The poor soul could only nod, mouth in a tight line, blood and sweat matted hair stuck to his forehead.

The Dark One reached out and gripped the locks on the poor boy's head.

"Many," his words splintered in the darkness like ice.

"Monster!" The prisoner screamed with all he had, writhing, pulling against his chains.

"And yet you still have fight in you! My, but the tales of your linage do not lie. You are a hearty one. Too bad only the sons hold the blood. That means Daphne wasn't one to inherit, was she? She would have been quite a fighter I bet."

The prisoner's face lit up fiercely. "You stay away from her!" His voice cracked at the end of his threat, unable to withstand the pain coursing through his body.

"My, my, overprotective?" An evil grin possessed itself upon his face. "I just want to have a bit of *fun* with her. If you won't tell me who Sealghair is, maybe she will. I wonder how she slumbers?"

"If you lay a finger," the prisoner tried to threaten.

"What will you do? I have you right where I want you," the Dark One taunted. "You poor, lost noble."

"No, she doesn't know anything! You leave her o-out of this!" The prisoner cried fiercely.

"Silence," the Dark One ordered stoically. He motioned for the Desdem servants to release the prisoner from the shackled machine.

The poor soul dropped heavily to the floor. He struggled to raise up, but collapsed.

"As it is, I am running out of time," the Dark One said wryly, worn with exhaustion, as the torturers dragged the prisoner over to the wall, securing the captive's hands with chained manacles. "You refuse to tell me who Sealghair is, you refuse to give up

Astralore's location. It's almost like you want me to kill all of your loved ones."

"Please don't hurt them!" The prisoner begged.

"Then you'll tell me what I need to know."

"No. I won't. I... I honestly don't know... I don't know where it is," he breathed, defeated.

"Liar," The Dark One seethed.

"No, I'm telling the truth. The location of Astralore was never revealed to me."

"This whole time you let me think otherwise?" The Dark One sneared.

"Yes. I was just trying to save everyone. Please don't hurt anyone else," the prisoner pleaded. His chains rattled as the torturers left him.

"So you're saying you're of no use to me?" The Dark One accused.

"Yes. Just... kill me. Please," he resigned himself to his fate. He had been waiting for this. He knew he had to die with the secret. His heart could only be strong for so long.

The Dark One came closer, and got down onto one knee, peering keenly upon his prisoner.

"You finally wish for death?" He murmured inquisitively.

"Yes." The prisoner swallowed painfully. He'd said his goodbyes in his heart. To his sister, and to his Adella. He would never see the outside world again. It was a sacrifice he would make over again in a heartbeat.

The dungeon was still, and not even the shadows dared to whisper.

"No," the Dark One's aphotic voice drove through the silence. "I still have plans for you." He violently grabbed the head of the prisoner and skimmed a small, crystal faceted vial along his neck, catching a trickle of blood from his new wounds.

The prisoner inhaled with pain. "No! Not again!" He cried, knowing the aphotic magic that the Dark One had in store for his blood.

The Dark One stood and smirked, tossing back his raven hair, and tucked the vial away. He chuckled wickedly and turned on his heels for the door, his cloak of shadows moving with him. "I suppose I'll just have to become more creative."

"You can't control them," the prisoner called hopelessly as the Dark One neared the exit. "You're dealing with forces beyond understanding. The Aphotic control you, not the other way around. They're using you, Braeden."

The Dark One reached the door, hand touching the cold iron frame. "My dear Prince Brogan," he turned to barely see his captive out of his periphery, "you know nothing of the power of Astralore. And don't you ever call me by that name again."

With that he strode out of the terrible dungeon, iron locks tumbling behind, and left his captive to wallow in despair.

He had barely made it halfway down the hall when a distorted and seductive voice spoke in the darkness. "Well that was certainly a show."

He halted as she came into the glow of a mounted torch. Her scarlet and ebony reptile legs, ending in terrifying talons, reached up to her human waist and chest; an artfully crafted breast armor and hip hugging sash were the only articles that covered her modesty. Her flame hair splayed out wildy from her reaching pair of footlong horns on either side of her head. They each were spiked to severe, spiral points. Her reptilian tail flicked around behind her, barely grazing her wings which were folded down her back. Her human arms were crossed in indignation, though her black taloned hands struggled not to bare down into her flesh. She was obviously irritated, as her queer green gaze on her peculiar human face bore into the Dark One's crimson eyes.

The Dark One scoffed at her greeting, "You're one to talk, Diamara. That stunt you pulled roasting that faire the other night was *show* enough."

"Uhg, faerie scum deserved it," Dia tossed her head back, shaking out her long red locks. "Besides, those ungrateful royals didn't come to my party. They blew me off. So I blew off some *steam*." She smugly stated.

"Listen, I know your *vice* is attention," Braeden reprimanded, "but that was too far. I mean just look at you," he nodded to the large bruise that was already fading on her cheek under her eye. "It's a good thing you're a fast healer."

"Not as fast as our guest in there," she bitterly retorted as she nodded her head down the hall to the prisoner's dungeon door. "Radiance blessed brat."

The Dark One sighed like he had had enough living for one day. "Let's go," he turned to continue down the hall, determination in his heavy steps, bringing his cloak of shadows up over his head.

"By the way," Dia began, keeping in time with him, claws lightly clicking on the ground. "May I ask why you are *so* obsessed with that Everheart girl? I thought the plan was to go after Vivian, the *empress*?" She pressed sourly.

"Shut up," Braeden snapped. "Adella's the key to Adamaris, as well as a great fighter. It'll be the ultimate betrayal to Brogan if I can sway her to join me," he explained. "Besides, I'd rather her be an ally than a foe." He added arrogantly, "Why can't I have both girls?"

"And me?" Dia arched an eyebrow, her ethereal face searching.

"Oh, you know *you're* my favorite," he looked to her, his cloak falling back to show his alluring gaze.

SLAP. Dia popped Braeden hard across his face. He stumbled back, holding his cheek, looking at her stunned. She could have killed him if she wanted. Easily. "That stupid spell charm won't work on me, Breaden. I showed you that magic, remember?" She reminded harshly. "And it's not working that well on Adella, either. She's strong. A *different* kind of strong."

"All the more reason to turn her," Braeden placated, rubbing his face. "I'd rather have her in my bed than face her on a battlefield. It's better this way."

Dia growled, the snarled sound strange coming from her human form's throat.

"Give it time," he attempted to mollify the tension. "We have a shard of Astralore already. We need to create alliances everywhere as we continue to find the staff. *Someone* has to know who Sealghair is," he reasoned tentatively.

"Vael doesn't have time," Diamara reminded flatly. Her tail flickered again, hitting the wall.

"Hey, you don't know what Vael wants either," he chided, frustrated fingers running through his ebony hair. "You've never been in the Astral realm. His pull on you is *vague* at best. We need the missing pieces to bring him and rest of the dragons into this realm."

Diamara had no retort to this. She sucked in her cheeks, staring The Dark One down. "I still don't like the plan we're on."

"Well, until we find out *exactly* what Vaeldar wants, then we need to play the game. Better to cultivate an easy foothold everywhere, than having to take all the kingdoms of Edenarth by force before we're ready. We barely have numbers as it is."

Dia's eyes never broke from him.

"Play the game," he persuaded once more.

She studied his face, thought's flickering across her eyes, then glanced down to the exit of the hall.

Suddenly, her body began to morph, and her dragon wings and tail flared out, then down and into her back. Her talons and scaled legs rescinded into her ivory skin, leaving dainty human limbs, feet, and hands in their places. She tossed back her hair as her horns hid themselves in their strands. "Then lead the way, *Brogan*," she sarcastically smirked, looking once again like the girl who walked the halls of Royal High.

At her words, a wicked smile worked its way onto Braeden's mouth. He brought the crystal faceted vial of blood out from his ashen robes, and locked it into place on his golden chain. He passed his hand over the ruby colored pendant, enacting the blood glamour. Brogan, the Crown Prince of Kelemer, manifested over Braeden's form, concealing his own darkness from the world.

# Appendix

Royals of Note:

Adella Olynia Gwendolyn Claire Everheart,
    Crown Princess of Adamaris

Brogan Greyson Thane Etherstone,
    Crown Prince of Kelemer

Vivian Deyanna Jaene Thelred,
    Empress of Varinth

Katherine Aurora Elise Fendraid,
    Princess of Daeleron

Blakely Kenneth Xander Telarn,
    Prince of Itheria

Jason Lancer Errickson Renlorre,
    Prince of Rivenlaes

Other Characters of Note:

Diamara, realm of Desevry, ancient name
    for Desochar.

Braeden, realm of Kelemer, exiled.

Duke Aedrian Aleksander Reyn Everheart,
    Father to Adella and Duke of Ardenthel

Duchess Olynia Rose Everheart,
    Mother to Adella and Duchess of Ardenthel

Sealghair, pronounced Shêll-kâr in the common
    tongue. Rumored protector of the Astralore
    staff.

Vaeldar the Bael Draconus, the title here meaning
    The God Dragon. Also known as Maugren in
    the tongue of fey. (see Maugren)

Maugren, the name given to Vaeldar by the fey as
    they refused to use his true name, believing
    that it gave him more power when mentioned.
    Maugren means The Destroyer, in the tongue
    of fey.

Bracke, the brogue alchemy professor of
    Royal High.

Lenroe, fey and alchemy assistant to
    Professor Bracke.

Baroness and Headmistress Bianca Gertrude Von
    Durdenmyer, of the realm of Cardiff

Lord Landin of the realm of Bydenvole

Arnold "Arnie" Kingsley, House of Renlorre, Duke
    in the realm of Rivenlaes, also said to be Lord
    of the Water Chests

Known Continents:

Nadromei (Monarch High, realm of Bydenvol)

Narcinion (Royal High, realm of Varinth)

Marrodar (Regal High, realm of Neymor)

Caroeninth (Supreme High, realm of Morrowaith)

Seasons: Tides

Green's Tide - Spring

Sun's Tide - Summer

Autumn's Tide - Autumn

Frost's Tide - Winter

Spirituality:

The Radiance, ancient form of the very first light in Edenarth. Created all things of life, light, and goodness. The ancient fey and humans were said to be the direct sons and daughters of this force.

The Aphotic, the ancient form of the darkest evil. Darkness incarnate, souls intertwined with this force become Maldeemed upon death.

Created all things malevolent and wicked. The ancient dragons were said to be the direct sons and daughters of this force.

Faerie Factions:

It is worth taking note that some unique forms of desirable magic are jealously guarded and abilities range from faerie clan to faerie clan. Some clans have a unique monopoly on certain forms of magic technology.

Nether Dusk Fey – A lesser fey clan, formed over the last few hundred years, responsible for much of the mischief and folly faeries can be known for. Always on the move in their disinctive carvaans, they set up and break down camp in the twinkle of an eye. Gifted with a pechant for tapping into the energies of all life, they easily alight mirth and wonder in hearts. They also specialize in manupulating kenetic energies, moving arond their patron's physical forms with ease on daring contraptions. Despite this apparent heart for fun and entetainment, outsiders of the clan are never to be trusted.

Collow Fey – Portals are often the work of the Collow Fey clan who control every Collocation Hall in Edenarth. The magical know-how on creating one of these rifts is heavily guarded by the Collow Fey. In addition, because portals are a difficult form of technology to create, even for the most skilled of Collow fey, to use a collocation hall comes with hefty fee to pay. Collocating can also induce a sickness that most refer to as "the ports". For mortals who aren't used to using portals somewhat frequently, especially for first timers, collocating can make one feel nauseated and ill for a good half day after. Due to these reasons, most peasants still travel in the old ways; by horse, cart, or however far their legs will carry them. Affluent and wealthy individuals, namely royals, are usually the only mortals who patronize colloction halls, for the obvious reasons just stated.

F.E.R.I. – Faerie Energy Revolution Incorporated. A faction of Nether Fey responsible for most of the crystal ball technology, magic mirrors, image orb capturing, and sound echos or sound replication. Anything that is media based most likely has the help of F.E.R.I. behind it. Any fey belonging of the F.E.R.I. faction is entirely forward minded. Forward thinking, technology expansion – always for the right price of course.

# ABOUT THE AUTHOR

Having been born into a family of nerds from a slice of the Shire in Northern California, Rachel Litfin cultivated a love of all things fantasy from a very young age. Inspired by dressing up with her family at renaissance faires, to losing herself in Tolkien, to playing World of Warcraft into the wee hours of the morning, Rachel created the very beginnings of The Chronicles of Royal High in her freshman English class. You can find her today in the realm of Southern California, often adventuring her way through Disneyland, reading by firelight, swimming in the ocean like a mermaid, and, of course, writing about the many stories that exist within Edenarth.

Made in the USA
Columbia, SC
07 February 2018